The role of criminal organizations in human trade has been put on a par with drugs and arms smuggling in terms of profitability and perniciousness.
—Interpol

Each year, an estimated 800,000 to 900,000 human beings are bought, sold, or forced across the world's borders. Among them are hundreds of thousands of teenage girls, and others as young as five, who fall victim to the sex trade.
—U.S. State Department

The United Nations lists Mexico as the number one center for the supply of young children to North America. The majority are sent to international pedophile organizations. Most of the children over twelve end up as prostitutes.
—Coalition Against Trafficking in Women (Fact Book)

Human life is the gift of our Creator—and it should never be for sale.
—U.S. President George W. Bush

For information write:
George Colton Publishing, Inc.
PO Box 375, Orangeville,
ON. Canada L9W 2Z7

Churches, schools, charities, and other not-for-profit organizations may acquire George Colton books by writing to the above attn: Ministerial Markets Department.

Library and Archives Canada Cataloguing in Publication

Clemons, Keith, 1949-
These little Ones / Keith Clemons.

ISBN 0-9731048-2-1

I. Title.

PS8605.L54T44 2006 C813'.6 C2005-907690-9

Printed in the United States of America

First Edition

06 07 08 09 10 11 12 – 10 9 8 7 6 5 4 3 2 1

Dedicated to
Kathryn Clemons
lifelong partner, wife, and best friend

Acknowledgements

I want to thank all those who contributed to the successful completion of this manuscript. Among them are two good friends who took time out of their busy schedules to review these pages in unpublished form and provide me with comment: Dan Schwabauer, author of *Runt the Brave,* a book I highly recommend, and Jamie Canivet, a super musician with an ear for fine tuning prose. I'm also indebted to the manuscript's editor Janet Dimond who, as her name implies, cut and polished the rough text until it became a true gem.

I would be remiss if I did not acknowledge the ministries of three men whose commitment to guarding our Christian heritage and worldview constantly inspires me to write: Dr. James Dobson of Focus on the Family, Chuck Colson of BreakPoint and Prison Fellowship and my own pastor, Rod Hembree of Good Friends Fellowship and Quick Study Television.

Finally, I want to express a personal note of thanks to Nancy Lindquist, author of many exemplary novels and Executive Director of the Word Guild, who is a constant example of how Christian writers should engage our world and our culture by working together to elevate the standards of Christian writing.

Other Credits

Cover Photo: Jyn Meyer
Cover Design: Laurie Smith

Also by Keith Clemons:

If I Should Die

Above the Stars

THESE LITTLE ONES

by Keith Clemons

GEORGE COLTON
PUBLISHING

They have given a boy as payment for a prostitute, and sold a girl for wine, that they may drink.—Joel 3:3

But whosoever shall offend one of these little ones who believe in me, it were better for him that a millstone were hung around his neck and he were drowned in the depths of the sea.—Matthew 18:6

PRELUDE

Seen from above, hovering overhead like a hawk, it was like someone had taken the green carpet of the jungle and given it a shake.

THE LEAVES that dangled and those shooting up from the ground, both large and small, broad and narrow, all of them spreading for miles, *trembled* all at once, simultaneously. But the people on the ground didn't notice. What they *did* notice was the silence. The animals were unusually still. Donkeys didn't bray, birds stopped mid-song, even the old rooster—that mangy cock who haunted Saint Christopher's taunting everyone to wring its neck—ceased its crowing. The sound of children playing was not to be heard, though with several of them having suddenly disappeared, that could be explained.

Overlooking the Pacific, the usually bustling village of Posada stood for a moment in silence. No one moved. The sides of granite outcrop forming the city's walls rose into the stillness, unswayed, but the leaves hanging from the dense foliage, the wall of green that encompassed the tiny Mexican town, shook again, ever so slightly, a billion leaves dancing in unison. And then all hell broke loose. Energy building for months beneath the earth's crust found sudden release. From the epicenter more than fifty miles away, the quake radiated along a brittle failure of rock in the earth's upper mantle, sending out shock waves and ripping the surface like a piece of dry paper.

The bell tower of St. Christopher's was the first to go. More than a hundred years it had stood, announcing births, weddings and funerals, proclaiming the festivals of the saints. It came down in slow motion, like someone had knocked the stilts out from beneath it, crumbling from the bottom, almost appearing to sink slowly into the earth, a gray cloud pluming from its base. Against the monstrous rumble the bell's clapper sounded a warning, *clang, clang, clang—get out of the way!* Roof tiles began to fly, and children to scream. The burros panicked and pulled at their tethers, kicking their heels and breaking loose, fleeing into the jungle. Parrots and parakeets, gnatcatchers and grosbeaks spread their wings in flight.

NICOLE HAD never seen a flock of birds so thick as the one that flew overhead. It was like confetti blowing in the wind, blotting out the sky. *Odd.* She meandered down a corridor filled with archways, bypassing the Portico of the Saints. It had been a lonely few days. The merriment that characterized the mountain village seemed subdued when Lonnie was away. And worship in the small Protestant church he pastored was notably uninspired.

She'd wanted to speak with the Catholic priest, Father Paulo Ceylon, hoping he'd heard something from Lonnie, but he wasn't in his office. She was about to make her way to the hospital, thinking she might find him there, when she felt the earth vibrating. She looked down. The tiles were lifting as the floor began to buckle. She turned into Father Paulo's office, and through the open window saw the bell tower starting to fall. She ducked under a thick router-leg table just as the giant monolith came down, crushing the roof, and the walls caved in around her.

The small space above her head filled with century-old brick dust. Her first thought as the chalky powder settled on her face was that she wasn't hurt, that the slab of heavy wood had protected her. But she opened her eyes and saw it was totally dark, and realized her limbs were pinned. She couldn't move. She started to open her mouth, wanting to spit up dirt, but there was—*something.* She probed with her tongue and felt a sharp shard of metal, or maybe it was glass. Her tongue followed the object past her teeth—*Oh God, no!*—it was sticking through the wall of her cheek. *A permanent scar!* Then a terrible pain shot up her spine, a pain so severe she knew she was either going to pass out—or die. *Why now, Lord? At least give me a chance to say goodbye.*

Atop a mountain of brick, many feet above the tomb in which Nicole was buried, a single butterfly with radiant red and blue wings emerged from the collapsed building, unharmed, and gently floated away.

ONE

Four Days Earlier

THE SUN was a dab of yellow butter melting on the hot blue plate of the Pacific. Lonnie stood at the edge of the world facing west, his arms outstretched to embrace the sea. If he slipped and fell he would hit the liquid surface a thousand feet below and be swept over the edge of the earth in a pounding waterfall—into the arms of Jesus. Someday, when he was through with this mortal toil, that's how it would be. But not now. He still had work to do.

His back was a silhouette to those who stood in the village behind him, a recognizable outline forming a dark cross. He drank in the musty air, the sweet smell of seaweed and brine lifting off the ocean, and thanked the Lord once again for bringing him home safely. He raised his hands in praise. His monthly forays into the Sodom of Tinseltown always left him with a deep appreciation of the life God had chosen for him. His returns were always cause for special celebration. *Thank You, Lord! Thank You, Lord! Thank You, Lord!*

He heard the bus approaching. The gnawing had been reaching his ears for ten minutes. He heard Father Paulo grinding the gears, and the engine whining as the bus tried to accelerate and then slow again at each tight turn. But the sounds were louder now, and if Lonnie figured right the bus would enter Posada at any minute. It would be good to see his old friend again. His three-day jaunts into civilization, the glitter and glamour of Hollywood, were all he could take. He enjoyed seeing his son, and his son's mother—to whom in spite of their tumultuous past he still felt inexplicably bound—but he also enjoyed returning to Nicole, with whom he planned to have dinner. That was their routine, something they'd done every Thursday for the past three years. His trips down the mountain were a necessary evil. He still owned fifty-one percent of Striker Films and chaired the monthly board meetings, though his son Quentin was officially installed as president and CEO. But nothing made him feel more like a seven year old anticipating Christmas than flying over the deep green jungles of the Sierra Madre del Sur, with the airport in sight, knowing Nicole would be there waiting—a feeling he dare not express since God had made it known he should marry someone else.

The rusty yellow bus rolled into the village, its paint looking tangerine in the wash of the setting sun. The brakes *screeeeched* as it stopped. It sat for a moment letting the dust float by. Lonnie heard the *clunk* of the parking brake and looked up, wiping moisture from his forehead and the back of his neck. Standing in the sultry sun, even in the evening, was as much perspiring as it was inspiring. He could see the kids climbing out of their seats, ready to exit. The field trips were a good idea. He supported the motion to buy the old bus, and had volunteered to pay for it out of company profits, but every time the children were away learning about life in the big city, he yearned for their return and was relieved when they made it home safely. Still, he had to let them go. It was important to let them know there was a whole other world out there, even if he preferred the privacy and seclusion of Posada for himself.

He pushed his red handkerchief into his pocket. The dust was thick and rolled in heavy as it settled on the cobblestones of the town's only road. A burro carrying gunny sacks filled with cornflour crossed his path, led by a peasant on his way to market with a dark woolen poncho draped over his shoulders and a soiled brown cowboy hat angled on his head.

The accordion door folded in and Father Paulo stepped down from the bus, his sandals leaving tracks in the dust. He turned to take the hand of each child, assisting them. Their sun-browned skin and glossy black hair shone in the late afternoon sun, but they wore

Western-style dress, polyester skirts for the girls and cotton T-shirts for the boys, hand-me-downs from church charities in the U.S. Lonnie noticed they seemed unusually quiet. He thought they'd be excited to be home, dismounting with glee. Perhaps they were tired. The big city was a befuddling place. "Oaxaca." Locals whooped it up over tourists who fumbled with the pronunciation. "You say it like, wa-haw-ca, señor." Lonnie was glad it was four hours away—couldn't be far enough—though it was less than a hundred miles. But it was a hundred miles filled with hairpin turns and lanes too narrow for passing. Stomachs would have churned as the bus wheezed its way around the mountain's oscillating curves. And the sun beating down on the metal roof would have made the inside as hot as an oven. The kids were probably in need of a good wash.

"¡Hola, Padre!" Lonnie cried, lifting his hand to wave as he continued over to greet the Father whose brown frock was wet under the arms. "What took you so long? I've been back several hours. Man, I gotta tell you, there's just no place like home. I know you're tired of hearing it, but if I never have to listen to another financial report, it'll be too soon." The priest did not smile. He nodded curtly, and continued helping children off the bus, one by one. Lonnie stood aside, waiting to be acknowledged. "Something wrong?" he asked. He'd anticipated a hug, or at least a swarthy grin. As the last child made his exit, Father Paulo turned to face his friend. His cheeks looked red and moist.

"Hola, señor Lonnie. It is good to see you as well. Come, we must talk." He held his hand out, indicating Lonnie should follow as he began taking strides toward the Catholic mission. Lonnie fell in step, his curiosity growing. Two shirtless men, their brown backs slick with moisture, were adding another coat of whitewash to the century-old walls. Domes graced the four corners of the compound with crosses at their crowns two in front and two in back. Where the building faced the road there was a tall tower that held the cathedral bell, with a pair of huge doors through which parishioners passed on their way to attend mass. The arches along the inner halls of the courtyard allowed the breeze—whenever they were fortunate enough to have one—to circulate. A few of the nuns who assumed responsibility for running the orphanage were herding the children into the yard. Sister Gabriela, a large woman almost as round as she was tall, in stark contrast to the two other sisters who were tall and lean, was counting on her fingers as they went inside. "Someone's missing!" she exclaimed. She put her hands to the sides of her face. "Where's Raúl and Mariana? Where's Sofía?" She looked expectantly at Father Paulo who had just arrived at the door. He held his arm out, extending it to include the sister, making sure she went before him as he crossed the brick threshold.

"Please, come inside. I will explain," the priest said calmly. They went into the chapel, the first room to the side of the entry.

Lonnie entered the building and followed him into the small room. It was always cool and dark in this part of the sanctuary. The thick clay held moisture even in the dense heat, and the brick and mortar emitted the earthen smell of lichen on damp stone. A large hand-painted plaster crucifix hung on the wall. Lonnie preferred to see the cross alone without the slain body of Christ. As a Protestant he felt since Christ was resurrected, the cross should be empty. But out of respect for his Catholic brothers who preferred a visual reminder of Christ's atoning act, he let it pass—though there were similar artifacts gracing the walls of the orphanage, the hospital, and the homeless shelter, and those were built with *his* money. But that was wrong-headed thinking. It wasn't his money. It was God's, and God's work was being done, and that was what counted. Two nuns sat on a wooden bench worn smooth from decades of penitence. They leaned in toward each other, conversing in private. They wore traditional black habits. Stiff white collars circled their necks, extending across their shoulders, looping down in front to provide a backdrop for their rosaries, and their flowing black dresses had billowy sleeves gathered into buttoned white cuffs. Across their foreheads were white bands attached to long black veils covering their hair, falling waist-length in the back.

Lonnie took a seat toward the rear of the small room. He withheld comment knowing an explanation was forthcoming, but his mind mulled over the obvious question: Where were the missing children?

He knew the ones Sister Gabriela had named. Sofía, the oldest, had been with them just over a year. She was now thirteen, considered practically a woman in the eyes of the culture, though she was really little more than a child. Lonnie recalled the day she was brought to him, her face unwashed, strings of greasy knotted hair covering her eyes, her clothing torn. A child of the streets. A runaway. He still didn't know the whole story, only as much as she'd been able to tell, but it involved an uncle who'd repeatedly raped her from the time she was seven. It was a tale that spoke of the depravity of man, one that made Lonnie ponder the blackness of an unregenerate soul. How could civilized man inflict such abuse on an innocent child? It was something he found impossible to fathom.

Lonnie had taken Sofía in hoping to find her a good home, but she wasn't comfortable around men, and the poor families in town didn't need another mouth to feed. He could only hope she hadn't run off again. She wouldn't open to him completely, but she responded to his counseling enough to make him believe progress was being made. Running away *would* explain the absence of Raúl and Mariana. He knew they wanted out. They were the two newest members of the group, having arrived only a few weeks earlier. Their father and mother had died in a fire, though the story raised more questions than answers. There was too much hostility, too much anger in little Raúl. He was only nine years old, but Lonnie perceived a hardness in those dark obsidian eyes. And his sister, only five, hadn't spoken a word since their arrival.

Sister Isabel entered the room and sat down. Father Paulo closed the heavy door and walked to the front. "As Sister Gabriela has aptly noted," he began, "there are fewer of us upon our return than when we set out this morning. I have the sad misfortune of reporting that three of our children are missing. We believe they've been stolen."

Sisters Fatima and Gabriela exploded out of their seats, their draped sleeves and loose dresses unfurling. Gabriela's girth blocked Lonnie's view. "What?" "Missing?" "Stolen? What do you mean?" "How?" "When?" Lonnie stood to see around the nuns, though he was sure he'd heard wrong. No one would steal orphans. No one wanted them in the first place.

"¡Silencio! ¡Silencio, por favor! I will try to explain. Sit!" Paulo commanded, and the women, caught off guard by his forcefulness, did as told. Lonnie remained standing. He put his foot on the bench and leaned forward, rubbing his hands. "I'm not sure I heard you right," he said.

"You did," the priest responded. "Now, if you'll let me do so without further interruption, I'll try to explain." Lonnie could see his friend was tense, which was to be expected. He stood in front of a large picture of Jesus, a familiar portrait emphasizing the Lord's sacred heart. Father Paulo folded his hands together and closed his eyes, taking a deep breath. "We were on our way back from the museum," he said, opening his eyes. He looked straight at Lonnie. "The children had a wonderful time exploring so many things they had never seen. We were walking back to the bus, and Sister Isabel and I were having a good conversation with some of the more curious ones. Their little minds had been exposed to so many new ideas and were full of questions. We were in the front, leading the group, while keeping a close eye on those behind. There was a van parked at the side of the road with two men, or maybe three, sitting there with the door open. We didn't think anything of it, though afterward we did recall the van had its engine idling, which was odd. Raúl and Mariana were last in line. That was to be expected. They've been slow at making friends. But we were keeping an eye on them, and I asked Sofía to stay back because we didn't want our little stragglers getting separated or lost. The rest happened so fast, I can only provide a few details. I was talking to Sister Isabel when I heard a scuffling behind us. I turned to reprimand the children and saw the men lifting Raúl and Mariana into the van, and when Sofía reached out to try and get them back, she too was pushed inside. The next thing I knew the van was speeding off down the road. I heard the door slam, and that was the last we saw of them."

Sisters Gabriela and Fatima were out of their seats again, both talking at once, one clutching her rosary, the other a cross. "What van? What did it look like?" "Who would do such a thing?" "What about the policía? Did you give them a description?"

"Silencio, silencio." Father Paulo raised his hands palms out as if to push the women back. "We went to the police. There is nothing they can do. They say it is a big problem, kids being stolen. Many thousands each year. The policía are underfunded and understaffed. They cannot follow up on all the missing person reports. And we had little information to offer. All we could tell them was the van was an older model, dark in color with many dents, but that could describe a thousand vehicles. We did not see the faces of the men, only that one was tall and thin and the other overweight, and Sister Isabel thought the thin one had a tattoo, but we couldn't even be sure of that."

Sister Fatima was working her beads so hard Lonnie thought she might break the string. She was of Indian descent, brown as any local, but her face seemed ashen white. "So, what do we do now, Father? Surely we don't give up and pretend nothing happened."

Paulo stood in the dank recesses of the small chapel. His face was an empty plate, void of expression, but if you looked close, even in the dim shadow, you could see fracture lines around his eyes, and a swell of moisture he seemed determined to hide. He turned, made the sign of the cross, and knelt before the image of Jesus—the one with the sacred heart. "No, Sister," he said. "No, we do not give up. We pray."

TWO

LONNIE STEPPED out of the cool building into a warm tropical evening. His favorite time of the day was when the sun, low on the horizon, painted the storefronts a bright ocher. It was like standing in first-century Jerusalem. The old inn with its potted palms, painted tiles and arched entrance, and the village store with its adobe walls, log beam ceiling, and windows through which cosmic dust could be seen dancing in the yellow light, in some ways resembled the architecture of a Judean town. He could imagine Jesus walking slowly across the cobblestones, and sitting on the edge of the cistern where the old pump stood with water shimmering in its basin like liquid gold. It had a mystical quality. Lonnie knew if he stood in the town's warm glow, watching the twilight sky popping with stars, and listening to the crickets praising their Creator, he would begin to feel like he was standing in the hallowed halls of heaven. But not now. Afternoon clouds had rolled in replacing the fallen sun, and through the webs of gray he saw cobalt blue, warning of night to come, with strobes of lightning in the east. The thread of peace had been broken, and with the descending darkness Lonnie knew all was not well on planet earth. He could hear the rumble of thunder in the distance. The humidity would soon turn to rain. He had to get on the road quickly. It was four hours to Oaxaca. By the time he got there, the children could be long gone. Paulo was probably right. There was nothing he could do—except pray. Still, he felt he had to do something, and he could always pray *while* on the road.

He saw Nicole approaching from the direction of the hospital.

She was wearing jeans and a white blouse, her hair fixed in a ponytail that swung back and forth as she walked. Lights were beginning to flicker on around the market. It was Thursday, the night traders kept their stalls open late. She caught up to Lonnie as he made his way to the small hut he called home.

Lonnie turned, acknowledging her presence, feeling a tinge of regret. She was a welcome addition to his staff, a breath of cool air in an otherwise harsh land. It would have been fine if he could have kept it at that, but his feelings had crossed over and he had to reel them back. She deserved better. He wished he could make up for the hurt his decision would cause, but the die had been cast.

Perhaps Father Paulo said it best: "It is not the prerogative of man to define what beauty is. That is the prerogative of God." But if Nicole *were* judged by the world's superficial standards, she would score high. With cosmetics hard to come by in Posada she rarely wore makeup, but was blessed with features that required little accent. Lonnie knew her use of lipstick and eyeliner was just for him, because she only wore them on Thursdays when they had a standing date, though in all fairness he always maintained a comfortable distance. Their interludes weren't meant to be romantic, at least not as far as he was concerned. It wasn't an intimate tête-à-tête. It was just a time to sit and relax and off-load the week's burdens, discuss the latest news and swap stories, without the strain of having to think in one language and speak in another. It was companionship. They would spend time together, enjoying the warm evening under the lights of the market, dining on barbecued pork in leaves of totomoxtl, sauce of jumiles, tepache, and a fresh-baked bread roll, and sipping espressos to the accompaniment of the town's marimba band. It was something Lonnie was fond of—and something he was going to miss.

They had met the year Lonnie inherited controlling interest of the company started by his father, a company which still bore his family name, "Striker Films." Nicole had been his brother's executive assistant, and as everyone knew, hired as much for her looks as her typing and organizational skills. But she had maintained professional decorum and distance. She had worked hard at being a good secretary, and had gained Harlan's respect. She wanted nothing more, and would accept nothing less.

If she had a weakness, it was that her life was a cliché. She was raised on the adolescent ideal of becoming a nurse in a Third World country, until not enough money, full-time work and a failed marriage caused her dreams to vanish like smoke over a dying fire. Lonnie inspired her to get her life back on track. Two and a half years and a nursing degree later, she joined him in his quest to bring the gospel to the lost tribes in the Sierra Madre del Sur.

"Hi, Lonnie. We still on for dinner this evening?"

Lonnie shook his head, and immediately regretted doing so. He had only just returned and here he was about to rush off again, but he was torn over how to break the news and this was not a good time. The kids couldn't wait. He went into his dingy hut and she followed him inside. "Afraid not," he said.

Nicole's eyes lost their smile.

"Sorry, something's come up. You'll have to have Father Paulo explain. I haven't got time. I'm about two minutes away from climbing on that bus and heading back to Oaxaca."

Nicole's eyes widened. "Oaxaca? What for?"

"I don't know," he said brushing past her, "and I haven't got time to figure it out. It's probably a fool's errand, but it looks like three of our kids got snatched, and I have to see about getting them back. Every minute I wait is another minute something bad could happen."

Nicole was following Lonnie, trying to keep up as he headed across the market, scattering a brood of squawking chickens. He reached the bus. "Sorry to be in such a rush. Go see Paulo and he'll fill you in on what he knows, which isn't much. Tell him I've gone to look for the kids. You're in charge of the hospital while I'm away." He climbed up and sat in the driver's seat, leaning forward to take hold of the large steering wheel. "I'll call as soon as I know anything," he said, turning the key. The bus fired up in a cloud of blue smoke, followed by a gurgling rumble from the engine. Then he shut the door. A puff of air fanned Nicole's face. She stepped back, and the bus lurched forward—taking Lonnie away.

THREE

Mamá, you are wrong! There is no God in heaven, no angels to protect you, no saints to watch over you. We are dirt to be stepped on and trampled underfoot. Your children, Mamá, are under the same curse as you and Papá. Yes, I watched you burn. What God would allow you to suffer so? I saw the inferno, the fires of hell consuming you and Papá. For what, Mamá? Because Papá would not go along. I know you tell me God loves little children, but where was He when these two burned your house with you inside, and stole your little boy and girl? If God exists—I hate Him! He is a cruel God who watches and does nothing while his creatures suffer! But have no fear, Mamá. I will do what I must. I will do what your God either cannot, or will not. I will kill diablo, myself!

RAÚL, MARIANA, and Sofía were sitting on an old ripped mattress that had cotton bleeding out the sides. It smelled of stale urine but the odor went unnoticed, being overpowered by the stench of human sweat. The passenger up front wore a plaid shirt, the driver a denim vest hanging open and bent cane cowboy hat. Raúl had seen him before. He was a scabby soul, little more than a skeleton with meat strapped to his bones. He had narrow yellowish eyes that reminded Raúl of a snake. There were tattoos on both his arms. The devil tossing a pair of dice on one, "*lucky seven*," and on the other a skull in a top hat with a reefer in its teeth. Raúl sat staring at the man, staying alert, looking for a chance to do what he had to do. He kept his little sister, Mariana, sheltered under his arm. The van hit a pothole the size of a moon crater and the three children bounced into the air and came down hard.

"¡Ay caramba! Easy, mi amigo, easy. You bruise the man's tomatoes, you see big trouble."

Raúl caught his sister, keeping her from bouncing against the metal wall. He looked for something to disable his captor. There were piles of dirty laundry, a filthy sleeping bag, jeans and old leather workboots. He could try to remove the hemp lace without being seen, but the odds of getting it around the neck of the driver before being pulled off were slim to none. And Sofía was undernourished, too fragile to be of any help. He needed a hoe, or a mallet, something to knock the man unconscious.

He'd have to wait until they stopped. There was no handle on the inside of the door, but the minute they opened it, he would slam his foot in their faces. He should have grabbed Mariana and taken off while they were still in Posada and run when they had the chance, but fear of the jungle always stopped him. The wild was hostile to those unfamiliar with its ways. He didn't want his sister ending up food for a cougar and, truth be known, he wasn't fond of snakes. That's why he'd welcomed the trip to Oaxaca. There should have been plenty of ways to slip into the crowd unnoticed, but every time he tried to escape, someone was watching. Then these two had tossed them into the van and he realized he'd waited too long. He'd made the mistake of thinking life in an orphanage might not be so bad. *Fool!* It had cost him. But if it did, it cost this crazy chica Sofía as well. They'd only wanted him and his sister. She'd put her nose where it didn't belong. Trying to help—*Hah!* There was a lesson in that. *Mind your own business.* Helping others only dumps their grief on you.

They were outside the city limits. There weren't any windows in back, but the many tall buildings he'd seen through the rain-spotted windshield had disappeared. Now Raúl saw trees. Miles and miles of trees. A pair of blue herons leisurely flapped their wings, crossing the road. Raúl had no idea what direction the van was heading, but he knew they were going deep into the rainforest. The road was still paved so, potholes notwithstanding, they couldn't be in too deep—at least not yet. Whatever their destination, it wasn't someplace nice.

They were slated to be sold, reduced to the level of barter goods like chickens and pigs. That much he knew from listening to their conversation. The men intended to recover the money their father owed.

Raúl recalled the scene vividly. The man had white hair and a white goatee, and was dressed in a matching white cotton suit with white shoes. He walked softly, spoke politely, and shook their father's hand with the formality of a man greeting a dignitary. And he smelled of scented perfume. The house only had two rooms: the living-eating-sleeping room and the bathroom, so it was impossible to be home and not be privy to the conversation, though they were supposed to be asleep. But they couldn't sleep. This man, so refined in speech and manner, was a genuine curiosity. He must have come from a city in the north to be dressed the way he was. They had never seen anything like it. Their own father was a fisherman whose nappy woolen clothes were disheveled and threadbare. He made his living on the sea with a net and scaling knife, but the fish harvest seemed to diminish each year while operating expenses were on the rise, so he'd put off making necessary repairs to his boat. When the engine finally choked and could no longer be revived, he'd gone to the bank but was refused. His credit was overextended. Apparently, this man had loaned him money and now wanted it back.

"I cannot pay you all at once," Raúl's father explained. "I can pay some now, but not all."

The man seemed unfazed. He nodded as though he understood. He told Raúl's father not to worry. He offered to let him work off the debt by using his boat to deliver merchandise to the U.S., but the fisherman declined. His boat would not be used for smuggling. About that he was firm. The man nodded, and stood. He didn't seem angry, or even upset. He just said to have the money ready by six the next evening. Then he left.

Raúl's father was a patient man, as fishermen and sea turtles are prone to be, but he'd seemed unusually anxious the following day. After an early dinner he'd forced money into the hands of his children and ordered them to the cinema. Only after the fact did it become clear to Raúl that he'd been trying to protect them.

Until that very moment, if it had been a snake slithering through the grass to bite his toe, Raúl would not have known evil. But that night he knew it. He saw it in the eyes of the man who confronted him in the alley on his way home. From beneath the shadow of a hat, looking cold and dark, the eyes leering at him were empty—*dead.* Without knowing why, Raúl sensed he had to turn and run. The eyes of the snake wanted him. At the end of the alley, behind him, was an unpainted cinder-block wall. The citadel of the fish plant. He grabbed Mariana and fled. The wall was ten feet high and topped with razor wire, but where a car had plowed into it there was a hole just big enough to squeeze through. The man came after them, just as Raúl knew he would. Raúl jerked Mariana along, forcing her to run faster than her little legs could move, and dragged her the last few yards when she stumbled and fell. The rocks pinched the soles of his bare feet, but he ignored the pain. Mariana was crying, but he reached the wall and pushed her though, then squeezed in after, cutting his hands and knees on the broken block. The man caught his foot and tried pulling him back, but Raúl kicked violently, forcing the man's hands to see-saw against the jagged concrete until they bled and lost their grip. Raúl stood, took a step back, and calmly dusted himself off on the other side, as the man groped through the hole trying in vain to grasp his ankle. He took his sister by the hand, limping off in the direction of the fish plant.

He heard the man grunting, and huffing, and scuffing against the ground, trying to squeeze through the hole, but Raúl knew they were safe. The hole was too small, and the plant was closed, the gates locked, and there was no other way in. He found a steel staircase on the side of the building and, with Mariana in front of him, began to climb. Over his shoulder, in the dark, he watched the man race to his vehicle and grind the engine to a start. The van squealed as it skirted the corner. Now Raúl had the advantage. This was his neighborhood. He knew where to hide. They continued up the stairs until they reached the top, then stepped onto the flat tar roof. They were high above the streets looking down and could see their house. But they couldn't believe their eyes. It was in flames. The fire rose like an inferno, one huge ball of blazing red heat. It was then Raúl knew why the man was there, and that he would not see his parents again.

He'd had three weeks to think about that night. Three weeks to sit and contemplate revenge. Even if he had trouble recognizing the man's face—it had been dark in that alley—there was no mistaking those eyes, or the telltale cuts and scrapes roping the man's wrists. It was the man now driving the van they were in. This was the man Raúl had to kill.

FOUR

THE OLD BUS lacked muscle as it slowly made its way up the grade. It *wheeeeezed* and *creeeaked* and *hissssed* with the sound of steam escaping metal. The bus had been retired from the California school system before being exported to Mexico in a sell-off of obsolete government hardware, and drafted back into service by Enrique for the transportation of his plantation workers. But now it was a school bus again, and though useful for short jaunts between villages, it was probably too old to take the scuffling and noise of adolescents over the long haul.

The headlights swept the road in front of Lonnie, bouncing off the thick growth of trees as he negotiated the turns. It wasn't dark yet, at least not completely. There was still a razor edge of light haunting the horizon, and an eerie purple vapor clinging to the mountains in a mist. A fog was forming as the warm moisture-laden air rolled over the cool ground. The turns in the narrow unpaved road were frequently too tight to keep all the wheels on the track. Occasionally a rear tire crept over the edge, but as long as there was traction, the vehicle moved ever forward. When the bus was heading into the mountain Lonnie saw the cotton-like haze in the trees, but when the road turned away the panorama of the Pacific opened up, and he saw the last remaining rays of purple light resting on the surface of the ocean.

Lonnie rounded another bend and found a family of peasants, or campesinos, traipsing back to their village. They hailed him from the side of the road. The men wore white pants with loose-sleeved white shirts and had on light-colored straw hats, which they held against the buffeting wind. On their shoulders were gunny sacks filled with beans and kernels of corn. They were heading home from the market. An old woman in a long skirt and brightly colored blouse held a squawking chicken upside down. The bird's wings were flayed out, beating the air. Lonnie knew every passing minute worked against him, but he had to stop. A flash of lightning brightened the sky. For a moment he saw sparks behind the clouds, pulsating east to west, followed by a rumbling of deep thunder. The wind tousled the branches of the trees.

The men were short and dark with broad flat noses and Beetle haircuts. Lonnie guessed them to be Zapotecs, though there were at least a half dozen other Indian tribes indigenous to the area. He cranked the handle, opening the door. No one bothered to say "Gracias." He was expected to stop. The troop climbed on board and plopped themselves on the empty seats. The chicken continued its *barrraakkk, cluck, cluck, cluck* of complaint. Lonnie was lucky to have left as late as he did because the later it got, the fewer people there would be on the road. The many stops would have detained him beyond reason. The last person climbed aboard. He was young, maybe twenty, and tall for an Indian, just under six feet with narrow shoulders. His straw hat held by the drawstring around his neck was twisting in the wind.

"Hola, Pastor," he said, grabbing the chrome bar to pull himself inside. "What brings you out so late?" Drops of water were bouncing off the bus' yellow paint. Rivulets formed and rolled down the windshield. An electrical flash whitened the sky.

"Hey, Felipe. Sit down, sit down, por favor. I'll explain but I'm in a hurry. I need to get moving." The sky broke with thunder, rumbling through the bus.

THE HEADLIGHTS cut through the rain, bouncing off trees whipped by the wind. The air smelled like wet wool. Lonnie held the steering wheel with a white-knuckled intensity. He passed the time quoting scriptures. *Take heed that ye despise not one of these little ones; for I say unto you, that in heaven their angels do always behold the face of my Father which is in heaven.* That's what Jesus said. The people who stole Raúl, Sofía, and Mariana were in trouble.

Lonnie dropped his passengers at the next village, all but Felipe, who decided to take advantage of a free ride to Oaxaca. He volunteered to drive but Lonnie politely declined. He now sat in the back of the bus, his head drooped forward and swinging from side to side as he dozed.

The bus continued to hiss, wheeze and pant, mile upon mile. There were no dashboard lights, a feature hardly missed since they seldom drove after dark and never at high speeds, but it would have been nice to read the temperature gauge just to make sure they weren't overheating.

Lonnie had made his way down to Mexico shortly after graduating from high school. He had hitchhiked from town to town, finally landing in Posada, a village with no cars where few people drove, so he'd never felt the need to get a license. Enrique Ramírez, the local coffee plantation owner and region's chief employer, had used the bus to pick up laborers and bring them to his camp for work. But the bus was over forty years old and spent as much time in the shop as on the road, so when he decided to put it up for sale and buy a new one, Lonnie bought the bus on the agreement Enrique would have someone teach him how to drive. Lonnie could handle the bus with enough skill to negotiate the mountains, but he still didn't have a license, and didn't feel he needed one since he rarely drove in traffic. The school used the bus for field trips, so the kids were learning about things they'd never had the chance to see before. The hospital used it as an ambulance. Many of the sick lived in remote villages and couldn't walk ten or fifteen miles down the road to see a doctor. And Lonnie used it to travel to other towns to minister. He held Bible studies right on the bus, standing up front, facing the congregants who sat in the seats like pews—the perfect mobile church. When it was running the bus was a Godsend, but any other time he'd just as soon roll it off a cliff and watch it sink into the blue Pacific.

They hit a pothole and the headlights bounced off and on again, but this time the dashboard lights came on too. The line on the temperature gauge was still below red. *Hallelujah!* Lonnie loved the convenience the bus provided but hated dealing with all the problems. Another bump and the headlights went out again. He pulled and pushed the knob several times until they flickered back on. Buying the bus had originally been Nicole's idea, but he was guarded about praising her for *that*.

Nicole? Now there was an enigma. One big question mark. He felt the magnetism, but it was misdirected. He had to remain true to his conscience. His emotions were in constant flux, the conundrum of having two beautiful women, one willing to spend her life in less than comfortable surroundings just to be with him, the other feigning love but craving the good life a little bit more. It was the nature of man to never be satisfied. The bird in the hand might be better than two in the bush, but woeful man seemed doomed to always chase the one that got away. But knowing this didn't quell his inner turmoil. All he wanted was the will of God, but how was he supposed to know what God wanted? Or maybe he knew, but didn't like the answer. Anyway, the point was moot. He'd asked Trudy to marry him, and that was that. He'd done the right thing. God created one man for one woman, not one for many, and once bound by the cord of intimacy man was expected to stay with his partner for life. *Been there, done that,* and like it or not, it couldn't be changed. The sin of his youth was a constant reminder of his frailty as a human being, and another reason he was guarded around Nicole—though there were times he wished he could let his guard down.

He struggled to change his mind and redirect his thoughts. Nicole was there, tending to the wounds of those who were hurt, providing for the needy, taking care of the children. And that was another thing. Trudy would never be good with the children, and the children were of paramount importance, which was why he was bumping and sliding along this treacherous stretch of dirt road in the rain and dark of night. But this was stupid. Such speculations were a waste of time, and the decision had been made. The question now was what happened to Raúl, Mariana and Sofía? *Stolen? Impossible!* No matter how it came together, the pieces didn't fit. They were orphans. No one wanted orphans. And if they did, all they had to do was ask. Lonnie couldn't imagine anyone stealing kids just to avoid the paperwork involved. Sofía didn't have a family, and Raúl's father had been a fisherman, not a wealthy landowner, so kidnapping was out of the question. You don't hold kids for ransom when no one's able to buy them back. It just didn't make sense.

The bus snaked its way out of the thick underbrush into the open plain of the valley. Headlights along the road were becoming more frequent. Rain dotted the windshield. The wipers flapped, *cachunk-eeeee, cachunk-eeeee, cachunk-eeeee.* Lonnie saw tiny spots of light coming into view, the city of Oaxaca nestled in a high valley, surrounded by the towering peaks of the Sierra Madre del Sur. His headlights painted the wet paved road with broad strokes of yellow. The tires whooshed, spinning up rooster tails of water.

Oaxaca was the second poorest and one of the most beautiful states in all of Mexico. Oaxaca City, the state capital, had settlements predating Christ by thousands of years. Subsequent civilizations were adept in math and astronomy, and were reputed to have devised the earliest form of writing on the continent. For centuries the Zapotec and Mixtec civilizations fought for control of the fertile valley. They were highly religious tribes that, like Israel's enemies the Babylonians and Chaldeans, had gods who demanded human sacrifice. *How could anyone do that?* Yet, even in thinking it, Lonnie knew God's own people, influenced by their pagan neighbors, had succumbed to the same practice.

Around the world, cultures and races of peoples with no physical connection involved themselves in the barbaric practice of sacrificing their children to the gods. Lonnie saw it as proof of satan's influence on planet earth. The devil wanted people dead—*wars, famine, pestilence, disease*—the method didn't matter. In modern times, when man no longer believed in gods made of wood and stone, and was too civilized to kill babies by passing them through the fire, he'd replaced sacrifice with abortion. Men and women still offered up their children. They reviled paganism, yet unwittingly slaughtered their babies all the same. And Lonnie knew the same false god was still behind the scenes, calling the shots.

Spain's conquest of Mexico brought Christianity to the Indians, putting an end to human sacrifice. In 1529, Hernán Cortés founded the city and gave it the name Oaxaca. Steeped in history and tradition, the town was a myriad of contrasts—old and new, rich and poor, cultured and unrefined. You could drive down la Calle Independencia and see modern commercial enterprises standing beside architecture from the seventeenth and eighteenth centuries. The well-to-do had villas with bougainvilleas and yellow adobe walls, arched walkways adorned with hand-painted tiles and potted red geraniums. But the other end of the economic ladder abounded with those who lived on the street, snuggling under their rebozos for warmth while boiling cabbage and baking bread over an open fire. Oaxaca was altogether a blend of the garish and ornate, the shabby and the sublime, which had earned it the designation of a national historic monument, and made it one of the most traveled tourist stops in all of Mexico.

Lonnie heard clomping footsteps and glanced in his rear-view mirror. Felipe was trudging toward him, rubbing his eyes.

"Hola, señor Lonnie." He stood, wobbling, grasping a chrome pole for support against the bouncing wheels. "Where are we?"

Lonnie looked over his steering wheel at the strings of electric bulbs criss-crossing the sidewalks, and the red streams of tail lights piling up in front of the bus. "Just coming into Oaxaca," he said.

"So, what will you do? I can look around and start asking questions if you like."

Lonnie shook his head. He geared down, slowing as they entered the town's populated core. "First I have to find a place to park. I can't pull up in front of the comisaria in a bus. Besides, I can't drive through the zócolo. It isn't accessible by car," he said, referring to the market square in the center of the city. "I'll see if I can get anything from the police, though Father Paulo already tried and didn't get much help."

Lonnie found a stretch of uninhabited road and pulled to the side, setting the brake. He cranked the door open and hopped down. "Felipe, I hate to ask, but I need you to stay here. I don't like leaving the bus alone in a strange place, and you may have to move it if someone asks. I'll only be gone an hour at most." The air was thick with the smell of overripe fruit. The rain was pelting Lonnie's white muslin shirt. He could feel the moisture seeping through the coarse cotton.

The tall young Zapotec removed his straw hat and wiped a sleeve across his forehead. His dark straight hair was moist and stayed glued to the sides of his face. He had thick Indian lips. "Sí. If you don't mind if I sleep."

Lonnie traipsed off in the direction of the zócolo, shaking his head. The drizzle continued unabated, running off his hairline, under his collar, and down his back. People were congregated in the streets. Fires burned sending sparks into the night. Off in the distance a marimba band could be heard over the bustle of conversation. A man sloshed by, bumping Lonnie's shoulder, and turned. "Hey, waaash where you're goin'." He wore a filthy poncho and smelled of vomit, but Lonnie didn't stop. Funny how there was never enough money to eat, but always enough to drink. A baby cried loudly, a shrill sound, like the screech of an owl. Lonnie walked through a corridor with a series of arches. Tourists kept the city busy at night, even in the rain. Crowds of sightseers milled about under their umbrellas. Street vendors abounded, hawking everything from jewelry, pottery and religious bric-a-brac, to hand-loomed shawls and blankets. Lonnie could smell tortillas smothered in assorted cheeses, and meat-stuffed tamales steamed in banana leaves being warmed over the coals of an outdoor pushcart. He passed buildings constructed of green volcanic stone and adobe structures painted turquoise and pink. He hoped the police station would be open. It should be. Crime didn't just happen during the day, though he felt safe—at least in this part of town. Most of the crime took place in the rookeries, the habitat of thieves, ragpickers and pulque sellers, where evil was committed with impunity.

He reached the door and held it back, the scream assaulting his ears before he stepped inside. There was a man on the floor with his wrists handcuffed behind his back. He tried bringing his knees up, curling into a ball before being kicked again. He looked up, pleading, his half-lidded eyes red and swollen. Blood poured from his nose. The room smelled of testosterone. Lonnie could feel the hostility. He approached the man sitting behind the front desk.

"Yes, señor, what do you want?" the man said.

Lonnie looked over his shoulder at the man on the ground, who groaned at another kick to the groin. "What'd he do?"

"¿Quién sabe? Who knows? I would not concern myself if I were you."

Lonnie nodded. "My name is Lonnie Striker. I'm from the mission in Posada. We've lost three of our children. Father Paulo Ceylon came in earlier and filed a report."

The man looked over his shoulder and then turned to the desk. He found a clipboard with a printed form on it. "Sí," he said, nodding as he held the sheet up to read, "the matter has been dealt with. The report is here. Okay, what can I do for you?"

"I was wondering what was being done, to get the kids back, I mean."

A grin slipped across the officer's face. "You want to know what's being done? Okay, I'll tell you. If the little muchachas and muchacho walk through the door, we will get in touch with you. Okay?"

"But no...I mean, is anyone out there looking for them?"

The man folded his hands and leaned on the counter, looking weary. "Señor Striker, children disappear every day. We have no way of finding them. When they disappear," he snapped his fingers, "they disappear. Like magia. And these were orphans, señor. No one is going to look for them. I suggest next time you watch the children more carefully. Now, por favor, I have work to do." The man turned and went back to his seat, picking up the magazine he'd been reading.

Lonnie could see he'd been dismissed. The victim of the police beating was being dragged by his coat to a lock-up in back, leaving a smear on the floor.

Lonnie left the acrid smell of sour sweat behind as he stepped outside. He loved Mexico. He loved the campesinos in the rural villages. They were an industrious and hard-working people. But the city was a world unto itself. A jailed man could wait more than a year for a trial and consider himself lucky to get one. Those believed guilty of capital offences sometimes just disappeared—*"I had to shoot him, he was trying to escape"*—but that was a problem for another day. He walked away. Then it hit him. He jogged his memory. *Where? Where was it? Oh, right!* He passed a kiosk with a public phone. The air smelled like straw passed through a mule. He picked up the phone. "Operator, can you connect me with the inn in Posada, and make it a collect call from Lonnie?" He smiled. "Posada" meant "inn." So he was asking for the posada in Posada, or the inn in Inn. When the line was picked up, Lonnie asked for Nicole's room. Nicole had opted to rent a permanent suite in the inn because it afforded her the luxury of a bath and electricity, rather than live in a more primitive adobe hut. She answered on the second ring. Lonnie explained his predicament, and gave her the number of the phone he was using. He asked her to go to his place, dig through his files, find the one marked "Modern Slavery," and then call him right back. He closed his eyes, shaking his head. *How could anyone stoop so low as to sell another human being?*

Lonnie stood tapping his toe. A little girl approached and held out her straw doll. He started to accept the gift, but a woman whose long braids were coiled in a bun and pinned behind her head came from behind and scooped the child up, scurrying away in a flurry of colored skirts. *Smart lady. If we'd done that, I wouldn't be standing here right now.* The phone rang. Lonnie snapped it up and Nicole read the information she'd found. It was a series of articles written by a journalist whose work Lonnie had come to admire. He'd clipped the articles and kept them because the writer alleged Mexican crime cartels were smuggling children across the border, and selling them into slavery and prostitution in the U.S.

Lonnie thanked Nicole and asked her to fax the articles to the police station. He knew what he had to do. He had to see William Best.

FIVE

I am so sorry, Mariana, so very, very sorry. You know I would have protected you if I could, but I couldn't. You saw, didn't you? I was waiting for the right time. I would have kicked the door in his face. I was ready to jump on his back. I would have bit off his ear. I would have gouged out his eyes before the stupid fat one knew what to do. But when he pointed that pistol at you...I could do nothing.

But I will, Mariana, you'll see. I will. He don't scare me. I hate him, and my hate makes me strong. I will kill him. I swear it on the graves of our mamá and papá. Someday—somehow—I will avenge their deaths. I will restore honor to our family.

RAÚL SAT peering into the eyes of his five-year-old sister, eyes innocent and large, accentuated by questions and fears. He wondered what was going on in her mind. She'd been there. She'd witnessed the evil, the lifeless look of the man, their dreadful flight. Seeing their home on fire with their parents inside. She'd not spoken since. For two weeks they had stayed with the missionaries in the seclusion of that remote village, far from the pain of the past, and agreed it wasn't so bad a place to hide, until the evil overtook them again. *What are you thinking, Mariana?* For the moment, he hoped she was praying because her prayers helped quell her fears, though he didn't believe in prayer himself. But if it made Mariana feel better, then bueno. He expected nothing beyond that. Raúl never prayed, even when his mother told him to, because he'd watched her pray and saw it did no good. She prayed for food, but they had little to eat. She prayed for money, but they never had enough. She prayed for their father, but... Raúl and Mariana would be in bed, supposedly asleep, and would listen as she pleaded with God until their father dragged himself through the door, his hair disheveled, his face unshaven, with nothing to offer but an apologetic smile proving, once again, her prayers were as empty as his hands. She even prayed for her children, and look where they were. All that stuff about forgiveness wasn't worth a dog's breakfast. Live by the Book, she'd said. Well, she'd lived by the Book, and see what it got her—burned alive. The irony was she would have prayed the whole time, not for herself, but for the man holding the match. God Himself would laugh at that! And his sister was possessed by the same forgiving spirit. She couldn't, or wouldn't, talk to anyone else, but she was talking to God, or at least trying to. In her innocence she believed what she could never understand, but that was fine as long as it kept her from giving up hope.

One thing Raúl was learning was that to survive in this world you had to be tough. It was his weakness that caused them to be where they were right now. He'd begun to think living with the missionaries, or at least the blond one—*because her hands were gentle, like a mother's*—might not be so bad. But that's what stopped him from leaving when they had the chance. Now he knew they wouldn't be safe until the snake was dead. He would do it himself. He would crush it. Someone had to stop the evil. He wished he knew what Mariana was thinking—*or praying*. He couldn't provide the words of comfort she needed to hear.

Raúl's mouth was covered with a strip of silver duct tape, as was Mariana's and Sofía's. Sometime during the night the van had stopped at the side of the road. The driver flicked on the interior light and, after shuffling under his seat, produced a handgun which he pointed at Mariana. She was pulled into his lap with the gun to her head, while his overweight partner flopped out the passenger door and waddled around to tie up Sofía and Raúl. Their hands were wrenched behind them and duct tape looped around their wrists, with a strip stretched over each mouth. Once they were secure, they did the same to little Mariana and had her join the others in the back where she was forced to sit facing her brother. He positioned Sofía so their legs intersected and criss-crossed the tape around all three pairs of knees, locking them together.

The door slid closed, leaving the children sitting alone with the *rat-tat-tat* of rain tapping the roof and the two men's voices dissipating as they disappeared into the night. Raúl could almost make out his sister's eyes, wide with terror, staring at him, begging his help even in the dark. He wanted to free himself not so much to escape, though that was ever on his mind, but to put his arms around her. For more than an hour he sat rubbing his wrists against the wall, trying to snap the binding, but it was hopeless. He wanted to be vigilant, but he knew he needed to conserve his strength for what lay ahead. He could tell by their breathing that Mariana and Sofía had drifted off to sleep, and with his head nodding under its own increasing weight, he allowed himself to doze lightly as well.

He awoke to the voices of the men approaching, his neck stiff and aching as his head snapped up. He shivered. Neither the T-shirt he wore nor the pink polyester blouse worn by his sister would keep them warm at night. He felt a *thump* as the men stumbled against the van. He heard the doors *screeeeeech* open, and then *blamm, blamm* as they closed again. The space filled with the hideous odor of smoke, liquor and unwashed bodies. He sensed the coming dawn, and recognized a faint glow in the back of the van that hadn't been there before. But he couldn't see the others clearly, nor tell if they were awake or asleep. The engine cranked a few times and finally caught, and the van lurched forward. The tires hummed over the open highway. He shook off his drowsiness, and once again set his mind to plotting a way of escape. *Why you doing this, God?* He tried stretching the tape, wanting to break it, but it was useless. The twisted material only bit into his flesh.

His mother had been a good woman, a praying woman, she read the Book—*Why you let this happen?*—and his father a decent hard-working man. His callouses were earned. Most days he was up before the sun, riding the first tide, battling white-capped swells with the wind biting his face and salt burning in the cracks of his hands as he labored with the net, hauling it over the side of his boat again and again, only to find it empty or filled with worthless kelp. *Why, God? Why do you let good people die?* Raúl flinched. A bug was crawling on his neck. He pressed his cheek to his shoulder but couldn't dislodge it. He judged it to be a spider by the way it moved. He tried rolling his shoulders, hoping to rub the critter off, but it slipped down his shirt, catching at the small of his back.

Spiders weren't so bad. He remembered the one he'd watched only a few weeks ago, back when life was boring. The spider had built a web in the corner of their house. Raúl watched, fascinated by the artistry of the creation, as the spider dropped on its own thread, linking it to a line spun in the other direction, tying it off, and starting over until it completed a net in which to catch its dinner. Then it crawled into a corner and waited. It didn't take long. A fly zooming recklessly around the room hit the web and froze on the tacky line. The spider wasted no time. It came out of hiding and began wrapping its victim in coils of sticky string. Just like what he and Sofía and Mariana were coiled in now. That was it! It wasn't about good and evil. There was nothing evil about a spider. The spider only did what spiders do. It was about the laws of nature, of predator and prey. This man was a spider. He had caught their mother and father, and now he had them. It was just the nature of some animals to prey on others, which also explained why God didn't care. He made the spider. But Raúl also knew when his mother found the spider in their house, she squished it. Whether God cared or not wasn't the issue. The issue was that some things were better off dead.

Another two hours passed before the van pulled to the side of the road. The others had been awake for some time, though both Sofía and Mariana seemed to keep their eyes closed more than open. The interior of the van was a morbid gray in the predawn light. There wasn't much to see. The driver leaned out the window, talking to someone outside, letting the moist chill seep in. Then the van pulled away and continued its journey.

They turned onto a dirt road with so many potholes the children had to lean forward to keep their backs from getting scraped as they bumped along. A sudden jolt sent Mariana up, but with her legs bound her flight was restricted. Her head crashed against the metal wall.

Once again, the van slowed and came to a stop. The men climbed out. They'd said little since returning, as though groggy from sleep, or lack of it. The front doors slammed, *blamm, blamm*, and the side door opened. The sun, just off the horizon, hit Raúl in the face, blinding him. He squinted and turned his head away. The heavy-set man used a machete to cut the tape from the legs of the three children. All three pairs of knees curled up, savoring their new-found freedom. Mariana was lifted from the doorway and set on her feet. Raúl wormed forward but the skinny one pushed him back.

"Slow down, mi amigo. You'll get your turn."

Mariana yelped as the tape was ripped from her mouth. Raúl struggled forward but was restrained again. The heavy man clipped the tape from Mariana's wrists and she was led away by a man Raúl had not seen before. He tried to wiggle out of the grip that held him and was backhanded across the face. He flinched, lessening the blow. The tape over his mouth absorbed part of the sting, but the shock, more then the slap itself, smarted.

"Don't be so anxious, perrito. Ladies first."

The fat man pulled Sofía from the back of the van. The tape was clipped from her hands and feet and she was led away, cowering. Then it was Raúl's turn. He felt the blood pounding in his legs as he stood for the first time in more than twelve hours, the numbness leaving his feet. The morning was brisk. He felt goosebumps on his arms as he examined his surroundings. They were in a large valley several miles wide, a basin filled with row upon row of tall green shrubs, all waving in the breeze. It looked like the jungle had been cut back to accommodate farming. The sky above had cleared and was hazy blue. The morning birds were joined in a cacophony of *ka, ka, kawing* and *kee-whipper-willing,* declaring to the world they'd survived another night. For one brief moment, Raúl was free. He could run if he wanted to, but he couldn't leave his sister. As his eyes adjusted to the blinding light, he saw they were not alone. Dozens of men were roaming the area, silhouettes moving against the bright sun streaming through the plants. All wore white muslin dress typical of campesinos, a few held guns, and all had large machetes fixed to their belts.

A hand squeezed his shoulder, prodding him around the front of the van. He winced, and vowed once more to kill the man who owned that hand. In the distance stood several rows of Quonset huts. Men were unloading carts piled high with crops. When a cart was empty and the plants carried into the hut, it was refilled with those removed from the hut that now looked brown and shriveled. In front was a small square office made of sheets of plywood with a screen door entrance. The sky in this direction was a satin sheet of magenta warming his shoulders. It felt good, but Raúl knew it was deceptive. Before long it would grow hot and the sun's warm blanket would be the last thing he'd want. He felt the grip on his shoulder tighten as he was turned in the direction they had taken Sofía and Mariana. He was being marched toward a large compound surrounded by a chain-link fence topped with razor wire. Inside the first fence was a second one. The space between the two housed dogs that continually barked.

He scanned the area, looking for his sister. If they were going to escape, it wouldn't be over the top. He'd have to dig underground. The pen held more than a dozen children. Raúl guessed their ages ranged from five to ten years old. He wondered if they could be counted on to help. There was human waste littering the ground and the stench wafting through the air was worse, if possible, than what they'd had to endure in the van. At the back of the pen, four posts held a square frame covered with wood slats that provided a shelter—of sorts. It was the only visible protection the children had against the burning midday sun or pounding overnight rain. A man held the gate to both pens open and Raúl was pushed inside by his tattooed escort. He stumbled and fell and jumped up with clenched fists, eyes filled with fire. Mariana ran to her brother's aid, but the evil one caught her arm.

"No, no, no, putita. Do not help him. He is no longer your brother. Where you are going, you will not see each other again." He spun her around and pushed her in the opposite direction.

"Nooooo!" Raúl launched himself at the skinny one, pounding on

him with his fists, knocking the hat from his head, and causing the glazed shine of his pointed-toe cowboy boots to become covered in a layer of dust.

"*Oh*, a tough one, eh? Okay, okay, we'll see." The man wrapped Raúl in a bear hug. "Hey, Diego, give me a hand, this one's slippery as a fish." He held Raúl down and the man who had unlocked the gate came into the pen with another roll of tape. They bound Raúl's hands and feet and picked him up like a trussed pig, carrying him to a post where he was tied, standing up.

"We'll see how tough you are after you cook in the sun," the man said.

Raúl's eyes grew hard and flat. He worked his tongue around in his mouth, scouring up saliva and, looking up, spat in the man's face.

This time the man did not comment. Instead he buried his fist into Raúl's stomach, knocking the wind out of the boy who fell forward, bowing over, gagging. The man yanked a strip of tape from the roll and slapped it on Raúl's mouth.

SIX

NICOLE'S EYES snapped open, her heart pounding. *Must have been a bad dream.* No, there was no dream, at least not one she could remember. Only apprehension. She lay still, gathering her thoughts. Something disturbed her sleep. *What?* Whatever it was it eluded her, but something was making her heart race, and she felt cold and wet like she'd been sweating.

The room was awash in the gray of a false dawn, the moon streaming in through the window, casting purple light on the dresser and mirror. She closed her eyes. There was something right at the edge of her thoughts, something she couldn't grasp. *Must not be important.* She rolled over, curling into a ball as she tucked the blanket under her chin, trying to fall asleep. She waited, willing the *thaathump, thaathump, thaathump* of her heart to quiet down, then turned away from the window and its light. It was no use. Ten minutes later she was still awake.

She sat on the edge of the bed, her toes searching for her slippers as she reached for her robe. There was a chill in the air, but it *was* the rainy season. She shivered, pulling the robe around her waist, tying the belt. She shuffled to the window, aching from lack of sleep. It had been a fitful night. The window was open, left ajar to circulate fresh air. She pushed it, letting it swing outward, and lay her forearms across the sill. The wood was rough and moist against her skin. She inhaled deeply, looking out over the town's market circle. The air smelled of moist humus and was filled with the sounds of night-crawling insects. Across the plaza a barn owl *whooo-hooo-hoooooed.*

The rain had stopped. The clouds were broken, shimmering brightly where the moon framed their edges. The light coming through was strong enough to make a quilt of the cobblestones on the road below. Parked off to the side was the old school bus, its yellow paint looking blue in the predawn light. Lonnie had said Felipe would bring it back sometime during the night.

That man was crazy, and she'd told him so. You don't fly thousands of miles to meet with someone you've never spoken to without first making an appointment. But he couldn't be deterred. Okay, it was irrational, but it was also bold and took initiative, and that was part of who he was. She'd been there when he'd walked into Striker Films and cleaned house, head-butting an industry bent on destroying virtue. He hadn't acted out of pride, or a pseudo sense of self-confidence, but out of a deep inner conviction. *Right is right.* He'd put his ministry and everything he loved on the line, but he couldn't let the company continue making films contrary to the kingdom of God, even if it meant losing it all. She'd wondered at the time if he was really that naive, or that selfless, or that—*real?*

Darn it all, Lonnie was a good man. He was decisive about other things. He could change the direction of an entire company without blinking, or build a hospital, or buy a bus. But when it came to affairs of the heart, he didn't have a clue. He was emotionally blind. *Can't you see it? Trudy doesn't love you. She's just playing you, boy.* Or maybe he was just too weak to do anything about it. With his words he'd acknowledge the need to cut himself loose, and then start thinking about Quentin and inadvertently pull the knot tighter. But it wasn't about Quentin. His son wasn't anxious to see his parents back together. He was smart enough to know his mother wouldn't leave her Malibu mansion, her manicures and make-overs, her social commitments and luxury limousines. She would never lower herself to live among the Indians. Nor could his father go along with the lifestyles of the rich and famous. Forced to live in Hollywood, he'd wither like a flower cut and left to dry on a hot porch.

Nicole watched the moon shimmering on the ocean. The nighttime waters looked inky from her second-story loft. She hated it every time Lonnie left to attend a board meeting, the tie that held him to his other life. She hated not knowing whether he would return.

His indecision was killing her. Maybe she should pack up and leave. She'd threatened to often enough, at least in her mind. She *should* do it. She should pack, leave a nice little note, and go. The only problem was she'd grown to love the people of Posada, so leaving wasn't an option.

The old bus sat like a huge blue boulder in the shadows. The bus that should have brought Lonnie home. *Darn it all.* She felt cheated—*again.* What was he getting himself into? She'd read the articles he'd had her pull from his files. This wasn't a game. Mess with the cartel and you were likely to end up in the trunk of a car with your brains leaking out the side of your head.

She turned, realizing now for the first time why she'd been awakened from her sleep. She was supposed to pray. She moved away from the window, sauntered back to her bed, and dropped to her knees.

THE SEA BLAZED crimson, reflecting the morning sun as the plane swept across the ocean on approach to Portland International. Lonnie struggled with his seat belt, trying to get comfortable. *Seat back up, table in an upright position.* He didn't need Nicole to tell him he was crazy. He knew it. There was nothing sane about hopping a plane in the middle of the night and flying off to a place you've never been, to meet someone you've never met, who doesn't even know you're coming. He'd wanted to call ahead but didn't have Bill's number, and the office of the newspaper where Bill worked was closed. So, here he was, on descent into Portland without knowing if the person he wanted to see had time for a meeting, or was even there. The jet banked to the east revealing a marvelous view of Mount Hood. The sun's spreading rays glazed yellow on the snaking Columbia River. The dense pines shouldering its banks were violet in the breaking dawn. The landscape was a cascade of warm magentas, purples and browns.

Nicole was right. He *was* acting foolish, but lives were at stake and he couldn't just sit and do nothing. He didn't know where else to turn, and, crazy or not, he had to do *something*. He had to meet this man in person. Call it a hunch, a whim, call it *stupid*, he didn't care. The man had to know more than what was said in the papers, and Lonnie was determined to find out what that was. He'd learned long ago not to fight his intuition, the inner voice that guided his life, though he hadn't been required to do anything *this* daring in years. Never mind. God had given him the strength he'd needed then, and God would provide the strength he needed now, though if the Hollywood film industry was Goliath, then this was the giant's big brother. And he'd already used his allotment of stones. But what choice did he have? He couldn't let Sofía be sold into prostitution. And what about little Raúl and his sister? They were young. Odds were they'd be snatched up by pedophiles and ravished horribly. It was barbaric. His stomach curdled just thinking about it. Lonnie held his breath as the wheels hit the pavement with a screech and a bounce, glad as always to be back on good old terra firma. But despite mulling over the possibilities for most of the trip, he still wasn't sure what he was supposed to do next.

THE TAXI meter read eighty-two dollars. He'd loitered in the lobby of the newspaper for nearly three hours waiting for Bill, but as the receptionist explained, writers were generally out chasing stories. Bill might not be seen for days, and no, she could *not* release his home number. It was company policy—a security measure. People were known to stalk reporters they disagreed with, making their lives unbearable. No amount of persuasion could change her mind. All she could do was call Mr. Best and leave a message asking him to contact his office as soon as possible. Lonnie didn't own a cell phone so he couldn't be reached, and in the three hours he was there Bill never called. So out of sheer frustration, Lonnie left to start his own investigation. He'd read Bill's latest column while waiting. It reported on an upcoming Special Olympics in which his daughter would be taking part.

Lonnie hired a cab to take him to the community center where the event was to be held the following day. There he insisted the pink-haired pin cushion behind the counter let him review his daughter's application. And the family name, of course, was "Best." Right there on her application were her parent's address and phone number. *Bingo!* He handed the form back to the clerk, wondering how she ate with that stud in her tongue. He headed for the door. If nothing else, Bill had to be impressed with his investigative technique.

The cab driver turned out to be a woman, which shouldn't have surprised Lonnie, but did nonetheless. She took the address and explained his destination was out of town. "Might cost much as a hundred bucks." *Ouch!* Thank God he'd remembered to bring the company credit card. Being chairman of the board did have *some* advantages.

But when she said "out of town," Lonnie assumed she meant a suburb close to Portland. He had no idea where they were going. They'd been on the road nearly an hour and the lady didn't look like she was planning to stop. Mount Hood loomed on the horizon with wisps of snow lifting like strands of white hair around its crown. They'd turned off the main road and were heading in-country, driving through miles of unending forest. Stands of spruce, fir, cedar, and pine stood thick at the road's edge, smelling of Christmas. A sign swept by his window in a blur, but appeared to have the name of the place Bill had used on his application. After another fifteen minutes the cab began to slow and Lonnie looked up, assuming they were pulling into town, but in actual fact all he saw was a log cabin standing alone in the middle of nowhere.

"This is it," his driver said, looking over her shoulder. "You want me to wait?"

Lonnie looked around for signs of life. *Rats.* Bill had used his cottage address to keep the hounds off his trail.

"Yes, definitely. I don't know if anyone's home."

Lonnie opened the door and stepped into a heavy breeze, his hair rippling along his scalp. He was standing in a grove of giant trees, some with trunks three feet in diameter. Sunbeams filtered through the branches, spilling yellow columns of cosmic dust onto the forest floor. The air smelled of cedar. Somewhere off to his left a squirrel was chattering. The cabin sat on the edge of a blue lake that was dappled with flecks of sun. It was made of logs and, except for its size, appeared rustic. It was two stories high with a cedar-shingled roof that held three dormers, each with its own gabled roof and window. Out front was a large welcoming porch with a rail and two high-back rocking chairs. This wasn't Bill's home. It was a hunting lodge.

There was no point in knocking. No one was there—he was sure of it—but he trudged up the wooden steps one at a time, making a pretense so the cab driver couldn't say he'd turned around without even trying. He paused, placing his hand on the edge of a chair, setting it rocking with the creaking sound of trees rubbing in the wind. He didn't see a doorbell. The door was tongue-and-groove pine, made of boards heavy enough to deaden sound. Lonnie wondered if anyone inside would hear him knock, assuming there was anyone there in the first place. He pounded on the door. Nicole was right. The whole idea was crazy. She had every right to say, "I told you so." He raised his fist and thudded on the door a second time. When he didn't get a response he turned and hopped down the stairs.

He could always have the taxi stop in the nearest town. He should have called. Bill wouldn't fake his phone number, would he? The people hosting the Special Olympics might need to get in touch with him. He took hold of the car door and started to crawl in, but something caught his eye. His head snapped up. Out on the water, back behind the house, a long red canoe approached the shore, and in it a man wearing a full beard and plaid vest. The man kept his paddle moving, taking long sweeping strides until he reached the smooth sandy beach. He pulled the paddle from the water as the canoe parked on land. Lonnie began to wish he'd left a few minutes earlier. The man didn't wave, nor did he look friendly. He stepped out of his canoe and scooped up a rope, tossing it around a tree before tying it off. The man was big, not just lumberjack big, but huge. *Why couldn't he just be a regular sized guy?* "I'm looking for William Best," Lonnie said.

"You found him," only it's Bill, the man said without looking up.

He reached into the canoe and retrieved a fishing rod and a string of trout on a line, and marched off toward the back of the cabin.

The cab driver stuck her head out the window. "Okay, bud, I gotta hit the road and the meter's still tickin'. How 'bout we settle up? I show a hundred thirteen on the meter plus the thirty dollar out-of-town surcharge, so that comes to a hundred forty-three bucks."

"Surchar—you didn't say anything about a surcharge."

"Read the sign, bud, posted on the back of my seat in plain view. I gotta charge extra to go all that way back without a fare."

Lonnie nodded, looking at the cabin again. He'd found his man. Should he let the cab go? What if the man didn't want to talk? He'd be stranded.

"Come on, bud, time's a wastin'. One hundred forty-three dollars, or get in and let's go."

Lonnie stood for a moment, waffling, his hand still resting on the door. *No!* He had to see Bill. He would do it for the children. He reached for his wallet and gave his credit card to the driver.

The man was back, hovering around his canoe. He reached out and pulled the free end of the rope, loosening it from the tree, and tossed the coils back into the bow.

The driver handed Lonnie a receipt and began backing away. The man pushed the canoe into the water. He placed his hands on the rails and stepped in, turning around as he crawled toward the rear, his weight raising the nose of the canoe. He used his paddle to push himself from the shore and cast off. "You coming? Or are you just gonna stand there till I get back?" The canoe began to turn into the water.

Lonnie took a step forward and suddenly his feet were running, splashing through the shallows at the edge of the lake. He stepped over the shiny red side of the boat, and plopped himself down.

SEVEN

Look at your son, Mamá. Look at me. Do not tell me God cares. Does He want me to hang here burning in the sun? If you are with Him, you tell Him to let me go. But you cannot. He is nothing, and so I must suffer. He must hate me. He knows I will not leave until I kill the man who put you there. Maybe He does not want me to kill. Ha! Killing this one is less than squishing a bug. The great God would not condemn me for that. And what about Mariana? She has done no wrong. She's just like you, she prays for the man. Yes, I heard you pray. You begged God to protect Papá, to keep the man away, that he would change his mind and not make Papá pay. You prayed for that man's salvation. Ha. You wanted him in heaven, and he killed you! Now Mariana's eyes are filled with the same...oh, Mamá, have they not shed enough tears? I know what happens to those who leave here. They become the slaves of rich American men. They are sold like animals. I try so hard, Mamá, but how can I believe in a God that treats us so?

RAÚL WAS delirious. His head was throbbing. The sun bore down hot and heavy on his scalp. There was a loud droning in his ears and his eyes burned, consumed by fire. He could no longer see anything but white. He was not seeing angels, though at times they appeared to be so, but angels would cut him loose, *wouldn't they?* His eyes were playing tricks on him, causing him to see what wasn't there.

The other children huddled in the small puddle of shade provided by the wooden scaffold. They had to relocate themselves as the sun crossed the sky, but at least they had protection. Breakfast, if you could call it that, had been served, though it was more of a feeding frenzy. The starving children mobbed the food like rats on a morsel of cheese, arms and legs and elbows flying. Mariana and Sofía stood back and watched. One grossly overweight child in a blue bulky-knit sweater had tried to squeeze in but his glasses were knocked loose and flattened underfoot in the fracas. He was pushed aside, tripping over his clumsy shoes, and left wallowing in the dust. He brought his knuckles to his eyes and began to cry. There was a time Raúl would have felt sorry for him—but not now. If gordo-boy didn't know how to fight, he'd have to live off his excess fat. Otherwise he wasn't going to make it.

It was during those early hours, while his mind was still clear, that he'd seen a glimpse of his future. A van had pulled up to the fence and the children, all but Sofía, his sister and gordo-boy, were prodded inside like cattle, a dozen or more kids crammed into the back of a hot tin box. The doors had slammed and the van lurched forward, a plume of dust trailing behind as they pulled away.

Raúl was young, but not naive. He knew this was his fate. The men probably wanted boys for hard labor, but that didn't mean his sister was safe. He didn't care about the work or about himself. He cared about Mariana. They had to stay together. If they came and took her while he was taped to this pole, he'd be helpless to do anything. They would have to let him go sooner or later. He resolved to wait. Come nightfall, he would tunnel under the fence and make good their escape.

EIGHT

LONNIE LIVED in a mountainous region of the Sierra Madre del Sur so he was used to seeing animals, like the doe and spotted fawn he now saw grazing at the edge of the lake. A few minutes earlier, a beaver had appeared out of nowhere, swimming straight for the nose of the canoe. Lonnie could see its eyes and little round ears above the water, and the tail that flicked a crystal stream into the boat as it veered off, chattering. Bill hardly seemed to notice, but did say the animal was letting them know they were passing though its territory and weren't welcome.

But what *was* foreign to Lonnie was being around so much water. Mexico was an arid land, even during the rainy season when the creeks were full. He liked it that way. He had only bad experiences with water. He never claimed to be a great swimmer, and the idea of being in the middle of a large body of water so far from the shore was unsettling. He didn't see any life jackets on board. He tried to be discreet, gripping the rails with white knuckles. The whole venture was taking *far* too long. He didn't consider where they might be going when he jumped into the boat. He just wanted answers. Only now it appeared he was stuck in the middle of a lake, at the whim of this burly bearded man, who could keep him hostage at sea as long as he wanted.

Lonnie shivered. In his hurry, he hadn't thought to bring a coat. The altitude was high, and the September weather cool. The wind skating across the lake rippled the water and made his face feel taut as paper. Bill Best had on a large puffy vest probably stuffed with goose down. He hadn't said more than a few words since they'd left, but Lonnie talked almost nonstop, explaining the disappearance of the children. The man just kept nodding, taking one long stroke after another, providing an occasional "uh huh" whenever it seemed appropriate.

"I see your point," Bill finally said, "but what's it got to do with me?"

"Everything, but we'll get to that in a minute. Can I ask where we're going? I don't want to seem pushy, but I'm kind of in a hurry to find my kids."

Bill nodded. "Un huh. We won't be long. See that waterfall over there?" He turned his head, pointing his beard toward the other end of the lake. "There's a falcon's nest on the face of that rock. She's got young. I've been watching her raise them, but the thing is she hasn't been around for a few days, and it's got me worried. I figure she must have got herself shot, or hit by a car, something or other. They're protected, you know. She's a peregrine, and they're rare." Bill took another stroke with his paddle. "I got to make sure those young are being fed. Won't take but a few minutes."

Lonnie stared at the cliff off in the distance. It didn't seem like a "few minute" job to him, but his plane didn't leave until seven and that would be time enough, or so he hoped. "It, uh, well, it never occurred to me I'd be sidetracked like this. I've got to catch a plane in a few hours. I've got to be getting back. There's no telling when my kids could be auctioned off, and if that happens, it'll make my job twice as hard. I could end up chasing them halfway around the world. You wrote about the abuse. You know what I'm talking about. These are my children, Mr. Best. I can't stand knowing what they might be going through."

Bill took another broad stroke. The canoe arced to the left causing Lonnie to think they were turning around, but it soon became apparent Bill had just altered his course slightly. "You have a daughter, don't you? I read that somewhere, a young lady in a wheelchair, isn't that right? You're a father. You must understand. What if it were your child?"

"If it *were* my child, I'd feel just like you. Maybe worse. As you said, my little girl's special. Fact is, I'd be tempted to put aside reason and go in there with guns blazing, not that I'd actually do such a thing, but I'd sure as heck feel like it. Don't think I don't empathize. I know how you feel, but I got a few critters to take care of, and I know what time your plane leaves. I should. Been on it enough times. Don't worry. You won't miss your flight."

The shoreline grew closer. Lonnie looked over the side and saw smooth round rocks glowing in the yellow shallows. At least if he fell in now he'd be able to walk. "Well, then I hope you understand my impatience. This whole thing has my stomach in knots." The canoe slipped into a pebbly cove. Bill stepped out, planting a boot in the water. He sloshed onto dry ground, pulling the nose of the canoe with him. Lonnie crawled to the front and climbed out, a bit shaky, but glad to be on land. The sound of the waterfall was deafening, pounding on the rocks so hard it sent clouds of white mist into the air. Above the channel feeding the stream a rainbow shimmered. The air was cool, but Lonnie felt good standing in the sun with its warmth on his shoulders. Bill reached into the canoe and grabbed a small backpack and a coil of blue nylon rope.

"I won't be able to climb the face," he said, "but there's a trail that takes hikers to the top of the falls. I'm gonna climb up and tie the rope to a tree and rappel down. I want you to stay here. You're actually kind of a Godsend. Things will look different up there. I want you to signal me when I'm over the nest so I'll know where to begin my drop."

LONNIE WAITED in the sun, keeping an eye on what was supposed to be the falcon's nest. All he could see were a few scrawny twigs. They could just as easily have been dead weeds. At least Bill assured him he'd reach the airport on time, but he hadn't yet received his commitment to help, though he felt sure the man would do what he could. He'd written articles exposing the cartel's activities, probably at great risk to himself. Still, they were spending more time on birds than humans, and there was something wrong with that, unless—unless Bill had a surefire way of getting the children back, in which case a slight detour wouldn't matter. There was no harm in saving a few birds as long as the children could be saved too. Then again, Bill had no way of knowing what had become of the children. They might already have been sold and shipped to some faraway place. But like Bill said, there was no point frustrating himself over things he couldn't control. His plane didn't leave for several hours so he wasn't going anywhere, and there should be plenty of time to talk before then. The trees were towering overhead. Lonnie looked up. God was watching. He raised his hands. The squirrels chattering in the boughs of an alpine fir joined him in prayer.

BILL APPROACHED the edge of the cliff, crab-walking sideways. The grade was steep, but he was able to get close enough to see Lonnie below. It looked easier from the bottom. From up here the ground was miles away. *Crud!* Bill backed away, looking for a tree to anchor his line. He'd done this kind of thing before. He should be okay. The closest tree large enough to hold a man was a fair distance back. He waved to Lonnie, who immediately pointed to his right. *Crud.* There was a large outcrop of rock that prevented him from tying off directly above the nest and making an in-line descent. He looked down. The skinny preacher was still flapping his arms. Bill waved again. *That boy's crazy. Wanting to take on the Mexican mafia. Absolutely, one hundred percent certifiably crazy.*

He turned and went back to the tree, measuring the distance as he paced it off, hoping he had enough rope. He secured his line around the base of the trunk, and hitched the rope through the belay using a carabiner to hook the device to his harness. He hadn't scaled a wall in years—when he was much younger, lighter, and far more daring. He fed out some line, stepping back to where he started, and waved at the tiny dot of a person he knew was Lonnie, who was still pointing right. *He has guts, though. And the nerve to do what's right. But that don't make him any less a fool.* The outcrop of rock was in his way. He moved along the top until he saw a clear path for his descent, turned around and slipped over the edge, planting his feet against the rock.

He pushed off, hanging in space, realizing the only thing between life and death was one thin rope. *I need to lose weight.* He pushed off again, swinging to his right, then dropped, swinging further to the right, and held again. Now he was directly beneath the overhanging shelf. He tried looking over his shoulder at Lonnie. The preacher was still pointing right. *Dang! Boy's got spunk, but even if he gets inside he'll never get out.* Bill pushed off the rock again.

The nest was further right than he thought, but after half a dozen tries, he got the okay sign from Lonnie. Planting his feet to hold his position, he unzipped his vest and retrieved a piton, unhooked his hammer from his belt, and pounded the spike into a fissure, creating a secure post. He looped his line over the peg to descend from there. *And he wants my help. Dang bust it. Why else would he be here?* Traveling to the right used too much rope. It was going to be close. At least the nest was below him now. He pushed off the rock, rappeling outward and swung back, hitting the wall. His knuckles scraped against the rock. He pushed off again. *This is an activity for young men.* He looked down and saw he was inches above a comfortable ledge. He decided to lower himself and take stock of his situation. *A few years ago this would have been easy.* Facing the rock, he still couldn't see the nest. He turned slowly, *very slowly,* and placed his palms flat against the wall. *Whew.* Mary would kill him if she knew what he was doing.

He sucked in a deep breath and tried to peek out over his toes. He could see a knot of branches directly below. They were covered with downy white feathers. The surrounding rock was awash in bird droppings. He was over the nest. Another five-foot rappel and he'd be there. He started to let out more rope but *dang!* There wasn't any left. *Dang it all! Shoot! Now what?* He knew it would be a problem. He was almost there. If he stepped off the ledge he'd get another few feet, but that would put his boots right about where the nest was. He wouldn't have enough rope to bend down and scoop up the birds. He'd have to rotate and hang upside down to reach them. *For crying out loud!* And he'd called the preacher crazy. He stepped off the ledge, keeping tension on the line. He could see the nest only a few feet below. A protruding piece of rock provided a place for his foot. He stepped down but his weight was too much and the shelf gave way. His knuckles slammed against the rock and he lost his hold, plunging the remaining three feet until jerked short by his harness, where he dangled, spinning slowly from the waist. His small nylon bag slipped off his shoulder and before he could catch it, spun toward the ground and landed on a pile of rock. One of the young falcons, frightened by the intrusion, panicked and fled the nest, but its wings were too short to keep it aloft. It got caught in the downdraft, sucked into the falling water, and slammed against the rocks below. *Dear God.* Bill was in pain. He'd have rope burns and a nasty bruise tomorrow, but he felt more for the loss of the bird. Nothing he could do about it now.

He took hold of the wall and turned his body till he was crawling down the rock head first. There were still two in the nest. They were backing against the wall with talons outstretched and their beaks open, crying without making a sound. He'd planned to carry the birds in his bag, but it was gone. He reached in and took one of the falcons, letting it claw and bite him as he shoved it into his shirt, and then grabbed the second one, doing the same. Saving two birds was better than saving none. He was sure now the mother was dead because she'd never allow an intruder to mess with her brood. At least he'd tried. If he hadn't the loss would have been four. His waist felt raw where the harness bruised his side. He held one arm against his shirt to keep the birds inside, and reached up taking hold of the rope with blood draining from his knuckles, righting himself till his feet were beneath him. *I'm too old for this.* With one hand he pulled on the rope, walking up the rock face till he was on the ledge again.

BILL UNHITCHED the rope and began looping it around his elbow until it was gathered together. He set it in the shade of a tree in a circular pile, and reached into his shirt to retrieve the two small falcons. They were full of down, but their pinion feathers were emerging and their markings evident. He set them in the coils of rope that now formed their circular nest. They weren't climbers, and they couldn't fly. They weren't going anywhere. They flipped on their backs, extending their talons to attack him if he approached again. A stab of pain wrenched his side as he removed his harness. That was going to hurt tomorrow. He wasn't the man he used to be.

He had taken off his vest to allow more freedom. The vest would have restricted his movement on the wall. He removed it from the limb where it was hanging and slipped it on. He tied the pull string around his waist and zipped the vest three quarters up. Then he pulled his climbing harness over his shoulder and stooped down on his haunches, looking at the birds in their blue nylon nest. They were still in a defensive posture. He picked up a twig and snapped it in two, offering half to each bird, and with the stick clenched in their talons, picked them up one at a time and placed them inside his vest. It would be nice having a shirt between himself and those claws. He slipped the coiled rope over his shoulder and stood, cautiously making his way over to the edge of the cliff to wave at Lonnie. Then he turned toward the trail to start down.

That crazy pastor was going to ask for his help. But he couldn't do it. It was Angie's day tomorrow, he'd promised to be there, and a promise was a promise. The sun was dropping into the folds of afternoon, the air cool, and the sky off to the east a porcelain blue. The birds snuggled into the soft welcome darkness of the vest. It was important to let Angie know she was special. The boys were demanding. They could find more mischief than any two boys he'd ever known. He had to keep them occupied, but that took time. So when Angie, who couldn't run, became involved in something, he had to be there by golly, no ifs ands or buts. Why, she'd never forgive him if he missed her event. Not that she was technically in an event, she was in the cheering section, but that was her part. She did what she could and he had to show his support.

What if it were Angie being sold into prostitution, or to a gang of pedophiles and forced to make filthy movies with other innocent children, or passed around and sexually abused? He grimaced. That's why he'd written the articles. He'd exposed what was happening, even though nothing had been done. It was obvious children were still being bought and sold like chattel. But that wasn't his fault. The only weapon he had was his pen. He'd done what he could. He'd write about this too, especially if the preacher got the kids out. Why, he'd tell the whole world their story. But what if he failed? Could he in all good conscience write about the preacher's tragic death knowing he'd sent him on his way with little more than best wishes and Godspeed? *Nuts!* There was no good answer. He had to help. Man, why did the preacher have to come at such a rotten time? Maybe Angie would understand if— Bill stepped on a log that lay across the trail, and then onto a rock on the other side, but the rock, which looked smooth and flat from above, was only partially in the ground. So as he stepped down the toe of the rock went forward, throwing him off balance. As his feet slid out from beneath him, the last thing he remembered was holding onto his vest to protect the birds and seeing a slice of blue, blue sky speckled with white cotton clouds. Then his head hit the log—and he was out.

NINE

LONNIE PACED around the trees. He'd gone into prayer mode after watching Bill nearly fall from the cliff. He saw no reason to stop. Bill had signaled he was on his way down more than two hours ago. It had only taken half an hour for him to reach the top. Coming down should be faster. Maybe one of the birds escaped. Bill was probably trying to get it back. But surely he'd given up the chase by now. The sun was dipping behind the mountains, casting the area into shadow. It was cold. Lonnie circled a tree and headed back. He'd been treading the same course for the last fifteen minutes. He was going to miss his plane. He knew it. *God, what are you doing? I need to get back. I need to find my kids.*

Lonnie went searching for the trail. He hoped to meet Bill coming down, but the trail wasn't marked and he couldn't find where it began. Someone had camped here previously. There was a ring of stones and charred wood. There were nails for hanging items on nearby trees, but no trail, just a pile of rocks at the base of the falls. The campsite would have looked great on a calendar. The falls and their misty rainbow, the pool beneath so bone-chillingly cold, and so *deep, deep, deep,* but he wasn't into beauty right now. Stopping to enjoy the wonder of God's creation would take his mind off his mission—and that somehow diminished his purpose. *God, what are You doing?* Lonnie felt his patience being tested, or maybe his faith. Why else would God keep Bill so long? *"Consider the ravens, they neither sow nor reap, and have neither storehouse nor barn; and God feeds them. Of how much more value are you than the birds?"* Bill needed to see that one. Birds were not more important than kids! But the rest of the verse Lonnie needed for himself. *"If you then are not able to do the least, why are you anxious for the rest? Consider the lilies, how they grow: they neither toil nor spin; and yet I say to you, even Solomon in all his glory was not arrayed like one of these. If then God so clothes the grass, which today is in the field and tomorrow is thrown into the oven, how much more will He clothe you, O you of little faith?"* It wasn't that he lacked faith. He had plenty of faith to know God would do whatever it was He wanted to do. He just wished he knew what God wanted because not knowing made him worry, and worry suggested a lack of faith. What if God wasn't of a mind to do what he was asking? Three innocent children would suffer. But God had to agree on this! *"It is impossible but that offences will come: but woe unto him, through whom they come! It were better for him that a millstone were hanged about his neck, and he be cast into the sea, than that he should offend one of these little ones."* Jesus said that! God had to be on his side, didn't He? He had to help him find those kids. *Where was Bill?*

Lonnie circled a large rock and headed back to the tree. *Be anxious for nothing, be anxious for nothing, be anxious for nothing,* but he needed the information he was hoping Bill would supply, and they had to get going or he'd miss his plane. Shadows blanketed the ground as the sun lowered itself on the other side of the ridge. He cupped his hands around his mouth and yelled up the mountain wall. "Bill! You out there? Can you hear me?" But he knew Bill couldn't hear or he would have already answered. The roar of the falls pounding on the rocks was drowning out his cries. What if Bill got lost? Maybe he'd taken a wrong turn somewhere. *Better not have.* Lonnie didn't fancy the idea of being stuck overnight. All his pacing around in circles was getting him nowhere. He had to do something. He'd tried to find the trail several times, but there was no indication of a footpath, no sign, no clear route, nothing but a pile of rocks. He decided to climb. The rocks were unsteady. He placed his foot on a shelf of loose gravel and lost his footing. *Ouch!* This was stupid. He was climbing a pile of rocks with no idea what was at the top. Bill could be coming down somewhere else and they'd miss each other completely. He got to his feet and took another step. The grade was steep. He leaned in, taking hold of the rocks with his hands as he climbed one slow step after another, grabbing the bag Bill dropped and slinging it over his shoulder on his way up.

The top of the pile was stacked against the mountain. There were only two choices: he could climb the sheer face of the wall, or make his way across the pile of rock to the left and hope something opened up. He started to his left, still ascending, but stepping up and down over rocks with his hand riding along the face of the cliff. He could see where the rocks ended and turned into a steep incline of mountain dirt. It wasn't really a trail, but it did make its way up along the wall, possibly going all the way to the top. It felt good to be on soil again. Lonnie took a step forward and reached for a tree to give himself support. He paused, panting to catch his breath. *Bill, where are you?* He pushed off the tree, shoving it behind him, and took another trudging step. If there was a trail up to the falls, this wasn't it. This might be a hike up the mountain, but it wasn't a trail. There was no point in turning back. He would try to reach the top. Bill might still be up there. Lonnie raised his hands, cupping his mouth, and yelled Bill's name again. With the falls behind him there was less background noise and, in fact, he heard his voice loud and clear, echoing off the valley walls. But there was no response. He kept going.

Ahead, a huge boulder was blocking his path. He would have to go down and around before continuing up. He started down, holding onto the rock as he came around the other side. *Ah!* There *was* a trail, or at least something that looked like one, and while Lonnie was thrilled to find it, he was not pleased with what else he saw. About a hundred feet up, Bill lay on the ground with his head propped up on a log like a pillow—fast asleep! Lonnie picked up his pace, planting his hands on his legs and pushing against his thighs to gain momentum. He was a dozen feet away before he said anything. "Bill, wake up. Hey, Bill!" The man's vest was moving and Lonnie could hear the *eeeeeeeyying* cry of the young falcons. "Bill, wake up!" Lonnie nudged the sleeping body with his toe. "Come on, Bill, time to rise and shine." He stooped down and shook Bill's shoulder, but there was no response.

"Bill?" He leaned in to check Bill's breathing. *Come on, Bill, wake up.* Lonnie put his hand behind Bill's head, urging him to sit. *Oh no.* Bill had a lump the size of an egg at the back of his crown. He was out cold. Then he heard a sound. *Right,* the birds. Lonnie lifted the flap of Bill's vest. There were two lumps of downy feathers nestled where the vest was sagging against the ground. He took Bill's duffle bag and opened it, then reached in and removed the birds, one at a time, placing them in the bag and closed the top. *Now what?* He slapped Bill's face, not hard, but enough to wake him. It worked. Bill's eyes popped open and his mouth gasped for air. He shook his head and started to raise himself, bringing a foot up for support. *"Ahhwww ouchhh!"* Bill grabbed his knee, wrapping it in his arms. *"Ahwww,* dang bust! I think I sprained my ankle. *Ohwww.* Shoot!" His hand began exploring the bump at the base of his skull. "How long was I out?"

Lonnie looked around. *Great!* There was no way he'd be able to carry Bill down that pile of rocks. "I don't know, couple of hours. I waited at the bottom a long time. You think you can walk?" It was a silly question, and one Lonnie regretted immediately.

"Not unless you're a miracle-working preacher. It's going to be hard just getting up. Where are the falcons? They okay?"

Lonnie nodded. "They're fine. They're in your bag. I got it back. I watched you drop it when you slipped. I nearly fainted. Thought you were a dead man. Anyway, once I saw you were alright, I retrieved it for you."

"Thanks. You wouldn't happen to have an aspirin, would you? My head feels like an overripe melon about to burst."

"Un uh. Sorry. What happened? Looks like you took a nasty fall."

Bill continued working his fingers through his hair, feeling the egg. "That's about it, I guess. I stepped on a rock on the downhill side of this log, and the next thing I know, you're here and I'm all busted up. Glad you could make it."

"Me too, only the sun's going down, which makes it about six, and I have a plane to catch at seven, and we're more than an hour from your cabin, and another hour to the airport, and I have a couple of lost kids that desperately need my help, which they're not going to get if I stay here overnight. But...well, I guess it looks like I'm stranded."

"Sorry about that. Okay, look, I'm going to need you to get me down the hill."

Lonnie surveyed the area. The fallen tree was large, sun-bleached, and dry—just what he needed. He walked over, placing both hands on a dead but sturdy limb, and pulled hard, snapping it off. Then he broke off the smaller branches until he had a long pole with a Y at the top. He handed it to Bill. "I think we should get going. It will be dark before long, and I don't want to spend the night on this mountain. Here, I made you a crutch. You think you can use your good leg to get up?"

Bill held onto the pole and reached out to Lonnie. "Give me a hand," he said.

LONNIE HAD been right. Though the distance wasn't far, it took them well over an hour just to get back to the lake, one slow, painful, agonizing step at a time. He unloosed the canoe, pulled it onto the shore, and waited for Bill to step in.

"I think you'd better get in first," Bill said.

"Me? I thought..."

"Sorry, but you have to paddle."

"Paddle? I've never paddled a canoe before. I've never even been in one before today."

"No problem. I'll tell you what to do. But I don't want to put pressure on my foot. I'll have to sit on the bottom and keep my leg stretched out over the side."

Man, oh man. Lonnie stepped into the boat and took a position on the rear seat, the way he had seen Bill do on the trip over, only Bill's weight had caused the nose of the canoe to rise out of the water. Lonnie's didn't. Bill tossed his crutch into the canoe, and started hopping on one foot while pushing the craft backward into the water. He stooped over and washed the blood from his hands, and then turned around and plopped into the canoe facing front so he could see where they were going. He pulled his legs over the side until he had one propped on each rail. He lay back and closed his eyes, breathing deeply, folding his hands across his chest to compose himself. He let out his breath. "Okay, here's what you do. Paddle backward from the right side, and the canoe will turn to the left toward the lake."

Lonnie began churning the water and the canoe turned, only he paddled too hard and the canoe ended up pointing back toward the falls.

"That's okay," Bill said. "Just keep going and you'll come back around. Whoa! That's enough. No, you're going too far. Put your paddle in on the other side and give it a stroke to straighten us out."

Lonnie raised the paddle out of the water and swung it across the canoe, flipping water on Bill's head which trickled down his nose.

Pspfftt. Bill wiped his mouth. "Okay, try to shake the excess water off the blade next time. Now, what I want you to do is stroke on one side, then the other. If you find yourself veering to the left, give an extra stroke on the right and vice versa. Make for the middle of the lake and just follow the length of it down. Don't go too close to shore, or you'll end up veering down a fork off to the side. Just keep going straight and when you get to where there's an island in the middle, get my attention. I'll tell you what to do from there. I'm going to shut my eyes and try to focus on something else."

Keeping the boat straight took some getting used to. Every time Lonnie took a stroke on one side, the craft angled the opposite way, but then when he put the paddle in on the other side and made a stroke it swung back, correcting itself. His real concern was that it was getting dark. He didn't know whether he was heading the way Bill said or not. Everything looked the same in every direction. He began to realize that in the fading light he might paddle right past the island and not see it. He shivered, warding off the cold. After about a hundred strokes, his hands felt puffy like they were filling with blisters, and his shoulders ached. He didn't like water. And it was *cold.* He didn't like the cold. And he didn't like that the delay was keeping him from his kids. And he didn't know where the heck he was. Lost on some foreign body of water. And he didn't like water. And it was *so* cold. *God, please?*

He was considering turning back, thinking he must have passed the island by now, when finally a lump began to emerge in the middle of the lake. It wasn't much of an island, more of a sand spit with a few trees, but it had to be what Bill was talking about. "Hey, Bill, I hate to wake you, but I think we're here."

Bill raised his head and looked out over the bow. "Yep, that's it. Now you have to veer left. The cabin is just a quarter of a mile down that channel." He pointed in the general direction, and laid his head down again. "Man, that smarts. Ever have a broken bone, Lonnie?"

"Don't know. Maybe, but I don't think so."

"I tell you, I hope I'm wrong, but I may have done more than sprain this baby. Man, my foot hurts. I can feel it swelling. I might have broke it. Couldn't have happened at a worse time. I was giving serious thought to going with you, but I'm obviously in no shape to tag along now. I don't know what's worse, not helping rescue your kids, or disappointing my daughter. There's a Special Olympics tomorrow. I promised to be there, and now I can't even do that. I'll probably be having my foot set by a doctor. And I have to get these birds to a sanctuary." Bill waved off the mosquito buzzing his ear. He got it with a loud slap, pulling his hand from his cheek to make sure the bug was squished between his fingers.

Lonnie smiled. Now there was something they had in common. Mosquitoes crossed all borders. So, Bill was thinking of tagging along. It would be nice, but that wasn't what he needed. He wanted information. "What event is your daughter in?" he asked, taking another stroke.

"Actually, she's not technically in an event. She has cerebral palsy. She can't control the muscles in her arms or legs so she can't participate directly, but she cheers, kinda, well, more like screams, but she makes a darn fine cheerleader."

"Sorry to hear it."

"Beg pardon?"

"Your daughter. Sorry about her handicap. It must be hard."

There was a pause. Lonnie sensed the mood change. "It's a

small point," Bill said, "but I'd rather you didn't call my daughter handicapped. She may not function the same as you and me, but she's every bit as proud. Handicapped implies something less, like she's subhuman. It may not seem like much, but I'm asking politely. That okay by you?"

Lonnie's face went blank for a second. Then his eyes drifted out over the water. How could Bill accuse him of being condescending? His own son was confined to a wheelchair, the result of a spinal injury sustained in a mountain biking accident. And what about little Sebastian? He treated him like his own flesh and blood, without reservation. But Bill didn't know any of that. "Ah, sure. Sorry, I...I meant no offence."

"I know. But you have to understand, I live with a beautiful young lady who has to work extra hard just to do things that are routine for everyone else. She's had to deal with it all her life. She's one brave little lady. If she's home when we get there, I wouldn't want you to make the mistake of treating her like she's inferior. I'll tell you this. In some ways she's better off than all of us. She's imprisoned by a body that won't let her go, but she enjoys more freedom than anybody I know."

The sky had slipped into twilight and the moon was on the rise. Lonnie could see lights glowing from a cottage far away on a distant shore. A corkscrew of smoke was twisting slowly from the chimney.

"Yep, they're home," Bill said. "You ever read Thoreau, Mr. Striker? He was put in jail for not paying what he felt was an unjust tax. A man after my own heart. Anyway, he said, and I quote, 'As I stood considering the walls of stone, two or three feet thick, the door of wood and iron, a foot thick, and the iron grating which strained the light, I could not help being struck with the foolishness of that institution which treated me as mere flesh and blood and bones to be locked up....If there was a wall of stone between me and my townsmen, there was still a more difficult one to climb or break through before they could get to be as free as I was.' The point he was making was that freedom is in the mind. You can be locked up and still be free. That's my little girl."

Lonnie thought about his children and their confinement. Maybe when they were being abused by some raging pedophile, they could escape to some far corner of their mind and be free, but he doubted it. He pulled back on the paddle. The yellow light of the cabin's windows swirled in the blue-black eddies of water. He wouldn't be leaving on a plane tonight, it was too late, but somehow, someway, he was going to see that his children were set free—truly free.

TEN

"Amazing Grace,
How sweet the sound
That saved a wretch like me.
I once was lost
But now am found
Was blind but now I see. . . ."

NICOLE HUMMED the tune softly, fighting to control her emotions. She had sung the verse dozens of times, an old church favorite, but now with Lonnie off trying to rescue the children, it took on new meaning. The words expressed agony and ecstasy. John Newton, who wrote the hymn, had been a slave trader. He'd come to realize that capturing and selling flesh was moral depravity. He'd relinquished his former life and found release at the foot of the cross. Nicole could only pray the same would happen to the men Lonnie pursued.

It was evening, and as she was accustomed in a town without televisions, e-mails or shopping malls—or as Lonnie was fond of saying, a place where the God channel was free from interference—she read her Bible. The book lay open in her lap beneath the glow of a small low-watt lamp, the thin, fragile, well-worn pages looking yellow in the dim light. She picked it up again. She had been reading the Book of Ephesians:

For we wrestle not against flesh and blood, but against

> *principalities, against powers, against the rulers of the darkness of this world, against spiritual wickedness in high places.*

Nicole understood there were unseen spiritual forces—those on the side of darkness, and those on the side of light—that warred over the souls of men, but this was different. Perhaps it was something John Newton could relate to, but she could not. One would have to be demon possessed to feel right about stealing children and taking pleasure in their abuse. Yes, there was no doubt in her mind, they were dealing with sadistic men, given over to lust and self-gratification.

She could relate to spiritual warfare, but on a totally different level. It didn't take great evil, or even a heart in rebellion, to be seduced. She'd learned the deceiver could afflict even a normally good-natured soul. She flipped the page to another well-known passage, this one from the first book of Peter:

> *Be sober, be vigilant; for your adversary the devil walks around like a roaring lion, seeking whom he may devour.*

For her, the lion had come in the guise of a husband who, after robbing her of every vestige of self-worth, took the hand of another woman and said goodbye. She knew about spiritual warfare. Inside the relationship she, like Mr. Newton, was blind, but from the outside, she could see. She had gone into the marriage strong in her faith, and had come out weak and ineffective. Ryan had moved on to destroy other lives while she was left to wallow in depression, unable to eat or even sleep. If she had any value, any worth, he would not have sought the company of other women. The roaring lion had pounced and devoured. And the destruction had been so great it had lasted, how long now? *My, how the years passed. Ten? Yes, ten years.* She was over it. She rarely thought of him at all, and then only when Lonnie was away and she was in a funk. Only now what she felt on those rare moments when she ventured that perilous journey into the past, was anger.

She had to control such emotions. She was supposed to forgive and forget and move on, even though what he did was unforgivable, and she had forgiven him, at least superficially. But subconsciously, whenever she abandoned needful control, her mind would drift aimlessly into a minefield of destructive thought, and she wanted him to suffer, just a little, because wouldn't that be justice? *Vengeance is mine, saith the Lord!* Fortunately, she didn't think about him all that much. The reconstruction process was underway, the fortress getting stronger. But she had wasted too many years caught in a barrage of self-deprecation, a casualty of war, captured and imprisoned in the quagmire of her maligned emotions, a worthless vessel in the kingdom of God. At least, that is, until God sent Lonnie to her rescue.

RAÚL KEPT digging, furiously hacking away at the hard clay. He had only a tiny stick to scrape with. It was all he could find. He filled his hands and pockets with dirt and crawled back to the opening, pushing it out, and hurried back to start again. The stick had been much longer when he started. It was breaking down. Soon there would be nothing left. *So what?* He would dig with his fingernails if he had to. Already they were numb and filled with dirt. Enough thinking, he had to work. It was only a few hours until dawn. If they didn't get out before the break of day, the guards would see the hole. He worked steadily, trying to be quiet. The camp was asleep. He could not risk discovery. Someone might inform the guards. Mariana was asleep, and the fat boy, and that chica Sofía too. He hadn't yet decided what to do about her. She'd tried to help him. He owed her something. But once they were out she would slow them down. He couldn't afford that. Besides, she didn't have anywhere to go but back to the orphanage. What kind of life was that? He dug into the wall, scooped another handful of dirt into his palm, and slipped it into his pocket.

He would grab Mariana and together they would run. The dogs were a problem. That's why the tunnel had to be long enough to take them into the fields. They had to surface behind the wall of plants. He couldn't afford to set the dogs barking. He had to get Mariana to safety, but then he would leave. He would go back. He would sneak into the barracks and while the men were sleeping, slice the throat of the skinny snake. That man could not be allowed to live.

Raúl lurched. Someone had grabbed his ankle. Someone was pulling him back, trying to drag him out of the tunnel. He was caught. *Noooooooo.* Raúl tried to kick himself free. Dirt was falling. He could feel it splattering his face. The tunnel was caving in. At least the evil man would die with him.

His eyes popped open. It was dark and cold. The man was still tugging on his foot. He could feel it. Bits of dirt were falling on his face, but there was air, lots of cool clean air. Something wasn't right. Was it dirt, or something else? No, it wasn't dirt—it was rain. He looked down his leg and saw the person holding his ankle. It wasn't the snake—it was Mariana!

She was dragging him across the ground toward the shelter, trying to pull him out of the rain. *Noooooooo!* He had to get back to the tunnel. He tried to kick but there was no strength in his legs. He tried to raise himself on his arms, but they wouldn't move. Why was she pulling him away from his work? Couldn't she see he had a tunnel to dig? He tried to remember. He'd been tied to the post. He couldn't recall anything beyond that. He must have passed out. Someone must have cut him loose. What about the *tunnel?* He had to get up. He had to start digging. Nightfall had come. They would only have a few hours in which to make their escape. *Leave me alone, Mariana!* He could not move to stop her. Where had his strength gone? Sofía joined his sister, and then someone else, the fat boy, grabbing his arms. He was carried beneath the shelter. Mariana sat down beside him, wiping dirt from his eyes. She too had drops of rain flooding her cheeks.

ELEVEN

LONNIE COULDN'T remember having been in a house with so many pleasant smells: cedar, pine, the musky smell of woolen blankets, and the crackling smoke from the birch fire. But right now the warm aroma of the oven had his full attention.

He was enjoying a feast. Never, at least not in as long as he could remember, had he eaten like this. The table was made of Western cedar cut into planks, fit together and covered with a thick coat of varnish, with the original bark still attached to the outside edge. The place settings were baked earthenware glazed with American Indian designs. And the chairs were constructed of cedar poles with seats made of soft leather. There were bowls of red sugar beets and northern cranberries, Idaho spuds and Columbia River corn, hot steamy rolls and a fresh garden salad, and the pièce de résistance, a platter of butter-basted trout fillets that Bill himself had caught that very morning out on the lake. Lonnie wondered how Bill's wife managed to fit everything else between the plates.

Bill and Mary sat across from each other at one end of the table, their daughter Angie within easy reach. Lonnie was sure Mary wasn't Angie's mother. No one said it outright. He'd just deduced it from the way Bill introduced Angie as *his* daughter. Mary was a handsome woman, with dark welcoming eyes and rosy cheeks that held a dimpled smile, but she and the other two children were distinctly brunette while Angie, like Nicole, was a first-rate blond. She sat in a shiny chrome wheelchair, doing her best to be part of the conversation. She was certainly well adjusted and happy, though she could not feed herself and jerked involuntarily from time to time. But for the most part she was poised and, whenever her face muscles relaxed, downright pretty. Two young boys sat across from each other. The one they called Ted was about six, and his little brother Josh, only four. Lonnie observed the family paradigm knowing this was what he wanted for himself. From Teddy's launch into his father's arms, which almost knocked Bill over as he crawled out of the canoe while trying to balance on one leg, to the welcome home kiss from his wife Mary, who frustrated him with her concern about his managing on only one foot while berating him for doing something so foolish as to scale a rock wall, to the affection he showed Angie as he took time, before even tending to his own needs, to ask how her day had been, right down to the blessing Bill said over the food—"in Jesus' name"—this was the epitome of a Christian family.

Lonnie's own parents separated when he was young. The only family he'd known was composed of he and his mother because his older brother Harlan was raised by his dad. The two families, though they shared the same blood and last name, never talked. Perhaps if he'd had a father, he wouldn't be so reluctant to get married. But upon their divorce his father chose Harlan and his mother chose him. Besides, he already had a son, though he hadn't known about it until after the boy was grown—his sin had seen to that—but at least his brother had stepped in and filled the gap. He could say a lot of unkind things about Harlan, but he couldn't say he was a bad father. He'd loved Quentin as his own, and the result was a maturity the boy possessed that made him a stalwart executive of the film company they now jointly owned. Still, Lonnie missed the privilege of raising his own child the way Bill was doing now. He tried to picture himself in Bill's shoes. The environment would be different, an adobe hut rather than a log cabin, and they'd be eating tortillas and maiz. The thought of Trudy as a mother was a bit of a stretch. She'd raised Quentin, true enough, but he couldn't quite picture it. Still, you don't pick a wife based on her qualifications as a mother. That was just one of the factors in choosing a lifetime partner. He also had to consider mutual interests, common goals, compatibility, physical attraction.

Okay, maybe Nicole *was* the better choice, but there was still one little problem. Trudy was the mother of his son, and that outweighed all the rest. If the sin he committed with Trudy, the sin that resulted in the birth of Quentin, consummated marriage, to marry someone else had to constitute adultery.

"...I'll probably end up in jail myself someday," Bill said, wiping his plate clean with a buttered roll.

"Bill! Don't talk like that in front of the children!" Mary scolded. She stood and took his plate and her own, then turned to Lonnie. "Don't listen to him. He isn't breaking the law. We still have freedom of speech in this country. Why don't you two get out of my way while I clean up. I have pie for desert. I'll serve you in the den when it's ready."

Lonnie, lost in his own thoughts, had missed what Bill said. "Jail... why?"

Bill stood on his one good leg and reached behind him for the crutch Lonnie had fashioned, only now there was a folded towel over the portion resting under his arm. "I'd help clear the table but..."

"Sure," Mary said, flicking her wrist, shooing him away. "Get out of here." She scooped up Lonnie's plate and stacked it with the others. "But as soon as we get Pastor Lonnie to the airport in the morning, I want you to see a doctor. You need to make sure nothing is broken. And you need a proper set of crutches. The lame duck excuse won't last long. Now, get out of my way. Scoot."

"Aye aye, Captain." Bill turned and began hobbling toward the den, his imitation crutch *thudding* as it hit the hardwood floor. Lonnie got up to follow, and Bill said over his shoulder, "No, I was just saying, sometimes you have to take a stand, even if it means sacrifice. It's like what I said about Thoreau. He wouldn't pay what he thought was an unfair tax, and was willing to go to jail for what he believed. I have to realize if I keep writing the way I do, I may end up doing the same. Thoreau said, 'Unjust laws exist; shall we be content to obey them... or shall we transgress them at once?' He chose to break the law rather than pay the tax, and wound up in jail. Like what you're trying to do for your kids. You have to right a wrong, regardless of the cost."

Bill reached his chair and took hold of the arm. He spun around and flopped into the overstuffed cushions, setting his crutch aside. His ruined foot wrapped in a stretch bandage looked twice its size.

The fire crackling in the hearth warmed the entire room. Lonnie found a seat on the couch. Ted raced in and looped his arms around Bill's neck, and Josh followed, receiving a pat on the head as he leaned on the padded arm of his father's chair. "Easy boys, don't step on Daddy's foot." A *scccreeeeech* was heard across the room. The boys looked at each other and then ran to the basket sitting on the coffee table. Teddy stuck his finger in, but quickly jerked it back.

"Careful, son. They may be small, but they can bite. He probably thinks that pinky of yours is dinner," Bill said, referring to the young falcons who found the weave of the straw basket filled with bits of cloth and twine a suitable nest. From the kitchen, Mary called the boys to their baths and both took off running.

"Wow, I don't remember being that anxious to get washed when I was their age," Lonnie said.

"Anxious? You've got to be kidding. They're running off to hide. You got kids of your own?"

"No. Yes. I mean, I have a son I didn't know about until after he was grown, an indiscretion of my youth, but he turned out alright."

"So, are you married?'

"Nope, never been. I'm thinking about it though." Lonnie yawned and pushed himself into the soft pillowy cushions of the sofa. His eyes felt heavy in the warm comfort of the room. It had been a long day. He hoped Mary planned to serve coffee with the pie. He crossed his feet and stretched. "You know why I'm here. I need your advice on finding my kids. I read what you wrote, so I know you've looked into all this. I'm just asking for a lead. Anything you have that can steer me in the right direction."

Bill's lips puckered as he looked out across the room, and smacked when he opened his mouth, creating a circle in his beard that looked like a knothole in tree bark. "Yep, I figured that's what you wanted." He leaned forward, took hold of his leg, and pulled it onto an ottoman. "Look, it's not that I don't want to help. The problem is, what you're asking involves someone else, and I can't volunteer their name without their permission. This whole kidnapping and prostitution ring is run by the Mexican mafia, and these guys are one mean bunch of desperados. It doesn't pay to mess with them, not if you know what's good for you. The guy in charge is Miguel Estrada. He's número uno—top dog. I'm not giving away secrets here, it's pretty common knowledge. The Federales have known about him for years, but he's above the law. You won't get near him. He keeps a security force around him at all times, though he doesn't really need it. No one wants to hurt him. He's kind of a folk hero. He employs half the population in the harvesting of his marijuana crop, and that makes him vital to the local economy so there's no incentive to put him away. But just to be sure, he has most of the judges and the local policía in his pocket." Bill leaned on his elbows, lifting his weight to get more comfortable. Lonnie noticed the red-blue welts of skin torn from his knuckles and cringed. "But this whole thing about trafficking children, that's only come to light in recent years, and already it's reached epidemic proportions. They say selling children equals arms smuggling as a source of revenue for crime families. And Miguel has it made because Mexico is one of the few countries that refuses to take the problem seriously. Look, I'm gonna call my contact and ask if they'd be willing to see you, but I won't pressure them to do anything. It has to be their choice. Personally, I think you're crazy, but I guess if the situation were reversed and they were my kids, I'd do the same. Hand me the phone, will you?"

LONNIE STARED at the moon. It was almost full, and heavy with light. The air rolled down from the mountain resting cool and damp on his arms. What kind of woman would risk her life to help a stranger save a bunch of kids she didn't know? Certainly one with a good heart. Anyway, thanks to Bill, he'd find out tomorrow. Bill had a friend who flew a sky taxi between Portland and LA bringing visitors up to explore the great Northwest, hunters and fishermen and the like. It turned out the man was heading back to LA in a few days to pick up a group of ornithologists set on tracking migrating birds. The pilot agreed if Lonnie would pay for the trip down, a fare he normally wouldn't have, as well as hotel and meal expenses for the extra night's stay, he'd leave a day early and take Lonnie with him, and they could leave at 7 a.m. That would put Lonnie in Los Angeles at about 10 a.m., allowing him to pick up a plane to Mexico City departing at noon. It would be a stretch, but with Godspeed he would be back on track, meeting Bill's contact without significant delay.

Lonnie looked at the stars. All his life he'd sought to know the will of God, but even now he realized His ways remained a mystery. He was going in blind, praying to confront a crime boss without a clue about what to say. The cool evening air made him shiver at the reality of his situation. Scripture admonished him to trust in the Lord with all his heart, even when he lacked understanding. And that meant in everything, including his relationship with Trudy. David had sinned with Bathsheba, but God blessed their union with Solomon. Lonnie had sinned with Trudy and was blessed with Quentin. But David married Bathsheba, while Lonnie had never actually done the honorable thing of marrying Trudy. And now, when he'd finally decided to make things right, he was having second thoughts. The world would insist he follow his heart, but the Bible said the heart was deceitful and desperately wicked, so there was folly in that. He felt divided, torn apart. He only wanted to do what was right. He rubbed the goosebumps on his arms. He couldn't guess what the dawn would bring. How does man at a crossroads know which way to turn? If he were destined to barter with the Mexican mafia, he wished God would at least tell him how to prepare. If Trudy were to be his wife, shouldn't God say so loud and clear? What if he were going about all this the wrong way?

TWELVE

RAÚL RECOILED as the morning sun broke across the hardpan of the earth, flooding the yard in streams of yellow. He raised his hand and curled into a shell in a vain attempt to keep the light from slamming into his face, then rolled away, crawling toward his sister, whimpering as though awakened from a bad dream. He buried his head in her lap. Mariana placed her hand on Raúl's forehead and began raking her fingers through his hair. After a few moments he raised himself, shaking off the sun, now fully awake—and ashamed.

A rooster crowed. Insects were buzzing in the fields. With the sun low on the horizon, the plants looked translucent and bottle green, their leaves shimmering in the morning breeze. The others were already up and about. The fat boy wandered off to relieve himself, leaving tracks in the pasty mud. His sweater was probably good for keeping him warm at night, but was too bulky to be worn during the day. It sagged on his overweight body like a potato sack. His hair was flat, parted in the middle and combed down on both sides. His monstrous black-framed glasses slid forward, too heavy to stay perched on his tiny nose. Raúl sat breathless, taking in his surroundings and gathering his thoughts. He remembered little of the previous day, just bits of a fragmented puzzle with some of the pieces missing and others that didn't fit. He could remember digging but saw no sign of a tunnel—no pile of loose dirt, no hole in the ground, no boards covering it over—*nada*. He couldn't seem to separate what he knew was real from images appearing only for a moment, and then bursting like bubbles when pricked by conscious thought. He *knew* he'd been strapped to a post. The offending block was still in the middle of the yard awaiting its next victim. And he felt weak. A small thing like crawling to Mariana had sapped his strength.

The campesinos were up and about. Men with machetes wrestled with handcarts, making their way into the fields. The gatekeeper threw the hindquarter of a monkey to the dogs who, growling, faced each other with bared teeth. As Raúl sat on the hard earth it suddenly occurred to him they were never going to escape. They were destined to be sold. At best, maybe he could convince whoever wanted *him* that his sister was part of the deal.

The gate opened and a man walked by carrying two wooden pails, one in each hand. He slogged to the center of the yard, dropping them one at a time, *thud, thud.* Water sloshed up the side of one, splashing onto the dirt. He turned and walked away. The fat boy got down on his knees, slurping from the bucket, spilling as much as he drank, and then stuck his hand in the other pail removing a fistful of pasty white tortilla shells. He looked up, his eyes buggy through his glasses, and ran off to sit by himself in the shade. Sofía looked into the pail and saw it was empty. Neither Mariana nor Raúl moved. Mariana sat with her hands in her lap, her large dark eyes asking the questions her lips were unable to voice. A shadow slipped in, quietly blocking the sun. It was Sofía standing over them. She started to sit down, but yelped as she was jerked away.

"No, putita. We have a need for you." The man turned, pulling Sofía with him.

"*Aaaaa*...una momento,"

But the man was already gone, dragging Sofía toward the gate by her elbow, her eyes bulging and her feet trying to keep up, struggling to catch their balance. They rounded the corner and disappeared, but not before Raúl heard her captor say, "It is time, little sister, for you to learn the trade."

NICOLE SAT at her vanity, staring at herself in the mirror. *Such an appropriate word*, she thought. *Vanity.* Was there a greater waste of time than sitting indulging yourself in your own beauty? She used her fingers to stretch her skin, smoothing the crow's feet lining her eyes. The women of Posada were thick-skinned, but constant exposure to the sun caused them to wrinkle early. How long would it be before her face began gathering into folds? And what did it matter anyway? There were no beauty contests here. No one cared what she looked like. Well, maybe one, but that was the problem. Lonnie might be only a friend, but still. Why was he always ogling Trudy? It couldn't possibly be about Quentin. He wouldn't court a woman he didn't love to father a boy who was already an adult. And he couldn't possibly love Trudy for her inner beauty. With all those New York designer dresses, Chanel-scented hankies, and five hundred dollar-a-pop hairdos, Trudy was the epitome of shallow. So if Lonnie wasn't looking on the inside, it had to be the surface he was enamored with. And that was why Nicole was declaring war on wrinkles. She massaged her face. Old age was coming *too* quickly. Soon her good looks would fade, and what then? *Vanity, vanity, all is vanity.*

She placed a rubber band in her teeth and stood, walking away from the mirror as she began brushing her hair. The room was organized and tidy, bed made, clothes hung, dresser dusted, and water pot shined. Not that she could claim *Good Housekeeping's* Homemaker-of-the-Year award, but when you had little to keep, keeping it neat was easy. She pulled her hair, twisting it back, and slipped the rubber band over her ponytail to fix it in place. It didn't really matter. Maybe she wasn't ready for a deeper relationship. But then again, she didn't want Lonnie to give up trying.

She reached out, opening the door, and stepped back, startled. She didn't expect to find Sebastian on the other side. He lay on the floor, looking at a book with big color pictures, his rubbery legs snaking behind him as though made of flesh without bone. When picked up the useless appendages dangled like a stringless marionette. He was eleven years old but the malformation of his lower limbs, parceled with a stunting of his growth, left those who didn't know him thinking he was only five. He glanced up at Nicole but something seemed out of place. His trademark smile—that enchanted keyboard—was missing.

Odd. That smile was ever present, as much a part of who he was as the syrupy chocolate of his skin. It was his smile that made Sebastian everyone's favorite. He'd been abandoned, left on the doorstep of Lonnie's house by parents who were probably still living in a town nearby, but you'd never know it by his disposition.

"Well, little man," Nicole said, "how did you get here?"

"Felipe brought me. My wheelchair's down there," he said, pointing at the floor. I was trying to scoot up the stairs the way señor Lonnie taught me, but Felipe saw me and carried me up. I was sent to find you. Father Paulo, he saw the bus this morning, but he no see el señor Lonnie. He say he has gone to find my sister, but he not sure. He say I drive him crazy with questions, but I worry, señorita, so he send me to get you, and here I am."

Nicole stooped over to pick him up. His frame was light and airy, like the hollow-boned skeleton of a dove. She looked into his eyes, dark and veined from lack of rest. "Well, I guess we'd better get over there then. It wouldn't do to keep the good Father waiting."

THIRTEEN

LONNIE SAT in an outdoor plaza, breathing the greasy smell of onions and fried tamales. He could hear the sizzle of the grill, the hissing and snapping of deep-fried grease, and the non-stop banter of tourists and townspeople waiting to be fed. The late afternoon sun cast a tint of red on the white plastic table, but around the square lights were starting to snap on. He slid his chair back to take stock of his surroundings, causing an abrasive *screech* as the legs scraped against the clay tiles. Lampposts and hedge rails were strung with banners and bunting in Mexico's national colors of red, white and green. He'd not been here before. He purposely veered away from tourist areas avoiding working girls, mescal sellers, and pickpockets as best he could. He wondered why Daniela would choose such a place to meet.

He'd arrived in the early afternoon, boarding a connecting flight out of LA, and had gone directly to the mercantile. As instructed, he'd asked for a copy of *The New York Times*. The woman behind the counter, in response to a pre-arranged code, apologized for not having the paper, but offered him a copy of *The Los Angeles Times* instead. He'd been cautioned not to hang around the store. He was to take the newspaper with him and read it for further instructions. Outside, he had opened the paper and found a note tucked inside directing him here. So here he sat and waited.

It was mild out, even in the waning light, and it made him glad to be back in Mexico. The local color, in spite of a bacchanal focus on wine, women and song, had a certain appeal. But that too was why he avoided such places. He rubbed his arms, pleased to see his silky blond hairs lying smooth and glowing in the sun, not standing erect and sprouting from goosebumps. Having just experienced the chilly north, reveling in the southern warmth was a welcome change. But he could not bring himself to unwind, even though he tried reclining. He stretched his legs beneath the table and leaned back. There was tension in the air. He could feel it. His fingers drummed the table's surface. He hated waiting. The woman had seemed nervous too as though intimidated by his presence, not the kind of behavior he expected of someone working inside the cartel, reputedly close to Miguel Estrada. He would've thought she'd be edgy and callous. But the woman actually seemed demure. Were she not undernourished, with a gaunt face and skin that seemed to suck into the hollow of her cheeks, he would have considered her attractive. She'd looked furtively around the room and slipped the paper onto the counter, then ducked behind the blanket that provided a door to the back without waiting for Lonnie to pay. He'd stood there, hoping she'd return, but she didn't, so he'd laid the money on the counter and left.

The sun dropped behind the horizon, leaving the buildings looking like piles of dominos stacked against the sky's yellow palate. He'd been there several hours, but he knew better than to expect the woman *too* soon. She had to close the store at the end the day and leave without looking suspicious. He picked up his newspaper, rereading the headlines he'd already read, realizing how odd he must look sitting there without a bottle of Corona or a platter of tortillas and frijoles in front of him, just occupying space, but his stomach was too agitated to eat and he couldn't leave. She might come while he was away. So he waited, but it was driving him crazy. Every minute without his kids was torture. He put the newspaper down and resumed tapping his fingers on the table. It was just that Bill had been a little *too* forthcoming.

Quoting statistics from the U.S. State Department, Interpol and the CIA, Bill explained how more than half a million kids were stolen from their parents and sold across international borders every year. *Half a million?* The number seemed staggering. His own kids were but a microcosm. *Half a million? Unbelievable!* And, according to Bill, the world's political machinery didn't have enough grease to do anything but pay lip service to the problem. He was trying to rescue two or three kids, when half a million needed saving. But there was nothing he could do about that. His kids were the ones he had to think about. *Sofía!* She'd just begun to heal. The thought of sending her back…no way. That wasn't going to happen. He brought his head up, rubbing the back of his neck.

Lonnie understood how sin consumed men from birth. He understood lust, greed and power. He'd fought a battle against all three during the attempted coup at Striker Films. It was one of the things he liked about Posada. He lived in a community where people had so little there wasn't much to covet, which was a good thing because unrestrained desire was what led to the Fall—Adam and Eve—*I know He said not to, but it looks good and*—and that was exactly why he had to stay away from Nicole.

But what Lonnie could not comprehend was the kind of lust that caused men to destroy other people's lives in their quest for self-gratification. Lust, greed and power were one thing. Every soul on the planet struggled with these to some degree. A man whose self-destructive nature led to his own ruination, he could understand. But when men let their unbridled lust run over others to get what they wanted, that was beyond him. What kind of man couldn't see the harm of abusing little children, *mere babies,* the innocent and undefiled? What kind of judgment would they reap at the end of time? *Forget that.* He needed justice *now.* He couldn't guess what his next step should be. He only knew he had to find the man who had his children and somehow convince him to give them back. If they were for sale, he would buy them. But he'd have to do it without letting anyone know how he felt. He'd have to hold his tongue. If he got in the man's face, it was likely he'd never see his kids again. Never mind, he couldn't even do that until this woman, Daniela, gave him the name and phone number of someone to call. He shivered at the thought. Maybe he could convince her to negotiate for him.

He rubbed his smooth long-fingered hands together. In spite of his labors for the Lord he still didn't have the calluses of a working man. He looked up and spotted Daniela wandering across the plaza. He wanted to wave, to flag her attention, but thought better of it. She did not seem in a hurry. She moved from table to table, talking to groups of men, taking a sip from a pitcher of cerveza when offered, holding it in both hands and laughing at something said as she wiped her mouth with her fingers, obviously well known and well received. She wore a red blouse made of shiny polyester, with short sleeves banded by sequined elastic that puffed out at her shoulders, and a low-cut front that revealed cleavage Lonnie hadn't noticed before. Her skirt was short and black and hugged her bottom as she squeezed between the chairs. A pair of large gold hoops dangled from the lobes of her ears, and her lips were painted bright red. She was prettier with her hair down, full, wavy, and dark brown with wisps of red that burned in the late afternoon sun. She stood behind a chair and placed her hands on the shoulders of the man seated there, leaning over to whisper something in his ear. Her hair fell forward, draping across the man's arm. He reached up, patting her hand, shaking his head with a toothy grin, and she moved on.

She was working the crowd. He should have expected it. Bill said she'd been a prostitute, though he'd somehow got the impression her hustling days were over. His lips formed a pragmatic pout. He wasn't her judge, but he couldn't help feeling disappointed. At least she'd volunteered to help. She finally reached his table and with a seductive smile, asked if he wanted to dance. The girl had to suffer some kind of split personality, from demure to brazen, from quiet to loud, from Dr. Jekyll to Mr. Hyde. Music was coming from a loudspeaker strapped to a telephone pole, accompanied by a male voice crooning love songs in Spanish. *She can't be serious.* What he wanted was to sit and talk, but she reached out her hand and Lonnie took it to be polite. She pulled him from his chair and turned. Looking over her shoulder, she puckered her moistened lips, beguiling him, but instead of moving toward the dance floor, she led him across the plaza, weaving in and out of tables where men sat chasing oily frijoles and jalapeno peppers with amber bottles of beer. Lonnie was trailing her like a child, still holding her hand as they entered a small inn off to the side of the market. His heart was pounding. What was she getting him into?

The room was buzzing. It was hard to tell which it had more of, flies or men. The bar at the front was crammed three feet deep with gringo turistas standing shoulder to shoulder, tipping back shots of tequila and shouting to he heard above the noise. Those fortunate enough to have seats had girls in their laps. Lonnie kept his head down, praying no one would recognize him. *Sí, I saw it myself, the padre was doing the rumba with...* He couldn't imagine trying to explain himself if rumors got back to his church.

Daniela led him down a long dark hall lit by a single red bulb hanging from the ceiling by a twisted pair of wires. Doors opened and closed on either side. They were passing couples coming and going, bumping into men too drunk to negotiate a straight line, and women with glazed and hollow eyes too high on cocaine to feel. She tried several doors, but voices on the other side let her know the rooms were in use, until they reached one at the very back. Lonnie found himself breathing through his mouth to avoid the rank smell of mildew and vomit. Daniela closed the door.

If Lonnie's heart was pounding before, now it was heading into fibrillation. This was not what he had in mind. Not at all! What had Bill got him into? There were no chairs in the room so he sat on the bed. The mattress sagged. *Gross*. The sheets were scratchy, stiff with dirt and dried body fluids. The smell of a thousand sweaty bodies wrinkled his nose.

"I am sorry. I know this is uncomfortable, señor, but it has to be. I thought very hard about this, but I'm being watched, so this is the only way. If someone comes in, I will throw myself on you. You must pretend to, you know, okay? Now, el señor Best, he asked me to meet with you. That is the only reason I do this."

Lonnie stared at the ceiling, afraid she might start to disrobe. He closed his eyes. "Bill told you why I'm here. I heard him. There must have been somewhere else we could meet."

"No señor, I am not free to go where I please." Daniela joined him on the bed, the springs of the bedframe squeaking under her weight.

"The man Bill told you about, Miguel Estrada, he owns me. I am his property. I work for him. I manage his store. This I much prefer—" A loud thump against the wall caused Daniela to grab Lonnie and roll into his arms, but when she realized it was coming from another room, she let go. "Sorry. Did I hurt you?"

Lonnie shook his head.

"Good. Please, I must ask you to forgive me. I do not want to be here. I swore I would never come back, but it was the only thing I could think of that would not draw suspicion. I work in the store during the day so I won't have to do this kind of thing. And I am old. Men do not pay much for me anymore. There are many younger girls to choose from. For this I am thankful, but I fear the day no one asks for me. They may decide it's time for me to disappear. So I think maybe this will help. You are a young American, and yet you buy my service, that maybe makes me one still desired. Please, I must ask that you pay me now." She held out her hand with her palm turned up.

Lonnie pulled his head back, narrowing his eyes.

"Not for my service, but the man who rents the rooms, he must pay Miguel, so I must pay him."

Lonnie removed his wallet and held it open, allowing her to remove a few bills. "Disappear? You can't be serious. How?"

"Sí, it happens. If someone doesn't earn enough, or holds back money, they, *poof*, gone, just like that. No one asks where they go. It is understood. So, what do you want from me?"

"How did you meet Bill?"

"Just like this. I was working. Señor Best was staying at the Palace Resort in Puerto Angel. The hotel is owned by señor Estrada. It is one of many legitimate businesses he owns. I was there to service men from your navy, and American men who say they are there to surf and fish, but are really hiding from their wives. To me, Bill was just another customer. I went over and offered him my services. I thought he was there for a good time, but the smile dropped from his mouth and I saw sadness. Then he said something that made my heart go stop, and I knew I had made a mistake. He looked at me and said, "Do you know God loves you?" That is all, but the next thing I know, my eyes are filling with water, and I have to run from the room so no one will see."

"He only said that one thing, so simple, but it made me *feel* something. And I had become numb. I did not want to feel. I went back to my room. My legs were shaking. I couldn't walk. I finally dropped to my knees and curled up and became a little ball, like dust on the floor. I was dead, señor Lonnie. I knew it. I was still breathing, but I was dead. Perhaps I had been dead for a very long time. It didn't matter. They could have carried me out and shot me. It wouldn't have made any difference. But something about what señor Best said made me feel alive. There's no way to explain it. I, I finally got up and washed my face and returned to the bar, but by then the place was empty. I was glad for that. I did not like what was happening in my head, *mi loco*. I thought I was going crazy. And then the next day he was there again. He grabs me by the wrist and drags me to his room. It was not like this, though. This was a nice hotel with clean beds. He took out his wallet and told me he would pay just to sit and talk. So that is what we did. Every day he would pay for an hour of my time, and before the week was out he had me calling on Jesus and...and...and," she choked and tried clearing her throat, "I owe him my life, señor, but he was telling me I had to quit working. I couldn't. I was owned, the slave of Miguel. If I tried to break out I would have been hunted down and shot. Less than a dog in his eyes. Bill, he stay in the hotel a week, and then, before he left, he told me to pray and trust Jesus, and he gave me his card and told me to call if ever I needed help."

"After he left, nothing was the same. I could no longer do what they paid me to do, though I tried. I was still forced to wait on customers, but I took no pleasure in it, and I'm sure I left many men unhappy. Then, it was like a miracle. A man with a mercantile died owing the cartel money. They took over his store and decided they would use it to get their money back. And since I was almost thirty, and not giving men much pleasure, they put me in the store to run it. You see, God had done just what señor Bill said. He gave me a way out."

She paused, biting her lip till it turned white. "Only I think now what I do is worse. Taking food to nourish men so they can destroy other people's lives, is that not like doing it myself? That's why I called this man, Bill. I told him if he would keep me secret, I would provide him with information to expose the cartel. I hoped what he wrote would pressure our government to shut Miguel down, but it didn't happen. He has too much power."

"So now I feed the men who sell little girls into prostitution. Little ones, innocent, forced to do hideous things while I stand by and watch. Many will die before they see womanhood. They'll be choked and dumped in a hole somewhere. They can't be allowed to live because they might talk and the secrets of the men who own them must be kept. And, since no one is looking for them, it's like no crime has been committed..." Daniela stopped abruptly, and Lonnie knew she'd seen the horror on his face. She shouldn't be so candid with someone whose children were missing. "I'm...I'm sorry, señor. What would you like me to do?"

Lonnie took a deep breath and exhaled. "I need you to find out if señor Estrada has my kids, and I want you to offer to buy them back. I'll pay whatever price he demands."

Daniela paused. She closed her eyes as though measuring her words, then looked at Lonnie. "No, señor, this I cannot do. I will do what I can, but I cannot do what is impossible. Only señor Estrada can negotiate a sale, and he does not talk to such as me. And even if he did, to say I have a buyer would suggest I've been talking about his business to someone he doesn't know, and for this, I would be shot. It is not done. You have to approach señor Estrada yourself. All I can do is direct you. Tomorrow—when I deliver supplies—we will do it then. I will drop you several miles outside the camp. You must walk in on your own. Miguel is heartless and cold. He would not think twice about killing you. But he is a greedy man. If you're willing to pay his price, perhaps he will accept your offer. Just leave me out of it. That is all I ask."

FOURTEEN

SOFÍA SAT in the dirt, her arms wrapped around her knees, rocking back and forth, tears channeling through the dust on her cheeks. Her long raven hair was tangled and her blouse had a rip at the shoulder. Mariana knew the hole hadn't been there before. She was too young to understand, but not too young to feel. She wanted to make whatever was hurting her friend go away. She sat beside Sofía, looking down, rolling a twig between her thumb and forefinger. She opened her mouth—but the words wouldn't come.

And Sofía couldn't tell her. She was reliving the nightmare, her mind filled with images of being tied to a bed, drawn and quartered, with a sock stuffed in her mouth while her uncle climbed on top sweating and smelling of stale tequila, week after week, and a mother who refused to do anything because she needed the shelter of her brother's house. The only difference was these men didn't bother tying her down. They just grabbed her arms and legs and pulled her apart, holding her while they repeated what her uncle had done, one after another in nonstop succession.

Raúl's face was stone, his eyes orbs of glass, hard and unseeing. His jaw was set, his teeth clenched, and the skin around his cheeks stiff as cardboard. He didn't know what he was feeling—*hate?*—yes, possibly, but it went deeper than that. He would *kill* the men who hurt Sofía. They did not deserve to live, *kill them*, along with the man who killed his parents. He shamed himself for not being more careful. *Why God? Why do you let this happen?* His sister did not need to be put through this. *What has Sofía done that You should hate her so?* She sat propped against the wall, eyes open, but not focused, staring at some distant point in space. What had they done to her? Now she bowed her head on her arms, her body heaving.

Raúl got up, mustering his strength. He began walking the perimeter of the yard, looking for a way to escape. The dogs followed, growling, nipping at the chain-link until the man guarding the gate ordered him away from the fence. He sat in the dirt, scraping the ground with his finger. The soil had dried in the sun, baked hard as kiln-fired brick. It would take a pick to crack the surface. He looked around the yard for something—*anything*—with which to dig a hole, but there was nothing. He gazed out across the vast expanse between himself and the field of crops, measuring how far he'd have to dig. He folded his hands over his biceps. His arms had lost their muscle. It would take forever. He let go, his knuckles scraping the ground. He looked toward the sky. There would be no escape. He closed his eyes, a tremor swelling in his chest. He needed to cry. He *wanted* to cry, but he couldn't. He had to be strong. His sister was depending on him. He felt a hand touching his hair and jerked back, falling on the palms of his hands. It was Mariana. She sat down, placing her arms around his neck, resting her head on his shoulder. He broke. The tears streamed down his cheeks as his body began to shake. Mariana held on, unwilling to let go. He grabbed her, pushing her away, holding her at arm's length.

"What do you want me to do, Mariana? What do you want me to do?" Strings of saliva clung to his chapped lips.

Mariana got on her knees, folded her hands, and rolled her eyes toward heaven.

"He's not going to hear me, Mariana. He doesn't listen."

Mariana kept staring at the sky as if some unseen force were about to intervene.

"If He listened, Mamá would still be here, you understand?"

Mariana's mouth was moving, her lips forming silent words.

Raúl closed his eyes and sighed, then slowly opened them again, shaking his head.

IN A BOX of cinder block walls, cool as the evening's heat dissipated over the ocean, Nicole sat on a hard slab of cement, praying. She was not alone. She sat in a circle of village women dressed in brightly colored blouses, each with her hair braided or rolled in a bun. Sisters Gabriela and Fatima, their black robes spread across the ground covering their feet, were also there, along with an old man in muslin pants with deep scars on his face hidden behind the salt-and-pepper stubble of a week-old beard. On the floor, lying on his stomach beside her with his legs wiggling out like the tail of a tadpole, was Sebastian. His elbows were planted on the ground, his chin propped up in his hands. This was the group Nicole had recruited to pray.

She was troubled by unfounded fears, the overwhelming sense of foreboding, the feeling that something horrible was about to happen, when there was no logical reason to feel that way. She could not argue with Father Paulo when he said Lonnie was in God's hands. The good Father did his best to reassure her. The kidnapping had taken place in Mexico. Lonnie had flown to Oregon, the opposite direction—far away. But Nicole still couldn't shake her anxiety. She had been wrestling with this unsettling feeling since Lonnie's departure. Father Paulo promised to pray for Lonnie, but that didn't satisfy Nicole. There had to be more she could do.

She gathered the townspeople—as many as she could rally on such short notice—to join her, and here they sat making their requests known before God, audibly, with everyone speaking at once. Waiting quietly upon the Lord was a foreign concept. It just wasn't done. They were groaning and wailing, and praising and weeping, making sure they were heard as one voice. The walls echoed with the jumble of sound. And they were animated. One of the ladies bowed on her knees, another lay spread-eagle on the floor, forming the image of a cross, one had her hands raised to the sky—and tears flowed as the supplications were made.

Perhaps it was Sebastian who had the most to gain from such a meeting. Even if Lonnie wasn't in trouble, Sofía was. She *was* his twin. They held each other up, a matched set of bookends, but now one was missing and either could fall. She was a sister to him, a best friend. It was Sofía who insisted on carrying him wherever she went. Her heart gave him legs. Their veins may not have flowed with the same blood, but they were certainly of one kind. Were she not to return, he would suffer more than any of the others. He would be losing his entire family, even if his real parents were still alive. Sofía was his sister, and Lonnie, the only father he'd ever known.

FIFTEEN

THE ROOM was windowless, somber and dark. Seventy-two small candles burning in red glass vases sent smoke up in small columns, leaving behind the smell of paraffin, their flickering lights causing shadows in the room to dance about the walls. Seventy-two flames glowing in front of a plaster statue of Mary holding the baby Jesus in her arms. But this was not a convent, nor other austere house of worship. This altar was erected in the sanctum sanctorum of a mansion. Miguel Estrada stood praying over the candles. They were a symbol. He crossed himself as he knelt. It bothered him there were so many, but it was the price of doing business, though he did wish people were a little more honest. When a man makes a promise, the promise should be kept. God would expect no less. The two newest candles were a perfect example. They should not have borrowed money they could not afford to repay. Sad. Very sad. But what really troubled him was their refusal to work off the debt. He'd tried to help but they rejected his offer and stubbornly persisted in breaking the contract. And now there were two more souls for which he had to pray.

"Mary, sweet mother of Jesus, look down upon me now and know that my hands have not shed innocent blood. It is the blood of the guilty I offer, and that alone. Pray to the Father. Acknowledge that I have helped in your quest to purge this world of evil. And if I have found favor in thine eyes, bless me with your peace." He crossed himself, and rose to his feet.

In another corner a square of white light burned from a computer screen. Miguel went to his desk. A *beep* let him know another message was being received, and there were several already waiting. He sat down, clicked his e-mail program and highlighted a recent delivery. It was a request for more children—one of many. This time the buyer wanted young girls, an easy order to fill based on his network of contacts. He had buyers and sellers strategically placed in every part of the globe: from Sri Lanka to São Paulo, from the Czech Republic to the good old U.S. of A. Children were a commodity, and one for which there was a sizable market, in spite of growing competition. He'd read the report published by Mexico's National Foundation of Investigations of Robbed and Missing Children stating a hundred and thirty-three thousand Mexican children were estimated to have been kidnapped over the past five years. He noted with some pride that by his calculation, his network of affiliates was responsible for about twenty percent. He was moving over five-thousand children a year. There were advantages to having his operations centralized in the great country of Mexico where there was little government intervention. On the books, of course, selling children was illegal. Those who occupied seats of power feigned, for the sake of international relations, that such trafficking was not sanctioned, but most in public office chose to turn their heads and look the other way. And anyone who didn't was either bought off or otherwise dealt with. This meant virtually every country in the world used Mexico as a channel for exporting children to the United States, making him the linchpin for all U.S. trade. And his agreements were bilateral. If a customer wanted an American, then he would reciprocate, but very few insisted on getting children from there. It was *too* expensive. Children from the Orient were a better deal. They were readily available, and cost far less. Of course those from Mexico were the easiest to obtain.

He typed in his password and brought up an image library, then clicked on the folder labeled "Little Ladies." Photographs of hundreds of young girls ranging in age from three to sixteen began to appear. He did a sort on ages three to seven, narrowing the field, and zipped the file to compress it. Then he clicked Reply, used Insert to make the file an attachment, typed a quick note promising availability as long as the order was confirmed within the hour, and clicked Send. Business was good, very good, and very profitable. One transaction alone could net tens of thousands of U.S. dollars. It hardly made the work of harvesting marijuana worth the risk. Drugs had to be smuggled. Kids, on the other hand, could be walked across international borders and no one was any the wiser because kids didn't require passports, just the word of the adult with whom they traveled. He was thinking of getting out of narcotics, but so many were employed in his farming operation and their families depended on him. *Caramba!* Did they think he was running a charity? Marijuana was the crop of the sixties. It was time to move on but—*mañana*, it could wait. He would think about it some other time. He still had six e-mails to read. He clicked on the next in the queue. A note from a worker. *What, Daniela?* Turned a trick—an American—he'd let her work the market because she wanted out. It might be nothing, but it was worth monitoring. He zipped off a note to his informant, hoping for the best. He did not relish the thought of having to light another candle.

SIXTEEN

LONNIE FELT the bruise growing as the truck hit another bump and his hip bounced against the steel floor. It was the most uncomfortable ride he'd ever taken. He lay sandwiched between gunny sacks filled with flour, cornmeal and wheat. Several liquid-filled cans were rolling around the floor. One had already hit his head, leaving a rather unsightly bump.

He'd climbed into the back of Daniela's truck in the dark hours just before dawn. She had instructed him to be discreet, staying in the shadows as he made his way down the alley while keeping an eye out for anyone watching. He'd been careful not to make a sound, though the gravel crunching under his feet was impossible to avoid, and the scent of adrenaline oozing from his pores set a dog to barking. *Dogs can smell fear—can't they?* Well, anyway, this one could, and it didn't shut up until long after he'd crawled under the tarp. She'd warned him the truck would be loaded with the supplies she'd be taking to the farm the next day, but failed to mention how little room there would be for him. The gunny sacks were stacked along both sides of the truck's bed leaving a narrow trench down the center for him to squeeze into. He could only crawl between the sacks sideways, so he had to lie on his arm, unable to move. This in afterthought was a blessing because had he been able to move, he might have disturbed the surface of the canvas stretched tightly over him, which might have been seen by someone outside. The steel bottom of the truck was cold and gritty, so he lay very still, his nose pressed against the burlap, breathing the smell of husked wheat until he finally fell asleep.

It only seemed like a moment before he heard the *creeeak* of a rusty hinge, and felt the weight of someone climbing aboard. He hoped it was Daniela. They weren't five minutes down the road when the bags began to shift, squeezing him even tighter. Now he bounced along hour upon hour, his arm being scratched raw against the rough metal, his nose wet and red from rubbing against the course jute fabric, and his head aching from the assault of the renegade can. It was bad enough when they were on a paved road, but it had become obvious they were now jogging their way down a dirt track.

The truck slowed. He could feel the wheels dipping in and out of holes as it came to a stop. He listened as Daniela rolled down her window and began speaking with someone. He missed most of what was said, but gathered they were crossing a checkpoint of some kind. The exchange seemed more conversational than confrontational. His heart was popping like grease in a hot pan as he lay there expecting the tarp to be lifted and a face to peer in exposing him, but the truck soon revved its engine and took off again. He had no idea where they were, or how much further he had to go to find his children. Or how he would get them back.

The bumpy ride bruising his ribs and punishing his nose continued for another few miles. The hammer in his head continued to pound. Then he felt the truck slowing for another stop. *Another checkpoint?* The door opened and *blammed* shut. He felt the truck rock as someone stepped off the running board. His heart caught in his throat. They were working the lashes that held the tarp in place. This was the moment of truth. Up till now he'd assumed Daniela was on his side. *What if she wasn't?* What if they knew about him? What if she'd turned him in? The thoughts ran rampant. *Oh God, please let Daniela be named among your saints.* The canvas was lifted. At first his eyes being used to the dark could not see the person standing over him. All he saw was a dark silhouette, but the voice he recognized. He released the breath he'd been holding.

"Okay, señor Lonnie, this is as far as you go. You must hide and wait until I return."

Lonnie raised his head, using his hand to shield his eyes. "How much further is it?" He looked around. They were surrounded by walls of green. "You think he'll be there? Mr. Estrada, I mean. How long will I have to wait?"

"I cannot say, señor, sometimes he is there, and sometimes not. Please get out of the truck, quickly. Your nose is bleeding," she said, as Lonnie crawled out.

"It is?" Lonnie wiped his face with the back of his hand, surprised at the amount of blood. "I didn't have room to keep my head away from those sacks. They pounded it something fierce."

Daniela finished stretching the tarp across the bed of the truck, fixing it in place, and went to the cab. She climbed in, shutting the door. "I will be gone as long as it takes to deliver the supplies. You must wait here until you see my truck return. I will not stop. When you see I have gone, then and then only can you come out of hiding. The camp is down that road," she said, pointing, "a few more miles. But please, señor, wait until I am safely gone. They will ask you how you found this place. Make something up. Tell them you bought the information. Many men work here. They drink, and when they drink, they talk, so who knows? They will want to believe you. They want your business, but they must be careful. Once, some American hippies came to our camp and said they heard we sold marijuana. They were questioned and threatened, but they got what they wanted." Daniela put her truck in gear. "One more thing. They will want to know why you are walking. Tell them your car broke down and had to be towed away. You must complain and say you did not know how far it would be or you would have gone back for another car. If they ask how you got by the guard, say you never saw one. Maybe they'll think he was asleep. He would not miss a car, but someone walking? I don't know if they will believe you. I must warn you of this before you go. And if they do not believe you...ah, it could go bad and I won't be able to help. From here on, you are on your own. Vaya con Dios, my friend. Go with God."

Daniela rolled up her window and the truck pulled away, leaving Lonnie standing at the side of the road fenced in by the sounds of the jungle.

Well, I made it this far. Now what? He turned, his eyes scanning the dense green for a place to hide, a place from which he could see the road, but not be seen. He scanned the area, and then it hit him. He was *alone* in enemy territory. His skin tightened. He snapped his head around at the sound of movement—*a monkey? A lion? A bird?* Sweat broke out on his forehead. He began to move away from the road. He had nothing to fear. He was doing good, rescuing little ones. It was knowing good and not doing it, that was sin. But doing God's will didn't guarantee God's protection. The church was full of martyrs. *Trust in the Lord with all thine heart, and lean not on thine own understanding.* That was the nut of it. He had to find a place where he could sit and pray.

SEVENTEEN

Mamá, I am lost. I have nowhere to turn. Your boy is to become the slave of rich fools. Can you see me, Mamá? I have prayed. I said, God, please, not for me but for Mariana, but He does not listen. I think He is mad because I want to kill the snake, but tell Him not to worry, it is impossible. I will not return from where they are sending me. The one they call Luis, he says I should be fat like him because then no one will want me. He said three vans have come and each time he has been left behind. But I cannot stay here, I must be with Mariana, even unto death. Maybe then we will see you again.

RAÚL STOOD beside Mariana and Sofía. They had been singled out and dragged from the pen, Mariana by the hand, he by his arm, and taken to this crude cube of a building. It was a hotbox with walls and floors of plywood, and a roof of corrugated tin that transmitted the noonday heat. He could feel pinpricks of sweat dotting his forehead even though he'd just been cleaned. He heard the word "camera" and "photograph," and knew without having to ask why they were there. He had never had his picture taken, so to be slicked up and stood in front of the large blue screen was a genuine curiosity. Were it not for the circumstances, he might have enjoyed the experience. The woman who washed his face, combed his hair, and helped him dress was nice, a lot like his mother. She hummed as she helped the three children get ready, introducing herself as Daniela. Raúl liked her. She was gentle. She took them one by one, snapping off pictures, and then was kind enough to let them see the images in the back of the camera. He thought they looked pretty good, even though none of the children smiled, and Sofía's gaze was a million miles away. When they were done, Daniela pulled a little plastic card from a slot in the camera and said, "Your pictures are in here now." The three children were then rounded up by a sombrero-wearing campesino and taken back to the pen.

DANIELA TRUDGED across the grounds to another building holding the wafer-thin disk so tight she risked snapping it in two. She loosened her fingers, trying to relax, but she couldn't arrest her feelings. She was contributing to the sale of these children. She'd asked them their names, but they'd refused to answer. They were the ones the padre was looking for. She knew it. They fit the description. And she'd been required to take their pictures, which proved they were new arrivals.

She rapped on the screen door and entered without waiting to be acknowledged. The man seated behind the desk looked up, his nose sniffing the air, his teeth visible even with his mouth closed. He wore thick glasses with black plastic frames. She hated the little man. Everyone called him "Badger" because he was small and vicious. He was Miguel's right hand—and the one who had robbed her virginity when she herself had been brought here as a child. He took personal responsibility for breaking in newcomers. He considered himself their teacher, their trainer, their mentor—but he was all things evil—a sadist, a rapist and a pedophile. Badger examined her over the top of his computer, his nose twitching. His eyes were watery and red, taxed by the smoke of the cigar that coiled up from the aluminum pie plate on his desk. He wiped his nose with the back of his hand and resumed typing. The spring recoiled and the screen door banged shut. Daniela went to the corner where there was a steel folding chair, and settled in to wait.

The man pounded on the keyboard with two fingers—or were they claws—peck, peck, pecking out his message.

"She's here now. Do you want me to keep her?"

"No, that won't be necessary. Tell her you need something and have her return tomorrow. I have a client who wants a special child, hand-picked, so I have to come out. I will question her then."

"Sí."

The man clicked the sign-off button and extended his hand to Daniela. She passed him the plastic card with the pictures on it.

He slipped the device into the card reader and opened each file to examine the photographs. "Muy bueno. Sí! This little girl, she has eyes, yes, these eyes...very good. Bueno. Bueno."

Daniela got up to go.

"Uh, uno momento, por favor. *Sniff.* We need you to come back tomorrow. *Sniff.* Our cook, he say you forgot to bring pinto beans, and we need pinto beans, and we could also use more coffee."

Daniela started to protest, "Tomorrow? Can't it wait until next week? I can't afford so many trips. Gas is expensive."

"Pinto beans, *sniff,* we can do without, but not coffee. The men would revolt. I must insist that you bring us coffee. Tomorrow. Gracias."

EIGHTEEN

LONNIE WATCHED the truck bounce by. The wheels dipped into a hole and came out spraying mud. He thought he saw Daniela waving. He thought she had her finger and thumb curled into an okay sign, but he was a fair distance from the road and there was too much dirt and glare on the window to be sure. He pulled himself from his place of hiding. His clothes were damp. Moisture was heavy in the air, creating a humidity so intense it rose up from the ground like steam. The jungle was alive with birds straining their vocal cords to be heard, *kooo-coo-coo, ka-ka-ka, ke-ke-keeee.* Lonnie picked up his pace, moving quickly down the dirt lane, stepping over water-filled holes and ruts. The cuffs of his pants were splattered and muddy. He was torn between wanting to find his children, and making sure he didn't cause suspicion by arriving too soon after Daniela's departure. But the children won. He couldn't stop his feet from moving. In only a matter of minutes he could feel beads of sweat rolling down his chest.

He'd walked about a mile when he heard a rumbling coming from behind. He turned just in time to see an old yellow Volkswagen filled with campesinos rounding the bend. *Putt, sputter, puftt.* The muffler had fallen off. He dove for the side of the road, ducking out of the way as the car bounced by, sounding like a tank. It didn't stop, but the man riding shotgun was talking to someone on a cell phone. They must've thought he had good reason to be there. After all, he'd already cleared one guard station. Or maybe they thought he was just another worker. But wouldn't they have stopped to pick him up? No, the car was already full.

Lonnie looked up, observing the sun through spaces in the canopy of leaves. It was the other side of high noon. He had set out before dawn, but Daniela's business had taken several hours. *It can't be much further,* he thought, hoping for the best. It was getting late, but Good Lord willing, he'd still have time to get his kids and be gone before nightfall. He stopped. A snake lay on the road in front of him, writhing. It had been run over by the Volkswagen—*jungle justice*—a serpent killed by a bug. Snakes could be poisonous. Lonnie was glad this one had moved and caught his attention. It was still able to bite. At the edge of the road, he picked up a stick and used it to push the snake into the bush where it couldn't harm anyone. There were supposed to be children around somewhere. He resumed his walk, paying more attention to the road ahead.

He was looking down and did not see the two men stepping onto the road behind him. Then he felt a stick prodding him in the back. He jerked around. It wasn't a stick. It was the barrel of a rifle.

"Eh, señor, can I help you?"

Lonnie's heart jumped to his throat. He raised his hands. The men didn't look unfriendly, but the gun presented a threat. "I...I...no, I mean, I'm looking for señor Estrada."

The two men looked at each other, shaking their heads. The man to Lonnie's left wore a red bandana around his bald forehead, knotted at the back with the tail hanging down. The man pumped iron. He had arms like ham hocks, and a chest like a sack of wheat. His mustache ran down both sides of his chin.

The man with the gun was shorter, but just as solid. He had long gray hair tied in a ponytail. "And what business would you have with señor Estrada?" He said, poking his weapon into Lonnie's chest.

Lonnie sucked in his breath and held it, trying to gain composure. He felt faint, like he might pass out. *Lord, please, help me here.* His hands were shaking, his chest starving for air. He'd never mastered the art of hiding his fear. He exhaled. "Tha...tha...that's between me and him," he said, gasping as air filled his lungs again. It's a...it's a personal matter. But it's urgent that I see him right away. Can you take me to him?"

"I am sorry, señor. You have wasted your time. Mr. Estrada is not here. And even if he were, he would not meet with you."

The man with the red bandana brought a cell phone to his lips and began talking.

Lonnie shot him a quick glance, but continued speaking to the man with the gun. "I'm sorry," he said, "but I must see Miguel Estrada. I've come a long way. I'm sure he'll be interested in what I have to say."

The man holding the rifle looked at his friend, who nodded.

"Okay, señor. You want to see señor Estrada? You *will* see señor Estrada. Turn around and start walking, por favor."

Lonnie did as told. He could hear the two men conversing behind him, keeping a distance of several yards. He wondered if he shouldn't duck into the woods and try to escape. But what for? It didn't seem like the men wanted to hurt him. They could have, if they wanted to. They had, in fact, offered to let him go. What point was there in trying to escape only to show up at the camp later? Looking back over his shoulder, he saw the man had relaxed the rifle in his arms. He closed his eyes and exhaled, breathing easier. This wasn't a death march—it was an afternoon stroll. He took a deep breath. *Relax.*

They had walked another quarter mile when the jungle opened into a lush valley. The tall trees gave way to fields of crops bustling in the breeze. It was a spectacular view. Purple mountains provided a backdrop for a valley filled with shimmering green plants. It was a crop to make the Green Giant green with envy. But these plants would not be canned or frozen. They were grown for an entirely different purpose, one of which Lonnie did not approve. This was a cash crop. The harvest was not food, the harvest was euphoria—*no*—the harvest was—*money!* Down the road Lonnie saw a complex of buildings arranged in neat rows, and the yellow Volkswagen that had passed him earlier was now heading back, making sounds like a tractor, but looking more like a lemon on wheels. When it reached the three men it stopped and backed into a small clearing, turning around. The two men came alongside, each taking one of Lonnie's arms as they escorted him to the car and shoved him into the back.

"Easy, *ouch!* Okay, okay, you want me to get in. I get it. Okay? *Ouch!*"

Lonnie rubbed his shoulder. The plastic seat was slick with the sweat of the previous occupants. Their odor saturated the air. The two men squeezed into the car and sat down on either side. The little bug took off with a lurch, rocking Lonnie so hard his head almost slammed against the rear window. One man took hold of his arms and crossed them, while the other bound his wrists with a cord. He pulled back instinctively, but his attempt to break the man's grip was futile.

The road continued down through the tall plants. Lonnie had no misgivings about what they were. As much as it pained him to acknowledge it, marijuana was the biggest export crop of the region. They pulled into a clearing surrounded by Quonset huts and other small buildings and came to a stop. Lonnie was lifted from the car and taken into a small wood building where he was shoved into a chair. A man sat at a keyboard, clicking away. He appeared small. Lonnie could barely see him above the monitor, but he did notice, as the man hunched over his work, that he was all but bald with a few ungainly hairs sticking out on both sides of his head.

The man looked up through Coke-bottle glasses that made his eyes look enormous. His face held the residue of a beard. His lips pulled back exposing huge incisor teeth. "Where do you come from, señor? What is your business here?" He ran a finger under his nose. *Sniff.*

Lonnie looked around, taking stock of his surroundings. The office walls were sheets of plywood. There was only one window and it was open to allow circulation of the stale air. There were cobwebs in the corners and the plywood floor was tracked with dried mud. The man working at his computer was typing even as he talked. Twists of smoke floated up from a hidden cigar.

"My name is Lonnie Striker."

The man continued typing. *She left several bags with fresh blood on them. This man's nose is bleeding. She was seen with an American last night. It's possible she brought him.* The man looked up. "You are American, are you not?"

Lonnie paused. He'd already thought about his answer. There was justification for lying. Abraham lied: *"Take Sarah, she's my sister, not my wife."* And David lied for the same self-serving reason: *"Hey Achish, ol' buddy, why kill me? I'm crazy,"* And what about those who hid Jews during the Holocaust? *"No sir, I haven't seen any Jews around here."* He could justify lying for a good cause, but it still didn't seem right.

"Yes, but I'm a missionary here." The man started typing again. "I run an orphanage. Three of my children have gone missing and it was suggested I speak to Mr. Estrada. I was told he might know of their whereabouts. I'm willing to pay him for his time."

The man sniffed yet again and wrinkled his nose. "Who said you should speak to Mr. Estrada?"

"I don't know. I didn't get a name. I was asking around. I asked if anyone knew where my children might be and one of the people I spoke with suggested I look for Mr. Estrada."

"And what made you think señor Estrada, *sniff,* would be here?"

Lonnie could see he was talking himself into a corner, but he couldn't bring himself to lie, so he stayed with the truth—*sort of.* "This is where I was told to come. Look, all I want is my children. I'm not here to cause trouble, and I'm willing to pay for their release. I'll even pay a little extra for your inconvenience." It looked like the man was recording everything Lonnie said. And it was also apparent someone was feeding him questions to ask.

"Is that Mr. Estrada? You're talking to someone, aren't you? If it is, please ask him if he knows anything about my children. Please!"

"The man stopped typing and looked up. The bald crown of his head reflected the light. *Sniff.* "I need to know how you found us. You will tell me, por favor, and you will not test my patience. Now I ask you again, *sniff,* who gave you señor Estrada's name and told you how to get here?"

Lonnie tensed. He didn't like where this was going. He couldn't give the information the man wanted, and the man seemed determined to acquire it. "I refuse to say anything until I see señor Estrada."

"You *will* see señor Estrada, that I can assure you, but not until you tell me what I want to know." The man stood and came around from behind his desk. He was barely half as tall as Lonnie, but was packed hard as clay, and thick—thick neck, thick wrists, thick chest, thick thighs. He walked to the door, his short businesslike legs pumping, the plywood floor creaking beneath his feet. He motioned to someone on the other side. The two thugs came in and grabbed Lonnie by the arms. They yanked him up and carried him outside to a post stuck in the ground in the middle of the yard. Lonnie tried to wiggle free. Over his shoulder he saw what he hadn't seen before. A large area was fenced off and there were children locked inside, but he only caught a glimpse before he was slammed against the post. The rope around his wrists was slipped over a large steel hook. The hook was attached to its own rope which was then tossed over a beam. Two men pulled on the rope, hoisting Lonnie's arms up till he was off his feet, balancing on the tips of his toes. He wanted to see if his kids were in the yard but they had him turned away from the fence. A man with a coiled whip stood in front of him, but he slowly moved around behind. *Oh God, give me strength.* The whip cracked the air, *whizzzzzz-snap*, and Lonnie felt his flesh rip apart. *Ahhuggggggg!* His face contorted. His body was as tense as a piece of stretched wire. Another crack of the whip sounded. His head snapped back. His skin shredded and blood gushed.

"Now I ask you one more time, señor Striker, who told you of this place?"

Lonnie hesitated, and the whip came down again.

LONNIE AWOKE on the dirt floor of a Quonset hut. Pain shot through his body as he tried to stand, but couldn't. Not just his back, but his head, his kidneys, his arms and legs, every part of him ached. He lay there, barely able to breathe. There were no windows to let in light. The hot afternoon sun was pounding on the corrugated tin, causing the room to feel like a can of beans simmering on an open fire. Lonnie tried getting up again and succeeded in wobbling to his knees. He looked around trying to figure out where he was. In the shadows he saw hemp plants laying in piles, criss-crossed atop each other, and as his eyes adjusted to the light, hundreds more hanging upside down from a grid attached to the ceiling. He wondered how long he'd been out this time. At least he was still alive. They hadn't killed him. Something moved in the corner. He turned his head, slowly, and caught a flicker of someone exiting through a door, the light streaming in before it banged shut. He tried one more time to stand but his legs were too weak. He flopped over and closed his eyes, wallowing in the dirt. It seemed like the man was gone only a few seconds, though it may have been longer because he may have passed out. He was awakened by a pail of water being tossed on his head. The cold cut him like a knife. He was hauled from the floor and dragged to a chair.

"Now señor Striker, *sniff*, if you will be so good as to tell me what I need to know, we can end all this."

Lonnie looked up through half-lidded eyes. The voice came from what looked like a pint-sized salt shaker, square and hard with a cylindrical cap, but through the glaze of water everything was a blur. And his thoughts were just as fuzzy. He could remember being beaten. He saw flashes of a fist pummeling his face. He tried blinking and realized his eyes were swollen. He probed his gums with his tongue and tasted blood. A stab of pain knifed his kidneys. How many times had he been through this? His head was about to explode. He'd passed out from the whipping only to be revived and beaten and knocked out again. How many times? *Two? Three? More?* He lowered his head and rolled it back and forth. Someone grabbed his hair and pulled his face down between his knees, while someone else poured something on his back. For a second it felt cool, but smelled like gasoline and burned like fire. He screamed. Then his world went black.

THE NEXT time he awoke it was dark outside. He knew because prior to this, minute strands of light had filtered through the cracks, providing at least some illumination. Now he was enveloped by black. It felt like the same room, the same distinctive odor of cannabis and machine oil, the same dirt floor. He thought about trying to get up but...*no*, the last time he did that, he was tortured again. It was better if he just remained still. He had no strength anyway. These men were evil to the core, probably unsalvageable. God might as well burn them now and save the world their stench. He envisioned fire falling from heaven. *Oh Lord, make it so.* A bevy of helicopters flying in low under radar, blanketing the hemp fields in napalm and defoliating agent orange. Miguel and his half-pint little henchman swinging from the gallows, birds feasting on their flesh, and...hadn't he learned anything?

His battle for Striker Films should have taught him God's judgments alone were perfect, and God judged in His own way and in His own time. A drop of water rolled down his face. The cross was about forgiveness. *Lord...they're here, Lord. Please, free my children.* He hadn't seen them, but he knew they were there—*right outside.* All he had to do was find a way. *Oh God, please. Remember Peter? Remember the angel you sent? I need one of those, Lord. If you can spare one. Please help me get my children back.*

He opened his eyes. A vision was silently hovering just above his head, waving at him, beckoning him to follow. The funny thing was, the vision looked just like Nicole—*but it couldn't be...*

NINETEEN

SOMETHING DREW Raúl from the gloom of sleep into the predawn light. He opened his eyes slowly, not anxious to face another day. A deep purple hovered over the eastern horizon, and stars could still be seen resting in the blue blanket of the west. He raised himself on his elbow, and then sat up. There it was again—a *rummmbling*. Turning in the direction of the fields, he saw a knife of light slicing through the tall plants, and as the vehicle turned the corner, a pair of lights sweeping the road. It looked like a phantom, a shapeless shadow with yellow eyes piercing the darkness. *Evil on wheels*. Spanish music shattered the silence as the van pulled up just outside the wire fence. The driver killed the engine and the sound stopped. Raúl's heart began to pound. Inside the cab there were shades of movement. Raúl heard the latch *click*, and saw the light come on. The driver hopped down and closed the door, making sure it didn't slam. The men spoke in hushed tones.

The skinny one made his way over to the fence where a guard was slumped in a chair. The dogs began to growl. One rose off his haunches with his teeth bared but the man snapped his fingers and pointed, staring the dog down, glowering, and with a yelp and a whimper the dog buried his head in his paws. The man kicked the guard's boot. "Hey, amigo, wake up. We have one more for you."

The guard's eyes opened lazily, as though pulled from a heavy dream. He stretched and yawned, thrusting his legs out straight. He pushed himself out of the chair, grunting, and joined the man in trudging back to the van. Both men disappeared around the other side of the vehicle. Raúl could hear the door *screeching* open, and voices, but not what was being said. The dogs were now prowling the line of the fence, growling. A few minutes later, a small boy was marched through the gate. He looked disheveled and confused as he shuffled by. He was short, but dressed smartly, not like anyone Raúl had seen so far. He wore a crested blazer with polyester slacks tapered down to hard leather shoes, his dark tie knotted in front of his white shirt twirled in the morning wind like the hands of a clock. His hair was neatly trimmed and curly and combed back with a part down the side, definitely not a child of the street. The man herding the child into the yard took no notice of Raúl, but Raúl noticed him. In spite of a chill in the morning air, he wore only a denim vest. His chest and arms were bare. His tattoos looked like dark blotches of ink staining his skin.

MIGUEL ESTRADA rode in the back of a white chauffeur-driven Lincoln Town Car reading *El Excelsior,* Mexico City's daily newspaper. The lead story had his attention. It ran under the headline: "Chip Implantation Promises Return of Stolen Kids."

> The "VeriKid" program, as it's being called, has been implemented in both Mexico and Brazil where the numbers of missing children have grown disproportionately large. A syringe is used to insert a tiny radio frequency identification device (RFID) under the skin, where it transmits a 125-kilohertz signal that acts as a homing beacon. A missing child can then be found when scanners, placed in strategic locations, are used to pick up the signal. Similar tests of the VeriKid program have been shown to both assist in child recovery, and serve as a deterrent to would-be kidnappers who face arrest and conviction when scanners are employed to determine where children are being held....

Miguel folded the newspaper. *Good!* Those who took children from their parents deserved to be hung. Putting them in jail would eliminate competition. He made it a policy to never harvest wanted children. He gathered street urchins. No one would be chipping them.

The sun came in low off the horizon, glaring through the dusty window. In the distance, mounds of Quonset huts sat like molehills on the landscape. He regretted being almost there. His ride was a bubble of isolation from the problems he would face when he stepped outside. In here it was cool, and comfortable, and quiet, leaving him time to think as he journeyed down the dirt track that divided the tall rows of hemp. He looked up. All this, he had created—one hundred acres of the finest Panama Red grown on the continent—an impressive achievement. Men were already in the fields working—*his men*—campesinos with machetes removing mature plants, followed by others replanting—an ongoing cycle of harvesting.

But once he stepped out of his chauffeur-driven ride, he would run smack dab into the wall of his conscience. Closing down the facility would put the men out of work. It wasn't the lack of profit to be made. There was enough. It was the distraction. He was here to examine the children, not the plants, but they would want him to inspect the quality of the harvest, review the efficiency of the new drying operation, and comment on their ability to maintain quota. And he couldn't care less. In his mind, all that mattered were the kids. They were the future. The rest, well, that's where his conscience was getting in the way of good business sense. He'd always felt a responsibility to the families of the men, but he wasn't running a charity, and their employment was costing him far more in terms of allocation of his time than the market justified. A relaxing of the laws north of the border had resulted in a significant decrease in demand, not because of a slowdown in usage, but because independent operators stateside were growing their own and supplying the market locally. Meanwhile federal customs officers were making it increasingly difficult to get product across the border.

C'est la vie. Times change. You either stay ahead, or get left behind.

When he was young back in the seventies, when profit from pot sales was at an all-time high, and he had the energy to work sixteen-hour days, seven days a week, it was worth it—but now? It took far less work to harvest children, and the returns were much greater. So in the final equation, the marijuana growing operation was really a drain of his resources. He had compassion for the men and their families, but he had to balance that with fiscal responsibility. Trends were shifting. Trafficking narcotics and weapons, formerly the mainstay of the cartels, was falling out of vogue. The primary interest now was the increased demand for young ones. Miguel was positioning himself to dominate this burgeoning segment of the market. He had a highly developed list of clients, an international network of suppliers, and a strategic location at the gateway to the Americas. He held all the right cards, and he wasn't about to fold. He wanted to do right by his men, but it was becoming apparent this businesses segment wasn't worth the effort.

And he was weary of fighting the moral battle. Drugs benefited the seller, but left an unsavory stain on society. He'd deliberately stayed away from growing poppies and coca plants. The world didn't need the kind of crime spawned by users of opium and cocaine. But in selling children, everyone benefited. The kids, for the most part, were homeless. They were taken off the street and given better places to live. They in turn brought pleasure to those who bought them. And he benefited from the money he received. It was *win-win-win*, all the way around. Not that he expected the missionary to agree, but healthy debate made life interesting. The padre was probably an educated man. Miguel was looking forward to their conversation. They actually had much in common. He was a religious man. By the Blessed Virgin, surely his guest would see that. He was doing his best to clean up the streets, improve the lives of the children, and, yes, make a profit in the process—but that was business. He slapped the rolled newspaper against his leg. He disparaged breaking into houses and stealing babies. He took his children from the streets where they didn't belong. Leaving them there to fend for themselves was cruelty. Perhaps the padre *would* understand, and if not, well, that would be unfortunate, but then his blood would be on his own hands. The greater concern was how to close the plantation without hurting anyone. Thousands of those he employed would be out of a job and their families left without food. As the car turned, he brought his hand up to block the killer sun. *Questions, questions, questions.* He fished in his pocket for his gold filigree pillbox and popped two aspirin into his mouth. Just thinking about it gave him a headache.

The car pulled into the yard. Dust scattered and brown chickens *cluck, cluck, clucked* with wings flapping as they scurried out of the way. The doors at the end of a Quonset hut were pulled open by two men in loose-fitting muslin pajamas and huarache sandals. It was an unwritten code that his plantation workers all dressed the same, not in pure white, which was reserved for him alone, but in the creamy off-white garb of the traditional peasant. The driver turned in, parked the car in the shade, then stepped out and opened the door for Miguel. Hot air rushed in. Miguel reached for his handkerchief. He turned and planted a pristine white, high-gloss patent-leather shoe on the hard-packed earth, and pulled himself from the car, smoothing the creases in his coat before heading out to the pen. Paco had called to let him know another shipment had arrived. He wanted to check the inventory. And he also wanted to get a closer look at the girl in the photo. This particular client was fussy, but with any luck, she might be just what the *doctor* ordered. He smiled, knowing the pun was intended.

LONNIE TRIED to blink. It was like watching black and white television, everything viewed in shades of gray. Scant light seeped into the room. He started to move, but his body screamed—like a white-hot knife had been placed on his back. He crawled to a sitting position, a stab piercing his neck as he rotated his head. He could see only the back of the man posted as guard. It looked like he was holding a magazine, skimming pages without taking time to read. Lonnie held still, keeping his breathing slow and even. He did not want to be noticed. He did not want to be tortured again. He turned his head, *slowly*, looking over his shoulder. Twelve long red lacerations criss-crossed his body. His eyes were puffy and filled with water. He was looking through narrow slits, making it hard to see. His fingers probed his nose. It felt broken. His lips were cut and swollen. A thousand plants were strung overhead, hanging upside down from a grid attached to the arched ceiling. He'd never tried marijuana, nor would he, but those who did said it eased their pain. He touched his lip. *Water water everywhere, and not a drop to drink.* He smiled at the irony, and felt his lip split apart again.

ACROSS THE compound, in a small wooden shed referred to by the workers as the "badger hole," Miguel Estrada was leafing through the new portfolio.

"Sí, very nice. This one, I saw her in the yard. She has eyes that hold you. My client will be pleased. Muy bueno," he said, shuffling the photograph to the bottom of the deck. The older girl was nice, but she wasn't worth much—*too skinny*—and the boy was pushing the age limit, but he could peddle him to someone looking for a good deal. He looked younger than he probably was. The little girl was by far the best, but he'd known that before loaning her father the money. She was collateral. He addressed the man sitting at the desk. "Tell me about our visitor," he said.

The thick little man continued to stare at his computer through big thick glasses. He pulled a cigar from his teeth but kept his eyes focused on the keyboard. "He has been very stubborn. He has not told us what we want to know."

Miguel was dressed entirely in white. From his shoes to his hair, he almost shone with brightness. His white clothes kept him cool in hot weather, but he wore them to emphasize his purity. He was a man of integrity and honesty, a man of his word. Sometimes the business he was involved in caused him to do things others might consider wrong. He did not see it that way. A man was expected to keep his commitments and if an obligation could not be kept, well, sometimes there were difficult decisions to make. But if he rid the earth of an irresponsible soul, then the earth became a better place for the rest of mankind. As for the children, he did not agree with the mongrels of media who claimed they suffered. It was not true. These children were taken off the streets, children without homes or families. They would be given to people who would care for them. What they had to do to earn their living was of no consequence to him. If they were to be fed, they had to work. And the kind of work they were being asked to do wasn't hard. Indeed, it could induce great pleasure. Perhaps his guest could be made to understand. Surely the mission needed money. And there had to be incorrigible ones they'd be better off without. It was a situation from which they both could benefit—*win-win.* But it had to be the padre's decision. Miguel did not need trouble. The judges and policemen he kept in his employ were at times, themselves, uncomfortable with what they were asked to do—the turning of the head, the wink of the eye. He wondered about that. The good he was doing far outweighed bad. And the policemen, who made only meager incomes for themselves, were able to buy nice things for their own children, and send them to better schools. How could anyone say that was wrong? In many ways, he was a philanthropist. *That* was why he wore white. He turned toward the door. "I want to interview this missionary," he said. "Bring him to me."

LONNIE SCREAMED. He was grabbed under the arms and pulled to his feet by two men who hauled him toward the door. The gasoline they'd poured into his lacerations burned like fire. It felt like the flesh had been stripped from his back. *Oh God, ohhh God, Savior, Lord, have mercy on me.* He tried to keep his feet under him but they were moving too fast. He stumbled, but they didn't stop and he ended up being dragged across the yard. When they came to the door, one man grabbed him by the collar and yanked him to his feet while the other knocked on the door's wood frame.

"Ah, sí, come in. Please, have a seat. Make yourself comfortable."

Lonnie was thrust into a chair, sighing heavily, gasping for air. "I pray my friends have not treated you too rough. Though I understand you have not been cooperative. Your name is Lonnie?"

Lonnie grimaced. He looked up. His eyes were too waterlogged to see clearly, but the man appeared to be dressed head to toe in white.

He tried to decipher the question. He tried get his mouth working, but his lips were held together by coagulated blood and when he pulled them apart, they split open and started to bleed again.

Miguel smiled. "I am told you are a missionary. Is this so?"

Lonnie's half-lidded eyes squinted, trying to see. He nodded imperceptibly.

"Sí, we have much in common, you and I. We are both religious men. This is good. I believe honesty is necessary for good business. Do you know why God has given us positions of responsibility? It is because we look out for the interests of others. Like you, I have many to care for. That is why I do all this." The man paused to make a grand sweep of his hand that included the entire room, and by implication, the plantation beyond its walls. "People depend on me. Children too. Not just those of my workers, but the homeless. Yes, I too care for orphans. This is why I think you and I are the same. I think maybe you and I could work together. I can find homes for children where maybe you cannot. You have orphans that need a place to live. This I can provide. And your mission would receive, ah, an anonymous donation to help you carry on with God's work, sí?

Lonnie could feel the pulse behind his eyes pounding, his brain throbbing with every beat of his heart. But he hadn't lost his mind. This man, the same man who had his children locked up behind a wire fence like prisoners, was confusing this hellhole with the kingdom of God. Was he *nuts?* "God forbid! No, no, I, that's not what we do. No. Never."

"Ah, I feared you would not understand. Perhaps you need more time to think, but sadly, for a man in your position, time can be painful. Most unfortunate. You have chosen a difficult path, my friend. I am truly sorry." Miguel nodded curtly at the two men who had taken up positions on either side of Lonnie.

TWENTY

He's here. He's here. I saw him. I know I promised I would not hurt him, but I did not think I would see him again so soon. Please tell God not to be mad, Mamá, but I must break my word. Please tell Him for Mariana. Tell Him for Sofía. Tell Him for the others. They should not be punished for what I do.

RAÚL WAS keeping an eye out, diligently scanning the yard for the one they called Paco. The oxidized blue and rust van was parked in front of the fence, so his parents' killer was still around somewhere. The morning sun was beginning to climb and the others, hiding from its wrath, had taken up places in the shade. Their once-a-day meal had been served. This time Raúl intervened, though not for himself, but because Mariana needed to eat. He stared gordo-boy down, who through his black-framed glasses looked like he was about to cry as he put back what he'd taken. Raúl divided the food up and passed it out equally.

He heard a loud *bang*, and turned to see the door of the small cube building fly open and men dragging the foreigner outside. He didn't know what the man had done. They had dragged him into the building, and now they were dragging him out. A man dressed entirely in white followed them outside, the same man who had visited his parents' house before they died. *Now* he understood. The knife the snake held was wielded by this man's hand. His heart began to flutter. And now, both men were together in one place. He moved closer to the chain-link, grabbing it, holding it, squeezing it in his hands as though he could melt it like butter and walk through to the other side, *free*. The dogs were jumping and barking and nipping at his fingers, but he was too mesmerized to care. The man stationed as guard yelled at him to step back, but Miguel waved him off.

"Let him be," he said. "I want the children to see this. Come children. This is something you should watch."

The small boy in his prim suit mindlessly but obediently began slowly migrating toward the fence, but not Sofía or Mariana. And the fat gordo-boy sat in the shade, refusing to give up his place.

"I know you are all good children," he said. "Good children are rewarded, and bad children are punished. That's the way the world is. This man has refused to follow the rules, so he must be punished." He snapped his fingers. The foreigner was shoved against the post. It appeared he was only semiconscious. His hands were tied and pulled up until he was dancing on his toes.

"See this man?" Miguel said, "He will stand in the sun until he's ready to do what is right. He does not have to stand there, but since he refuses to obey the rules, it is his choice. All decisions, be they good or bad, come with consequence. He will become delirious in the heat and eventually agree that we have his best interests at heart." He motioned for the men to stand aside.

Raúl stared at the man. He'd watched him being whipped the day before, a dozen stripes, only then his back was to the fence. Now, he was facing the children and Raúl could see his face. He knew that face, bloody and bruised though it was. It was the face of the missionary of Posada. Where had he come from? Was he there to negotiate their release? If so, he should have brought an army.

MIGUEL KEPT glancing out the window at his captive, marveling at the amount of pain he seemed able to endure, but it was foolishness. They would get what they wanted sooner or later. Finally, when it looked as though the missionary had passed out, Miguel gave the order to have him cut down. He didn't want the man to die, at least not yet. He would wait until he recovered and then proceed to extract more information. Of course the man would have to die eventually, but by cooperating now he could avoid a lot of unnecessary grief. He should have at least considered the proposal. It would, if nothing else, have bought him time.

LONNIE WOKE again. His world was a blur, like looking through glass smeared with Vaseline. A shaft of light streamed into his face. He felt warm, and squinted to improve his focus. He was seeing things. Nicole was standing in front of him robed in light—like an angel. She was beckoning him with her hand, *Come, come quickly.* He curled into a sitting position, propping himself up on his arm. As he moved, the dried blood on his shirt ripped away from his skin. He turned his head. It looked like the guard was asleep at his post. Lonnie did not want to get up. He could think of a dozen reasons why he should just stay there, not the least of which was it hurt to move, and if he woke the sentry it would activate another sequence of scourging. But the vision was persistent, her white hands beckoning—*come.* The beam of light slipped across the room to the other side. Lonnie struggled to his feet, his legs wobbling as he followed the shining object—*or was it a person?*—to the door. Then the light disappeared, seeping through the wood like water. He reached out and tried to turn the latch, but it was locked. The man in the chair grunted and snored, but didn't wake up. Lonnie put his shoulder to the door, but it was a hapless attempt born of little strength. It wouldn't budge. He turned around, looking for direction from the person, angel? Nicole? whatever, but the light was gone, *poof,* vanished. The mind plays tricks when tired. He closed his eyes and exhaled, now sure he'd imagined the whole thing.

He withdrew and sat on a stack of empty pallets, bracing himself with his hands. The sun was pounding on the metal roof, which was torture enough. Sweat rolled down his chest. He felt himself shaking—*no*—he wasn't shaking, the pallet was. At first he thought a tractor was rolling by, making the earth rumble, but then the ground beneath him began to move. Not just move, but shudder violently. The corrugated walls of the Quonset hut were undulating, the aluminum curling in and out, and the ground was bouncing.

Suddenly the door twisted loose and fell from its frame. He had to be dreaming. This couldn't be real. But if he were dreaming, he didn't want to wake up. The pallets were shifting beneath him. He stood, turning. The guard was nowhere in sight. Yellow sun burst through the open portal illuminating billions of flecks of cosmic dust pounded from the earth. Lonnie moved to the end of the building, placed his hand on the doorframe, and looked out. Then he stepped across the threshold—into the light.

TWENTY-ONE

ONE BY ONE, the two-by-four and plywood buildings, which were never well constructed in the first place, popped their nails and collapsed. Men were running in from the fields, their straw hats leaving their heads, machetes flopping at their sides. A crack in the earth had opened up leaving dozens trapped on the other side of a chasm. The world was ripping apart. Everyone was running somewhere, but no one knew where to go. Those who sought refuge inside the corrugated walls of the Quonset huts found them heaving and buckling with the warped sound of a vibrating saw. The dust floating in the air was at times so thick you had to wave your hand in front of your face to see.

Through the din, Lonnie saw Miguel standing in the room where they'd met. The plywood front of the structure had buckled and snapped off, leaving him exposed. He raised his arms as the walls caved in around him. A joist held the roof as it broke apart and formed a triangle overhead, saving his life. The miniature man crawled between his legs and fled into the yard. Miguel started to follow, but his pristine white suit caught on a nail and held him back. He threw his hands out like a boxer flailing the air, ripping his jacket as he pulled free, and hustled out to the van, climbing inside. His short-legged friend crawled through the side door into the back. A third person was already in the driver's seat. Lonnie recognized him—the man with tattoos and malevolent eyes—the one who had doused him with gasoline and stood there with a lit cigarette, threatening to set him on fire. Miguel began screaming, *"Go, go, go!"* The engine was already cranking, *rurr uuurrr, rurr uuurrr, rurr uuurr.*

The earth had a tear running the length of the yard with yellow dust ascending like debris from the pit of hell. The children were screaming. The fence surrounding them twisted and fell forward in a tangled pile. Lonnie struggled to reach them but was stopped by the sound of the Quonset hut behind him imploding. He turned and ducked. An explosion of dried brown plants billowed into the air and settled like autumn leaves. *Whew, too close.* He hobbled off-kilter, fanning away the pollen, each step a lesson in pain. He could hardly see. His eyes were swollen, full of water, and the haze was thick. In one section it looked like the fence was completely down. The children were free, they should be running, but they stood huddled together. Lonnie saw a girl sitting on the ground whom he thought was Sofía, but she was looking the other way. The children were a blur. As he got closer, he recognized Mariana, but didn't see Raúl. He turned, searching the compound, and found the boy. *Oh no, where did he get that?* He was heading toward the van with an AK-47 wrapped in both arms. A man in a cowboy hat was cranking the engine, *ruurrrr, rurrrrr, rurr-uuurrr,* over, and over, but it wouldn't catch.

Raúl stopped and raised the gun. The man behind the windshield kept his eyes focused on the ignition, turning the key, trying in vain to get the engine started. He looked up and saw Raúl, and then the gun, and raised his hands. Miguel's face was white as his suit.

For a fraction of a second—that frozen slice of time you wish you could take back because it's wrong, yet you know it's instantly before the throne of God—Lonnie was glad. *Blow 'em away, Raúl.* But in that same moment he found his mouth screaming, *"Noooooooo!"* He was too late. The cry went ignored. Raúl pulled the trigger.

FIFTY MILES away, straight as the arrow flies, the earthquake hit Posada. Caught off guard, Nicole ducked under Father Paulo's table and—lights out—her entire world went black.

She awoke coughing. Dirt was lodged in her throat, blocking her windpipe. She tried to get it out, but it was impossible. Something was in the way. *Glass? Where did that come from?* Then she realized she was choking on a piece of glass from the framed photo of Father Paulo's family. It was a prized possession, the last remaining vestige of a life now gone, dashed when the small twin engine aircraft went down over the Pacific on its return to LA. *Poor Paulo*. He would be rightfully upset but—*wait a minute.* It was sticking in *her* cheek, a permanent scar, one hundred percent guaranteed to be an old-maid maker. *No, no, no, no, no! What happened?* The ground rumbled, the walls shook, the tower fell, she ducked. She was buried alive. *Please God, no!*

Her eyes were heavy. She let them close, her mind drifting between lucid thought and the deep void of space, only semiconscious. She forced her eyes open. She had to stay awake. If she passed out, it might be forever. She tried to think about *something*, anything, her past, but that was bad, and she had to avoid the present. How about the future? Anything, just keep the thoughts rolling. Life, the good, the bad, the ugly, vignettes that produced little movie clips of entertainment, anything that might keep her alive. She tried moving but it hurt *sooooooo* bad. She took inventory. She could wiggle her toes and feel the bottom of her shoes, her socks. At least she wasn't paralyzed. She tried moving her fingers but her nerve was pinched and pain shot up her arm. No problem with sensory impulse, she could feel everything, but was engulfed by darkness and couldn't see. The table she'd crawled under saved her life, *Thank You, Lord*, but the walls of Father Paulo's office were now piled on top of her, cutting her off from the outside world, and the pocket of air between her body and the table's surface was probably all there was. She tried to slow her breathing. Sooooo tired. Wake up.

Where was Lonnie? *Here I am, your damsel in distress.* She laughed, choking and spitting up dirt. She didn't know if her tears flowed from her weak attempt at humor, her pain, or simply because there was dirt in her eyes. She hoped it was the latter, because the former wasn't funny. Her knight in shining armor wasn't there. He was off fighting battles in another land. Story of her life. Her men were never there when she needed them. Dr. Ryan, that sorry excuse for a part-time lifetime partner, and Lonnie, always off visiting Trudy and their son.

Two men, so very different, each in their own way, had brought her to the place she was now. She had dreamed of becoming a missionary, nursing the unwashed, disease afflicted, undernourished masses. It was the passion of her young life, complete with maps on the wall and multicolored stick-pins marking preferred locations—though she really didn't care as long as it was somewhere she was needed. Perhaps the dreams she'd fostered as a child really were programmed by God to get her where He wanted her to be. If so, it was God who brought her here, not Lonnie—*nor Ryan*—but her men each played a part. One to hasten, and one to delay. *Ryan and his overinflated ego*. That's where it all went wrong.

She'd been in university studying for her nursing degree, sidetracked by the occasional short-term infatuation, but nonetheless committed to one day venturing into parts unknown. She had no idea where that would be. Any flag on the map would do as long as she'd be able to minister to those in need. But her dream had been shot down, blown apart two years from fruition. She rued the day. Her eyes drifted closed, but then snapped open. *Come on, stay awake. Think. Think...*

It was the end of the semester, finals were over, time to let her hair down, pursue social interaction—time to party. She could look good when she wanted to, very good, and this night, for whatever reason, she wanted to. And the adrenaline-pumping young men, wheezing testosterone and smelling of musk, were receptive, lining up to vie for her attention. One by one they zeroed in, asking her to dance, but she kept her distance keeping them at a cool arm's length, even when dancing slow. Their goals and aspirations were to practice pediatrics, optometry, psychology, which didn't line up with her desire to do mission work. Besides, they ran the gamut of disgusting behaviors, from the childishly insecure, "I, uh, I...I almost didn't ask, uh, I didn't think you'd want to dance with me, you know," to the "Hey, girl, you ready to get it on?" oversexed chick magnet whose only goal was to get her in the sack. But there was one who did catch her attention, a young man whose blue eyes seemed to catch hers several times. She could feel the attraction, a physical, though completely invisible, desire to connect. They would be in different conversations with different groups of people, he usually surrounded by young women, and she by young men, when their eyes would find each other across the room.

She was standing in line to refresh her punch when she felt his breath, warm and sweet, on her neck.

"Want me to stiffen that up a bit?"

"No, thank you," she replied. "Frankly, I don't care for the taste."

He wore a brown tweed coat over an off-white turtleneck, the thick kind with a diamond pattern woven into the front, and his hair, fashionably long, rode just over the collar. His blue eyes widened, his eyebrows arching, but he screwed the cap on the silver flask without comment, and slipped it into his vest pocket. "I don't remember seeing you before," he said.

"Nor I you."

"I mean, you're not a regular, are you?"

"No," she said. "My work and studies keep me busy. I have to make parties an exception, not the rule."

In spite of the shoulder-to-shoulder crowd that denied them privacy, they spent most of the evening together. That is, until she was elbowed out by an overly flirtatious ex-something-or-other who made a point of stealing her new beau's attention. Nicole used the excuse to retreat like Cinderella missing a shoe. She was earnestly involved in her studies, and love wasn't good for the GPA—but friends with loose lips thought it in her best interest to be dating, so he was able track her down, glass sipper in hand. He called, and called, and called, until she finally agreed to have lunch just to shut him up. That's how it started—the beginning of the end. Ryan with his blue-eyed boyish good looks, his sandy too-long brown hair that kept falling in front of his eyes, causing him to constantly sweep it aside, his wit, always ready with an in-your-face comeback that his giggling girlfriends seemed to love, and intelligence. He was on the dean's list, Omega Delta Phi, pie-in-the-sky, or something like that. And charm. Talk about God's gift to women. He had it all, and like it or not she was doomed from the start. One year later they were married, regrets all the way around.

She never saw him much after that. Ryan, now a graduate, was ready to enter the intern program. His residency would keep him occupied twelve to sixteen hours a day, so children were put on hold, a mutual decision—or, so she thought—and because money was so very tight, and an intern's salary next to nothing, and her school tuition, books and living expenses high, they agreed she should drop out and go back to work, just until his residency was finished and he'd established a small practice. Then she could return to school, graduate, and work for him. They would be a team—*Dr. Ryan and nurse Jensen—Dr. and Mrs. Jensen—Mrs. Nicole Jensen*—she would be his nurse and office administrator. But people can't communicate when they're apart, and well, Ryan's schedule prevented him from being home much. And the foundation upon which they would build, the promise of attending church, which was so vitally important to her, was never laid. His schedule was filled most Sundays. Every now and then, as she sat alone in the pew, isolated, the proverbial island unto herself, his absence set the alarm ringing, and she had to pray it would stop. *Methinks, John Donne, that thou wast wrong. The bell dost not toll for me.*

TWENTY-TWO

N*oooooooo!* THE WORD was still echoing from Lonnie's lips as the trigger was pulled—but nothing happened. For a moment there was silence. Raúl stood mystified, the gun tilting forward. He started fumbling to see if it was loaded, trying to find the chamber with the bullets. Lonnie limped over and grabbed the weapon. He yanked it from Raúl's arms and with both hands around the barrel, flung it across the yard. Raúl looked up, bewildered. He turned to lunge for the gun, but Lonnie caught him by the T-shirt and held tight, reeling him in. He wrapped him in a bear hug to pin his squirming arms. The two men behind the windshield didn't seem to understand. They'd been a hair's breadth from death, their lives spared by a gun parked on safety. Lonnie wrestled with Raúl, carrying him kicking and screaming back to the twisted wire. The dogs barked incessantly. The twin fences forming their kennel had collapsed on top of each other, pinching off their escape. Lonnie held Raúl, squeezing harder every time the boy struggled. Part of him wished the gun had gone off—but that was wrong-headed thinking.

He spoke to the two boys he didn't recognize. "I came to get this boy and his sister. I can't leave them here. They're my responsibility. We're leaving. You can come if you want. I'll do my best to get you to safety. If you're with me, we have to go now." He turned, carrying Raúl as he stumbled off in the direction of the fields. The boy was still squirming, making walking difficult and adding to his pain, but Lonnie refused to let go. He wished those men were dead—they deserved to die—but he could not let a nine year old become a killer.

Vengeance is mine, saith the Lord. He turned to see if he was being followed, but no one moved.

"Sofía! Come on!"

Sofía sat in the dust with her knees tucked up under her dress. Her arms were wrapped around her legs and her head was bowed so that her long black hair hung down, covering her face. Mariana looked at Lonnie, then at Sofía, and then at Lonnie again. She took Sofía's hands, helping her to her feet, and led her over to where Lonnie stood. Sofía stared blankly into the fields, her eyes glassy and distant. Lonnie glanced at the remaining two boys, but they managed to avert his gaze, refusing to move. He shook his head. What did he expect? His face was a bloody mess, and he was holding Raúl against his will. He probably looked more like a monster than their jailers did. He turned and started walking. He couldn't make them follow—they had to come of their own volition. Mariana fell in behind with Sofía in tow. Raúl was still kicking and squirming as he carried him into the rows of tall plants and disappeared behind the curtain of green. That broke the spell. The boys bolted into the field, quickly catching up. The heavy-set child with the outrageous black glasses took hold of Lonnie's shirt, content to let him lead the way. Lonnie tried to pick up his pace. He broke into a limping run, causing the boy to lose his hold. Mariana grabbed him with her other hand, a five year old taking responsibility for two bigger kids. Sofía broke her grip and picked up the little doll-boy, carrying him with her. The branches were slapping Lonnie's face, clods of dirt breaking under his feet. Raúl was screaming, "Put me down! Put me down! I can run by myself! Put me down!" Lonnie did, watching to make sure he didn't turn back. Raúl took his sister's free hand, adding to the chain, and pulled them along. The ground was still rumbling. Lonnie stumbled but caught himself. He didn't have time to think about his deliverance in theological terms—that would come later. They had but one chance to escape and he had to take advantage of it. He plowed through the rows of hemp, limping, ignoring the pain, gaining momentum with each step.

He was winded, his lungs hollow and raw. They must have run

half a mile. Ahead he could see where the field disappeared into the jungle. The bushes snagged his clothes and slapped his face, and the rocks pulverized his feet. He wished the earth would stop moving. The uneven forever-changing landscape made it doubly hard to run. Lonnie could see Sofía pausing at the edge of the jungle, questioning. He caught up, slowing to a stagger, and then saw why she'd stopped. She'd reached the bank of a river. He had to catch his breath. He sat on a boulder, placed one hand on the cool rock and the other on his chest, breathing erratically. They were at the edge of the jungle. Crossing the stream would introduce them to a whole new world of danger. The others fell to the ground around him, propping themselves up on weary arms. Lonnie tried to speak, but his voice faltered.

"We, uh, we...we can't rest long," he said. The words barely escaped his lips when he heard dogs barking. They were chomping at the bit, like someone was prepping them for a race. And then the howling accelerated and he knew they'd been released. The hunt was on. The men would be close behind. Lonnie stood and urged the children into the water, sending them downstream to avoid fighting the current. Raúl stayed with his sister, waiting until Lonnie passed. Every step hurt, from one slippery rock to the next, as Lonnie strained to keep his tennis shoes fixed against the rushing tide. The round boy lost his footing. He plopped into the water, his giant sweater ballooning in the eddies of foam. He crashed into a rock and careened around, swirling through the rapids until he was able to grasp an overhanging branch. The whitecaps were breaking against his face, but he held onto his glasses and managed to right himself and regain his footing, his sweater now soppy, hanging below his knees. The current surged. Lonnie drew in hard breaths, trying to relax. He was wound tight. Just one more thing—just *one* more—and he'd snap. The water roared, swirling around his feet. The air smelled of wet lichen and moss. *Calm*, breathe easy, *calm*.

Lonnie looked over his shoulder. His heart sank. Raúl was taking Mariana off in the other direction. He yelled for the boy to come back, but his voice was drowned out by the pounding water.

Raúl had his sister's hand, pulling her behind him as he made his way upstream. Mariana slipped and dipped under the whitecaps and came up soaking wet, but Raúl pulled her to her feet and kept going. Lonnie went after. He had the advantage of a longer stride. He caught up and took Mariana by the waist, lifting her, wrenching her from her brother's hand, and once again started moving downstream. Raúl spun around, splashing the water with balled fists. He lunged at Lonnie and climbed onto his wounded back. Lonnie reached behind, struggling as he slipped on a rock. He twisted to steady himself, and was able to grab Raúl's arm, pulling him off. The boy slipped down but latched onto Lonnie's leg. "Raúl! Stop it! We have to stick together."

Raúl's head dipped in and out of the foam, there one minute and gone the next, but he held on, trying to pull Lonnie back. Lonnie kept trudging ahead. He pushed one leg forward, secured a footing, and dragged Raúl up with the other. "Help me!" Lonnie yelled at the fat boy who was standing beside him, holding onto a branch for dear life. The boy only shrugged as if to say, "What can I do?" But lifting his arms caused him to lose his balance, and the surging water swept him off his feet. He landed squarely on Raúl, breaking his grip.

Lonnie felt the release. Looking over his shoulder, he said, "Muchas gracias, muchacho." He didn't even know the child's name. He forged on ahead, picking up the lead again. Raúl was on his hands and knees being battered by the water pouring around him. "Give me my sister!" he screamed, but Lonnie kept walking. They plodded through rapids broken by stones, hampered by moss-covered rocks and fallen trees, but they stayed in the flow. The dogs wouldn't be able to track them through water. And the men wouldn't know if they'd gone right or turned left, so they'd have to split up. One dog would have to be used to look upstream and one down. At least that would reduce their foes by half.

The howling was louder now. Lonnie perceived the dogs were at the river's edge, anxiously milling about, trying to pick up a scent to follow. They were whining in confusion, not that far behind. Lonnie urged the children on, but the water slowed them down. The men might split up, but they would keep to the shore and move faster. It was time to leave the stream. "This way!" He turned, stepping onto the shore and started up a steep bank, still holding Mariana in his arms. The children raced alongside using their hands and feet to climb. Fifteen feet up, the rise leveled off and they found themselves standing on the shoulder of a dirt road. It had to be the one he'd come in on. "That way," he said, pointing. The children turned in unison and began to run, but the first child to make it around the bend suddenly stopped. The others slowed too, hesitating. Lonnie's heart was pounding. Now what? *A roadblock? An ambush? Men in a Volkswagen with guns?* But when he caught up he saw what they were looking at and breathed a sigh of relief—*Thank You, Lord.* It was Daniela's pickup, sitting with one wheel stuck in a hole. The earthquake had taken out a portion of the road. She was trying to get the vehicle out of the ditch, but there wasn't enough traction. Lonnie reached her with the kids in tow.

Her window was rolled down. She looked startled at the sudden appearance of his bruised face. "Looks like you could use some help," he said. He pointed at the truck. "Lady needs a hand. See if we can't get under that bumper and lift her out." Lonnie, with the three boys and two girls, took up positions behind the truck, lifting and pushing until the tire found dirt. The truck lurched forward, and Daniela slammed on the brakes. Lonnie began hefting the smaller children into the back as the larger ones scrambled over the rails, falling on sacks of coffee. Lonnie handed Mariana to the chubby boy already in the truck, and Raúl dove in after. Then he ran around and jumped into the cab. "Hurry! They've after us," he said as he slammed the door." Daniela revved the engine and hit the gas. The wheels started spinning. The truck lurched forward, the tires tossing dirt, fishtailing with the rear sliding sideways. Lonnie glanced over his shoulder. A dog was lunging toward them, full stride, barking. Two men rounded the corner. One leveled an AK-47 at the side of the truck. Lonnie did not hear the discharge, but saw the glass shatter as blood splattered against the windshield.

TWENTY-THREE

THE LEAVES were changing color, yellow, orange, red, many already brown, spinning off the trees. It was the second cold front of the season, and it hit with a vengeance turning the sky slate gray, scattering chips of ice across the yard, and flexing branches in the wind. Bill stared out the window. He wasn't looking forward to it, but he was prepared. He had three cords of wood cut and stacked at the side of the cabin, his cellar stocked with food in case the roads became impassable, and the generator full of fuel with extra gallons stored in the shed. Cold and dank, it was an appropriate expression of his soul. How could men, created in the image of God, even *think* of doing such things? What possessed—*possessed?—yes, that was the operative word*—whatever possessed men to seek fulfillment in the abuse of children? What insidious mindset, what quirk of nature could make them stoop so low? They were blind. They couldn't see the evil because they were part of it. And the shadow was spreading across the land. He'd been in prayer all morning, donning the armor of God, readying himself for battle. But the gloom he'd felt was so intense, he'd had to light a fire just to drive out the chill. Now he sat in the warmth radiating from the hearth. A light shining in the darkness.

He sat in his refurbished slat-back chair, a favorite he'd discovered at an auction of old school furniture. He'd got the desk, credenza, file cabinets, and a large round wall clock all for fifty bucks—*such a deal.* Solid hardwood, not veneer. He swiveled, and leaned back in a reflective pose. Comfortable too. He called it his "derrière chair" because it had a seat contoured to fit him perfectly. But more than that, it was an image of who he was. There was strength in that chair, made of seasoned red oak, wood old as time, cut down and reshaped and made better by refining. Surrounding the heavy seat were arms with rounded ends his large hands could grip comfortably, a curved back with a high rounded board at the top wide enough to fit his shoulders, a star pattern radiating from the bottom with five casters so he could roll across the hardwood floor, and a heavy-duty spring underneath allowing him to sit back and repose in thought. He rocked forward, gripping the arms, being careful not to hit his damaged foot as he spun toward his desk. *Man, they just don't make 'em like this anymore.* He looked at his monitor again. He had dredged up every note, interview, and piece of research he had on Miguel Estrada, reviewed all the articles he'd written, trying to uncover something, *anything*, that might help Lonnie get his kids back. It was something he *had* to do—because—he glanced up over the screen at his daughter sitting across the room in her wheelchair—because the defenseless needed defending.

Angie dropped her hand onto a sponge, getting her palm moist so se could sweep it across her book and turn the page. It took four tries and excessive grunting, but she finally achieved the task. She smiled at her accomplishment. She loved to read. She had taught herself to turn pages by sweeping the book with the heel of her hand, not always successfully and not always without help, and frequently accompanied by much groaning, but an amazing feat nonetheless, considering her almost complete lack of muscle control. Her head rolled side to side as her eyes scanned the page. Years ago Bill had adopted the slogan of the United Negro College Fund: "A mind is a terrible thing to waste." He'd determined not to waste Angie's. He'd sat hour after hour helping his daughter learn to read, teaching her the alphabet and how the letters fit together to make words. She was one smart kid. Limitations of the body did not necessarily translate to limitations of the mind. To her credit, she already had her high school diploma, and was preparing to enter her first year of university. With Bill's assistance, her schooling was done online via the Internet.

Bill took pride in knowing her work was graded without prejudice or favor, because most of her teachers didn't even know their student had cerebral palsy.

His involvement with the disadvantaged, which started with wanting the best possible life for his daughter, had evolved into a personal quest. Somewhere along the way, Bill had become a crusader, the champion of the downtrodden, defender of the defenseless. He did battle on every front—shielding the innocents, the physically frail, the mentally slow, the elderly and impoverished—from those who subtly suggested by offhanded dismissal that these subhumans should go away, that the planet would somehow be better off without them. His weapon was the printed word. The pen *is* mightier than the sword. Angie had taught him to never underestimate the value of a human life, regardless of how it looked on the outside. Take yesterday. The basketball game had been composed of children with Down syndrome, pop-eyed, drooling and bent, those society disparagingly labeled "Mongoloid." They were kids with mental deficiencies and physical shortcomings, but while the challenges were wide and varied, the one thing they all had in common was heart. They played like pros. And Angie had done her part. She couldn't play, but she could cheer, regardless of how distorted her cheers rang out. The kids were energized and excited, delighted to be part of something bigger than themselves, a team, egged on and encouraged, entering the fray with the ball in both arms, some trying to dribble, others content to carry or roll it downcourt, tossing hoops underhanded. So what if the rings were lowered? They weren't seven-foot giants. Most shuffled more than ran as they clung to the ball, hoping for a shot at the basket. They had fun. That was the main thing. It didn't matter who won, it was about how they played. It was a day to make parents proud.

Angie looked up. Her dad was staring at her and it made her self-conscious. Her head lobbed to the side. She smiled, the spitting image of her mother when her face relaxed. Bill had explained what he was trying to do. The preacher was heading into a dangerous situation. He needed to solicit all the help he could get. He knew the cost of engaging the forces of evil. Angie's mother had gone into a seniors' home were the elderly were being put down like animals, supposedly under the guise of assisted suicide. She was determined to expose the abuse. The men she had gone up against were now in prison serving twenty-five to life, but she had paid the ultimate price, struck down in her prime, a soldier fallen on the field of battle. She deserved the Congressional Medal of Honor. Instead she was a mere footnote on a dusty page of history. Service to the King was its own reward. But now, the preacher was facing the same kind of trouble.

One of the advantages of being a writer was having good contacts, and Bill planned to use them. He knew people in the State Department who could help. He was promised measures would be taken to bring child trafficking to an end after his first series of articles. But it was politics. Other governments were involved. Things moved slowly in the international realm. It had been nearly two years, and as far as he could tell, not a single thing had been accomplished. But not this time. This time an American citizen was involved. An American trying to rescue young children. They had to do something about that. He reached for the phone. A hurricane blew in, taking the form of two mop-headed youths. The older boy held what looked like a large candy bar out of reach of the younger one.

"Daddy! Daddy! Teddy won't give me the remote! It's my turn, Daddy! It's my turn!

"No it's not!"

"But he wants to watch..."

"Shut up! I do not."

"Yes he does. He was..."

"Don't tell your brother to shut up. We don't talk like that around here." Bill frowned, puckering his lips. It was hard to communicate large truths to little minds. He couldn't tell them what kind of society evolved when in the name of freedom, people abandoned rule and discipline and gave themselves over to satisfying their lustful desires. Much of what was on TV was the vanguard, but such things were over their heads. Bill was familiar with the destructive nature of lasciviousness. He'd seen it firsthand. He'd been in Vietnam, the Netherlands, and most recently covering the tsunami in Indonesia, places where red-light districts were commonplace, where pedophiles took their vacations so they could have sex with young children, where women were treated like animals, used, abused, and degraded beyond measure. It was the very reason the preacher's kids needed rescuing, because somewhere morality had gone off the rails. His sons were about the age of those the preacher was trying to save, and there wasn't anything he wouldn't do for his own. But there was no way to communicate that to a five-year-old boy.

"Okay, no arguments, hand me the remote. No more TV. You're not gonna be couch potatoes. God gave you a life, and a brain," he said, tousling Joshua's hair. "I want you to use them both. How are you coming with your reading? Have you finished your book?"

"No, but I was gonna."

"Finish the book. Tell me how it turns out. I want the TV off. Now! And I want you boys to be quiet. I have a call to make and it's very important. Okay, can you do that?"

The boys looked up, their large eyes nodding. They took a step back from his chair, turned, and started to walk away. They didn't get three steps when one started to run and the other chased after, squealing all the way.

Angie looked up and smiled.

"I'm glad you were never like that when you were a kid," Bill said.

Angie giggled, and Bill picked up the phone.

TWENTY-FOUR

THE EARTH settled, the shifting sands coming to rest and compacting again. Nicole tried closing her lips to keep the dirt from falling into her mouth, but the shard of glass cutting through her cheek was in the way. She couldn't spit the dirt out. All she could do was swallow it, gagging as it went down. Her legs and arms were buried. She lay on her back staring into blackness. Whatever pocket of air there was, it wasn't large. Death by slow suffocation. She considered what it would be like struggling for that last gasp of air when there was none left. She wanted to scream, but it was impossible with the shard in her teeth, and would be a foolish waste of air. The sound wouldn't transmit through dirt. *Oh God, if I'm going to die, let me go peacefully right now.* She was drifting, light as a cloud. Her eyes were closed but she couldn't really tell. The darkness was the same either way. *No! Wake up.* She began to sob, choking on the dirt in her throat. She had to stay awake.

Think of something—*a song*. She began humming. *I love thee in life, cuff, cuff, I will love thee in death, and, cuff, cuff, praise thee as long as thou lend-est me breath.* She smiled faintly and swallowed. How appropriate, *cuff, and say, cuff, cuff, when the dea-ath dew lies co-old on my bra-ow, if ever I loved thee, my Je-e-sus 'tis now.* But the pain was overwhelming and it seemed even the vibration of her breath caused more dirt to fall into her mouth. *So this is what it's like to die. No white light, no cloudy mist-filled tunnel, no angels reaching out to take my hand, cuff, cuff.* But that was because she wasn't going to die. She couldn't die. Only yesterday she was a child, sitting on the seat of her bicycle, pretty in pink, with white training wheels and pink streamers flowing from the handlebars. She could see it, holding her Barbie doll, also dressed in pink. "Blondie," that's what her father called her. Blondie. "Come on, Blondie, you can do it." Her hair, flowing behind her, had been full of the sun, shining bright and beautiful. Oh—but that's what purchased Ryan's attention...

"First time I laid eyes on you, it pulled me in. It was like gravity drawing me in toward the sun."

Yeah, well *that* sun went supernova. Now there was just one big black hole.

"Come on, you know how it is, we have to have money to live. It's just for a little while, just until I complete my residency and get the practice going. Then you can go back and get your degree. Come on, don't be selfish. There's more than just you in the picture now. We have to do what's right for both of us. You drop out of school and support me, and as soon as I get things going, I'll support you. That's the way it works."

Which might have been fine if it had turned out that way. If he hadn't insisted on buying that jet-black, leather-upholstered, 225 horsepower, in-line, ragtop monster with the upgraded eleven speaker Harman Kardon sound system. And they couldn't *afford* a house. But then the Beemer was just a symptom of the disease, not the disease itself. In fact, the disease was—*self.*

"Hey, Nicky Girl, come on, don't be upset. It'll only be a few years and we'll have it paid off. Look, it isn't just about me. I'm doing this for you too, to give you a better life. I mean, sure I'll be driving it. I have to do something for myself, I deserve it, but it's really about getting my patients to think I'm successful. Success breeds success. And the sooner I get more patients, the sooner you'll be able to go back to school, or just live the life and do whatever you want. But until then, we have to make sacrifices. I'm a doctor now, so image is important. I can't be seen driving around in that old hunk-a-junk Chevy of ours. I'll look like a rookie. Think of my patients. I have to earn their trust. Besides, you won't believe the deal I got. It was unbelievable. The man practically gave it away."

Hear the alarm bells? Loud as St. Christopher's when the walls fell, but she ignored them. It was only a hiccup, a slight blip in their original plan. She'd get back to school soon enough. At least that's what she wanted to believe.

Nicole almost laughed, and nearly choked trying not to. How many years had she ended up working to support her man, *five, six,* and for what?

TWENTY-FIVE

THE TRUCK began to slow, coasting to a stop. The man lowered the weapon, his fingers still on the trigger. The dog was lunging full speed ahead, now less than a dozen feet away and closing. One good leap and he'd be inside the truck with the children. Lonnie grabbed Daniela's hands, pulling them from the wheel. He slid over, shoved her foot off the pedal, and jammed his own down on the gas. The wheels started to spin, the rear end of the truck fishtailing left. He glanced in the rear-view mirror, watching as the children were thrown to the right, grabbing each other. The truck was sliding sideways. He jerked the wheel back to straighten it out. A string of bullets hit the side of the truck, *ping, ping, ping, ping, ping. Lord, please! No one else!* A bend in the road loomed ahead. *Just make the curve.* He was skidding toward the trees as they skirted the corner, putting distance between himself and his pursuers. He heard the gun going off again, *puft, puft, puft, puft, puft,* but the bullets whizzed by without finding their targets. He checked his mirror again. No one in sight. He backed off the gas, but couldn't find the brake with Daniela's foot in the way. The truck slowed enough to make the next turn, *so far so good.* He'd have to find a way of moving Daniela over so he could sit in the driver's seat. Her head was in his lap. He looked down. The side of her face was bubbling blood, her eyes fixed open, her mouth ajar about to speak. *Oh God.* Dead.

Trees were racing by, the truck bouncing over ruts. The steering wheel wanted to shimmy out of his hand every time he hit a hole in the road. He checked the speedometer. They were only doing thirty.

He would've guessed more like a hundred. He didn't know where he was heading, but he had to keep moving. Whatever road they were on, it had to go somewhere.

He took another bend to the left, the truck sliding on the soft shoulder as he hit the gas. He'd been driving that way for a few minutes. They had to have gone at least a mile. It was far enough. He had to pull over and get things situated. He let off the gas, slowing the truck. His pants felt wet. He looked down and saw his leg soaking in Daniela's blood. When he looked up, he went for the brakes, but her foot was still in the way. *Too late.* The front of the truck plowed over a ledge. Lonnie slammed into the dashboard, the wind exploding from his chest. The kids in the back crashed against the cab squealing through a cloud of dust. It was seconds that seemed like hours *wheezing* before Lonnie could get his breath back. He pushed Daniela off his lap leaning her against the door and sat upright, dazed, dust filtering in through the window. The kids in the back began to untangle, picking themselves up checking for cuts, bruises and broken bones. Sofía dug in her heels and inched away from the pile waving her hand in front of her face, coughing. Lonnie leaned to the right scooting over, reaching for the handle and when the door popped open, practically fell out. He tripped over the running board, crashed to his knees, then rolled onto his lacerated back where he lay looking up at the trees, still trying to catch his breath.

Now that was more like it. Beautiful, peaceful trees. Birds criss-crossed his field of vision darting point-to-point, chattering in the branches. No earthquake here, just green leaves flickering in the breeze and sun-drenched clouds bright and white. The garden of God. He wished he could lie there and die. He groaned. *What now, Lord? What now?* How was he supposed to help these kids? They weren't supposed to be here. They should be home skipping rope and chasing chickens, playing with straw dolls and drawing stick pictures in the dirt. They should be playing with toys, not running from men who wanted to turn them into toys to be *played with.* How was he supposed to get a pack of kids through the jungle, a place every mother warned her kids to stay away from, and somehow get them to safety? Little kids, emotional babies, with short little legs that had to climb rocks, crawl over moss-covered trees and wiggle through tangled vines, while staying ahead of long-legged men with dogs? They were depending on him. *Oh God, I need help.* He needed Daniela. *Why, Lord, why? She was just starting to live. Why did you take her?* How was he going to explain this to Bill? He didn't have it in him. He struggled to sit up.

The truck had fallen into a fissure in the earth opened by the quake. The front end was now stuck in the ditch and the rear tires were off the ground, spinning. It was the end of their joyride. Even if he could get the boys to lift the front, which would be a much bigger job under the weight of the engine, they would never get across the chasm. *Why Daniela, Lord? Why our only means of escape?* He rolled to a crawling position and tried to stand. His legs were wobbly. He leaned over with his hands on his knees. *Not good.* They would have to go on foot. He could still hear the dog barking. The men were on their trail, but they were a good distance back. He looked right and left. To his right was a mountain. To his left a valley. If they stayed on the road, they'd be easy to find. Traveling downhill would be faster. It was probably the way they'd expect him to go, but he'd be lost. If he climbed the mountain, perhaps he could find a vantage point high enough to look down and spot a town or some other landmark, and get a fix on their location. Whatever they did, they had to do it quickly. The dog would soon pick up their scent.

The children were already out and starting to wander. He stumbled forward holding his stomach. "Sofía, could you come here, please. You too, Raúl," he said, drawing them away from the truck. They didn't need to see Daniela. "We have to move quickly. Sofía, round up everyone and take them over there." He raised his hand pointing at the mountain. "I have something to do. It will only take a second. I want you guys to go ahead and start climbing. I'll catch up fast as I can."

He turned and walked across the road, but stopped when he heard one of the children starting to cry. It was the large boy again. *Oh no!* Lonnie loved kids, but getting five of them over a range of mountains to safety was more than he was capable of, especially when he was too weak to make it himself. *Why, God? Why?* Sofía took the boy by the hand and stood there with the smaller boy already in her arms, holding him the way she used to carry Sebastian. Her long loose dress was wet from the waist down and covered in dirt. She started up the mountain towing one boy and carrying the other.

With his hand on the truck to provide balance, Lonnie hobbled to the driver's side, and sidestepped his way into the ditch. In getting Daniela off his lap, he had propped her against the door. She was resting there, her hair half out of its bun, hanging out the window, shiny and black. He pulled the handle and her body fell into his arms. This did not make sense. *Why, Lord? Why, why, why, why, why? Trust in the Lord with all thine heart, and lean not on thine own understanding. Okay, but this?* His back was screaming as he struggled down the ravine, carrying her cumbersome weight with his arms wrapped around her waist, tripping over loose rocks, trying to stay on his feet. He couldn't leave her there. These men were evil. They might in some nefarious way abuse her body.

The crevice soon became too narrow to pass. Lonnie lowered Daniela into the space and began covering her with dirt, shoveling rocks and topsoil into the hole until Daniela's body was completely concealed. It took only a few minutes. Lonnie gathered an armload of brush and scattered it over the grave, then added sticks, grass, and larger rocks to make the spill look natural. He stood back. He couldn't tell it from the surrounding damage done by the earthquake. One last thing. He took two large branches and laid them over each other in the shape of a cross. It looked natural. They could have fallen that way. It was the best he could do. He folded his hands and raised his eyes to heaven. He knew the litany of a funeral, knew the words by heart, but all he said was "Father, into your hands I commend Daniela's spirit." Then he looked at the makeshift grave. "Vaya con Dios, Daniela. Go with God."

Lonnie turned and saw Raúl standing there. His lips were taut and white, pressed together, his gaze glassy and hard.

"That lady was nice to me. You...you killed her! You shoulda let me shoot those men."

"Raúl, I..."

"My sister and I will be going. I'm taking her with me."

"Look, Raúl, there are things..." but he was interrupted by the howling of a dog. "Look, we have to stick together. Your sister's already halfway up the hill." Lonnie pointed and Raúl turned to see the small pink dot climbing with the others. "By the time you get her and bring her down, that dog will be here. Now come on, we have to get going."

THEY WERE following the fault up the side of the mountain. The crack in the earth seemed to go on forever, splitting the mountain in half. Lonnie stayed back to keep an eye on the children—climbing, stumbling, pulling themselves up with bushes and branches. They were leaving an easy trail for Miguel's men to follow. They hadn't gone a quarter of a mile when the breach in the earth turned and crossed in front of them, blocking their path. Looking through the dense green jungle Lonnie couldn't see where it ended and at that particular point the gulf was deeper and wider than ever, impossible to cross. They would have to turn around and go back. A dog started barking in the valley below. It had found the truck.

EVERYTHING OLD was new. The Bible spoke of a time when "every thought and intent of man's heart was only evil continually." It had brought disaster, but man didn't learn. In another passage, written much later, it said the world regressed to the point where "every man did what he thought was right in his own eyes." In Bill's mind, they had come full circle. "What may not be right for you could still be right for me, okay? We have to be tolerant of each other." Every truth tried in the court of public opinion. Whether something was right or not depended on the circumstances. Bill didn't buy it. Not having a standard, an absolute truth by which all others were judged, was akin to everyone setting their watches to whatever time they thought was best. *Chaos!* Situational ethics were no ethics at all.

The fire in the hearth snapped and crackled, taking the chill out of the air. He'd been on the phone all morning. He was working his contact list, calling senators and congressmen, the State Department, Interpol, anyone who would listen. He'd told his story a dozen times. And always with the same response. "We're sorry, we really are, but there's nothing we can do. Mexico is a sovereign nation. We have to go through the embassy. Let the ambassador handle it."

But that wasn't good enough. He didn't like calling in favors, but he had no choice. So now he was talking to Alex Grisham, Field Director, Western Hemisphere, CIA. The man had operatives in Mexico and the clout to get things done. More than that, they'd fought together in Vietnam. He was Bill's last hope.

"Come on, Alex, you know better than that. We can sit and quibble all afternoon. But there's an American citizen down there and he's likely to get himself killed. You've got to do something."

"Of course, of course. We're working with State, but we have to go through channels."

"Oh, give me a break! You're talking like a politician, Alex. You know if it's up to them, nothing will happen." Bill closed his eyes, pinched the bridge of his nose, and took a long, slow breath. "How 'bout we do a quick in and out? Get a 'copter, slip in under radar, pick up those kids, and duck out. We could be back over the ocean before anyone even noticed. Even if they did, they wouldn't say anything. The Federales have been denying such an organization exists. If they raise flack, it will be the same as admitting they knew Estrada and his bunch were selling children all along. Think about it. This story is going down one of two ways: either I'm going to write about how our government stepped in and saved a bunch of innocent children, or that a missionary, an American citizen, went in there, and we did absolutely nothing to protect him. How's it going to spin if he dies because a bunch of bureaucrats refused to get involved? I'd hate to write it that way, but if I have to..."

"Nice try, Best, but no go. You won't compromise national security. Not you."

Bill shook his head. The truth was, he probably wouldn't. But then again...

TWENTY-SIX

NICOLE OPENED her eyes, and saw nothing. There was no discernible difference between open and closed, except when her eyes were open, they were dusted with tiny bits of dirt from the fallout. When they were closed she kept drifting off to sleep. For that reason, open was better, despite the dirt. Either way, all she saw was black. Maybe she was blind. She hadn't thought of that. For all she knew she could be lying in the plaza in plain sight, unable to see. But they'd be helping her, wouldn't they? *Unless*—unless the whole village had been wiped out. But if that were true, she'd feel the sun touching her skin and be breathing fresh air, not this musty chalk smell that embalmed her. How long had she been there? Time was nebulous. One hour in the blackness was like a day, *or two—or three.* She couldn't see the space that surrounded her. She didn't dare breathe easy. She continued to sip air, just short tiny breaths, working at keeping her mind alive—excising Ryan...

"Flyin' Ryan." That's what they'd called him. Flyin' Ryan. Because he *was* flying. He was going to the top, no limit but the sky. Nothing could prevent him from achieving his goal. But that was the problem. He wasn't about to let anyone stand in his way, which was exactly where she so often found herself. She was forever having to duck because, with or without her, like it or not, one way or the other, he was coming through. He never said it outright, but it was clearly understood. If she wasn't on board, she'd be left behind.

Talk about blind, that was real blindness, blinded by all his superficial hopes and dreams. Yet at the same time, she knew she was never really blind, no more then than now. She'd gone into the marriage with eyes wide open, knowing what kind of man he was, but hoping he'd change. Not! It was always about *his* goals, *his* objectives, *his* plans, *his* carefully choreographed life. She was just a prop on a skillfully designed stage. But that didn't make her any less affected by the spell, the mystical incantation of the dream weaver, always larger than life. He had a way of making the future sound magical, elusive and downright romantic.

She should have bailed the first time he used that disgusting endearment. Weren't endearments supposed to bring people together? *Ha, ha,* big laugh! No, his were meant to separate. They were a declaration of position. "Nicky Girl," that's what he called her. She hated it, though she never bothered to tell him. "Nicky Girl," so demeaning, so trite, so blatantly subservient. "Nicole" was too formal, he said, but he really meant it was too eloquent, too lofty. He needed a way of showing she was beneath him. He claimed the nickname implied intimacy, but she saw it for what it was—a devaluing of her person. He tried other endearments—Nicky Honey, Nicky Baby, even Nicky Poo—but Nicky Girl was the one he liked. Said it had a nice ring to it. It didn't matter, they all had the same purpose, though Nicky Girl definitely said it best. He was the "Doctor" and she was his "girl."

When it came right down to it, they were at loggerheads about almost everything, but mostly about money. He liked to spend, and she liked to save. Their apartment had been a blasé affair, a Formica-topped chrome-legged table in a world of lacquered wood. He hated it, felt it conveyed an image of poverty, a visual declaration of the success he hadn't yet achieved. "You have to acquire nice things, and believe you have the power within yourself to achieve the means to keep them." Nicole disagreed. She draped the table with a tablecloth to hide its fifties appearance, and folded a matchbook cover under the leg to keep it from wobbling. She had always lived frugally. She hated spending money on things that didn't really matter and refused to use credit to buy what she could not afford. Ryan was the opposite. He wanted an apartment full of new furniture to go along with the grandiose vision of who he was, but Nicole put her foot down, standing in the way, again. If she were going to quit school to support him, she insisted they live on a budget, so the walls were apartment white, the kitchen counter had only two stools, and no, he could not keep a bar in the house, not even for entertaining. It was an affront that he would even ask...

Ryan stood looking at a pile of paper strewn across the dining room table. "Nicky Girl, come here. I want to show you something."

Nicole, who had been at the kitchen sink with her hair in a bun to keep the moisture from removing her curl, walked over, wiping her hands on a dishtowel. She pulled the pin and shook her head, letting her hair fall loose and bright so Ryan could see her at her best. The dinner dishes were now washed and put away, without help, because this was "her" job. She stood behind her husband looking around his shoulder. The table, the one he absolutely hated, was cluttered with pamphlets and brochures, and what looked like a legal document and a blueprint. "What is it?" she asked.

"It's my new office. What do you think?"

"New office? Someone vacate space for you at the hospital?"

"No. No, I won't be working there anymore. This just came up and I had to jump on it. I'm being offered a once-in-a-lifetime opportunity."

Nicole began to study the diagram. It was an office layout with rooms outlined in blue ink. "Looks alright, I guess. Can't tell much from this."

Ryan reached out and handed her a color brochure, pushing the bangs out of his eyes with his manicured fingers, his baby blues clear as a morning in spring. The coated paper had glossy photos. On the cover was a tall high-rise made of glass and brushed aluminum. It stood in a park with trees on a carpet of green, and was crowned with white clouds dotting a blue sky. "It's an existing practice. I'm buying it from a doctor who wants to retire."

"Buying?"

"Yes. Dr. Osteroff, a physician I met at the hospital, wants to sell his practice. He's ready to retire. All I have to do is step in and take over. That's the beauty of it."

Nicole opened the flyer and scanned the rest of the photos. The office was decorated in chrome and leather. There were floor-to-ceiling windows and tall plants, mauve wallpaper with a pattern of multicolored leaves—greens and reds, yellows, tans and browns—the art was contemporary, colorful flowers framed in chrome with track lights illuminating nonglare glass. The carpet was luxurious and thick, and the chairs padded in a supple tan leather that reminded Nicole of Ryan's beastly car. It was first-rate decor, assembled with a designer's touch. "Looks expensive."

"It is, but I ran the numbers and we can afford it."

Nicole furrowed her forehead, turning her eyebrows into question marks. "How expensive?"

Ryan turned away and began shuffling papers on the table. "Four hundred and fifty thou."

"Four hundred and fifty thousand *dollars?*" The tone—the temper of her words—carried a message, but she was looking at his back. She tapped his shoulder.

He turned. "Yes?"

"We don't have four hundred and fifty thousand dollars! We don't have four hundred dollars! What are you thinking?" Here she was, standing in the way again, unable to step aside.

"Relax! Don't get all hyper. Like I said, we can afford it. I've got it all worked out."

"That's ridiculous. The bank will never loan you the money. We haven't got collateral. You're not employed. And they're sure not going to do it based on my salary."

Ryan shook his head, causing his sandy hair to fall across his forehand again. "There you go, jumping to conclusions without hearing the facts." He brought a narrow finger up and pointed at her chest. "Now listen, just hear me out. Doctor Osteroff owns the building, and he's willing to carry the paper. I don't have to go to the bank. We've already worked out the deal."

Maybe it was stubbornness, maybe it was pride, maybe it was rational common sense, but whatever it was, Nicole just couldn't seem to get out of the way, so she stood her ground, blocking his path. "Worked out the deal? Without talking to me?"

"I am talking to you—now. I would have done it sooner, but I had to act fast."

And her alter ego, the part of her she hadn't known existed until after they were married, advanced on her husband, getting ready to push. "Let me get this straight. First you bought that, that, *car*, and now you want this? No way. You go right back and tell the man the deal's off."

Ryan raised his hands, palms out. "Relax, will you? Calm down. I'm not gonna go back and tell the man anything. I've already signed the papers. This is a great opportunity. It's gonna solve our financial problems. The business comes with the patient list included. And his current patients provide income enough to pay the mortgage with money left over for the car. And what you make covers the rent on our apartment, so we're covered. It's all there in black and white. We're buying the goose, and the golden egg. His patients come from all over Hollywood and Bel Air and Malibu. Rich old ladies that call him every time they hiccup. His billings are astronomical."

And push came to shove. "You want to pander to wealthy widows. I thought you entered medicine to help people. Taking money from little old ladies who don't need help isn't medicine. It's larceny!" Her headstrong demeanor was driving them apart.

"Oh for love of..." Ryan snatched the brochure out of her hand and threw it on the table. "What is your problem? I never said I didn't want to make money. Medicine is medicine. There are two kinds of patients a doctor can treat: rich ones and poor ones. I've decided to take care of the rich ones. So what? The way I see it, rich people need medical attention just as much as poor people. Only rich people pay better." He closed his eyes, took a breath, and opened them again, slipping back into his innocent baby blues. He took her hands in his own, mollycoddling her with compassion. "Look, I'm doing this for us—well, actually, more for you. I want you to have all the finer things in life. You're going to have everything you ever wanted."

Only what Flyin' Ryan hadn't considered was that Nicole wanted to minister to the poor and needy. That had always been her dream. She'd explained it while they were dating—was he even listening? Not! Because here he was heading off in the opposite direction, acquiring a debt load too big to even comprehend. The marriage was doomed from the start.

That practice, that "golden egg," had been the second loop in a downward spiral, the car being the first. It didn't matter that over the years he'd proved he was right by turning the risky venture into a walloping success. It was that he'd made the decision without talking to her. Marriage was supposed to be a partnership, a mutual endeavor. They were supposed to share, husband and wife. But no! He was the "Doctor," and she was his "girl." Now here she was with her feet planted firmly on the ground while he was off soaring through the sky.

To support her man, she'd taken a job at Striker Films, working as an administrative assistant in the small but growing company, run at the time by Lonnie's older brother Harlan. She went to work because Ryan claimed they were struggling. It wasn't until much later she learned he kept a separate bank account for himself. His real goal was to keep her occupied and out of the way, but not with school. That would mean she'd eventually want to join his practice, which might clip his wings and impede his ability to fly.

She ended up working for a man with a fold-out couch in his office, which he claimed was for emergencies. "I won't be home tonight dear, I have to work late. We're in the final stages of production. You know how it is. I have to be here twenty-four-seven." Words that were usually said in the company of another woman who sat and smiled and polished her lips while waiting. Harlan's door was usually ajar, leaving the words to echo in Nicole's ear, only she heard her husband's voice. "I have an emergency. Miss Natty fell and broke her hip and the operation couldn't be scheduled until 1:00 am." The thought of her husband fooling around bubbled like acid in her gut, making it impossible to sleep.

So while Ryan was flyin', she was slowly dying.

TWENTY-SEVEN

LONNIE SCANNED the long narrow divide. He couldn't see where it ended. The barking got louder. His heart was pounding as the minutes passed with the dog scrambling up the mountain, closing the distance in hot pursuit. They were cut off in front, and behind. *Man, what are You doing, Lord? Could you give me a break? I've got a pile of kids here. Think You could do something besides block the way? Please!* He looked around. The lichen-covered tree behind them was termite infested. The top half had broken off long ago, and its base looked like someone had taken a drill and filled it full of holes. *You can't possibly mean—oh, come on*—he made his way over and started to push. The tree was creaking and teetering, ready to break. The children joined in, placing their hands against the trunk. Lonnie turned around, putting his wounded back to the job. With a *snap* and a *crack,* the tree started to come down. It fell, sluggishly, its branches crashing against the dense jungle foliage with a muffled *whafffump*. Unbelievable. They now had a bridge. It wasn't a particularly large tree, but wide enough to cross on foot without crawling, and the remaining branches offered something to hold onto for balance. "Okay kids, this is it. Climb aboard."

If he thought the children might be afraid, his concern was unwarranted. They scampered across one at a time as easy as playground toddlers scaling a jungle gym. Sofía hiked her dress up above her knees to keep it from snagging on the branches. Lonnie went last behind the heavy-set boy whose sweater still dripped water. On the other side, he stepped down, grabbed a thick limb, dug in his heels, and pulled the tree forward until the trunk fell into the breach, then walked toward the edge turning the tree sideways until the rest fell in. *Unnn-believable!* Just like Moses crossing the Red Sea. *Trust in the Lord with all thine heart...and he shall direct thy paths—yes.* The dog was getting closer. Lonnie could hear twigs snapping and see the rustling of the leaves as it channeled its way through the brush. "Okay kids, let's move. Let's see if we can reach the ridge by nightfall."

THE DUST finally settled. In the aftermath, Miguel Estrada surveyed the damage. The earth had opened along a fault running through the center of his property. The river, formerly used for irrigation, was intersected opening the bottomland to flooding, washing out twenty-five acres of crop. The cost of backhoes and bulldozers to fill the crevice would be enormous. And it would demolish the remaining plants on both sides until the work was done. Many of the Quonset huts were flattened or in need of gross repair. He stood with Badger beside him, notepad in hand, calculating the cost. Thirty years of work brought down in a few minutes, and it wasn't the kind of business you could insure. It saddened him, but it was a mixed feeling. He'd been thinking of closing the plantation anyway. But seeing it happen so abruptly left him feeling numb. *Sweet Mother of God.* Now he was faced with how to handle the layoffs.

Miguel reached for his handkerchief, mopping his brow. The yellow sun burned hot and hazy through the residual dust. He sneezed, covering his mouth. He'd be on his way home, resting in the air conditioned luxury of his limousine, if the Quonset hut he used for a parking garage hadn't been one of those that collapsed. Men in white muslin outfits were busy cutting away sheets of corrugated aluminum, trying to free the car. It would be severely scratched, but that didn't mean it wouldn't run. He was still waiting for a final tally on the number of men he'd lost, but *he* wasn't hurt—*thank the Blessed Saints.* Sí, in some ways the earthquake had been a blessing. Had he not that very morning contemplated what course of action to take? Now God Himself had intervened and made the decision for him. Now he could devote all his energy to helping unwanted children find new lives where they would have roofs over their heads, and food to eat, and nice American clothes to wear.

The livelihood of the children was paramount. They had to be found. Daniela's death had been reported to him, and though her body was still missing, the blood found in the truck was proof of her demise. Sad, *very sad,* not that she was dead, but that she'd turned on him—after all he'd done for her. He'd been like a father. Hadn't he provided everything she needed? She'd had food to eat and a place to live. He'd even given her additional responsibility, her own store to manage, and increased freedom. Her betrayal was something he couldn't fathom. Why put her life on the line to help a dishonest priest? The man was corrupt, a liar and a thief. He was taking what didn't belong to him. But, once again, God had spoken. She had met her just end. The missionary would too. It was just a matter of time. His men had chased the children all the way to the edge of a canyon, but then the trail disappeared. The dog ran around in frenzied furor, barking, howling and chasing its tail, completely baffled. The scent of the children had vanished. They'd gone a quarter mile further on, but there was no new trail to be found, and he'd been assured the gulf was too wide to cross. Miguel responded by sending a few of his most trusted campesinos on ahead to wait. Patience was a virtue. The children would eventually turn up somewhere. He needed them back. Not so much that fat boy, or the tall girl, but three of those missing had to be found. The missionary, because he was a thief. He had stolen from Miguel and for that he had to pay. That one little girl with soulful eyes, because she was there to square the fisherman's debt. Just before the earthquake he had e-mailed his client who immediately responded with payment. The money, transferred to his account, was already in the bank, and ethics dictated he deliver the girl as promised. And for obvious reasons, he needed to find the boy in the blue blazer. *Stupid, stupid, stupid.* That Paco was one estúpido hombre. He had broken the rule. Only street children were to be acquired. When children were taken from families, complaints were lodged with the police. That was bad enough, but *this?* Paco was a fool. Pulling a knife on someone in a bar was criminal enough. He was lucky the authorities only held him overnight. But to swear a vendetta, to steal the son of the chief of police just to get even, was unconscionable. Now Miguel was forced to make sure the boy never returned. He could deny having anything to do with the child's abduction, other organizations could blamed, but the boy had seen his face. If he were allowed to return home, the consequence would be unthinkable.

TO LONNIE, the rounded shapes of the children sleeping in the moonlight looked like smooth blue stones. The depth of night had enveloped them. They had pushed on, climbing the mountain with every ounce of strength they possessed, but it was slow slogging. At times he'd had to beat down the tangled brush with a stick, or prod his way through, or wait while others held the vines back so they could pass. Other times, they had to detour around growths of markweed and nettles, while avoiding colonies of ants and wasps. He was darn proud of those kids. They'd taken to the mountain like it was an adventure. In spite of the perils, they'd made it to the top of the ridge and while the sun was still on the horizon, stumbled upon one of the many well-worn trails linking the remote mountain villages. The landscape of the Sierra Madre del Sur was a regular connect-the-dot drawing, penciled with trails that criss-crossed the countryside, providing the means by which the Indians conducted commerce.

Lonnie had pushed the children hard, despite the fact his wounds felt like they'd been seared with a hot knife. His head was pounding. He felt it more now while resting than he had while they were on the move. Under the dark blanket of night, the children had fallen asleep quickly. A clearing surrounded by figus mecianos provided a natural shelter. He didn't have to tell them to go to sleep. Their eyes closed with exhaustion as one by one they curled up, snuggling together like a pile of puppies. Lonnie felt the guilt of a parent unable to provide the most basic necessities. His children had no food to eat, no water to drink or even a fire to keep them warm, and yet no one complained. Not even Raúl.

Lonnie grimaced as he stood. There wasn't one part of his body that didn't hurt. He felt faint and stooped over, placing his hands on his knees to catch his breath. His shirt, clotted with blood, pulled away from the wounds on his back, opening the sores to bleed again. His arms were cut from squeezing through the brush and riddled with welts from insect bites. His legs trembled from the hard climb. What had he accomplished? He'd saved his kids, but at what cost? Daniela was dead. And wouldn't Miguel simply replenish his stock by going out and capturing more? Would the freeing of his children bring suffering upon others? How could a man like Miguel live with himself? Worse still, how could he call himself a Christian? Lonnie always wondered how S.S. officers serving under Hitler could justify the atrocities they'd committed in the death camps, stuffing thousands of human beings into the ovens throughout the week, and on Sunday morning still sing hymns with their children in a local Lutheran mass. How could they go home and after dinner read to their children under a light that had a lampshade made of human skin, and then kiss their babies goodnight as though, *all in a day's work*, they'd made the world a better place in which to live? It was a phenomenon old as time. Christ said a day would come in which men would kill His disciples and think they were doing God a favor. If men could justify *that*—they could justify anything.

He wondered too if Miguel had called off the chase. Shouldn't they have heard the hounds on their tail? They had plunged into the jungle, stopping only for brief moments to regroup and catch their breath, pausing to listen for anything that might reveal they were being followed. The jungle was alive with *cuckoo-cooing* and *ka-ka-cawing*. They'd disturbed a bevy of pauraque hiding in the brush, and sent a hundred pairs of wings into the air with the sound of rushing water. The hairs on his neck stood on end when he realized their location had been compromised, but he'd waited, and in the stillness that followed, no dogs could be heard. Nothing but the wind in the trees. The quiet had been unnerving. He didn't know Miguel, but the man didn't seem the kind to give up, yet it appeared they had escaped. Once they found the trail, Lonnie knew he could go either direction and eventually come to a village. From there he could get a fix on their location and determine the best route back to Posada.

He couldn't begin to guess where they actually were, just somewhere between Oaxaca and Mexico City, which was an area spanning hundreds of miles of unmapped forest.

His head ached. His swollen face was throbbing. A blue-gray fog was rolling in from the ocean, a sign they weren't far from the coast. He rolled his eyes toward heaven. *God, give me strength.* He straightened himself and took a few plodding steps toward the woods where the night insects were making their presence known. He brought a finger up and touched his lip. It was puffy and numb. He wondered how he'd look in a mirror. But at least he could feel. Pain was a blessing. Daniela no longer felt anything. What was he supposed to say to Bill? There were so many things he didn't understand. *Why did she have to die? She'd just begun to live. Why her and not me?*

Lonnie found a large boulder, an outcrop of rock overlooking the valley. The flecks of granite sparkled in the moonlight, but its surface was rough and felt like sandpaper under his knees. Slowly he raised his hands. His arms felt heavy and his shoulders weak, but he forced them to reach toward heaven. The sky was midnight blue, crowded with a nebula of stars, a billion pinpoints of light as numerous as the sands of the sea. It was time to stop whining and start thanking the Lord. He'd complained every time they confronted an obstacle, and God had always provided a way. He'd asked the Lord for a miracle, and got it. *They were free.* God had shaken the doors off his prison. Lonnie closed his eyes, seeking forgiveness. In spite of the miraculous undertones, including the vision of Nicole that lead him to the door, there was a side of him that still wanted to attribute the earthquake to natural phenomenon.

Had such a thing happened since the days of the apostles? He struggled with knowing. After all the miracles God had done in his life, his faith was still weak. When their path was blocked he'd doubted, but now saw how God had used that chasm and an old rotted tree, not to stop them, but to prevent them from being followed. And he'd doubted when their truck fell into the ditch, but now saw there was a reason for that too. Daniela was probably on her way in to see Miguel. If they'd kept going, they would have ended up back at the camp, and then Daniela wouldn't have been the only one dead. *Poor Daniela.* But was it the will of God that Daniela should die? See, that *too* was a conundrum. He couldn't shake the feeling her death was somehow bad. If he truly believed what he preached, shouldn't he be rejoicing? Only a moment ago he had felt pain and said it was a blessing, like living on earth with all its toil and strife was a good thing. He had to get a more eternal focus. He might, at a funeral, be justified in mourning the loss of a loved one because those left behind would miss the one sent on ahead, but as far as he knew, Daniela didn't have any family. And she'd not been able to fully eradicate herself from the life she so hated. Now she was truly free, the virginity stolen from her was now fully restored—*the virgin bride of Christ.* No longer would she wear frilly seductive blouses, constrained to sell what belonged to God. No longer would men rape her with their eyes. Now she was dressed in robes clean and white. He'd read the passage in Isaiah at funerals, the one that said God sometimes took people off the planet to deliver them from evil.

The righteous perish,
and no man understands:
that merciful men are taken away,
none considering that the righteous
are taken away to spare them from the evil to come....

That was the truth of it. The *absolute* truth! It was about time he got it through his thick head.

TWENTY-EIGHT

Are You there, God? I don't see You. How do I know You even exist? We are here, my sister and me, and she prays that You will set us free and here we are—so, maybe? Does Your breath shake the mountains? Do You build bridges out of trees? Are trucks and people like toys in Your hand? Okay, then, why kill one to save another? Why not save everyone? Listen, all I ask is that You keep Mariana safe. You can do that, can't You? Please! She never hurt anyone.

THE MOON stretched blue shadows across the landscape, a cooling of the ground aided by a breeze rippling through the trees and scattering leaves around the hilltop. The children lay motionless, stationary as a pile of rocks, the endless *chirrrrrping* of the crickets lulling them to sleep. But one pair of eyes remained open, two white orbs scanning the night like beams of light. Raúl waited until Lonnie was out of sight, then slowly propped himself on his elbow, looking around, careful not to disturb his sister. The brightness of the stars made the ground clearly visible. He could see leaves, foliage and rocks. He wouldn't have a better chance. He sat up, pulling Mariana into his arms. Her head rolled back, her eyes opened sluggishly, half-lidded. He put his finger to his lips, *shushhhh,* and then realized the gesture was pointless. She hadn't made a sound in weeks. He pulled her into his arms and stood, snuggling her against his chest. Mariana's eyes closed again, secure in the warmth and rhythm of his heart. Within a few seconds her breathing grew heavy and she slipped back into the sleep from which she'd awakened.

Raúl paused to see if he'd unsettled anyone, but the bodies remained still. Stepping lightly as possible, he crept through the clearing to the trail, using the light of the constellations to avoid stepping on twigs and leaves that might snap and crackle. He continued down the well-traveled path, heading in the same direction they'd established before nightfall. He wouldn't risk going the opposite way. Miguel's men might be on their tail.

After walking the better part of a mile he was getting used to the bats. The first one swooped around his head, veering off at the last second, giving him such a start he nearly dropped Mariana trying to wave it off. But he no longer felt threatened by their presence. He sensed they were harmless. They were as anxious to avoid him as he was them, though he was surprised by how many there were. Somewhere off in a shadow primeval, an owl *whoo-whooo-whoooooed*, and the wind picked up, buffeting the trees, but he was determined to brave it out. He was glad to be walking. He'd seen fleeting glimpses of yellowish eyes skittering into the bush too many times. He couldn't imagine what it would be like sleeping on the ground with a bunch of rodent-toothed critters burrowing between them, looking for food.

He had to stop and rest. Mariana was getting heavy. He trudged another hundred yards before finding a rock large enough to sit on. He shivered, wishing again he had more than a T-shirt to wear. He felt his skin tighten and the goosebumps rise. While walking, he hadn't noticed the air cooling, but now sitting on stone, he felt cold. He leaned in, sheltering Mariana, snuggling her in his arms to keep her warm, her head turned toward his chest. Her eyes opened for a moment, then closed. With the stretch of distance they'd covered, and the sounds of nocturnal noise, he wasn't concerned about being heard, but spoke softly nonetheless.

"We had to leave, understand? The others can sleep if they want, but we can't stay with them. They'll slow us down. Understand?" Mariana's head was drooping. She was only half awake. The earthquake had struck early the previous morning, causing them to flee through the fields and down the river and then up the mountain, and in all that time, she'd had no rest. Raúl waited, trying to regain his strength but his vision became dull and his eyes grew heavy, and when his eyelids began to close, he stood, holding Mariana close, and continued on.

The moon was now directly overhead, much smaller and brighter than before. The shadows were shrinking. He kept plodding on, shoving one foot forward and dragging the other up from behind. He wasn't sure how much further he could go. His strength was failing. He'd already accomplished what he'd set out to do. Now that they were away from the group, they were safe. If the dogs were able to ferret out the others and their absence *was* noticed, they would assume the two of them had become separated and wandered off into the woods, and were lost—or so he hoped.

It was time to stop. The night was alive with the sounds of flying-crawly things everywhere but there was no way to get away from it. He was out of options. He had to rest. Tomorrow morning he would get his sister to a village, and leave her with a sympathetic soul while he went back to finish what he'd started. It would already be done if that crazy padre hadn't interfered. The man was muy loco. He'd tried to buy their freedom. *Fool!* You can't barter with el diablo. A real man of God would know that. If he wanted to do what was right he would have helped kill the two men—not save their lives. Didn't he care what they'd done to him? One more second and *bang-bang-bang-bang-bang,* they'd be dead and everyone would be safe, instead of wandering around the mountains in the middle of the night. *Fool! Coward! Weak!* Not a man he could trust.

He was still trudging ahead, looking for a suitable place to stop when, after another quarter mile, he began to see glints of light filtering through the leaves. He pressed on, his heart accelerating, feeling the adrenaline, the hair on the back of his neck beginning to bristle, but he was careful not to make a sound. He rounded the corner. The path opened to a wide clearing. Set back in the distance between several domed huts were moonlit walls of adobe. A warm glow poured from an open window. He'd stumbled upon a village. He glanced around the courtyard. The buildings appeared to be standing. The huts were made of sticks covered in mud, a resilient combination. The only permanent structure was the log tavern surfaced with brick clay, the central meeting place of the town. He didn't see any damage. Maybe the earthquake only shook the valley below. His first inclination was to march in and seek asylum, but his survival instinct raised a flag of caution. He stepped off the trail looking for a flat space covered with grass. The brush near the village was well trampled. He saw a large chunk of gray granite poking out of the earth like a pointed finger, and at its base found the perfect place to leave his sister. Still holding her in his arms, he squatted on his haunches and began flattening the grass. He unearthed a jagged stick and tossed it aside along with a few lumpy stones, and lay Mariana in the bed, making her as comfortable as possible.

"Mariana, wake up. Listen to me. There's a light ahead. I think it's a village, but I'm not sure. I want you to wait here until I find if it's safe. Can you do that?"

Mariana's eyes were droopy. She covered her arms and rolled over. She was one tired little girl. "Okay Mariana, stay here, okay?" Raúl stroked her hair with the back of his fingers. "Do not move. I'll be right back." In the shadow of the rock the moonlight was thin. He felt more than saw her nod. She brought her knees up and curled into a ball.

Raúl slipped into the village, working his way toward the light burning in the window. Everywhere else was dark. The town was in a hollow, an antediluvian enclave of the Sierra Madre del Sur. There was no electricity—no television, radio, nor other forms of electronic entertainment. People went to sleep early. The one room glowing in the darkness flickered and danced in the shadows as though the light from its portal emanated from a fire. As he moved toward the building, Raúl heard someone grunt and laugh. He crept up cautiously, peeking over the sill, his heart pounding, *wawhump, wawhump, wawhump*. Two men sat at a table eating bowls of guisado with long-handled spoons, a bowl of chili peppers and corn chips between them. They drank beer from amber bottles, of which there were a dozen standing on the table interspersed with a half dozen shot glasses, two spilled over sideways, and a half-full bottle of tequila.

Their arms were propped up next to a can of salt and a pile of lemon rinds. They were dressed in white muslin pants, probably local campesinos. Their brown faces gave off a deep ocher glow, reflecting the flames in the stone hearth. A man in a long-sleeve plaid shirt and soiled apron stood behind a polished bar. He had a stomach round as a pomegranate, and a face just as red. He popped a hard-boiled egg into his mouth, and leaned in to wipe the counter with a cloth, chewing with his rosy cheeks ballooning. Raúl could feel saliva secreting from his glands. The two men hovering over their hot bowls of stew made him realize he hadn't eaten in days.

He got down from the stoop. It wouldn't be wise to beg food from the men, but around back the bartender would throw out scraps. He waited until his eyes adjusted to the dark and crept around to the rear of the building, the stars overhead providing enough light to identify shapes and shadows. There were two large aluminum trash cans, dented and lopsided with their lids askew, overflowing as though they hadn't been emptied in weeks. He stepped lightly with his heart in his throat. He removed one of the lids, but his hand was shaking and he knocked the other off, sending it *clanging* to the ground. He froze, eyes fixed on the back door, ready to run, but the tavern remained quiet. Nothing else moved. He turned his attention back to the can. The light from the moon revealed a king's feast, enough for both himself and Mariana. There, right on top, was a half-eaten frijole-filled tortilla wrapped in a corn husk, and an ear of corn with half the kernels still on the cob. He scooped up both pieces and turned around—right into a huge stomach. His nose was pressed against an apron stinking of sour milk.

"Hey, look what I found, a little raccoon come to steal my garbage."

Raúl started to stammer, but a hand came down, grabbing him by the shirt.

"Sí, a thief. And perhaps a little escape artist too, no?"

Raúl panicked. He tried twisting out of the man's grip, but the man held tight.

"No, muchacho, first we find out who you are." He turned,

holding Raúl with one hand while wiping the other on his apron. He raised his free hand, cupping his mouth as he yelled to the men in the tavern. "Eh, señors, come here. I think I have one of your children."

A moment later a man dressed in muslin shuffled out. He was tipsy, teetering, moving with halting belabored steps.

The meaty bartender turned Raúl around. "Look what I found. Do you recognize this one? I think he's one of yours."

The peasant looked at Raúl, then at the bartender. His eyes were waterlogged and heavy. "This is but one boy. Where are the others? I want them all, and...and the missionary priest." He turned to address Raúl. "Eh, muchacho. Where is your father, and your sisters and brothers? *Eh?* Tell me."

Raúl's lips were quivering. He tried to break free, squirming with such force his captor had to wrap his elbow around his neck, locking him in a scissor hold. The sleeve of the man's shirt was moist with sweat and grease, and his arm so thick it nearly covered Raúl's face. The man grabbed his wrist and pulled it up behind his back. *"Ohwwwww!"*

"Hey, be careful. You don't have to hurt him. He's just a boy."

But Raúl continued to squirm, and the fat bartender could barely hold on. "Then you take him. Child or no, this little one is slippery."

The campesino leaned in toward Raúl, his breath smelling of chilies and beer. He was a thin man, with the stubble of his gray beard poking through his creased brown skin. His eyes bulged and his eyebrows turned every way but straight. His Adam's apple bobbed up and down as he spoke. "It will do you no good to fight, little one. We have men in every village. They are offering a reward for your return. Do not expect to find help, okay? Okay, we have you, so now maybe you can tell me where the others are, and I will see you are not punished for trying to escape, eh?" He reached out and took Raúl by the arms. "I can give you food. Sí, you are hungry. Come inside and I will get you something to eat."

The man's eyes were runny but, though his lips were cracked and he had a chipped front tooth, his smile was broad and disarming.

Raúl relaxed.

"Good, we understand each other."

The bartender held out a puffy red hand. "Fine, you got your boy. What about my reward?"

"That is for Don Estrada to say."

"But you said the Don would pay mucho dinero for the return of his children."

"Sí. For all his children. Not for one scrawny bean such as this."

"But I should get something. I caught him."

The man shrugged. "Perhaps. We will see."

The fat bartender turned and stomped off, grumbling. The screen door slammed, scattering the June bugs that had collected there, attracted to the light. Raúl could hear him talking to the man inside. He looked at the campesino. This man was old and frail, and probably drunk. Raúl had but one chance and that was to put every ounce of energy he could muster into one gargantuan attempt to break free. He took a deep breath, flexed, and began twisting with the force of a gale, spinning and jerking and kicking, his fists flailing the air, sometimes hitting flesh, a whirling dervish in the making. The smell of beer invaded his face as the man huffed and puffed trying to hold on. Raúl jammed his fist into the man's groin and the man lost his grip, wide-eyed, wind-gutted, staggering backward, unable to speak. Raúl seized the moment. He plowed his head into the man's stomach, shoving him further back into the garbage cans which toppled over, taking the man with them as they fell. Raúl turned and ran. He picked a moonlit track between an outcrop of rock and the rusted hull of a pickup sitting on its axles. He ran fast and furious disappearing into the night. He could hear cans clattering as the man tried to get up, but he didn't dare look back. He had to save Mariana.

The bartender and the other campesino came flying out the door, but it was too late. Raúl was gone. The thin one teetered, trying to get up, straining to catch his breath. He leaned over, placed his hand against the wall and began to vomit.

"You want me to go after him?" his partner said, peering into the dense foliage.

The man shook his head.

"What about my reward?" The bartender had a towel in his hand, pointing at the trees and the blackness beyond.

The campesino grabbed the towel and used it to wipe his mouth, pressing a hand against his side, trying to breathe as he began a slow shuffle back to the tavern.

BY THE TIME he reached Mariana, Raúl was out of breath, wheezing, trying to draw air from a chest on fire. He collapsed to the ground, rolling onto his back, listening for the sound of someone following. He'd checked several times as he ran, going far into the bush in the opposite direction of Mariana, before doubling back to find her. If there was any chance they were after him, he wouldn't have come. He felt the sweat he'd worked up hit the cool night air, giving him a chill. He shuddered. His breathing was loud and uneven. They were surrounded by the buzzing songs of the insect choir, but other than that, the night was quiet.

Raúl looked up into the eyes of his sister standing over him with the moonlight on her shoulder looking like pink geraniums. A bat darted by, causing her to be momentarily distracted. He wondered if she realized what was going on. "These men," Raúl wheezed, "are evil. They tried to catch me." He struggled to sit up. "They are here. We have to go." He tried to stand, his body faint. He reached out, taking Mariana's hand, and started to move forward, pulling her with him, but she held her ground.

"Come on, Mariana. *Now!*" he said, holding his voice to a pronounced whisper.

Mariana was shaking her head. She jerked her hand free. "No! We have to go back and warn the others."

"We can't go back. We'll be caught. They can take care of themselves. We have to go on." Then Raúl stopped. He grabbed his sister by the shoulders and dropped to his knees. *She's talking.* He put his ear to her chest, listening for more, the air wheezing from his throat. *Oh, this is, oh.* He was fighting not to cry.

Mariana crossed her arms. "We have to help. If we don't, they'll walk into a trap." She turned, breaking Raúl's embrace and marched back down the trail. Raúl struggled to his feet. What could he do but follow?

A FAINT RIBBON of purple light was breaking on the crest of the mountains, so faint it was hard to distinguish from the darkness, but it was there, the first sign of approaching dawn. Lonnie stretched, rubbing his arms, feeling the goosebumps. The wind whistled through the trees, whipping the leaves. It was cold. He hadn't slept with the children. They were able to snuggle and share body heat, but out of a sense of propriety he'd slept alone. Maybe it was a foreboding he felt, the dreams that woke him throughout the night. He'd caught sleep in short bursts filled with images of ordeals yet to come. Nicole was beckoning to him from a dark place, or so it was in his dream. And where was Trudy? Why would God send Nicole to him instead of his fiancée? He yawned and shivered, shaking it from his head. *Dreams are just images projected by the mind to keep it active while the body is at rest.* He regretted having to start moving again. His own body was rent and worn. He felt an anxious tension, his muscles aching. He woke the children. It was time to go.

They stood huddled in a group rubbing their arms and shuffling their feet to keep warm. Lonnie wanted to introduce himself and fill in the missing names. Sofía held the little boy. It was a symbiotic relationship. She and the boy drew strength from each other. But she was troubled about something. She wouldn't look at him. He'd made numerous attempts to garner her attention, but she'd always averted her eyes. And when he did make contact, even for the briefest moment, her eyes began to fill with tears before darting away. She hadn't said much since their escape. Perhaps the boy filled the void left by Sebastian. It was clear the little guy was leaning on her for a mother's touch. The children were waiting for him to say something. He began to pace, scanning the area, fearing what he already knew. Raúl and Mariana were missing.

"Has anyone seen the little girl and her brother?"

The fat one raised the hem of his dark sweater and slipped his hands into his pockets. Behind his huge glasses, his face was blank. He looked down.

"You, what's your name? Did you see them?" he asked, addressing the boy directly.

"Sí, señor. Last night I saw the boy take his sister and go." He brought his toe back and kicked a clod of dirt.

Lonnie's eyebrows rose, and settled again. "Why? Why didn't you say something?"

"I did not think, I mean, I thought maybe she had to go, you know, and he was taking her."

Lonnie closed his eyes and shook his head. *God, I don't need this.* The boy was a problem. If he was determined to travel alone, then so be it. At least he'd helped them escape. Hopefully, they would be traveling the same direction. Maybe they'd hear news of them when they got to the village. And if not, all he could do was pray.

"I'm Luis," the boy said, almost as an afterthought.

"Okay, alright, Luis, thank you. I guess they've decided to leave us. We'll have to go on and hopefully catch up with them later. And who's this one?" Lonnie asked, addressing the boy in Sofía's arms, but he turned his head away, tucking it into her bosom.

Lonnie waited, but when the boy remained silent, he turned to walk away.

The boy's head rolled, one eye poking sheepishly out from behind Sofía's arm, then two. "I'm Juanito," he blurted out.

"Okay. Juanito, Luis, that's good."

They were on a hilltop. The sky was faintly purple, and their hair was being tousled by a brisk morning breeze. Lonnie made sure the children were together. They were down to three, and two of them weren't even his. He placed himself in front so he could lead, with Luis in the middle and Sofía in back.

They'd only been walking about twenty minutes when Lonnie heard a voice. He motioned the children off the trail and into the bush just in time to see someone rounding the bend.

It was Raúl and Mariana. Lonnie released a heavy sigh, and stepped onto the trail.

Raúl was holding his sister's hand. When he saw Lonnie he stopped, studying the dismay on the faces of the group, and then lowered his eyes. "I was hungry," he said. "I thought maybe I could find the town and get us something to eat. But the men there are looking for us. They've been offered a reward."

Great! "What about the name of the town? Did you happen to find out where we are?"

Raúl looked up. His eyes were red. Whether from tiredness or tears, Lonnie couldn't say. "No, señor."

Lonnie turned to the group. "Alright, at least we're together again." He looked back over his shoulder. "Thank you, Raúl. You've been a big help. We'll have to be careful. It's getting light. How far is the town?"

"Not far. Maybe another hour, that way," he said, pointing.

"Alright," Lonnie said, "let's stay together and when we near the village we'll slip off the trail and go around."

The outline of the forest was taking shape in the predawn haze, the plants dripping with crystalline dew. Lonnie felt a tug on his sleeve and looked down to see Mariana. She was looking up at him with big button-brown eyes.

"Be careful, señor. There are many bats."

TWENTY-NINE

FATHER PAULO stood with his hands behind his back, the looping sleeves of his frock trailing beyond his waist, his brown robe, now blotched with white powder, covering his sandaled feet. He stood staring in disbelief at the pile of rubble that was once a bell tower, covering another pile of rubble that used to be his office—a hundred years of history come to ruin in minutes. Holding on was foolishness. All things come to an end. Such was the nature of the world, and everything contained therein.

He was a man of patience, refined in the fire. He'd been through the cholera epidemic. Thirty lives were lost before they were able to bring it under control, but that was before they had a hospital. He'd been through the mudslide that buried a whole family and wiped out Enrique's coffee crop, putting most of the townspeople out of work. He'd been through snakebites and infectious diseases. In Posada, hardship was a way of life. It had a way of defining a man, of making one stronger and better if handled properly. *"Take, my brethren, the prophets, who have spoken in the name of the Lord, for an example of suffering affliction, and of patience. Behold, we count them happy which endure."* Ah, Saint James was truly a comfort.

He refused to feel sorry for himself or waste precious time wallowing in pity. To the best of his knowledge, not one person had been hurt. The bell tower, and by extension his office, incurred the only major damage. The cistern in the middle of the plaza had a crack from which water now leaked, soaking the dry dust and turning it to mud, but that could be fixed. All the other buildings and homes seemed intact. He'd taken inventory. The sisters were accounted for, as were the children under his care. He'd been from family to family in the small community with no one reporting a loss. So, instead of fretting about the destruction of a building, his furniture, his desk, or other items that might inconvenience him until they could be replaced, he had reason to rejoice. Bell towers could be rebuilt, offices rebuilt. But human life, once lost, could not. Gracias a Dios! *Praise the Lord.*

He caught a glimpse of movement across the plaza, a glint of light sparkling off chrome, and heard metal clanking. He looked up. Sebastian was rolling toward him, his wheelchair bouncing over the cobblestones of the main road. His wheels were dusted with the same white powder that covered Paulo's robe. He was a royal prince in a flashy silver chariot, but the chair wasn't made to negotiate such a rough surface. Sebastian had to work at keeping the contraption moving forward over the bumps and grinds, his skinny arms with raised elbows looking like the limbs of a grasshopper jacking up and down on the wheels. His legs may have been weak and useless, but his arms, though thin as straw, were surprisingly strong. Father Paulo smiled. *Yes,* he had much to be thankful for.

He looked at the pile of brick again, and rubbed the side of his long nose. The smell of chalk still filled the air. A butterfly was resting on a piece of clay, its wings folded flat, sunning itself. Perhaps things would get better. This particular butterfly, the agrias, was rare. The Indians considered seeing one a sign of good luck. Folklore was a way of life in the village, and the Indians had much to say about the glittery insect with the bright red and blue wings, stories usually mixed with intrigue and superstition. Paulo didn't bother correcting the error. Instead, he enhanced the stories and applied spiritual principles. He attributed the luminescent red on the butterfly's wings to the blood of Christ, an example of the transforming power bringing newness of life. And to the neon blue he ascribed the radiant glory of life on the other side. The butterfly slowly raised its wings and flattened them again, yawning in the warmth of the sun. It was a sign of hope—not luck. Paulo turned to acknowledge Sebastian, who bumped up alongside.

The boy usually had a mouth full of teeth, white as an egg, but he wasn't smiling. Paulo hadn't seen him smile since the disappearance of Sofía. "Father, have you seen la señorita Nicole? I've looked everywhere, but I cannot find her."

"Ah, Sebastian, and how are you faring today?" Of late, the young man seemed to be continually fretting about one thing or another. His eyes were pleading with the priest.

"I'm fine, Father, but I cannot find la señorita. Have you seen her?"

Paulo turned, his hands still folded behind his back. He did not have time for games of hide and seek. There was much rebuilding to do. He needed to get the work started. "No, no, I can't say I have."

"Me either. I've been everywhere and she cannot be found."

"Did you check the hospital?"

"Sí, of course. And I check her room. I even had el señor Alejandro open the door to see if she'd fallen asleep but she wasn't there. And I went to your house as well. She disappeared."

"Ummm, well," Father Paulo said, turning. "I'm sure she's somewhere. Come, let us go look for her." His hands took the grips of Sebastian's chair, rolling him toward the plaza. "And perhaps we can find a few volunteers to help us move this pile of bricks."

NICOLE WAS in a sarcophagus, buried alive in the belly of a pyramid, an Egyptian queen given the honor of following her master into the next life, waiting to die. She could neither see nor hear the men standing above her discussing her whereabouts, and if she could she would not have been able to respond. Dirt was clogging her throat and plugging her nose, reducing her breathing to short gasps. She saw only the blackness of death, the deep, deep, dark of nothingness. Was this what death was like? The Bible said darkness or blackness was for those who refused God. But that wasn't her. She was destined for the glorious light of Christ. Darkness and blackness were reserved for people like Ryan. *Ryan?* There, *you see,* she was thinking of him again. It made no sense at all. For the past few years, she'd spent most of her waking hours trying to be noticed by Lonnie. So why now, at death's door, was she so fixated on Ryan? She hated to admit it, but Ryan still controlled her subconscious, and she knew why. She hadn't forgiven him. She'd tried. She'd made a conscious effort to release her anger, but in the black hole of her inner being, a place she didn't understand, he was still there—*tormenting her*—so when faced with death, it was his image that surfaced. He had some kind of supernatural stranglehold on her, so dark and cruel she wondered if she'd ever break free. The last thing she wanted was to die with Ryan on her mind. But no matter what she did, that's where her thoughts took her. It wasn't fair. She took comfort in knowing that unless he did a complete turnaround, the blackness of darkness was reserved for him—*forever.* But see, that wasn't forgiveness. That was anger. That was resentment. That was *hate!*

She struggled to take a breath. The air around her was slowly evaporating. She felt like she was sipping through a pinched straw. She knew oxygen had to be seeping into her little space from somewhere. Otherwise, she would have suffocated long ago. But it was only a small amount. She wondered how long it would last.

She searched for something else to think about. Anything but Ryan. *Lyin' Ryan.* That's what *she'd* called him...

"I won't be home tonight, Nicky Girl. I'm in surgery at the hospital."

"Ryan, that's the second time this month. You're not even a surgeon."

"I know, Nicky. We've been through all this. I'm low man on the totem pole at the hospital, last on the list. The senior surgeons book all the best times for themselves. We have to use the facilities whenever we can, and that's usually late at night when the hospital isn't busy. And I have to be there. You know my patients don't like being handed off to other doctors. They want me to dote on them, hold their hands, be there when they wake up, you know? They don't have anyone else. That's part of the recovery process. It's therapy."

She should have known. She shouldn't have been so naive. But she *had* known, hadn't she? How could she not? She'd known all along, but refused to believe. It was a self-imposed blindness, as dark as the one surrounding her now. She didn't mind having to work to support her husband. It meant putting her own career on hold so he could further his, but letting her wants and needs be second to those of her spouse was the definition of love, so she tried to do it with joy.

What she did mind was spending so many nights alone. What began as one or two nights a month soon became one or two nights a week. It seemed Ryan was never there. And when he *was* home, there was little conversation. He would arrive tired, eat something, read for a while, and fall asleep. That was his routine. She'd put in a full day and come home tired, but when she got there, she faced mounds of laundry, a house to vacuum, dishes to wash and toilets to clean, because those were *her* jobs. All the money she earned went into the family bank account to pay bills. It paid the rent on their apartment, it paid for their food and their electricity, it paid for insurance and the gas in their cars. The income Ryan gleaned from his medical practice paid the mortgage on his office. It paid for his equipment, his nurses, his administrative staff, and his car payments. He claimed he had nothing left to contribute to the family account.

She should've faced facts. The telltale signs were obvious, a blinking neon billboard of admissible evidence. The faint smell of strange perfume, traces of pastel lipstick, a strand of dark hair on the lapel of his coat, proof something was amiss. But she didn't want to believe it. So when he said his patients, those dear sweet little old ladies, wore that "horrible" perfume and hugged him, leaving hairs on his coat, or gave him a peck on the cheek smearing lipstick on his collar, she chose to believe it. The Bible admonished her not to think negative thoughts. "Whatsoever things are honest and lovely and of good report, think on those things." She didn't want to think ill of her husband, but her boss was lying to *his* wife day in and day out, week after week, and when she heard her husband's voice, it sounded like an echo.

"Lyin' Ryan," that's who he really was. She didn't know the office suite he'd purchased included an apartment in the same building, furnished to the nines. The second life he lived fulfilled the image of the man he aspired to be—a cosmopolitan, Wilshire District, upper echelon, world class, looking-down-on-you snob, living in a private bachelor suite, fully furnished with a closet full of Jack Perry and Victor Ellis designer suits. She didn't know, or didn't want to know, that there were two faces to the man she loved.

Lyin' Ryan. He was making money hand over fist from his practice. Those rich little old ladies paid well. He was covering his mortgage, and his staffing, and salting money away. That son-of-a... liar. Her dear, sweet, precious—*no good, filthy, rotten Lyin' Ryan.*

THIRTY

MARY SHUFFLED into the kitchen in her nappy pink bathrobe and fuzzy pink slippers, drowsy eyed, her dark hair tousled. She stood with both hands gripping the sink, staring out the window as if wondering why she was there. Her unadorned lips were dowdy and pale and the somber morning light exposed fracture lines around her mouth. She raised the back of her hand, stifling a yawn, looped a lock of hair around a finger and tucked it behind her ear, then reached sleepily for the coffee pot. The aroma was a wake-up call reviving her as she poured coffee into her waiting mug. Taking it in both hands, she brought the steaming cup to her mouth and turned to lean against the counter, staring at her husband.

Bill pretended not to notice. He sat the kitchen table, triangulating maps.

"What's the matter, couldn't sleep?" she said.

Bill looked up, acknowledging her, his droopy eyes dark with shadows. "No, actually I couldn't. I was restless most of the night."

"You're obsessing."

"No, I'm not."

"Yes, you are."

"Am not."

Through the window a drab gray blanket of light fell on Mary's shoulders, the low morning sun struggling against a thick fog. But the kitchen table, under a stained glass lamp hanging from a brass chain, was brightly lit. The yellow light illuminated Bill's work. His hair was disheveled, his eyes heavy. He'd been up most of the night.

"Bill, I know you. You're obsessing."

"Look Mary, I..."

"I can see what you're doing."

"You have no idea what I'm doing."

Mary thrust her hand out, waving her fingers. "What? All those maps, Mexico all over the place, weather reports, flight schedules, hotel pamphlets, and I'm not supposed to know what you're up to. You must think I'm blind, or stupid, or both!" Her face was sullen, her eyes focused on her cup. She took it in both hands, bringing the hot liquid to her mouth to hide behind its wall of steam.

"I'm just trying to figure out where they might be."

"Uh huh." Mary blew across the rim, sweeping the vapor away before taking a sip. Cast iron skillets and copper ladles dangled from hooks over the island stove, spinning like a mobile. She reached up and turned a shiny pot that mirrored her reflection, the metal clanking against a long-handled spoon. "And if I believe that, I bet you got land to sell in Florida."

"Mary..."

"Bill, that's not it, and you know it. You want to be there. You miss the action."

Bill eyes were heavy, bolstered by bags, puffy and red. "Mary, I tried to get in touch with Daniela. I couldn't reach her. A man answered the phone, said he didn't know a Daniela and hung up. I tried the police but they didn't know anything. I tried Lonnie's mission but I couldn't get through. I gather the earthquake hit them pretty hard. I've tried everything I can think of, God knows I've tried, but everyone seems to have disappeared, and frankly I'm worried."

"You're obsessing."

"I am not. I'm concerned, that's all."

"You're obsessing."

Bill dropped his face into his hands, rubbing his eyes. His pencil was sandwiched between his fingers, bouncing up and down. He was still smoothing his beard as he raised his head. "Look, you met that pastor, a nice guy, right? Well, right about now he's down there messing with a bunch of guys who would just as soon slit his throat as look at him. I can't help being concerned."

Mary shook her head, then raked her fingers through her tangled hair. "Oh boy, and that's supposed to make me feel better, knowing you want to go down there. Bill, I know you. I can read your mind. You think you should be helping."

Bill's brows narrowed, an exasperation emphasized by eyes already watery and red. "And you think otherwise? Mary, you know what will happen to those kids if someone doesn't intervene? You read the articles. You said they were nauseating. Little boys being sold to pedophiles, hidden in basements and forced to have sex with grown men, passed around from one pervert to another. You know most of them don't live till their teens. They're just castaways, the unwanted lower hordes of humanity—*right*—so who cares? No one's looking for them, strangled and buried in some backyard, used, abused and tossed aside, and then another child is brought in to take their place, keeping the market alive and healthy. And the girls sold as prostitutes. Remember the article I showed you, the one about that fourteen year old they found in Florida being used to service as many as thirty men a day? And you don't think it's right to want to help them?"

"I didn't say it wasn't right. I just don't want you involved. You said the problem was so big there was no way to attack it, remember? 'One of the largest criminal industries in the world,' you called it. 'Absolutely massive.' Saving these kids isn't going to stop what's happening. It won't even make a dent."

"Yeah, so Corrie ten Boom and Schindler and the like shouldn't have hid the Jews they did because they couldn't stop the Nazis from sending millions of others to the ovens, right? Yeah, that makes sense."

"Bill, I won't have you running off half-cocked into some situation where you could get yourself killed."

Bill laid his pencil on the table and pushed back, his chair scraping across the kitchen tiles. "Look, Mary, I'm not going to do something stupid."

"You're right, you're not. I won't let you. If you really want to do what's right, you'll think about your family. You'll put us before someone you hardly know. It's not that I don't feel sorry for those kids, or for, what's his name? Lonnie. I met him, remember? I'm sure he's a very decent person, but I have little ones of my own to think about. And you need to think about them too. What's more important, a bunch of kids you've never even met, or your own children? And I'm talking about Angie too. She needs you. If something were to happen to you, I don't know what she'd do. I want you to think about that. Then I know you'll do the right thing." Mary picked up her steaming coffee and shuffled her pink slippers past Bill into the living room, ending the discussion. Bill could hear the little boys squealing to get her attention, *"Mommy! Mommy! Mommyeeee!"*

He stretched out. His Levis needed washing and his plaid flannel shirt was frumpy from a two-day wear. He folded his arms across his chest and crossed his legs at the ankles, looking down at his damaged foot, a ball of wadding bound up in a fat knitted sock. He could think of a lot of reasons for not going. What could he accomplish on crutches anyway, though he hardly ever used the crutches despite Mary's constant reminder about what the doctor said. The problem was, she was right. That's what made it so hard. It wasn't like he had to go, but if that preacher or Daniela or those kids got hurt, or worse yet, killed, how could he live with himself?

THIRTY-ONE

LONNIE OBSERVED the village from behind a wall of needle leaf palms and scrolling vines. He'd made mission trips to dozens of remote communities in the Sierra Madre del Sur, but this one he did not recognize. There were no telephone lines, which was not unusual, but it meant there was no way to call for help. The only building of substance was the one Raúl described—the tavern. Perhaps the owner had some kind of two-way radio. He'd seen that in other villages, but he didn't see an antenna. Even if there were such a radio, he wouldn't know how to use it.

A man in the courtyard was loading gunny sacks onto a train of burros tethered to a post. There were no farms nearby, a few small gardens perhaps, but the land was too steep and the soil too rocky for growing. The man was probably a trader. Village women were adept at weaving baskets and looming colorful jute blankets sought by tourists, commodities they could exchange for staples like corn, beans and flour, but their husbands probably worked for Miguel on the plantation. Lonnie watched as the man hefted the bags over his shoulder and then flipped them onto the backs of the animals one by one, lashing them securely in place along with a conglomeration of wicker bowls and hand-painted pottery. He loosed the anchor and coiled the rope in his hand as he began to walk. The other end was hitched to the lead donkey's bridle. The animal waited until its neck was fully stretched before yielding to the tug, but then lurched forward. Before long, all three donkeys were following him out of the village, meandering down the same trail Lonnie and the children would be using. They would have to be careful. Should they encounter the man he might share their whereabouts with others in a nearby village, but he could worry about later. What he needed now was to find the name of this town so he could pinpoint their location.

Lonnie scanned the area for other signs of life. There were goats in one pen, chickens in another. A robust smell of donkey dung invaded the air. He caught movement to his right and ducked, but it was just a denim shirt hanging on a broken limb in the breeze—*a shirt?*—man, a clean shirt would be nice. His own was soaked with blood and had dried stiff as cardboard. His back looked like a brown tie-dye stain. Perhaps he should borrow the shirt. Whoever hung it there probably didn't need it. They'd left it outside. But that would be stealing. He pushed the thought from his mind.

The sun, like a yellow haze filtering through the village, was warm on his shoulders. Lonnie saw smoke rising from several of the stick huts. Fires were lit, meals were being prepared, people were getting ready to start the day. But the man with the donkeys was the only one he'd seen outside so far. Chickens clucked and scratched, and goats bleated with bells clanking.

There wasn't much else to see. The tavern was Lonnie's only hope. It was the only building of any substance. People had to receive mail, and it was not delivered door-to-door. It was dropped at a central location, which in this case had to be the tavern. Somewhere in that building was a letter with the name of the town on it. *Had to be.* And such a letter would let him know where he was.

Lonnie turned and limped back to the waiting group. He lined them up and headed down a narrow ravine until he was sure they could no longer be seen from above by anyone on the trail. They stopped when they encountered a wall of vertical rock. It was a natural fortress surrounded by trees. *Perfect!* He herded the children inside.

"Okay Raúl, I need your help." Calling upon Raúl for the task he had in mind defied logic. The boy had refused to acknowledge his authority. And Luis had only shown subservience. But that was the point. Luis would obey him, but it was not likely Raúl would obey

Luis. Then again if Luis saw that Lonnie left Raúl in charge, he would comply obediently.

"I want you to watch the kids. I'll only be gone a few minutes, half an hour at most. If I don't come back, take the children and do your best to get them to safety." Then he turned to Sofía, whose eyes skittered away. "Sofía, you're second in command." Then to everyone else he said, "I want you all to stay here. Just do what Raúl tells you, and be quiet."

LONNIE CREPT up to the village. The tavern was made of logs covered with clay painted cream yellow. The sun glared off the walls brightly. He kept his footsteps light, moving quickly toward the tavern, trying to avoid being noticed. He doubted the building would be locked. The village was too small to have a problem with thieves. He approached the front. An arch formed an extended porch over a door that was slightly ajar. He slipped into the shade and used his knuckles to push lightly on the wood. The door slowly *creeeeeaked* open. He tensed, his body coiled to spring, waiting to see if anyone responded to the sound, but the room settled back into quiet. He walked in. If the men Raúl reported seeing were around, they weren't in sight, which meant they were either asleep in the back or had taken up shelter in one of the huts. The five or six tables in the room were cleared and wiped. He glanced about, trying to determine where they might keep letters. There were only two possibilities: behind the bar, or behind the cash counter. He tried the bar first.

Though most people in a town such as this would only want tequila and beer, the bar contained the ingredients for making an assortment of drinks. There were spoons and swizzle sticks and stainless steel shakers, and cans of salt—but no letters. At least none he could see. He was moving quickly when he heard loud snoring. *Yikes*, someone was sleeping in the room on the other side of the wall. He could feel his heart pounding. The snoring was so loud it was like they were in the same room, which made Lonnie realize any noise he made could be just as easily heard. He envisioned two pistol totin' bandolier wearin' desperados, descending on him with guns blazing—*but they wouldn't have guns, not in a small village like this*—would they? He tiptoed to the cash counter. *Ah*, lots of paper here. Newspapers, a few magazines, receipts, and *yes*, a letter. He slipped it out from beneath the pile, but it turned out to be an empty window envelope. Whatever was inside had been removed, taking away the address. He set it down and at the same time saw the corner of a piece of paper sticking out with a logo printed on it. There it was. He reached for the letter and shook it open. It was an order confirmation from a liquor distributor in Mexico City, and right on the front was the address: Terciopelo's, Peñasco, Mexico. *Peñasco?* He'd heard the name before, but couldn't say he'd been there. In his mind he could see it on a map. He used his imagination to connect the dots back to Posada. If he was right, they were about forty miles away, a good distance more than they could cover in a day. And that was assuming the trail was well marked and easy to follow. It also assumed they would not encounter anyone with the notion of turning them in, but he didn't want to think about that. At least now he knew where they were. That was the important thing. Posada was southwest of their current position. If he had to, he could follow the sun. It would set in the west over the ocean, and from there it was turn left and head due south along the coast. He would get these children home.

I don't like this, Mamá. It doesn't feel right. Don't you see? We're being led by a foolish man who doesn't even know where we are. How can we get where we're going if we don't know where we're at? Right now he's down there walking into a trap, and he wants us to wait and be caught with him. It would be better if we all split up and went different directions. At least then some of us would get away. When Mariana is praying, do you hear her prayers? Can you maybe break in and talk some sense into her, Mamá, please?

RAÚL SAT by himself, wondering what would happen if he just took Mariana's hand and walked away. She'd probably refuse to go. *Why?* Blame it on the missionary. The madman had mesmerized her. She was under his spell. Maybe she was intrigued by how much pain he seemed willing to endure. But that didn't make him a friend. A friend would have helped him confront his foes—not cower and run like a dog. A coward, that's what he was, afraid, a man who would rather let himself be beaten up than stand and fight. Maybe she felt sorry for him. Maybe he should leave Mariana with the missionary while he went back. Those men still had to pay for what they'd done. His parent's death had to be avenged. But what if he couldn't find her afterward? No, it was a dumb idea. He wouldn't even know if she'd made it to safety. The missionary was crazy, down there marching around in broad daylight with a banged-up face. It was bound to draw attention. You can't trust a crazy man. What if he were captured? He'd be forced to reveal their whereabouts. Raúl jumped to his feet.

"Okay, I want everyone to get up. We have to move." The group sat looking at him, their eyes white against their burnished brown skin. Raúl looked at Sofía, then at Luis. "Tell them to get up! Now!"

Luis was twiddling with a stick, doodling in the dirt at his feet, the shoulders of his dark sweater powdered with dust. He raised his eyes, his huge glasses slipping down from his nose. "The man said to wait here."

"He put me in charge, and I say we move."

"We need to stick together. These woods are full of animals and he's the only one big enough to scare them away."

"What animals?" Raúl raised his arms with his finger curled like claws. "Ooooh, lions and tigers. You better hope not. Not the way I see you run."

Luis stood and raised his stick like a club. "Go! You're the one who wants to leave! You've wanted to leave since we started! Go! Go on! Get out of here!"

Raúl raised his hands defensively. "I'm not going anywhere. I just want to make us safe."

"How? By going somewhere else? You want to get us lost? People get lost in the mountains all the time! And it's the rainy season! The weather can change in just a few minutes and if we're caught in a storm the trail could wash out and..."

"Keep your voice down. You want everyone knowing we're here?"

"If we move, the padre won't know where to find us."

Raúl puckered his lips. His eyebrows furrowed in. "I can take care of that. We'll move to a different location, but someplace close, and as soon as we're settled, you come back and get him. Look, we have to do this. If he's captured, they might force him to talk, and he'll lead them right to us."

"He would never do that!" All heads turned toward Sofía. It was the first time anyone had heard her speak in days. Her dark hair fell around her face, accenting the fire in her eyes.

"You don't know that. They have ways of making people talk, drugs and things like that."

"I don't believe it. You saw what they did to him. He would never betray us."

Raúl's lips puckered again, his eyes hunkered down. "You don't get it, do you? If he'd let me kill those men, we wouldn't be here. He's the reason we have to hide. He's just a coward."

Sofía placed one hand on her hip and brought the other up, tracing circles around her ear. "You muy loco, that's what's wrong with you! That man risked his life for us! Look at his face! Don't you see what he did? Look at the blood on his back!"

Raúl could see she too was duped by the missionary's magic, but he didn't have time to argue. "Okay, maybe you are right. I hope so, but why take a chance? Look, all I'm asking is that we find another place close by to wait. Luis can stay here. If anyone else shows up, he'll come and tell us, and we'll sneak away. But if the padre comes back, fine. We'll regroup and leave together."

Jaunito stood and bent over to dust the legs of his dark blue polyester slacks, his loosened tie hanging to the ground. "Maybe he's right. It can't hurt, long as we don't go too far."

Mariana took Raúl's hand, implying she was ready to go with her brother.

Luis shrugged his beefy shoulders. "I guess I *could* come back and get him."

Sofía looked around the group. She rolled her eyes and sighed.

"This is crazy," she said.

Raúl took off, leading them further down the ravine. They were in a dry creek bed. They had to climb over large stones and lower each other down from rock ledges. Sofía complained that her dress wasn't made for climbing and Juanito's suit sprouted a hole at the knee. At least he and Mariana and Luis wore jeans. He found a place where they could scale the hill, turned, and started ascending a large shelf of granite, their feet sending loose dirt and gravel down the slope with the sound of rain. They came to a place where the ground leveled slightly, and found themselves in a clearing surrounded by yucca, palm and Mexican ficus.

"This will do," Raúl said. "Luis, you go back and wait, but stay out of sight. If the missionary comes, bring him here. Give him half an hour, but if he doesn't show, we leave. Okay?"

Luis nodded. He spun, skittering down the steep mountain, his bulky legs sliding in the loose gravel with dust pluming at his heels. He reached the bottom and disappeared into a tunnel of green.

LONNIE HEARD heavy footsteps, then a thump against the wall and a low-throated grunt accompanied by a flash of movement. Suddenly there was a man filling the back room door, a large man, huge by Lonnie's estimation, even bigger than he'd imagined from the description given by Raúl—*the bartender.* The man stretched and yawned, his eyes filled with sleep. He didn't seem to notice Lonnie standing there. Lonnie quietly dropped the letter and turned, ready to run. He didn't want the man to see his face. The bruising would be a dead giveaway, but then so was his bloody back, though in the shadowy light it might look like dirt. He took a step, heading for the entrance.

"Hey, what you doing, amigo?"

Lonnie kept walking. He raised his hand, indicating there was no cause for concern. "Just looking for a letter. Hasn't come. Gracias." He walked to the door, keeping his back to the man.

"Uno momento, por favor."

Lonnie didn't stop. Outside the door, other people were out of their huts. A woman was scattering seeds to chickens, and a man was shaking out a blanket. Both had their backs to him. Lonnie brought a hand up to cover his face and turned away, but neither seemed to notice. He rounded the corner of the building, saw the rusted hull of a pickup, and headed for the ferns, fading quickly into the forest.

The tavern owner came out looking both ways, but the intruder was gone. He stretched and yawned and went back inside.

Lonnie was scurrying fast, heading back to where he'd left the children. He looked over his shoulder to see if he was being followed, but when he turned back around he tripped and fell, skinning his knee. His face came within inches of a pool of water left by the rain. He was thirsty. He drank a minuscule amount, skimming off the surface, but mosquito larvae and other slime made the draft uninviting. He lay there a moment knowing he had to pick himself up and hurry on, but not wanting to suffer the pain of struggling to his feet. His body wasn't made for this kind of abuse.

The rings of water settled, mirroring his face. His countenance was bruised and swollen, grotesque as a matinee monster. What would Nicole think of him now? And shouldn't he be thinking about Trudy? He should have asked her to marry him long ago. She was the only woman he'd ever known—in the Biblical sense. She was the mother of his son. He was obligated to work things out with her.

He pulled himself up, struggled to his feet and continued on, stepping over one rock after another, bending one tree limb back, then one more, sweeping tangles of leaves, moth cocoons, and spider webs out of his way. At times the brush was so thick it gripped him like a pair of hands holding him back. But always he escaped. He pushed through another vine, breaking free, and struggled forward again, looking back, though he was sure by now he wasn't being followed. Still he had to hurry. The man had seen him—the same man who tried to hold Raúl for ransom—and just because he wasn't chasing him didn't mean he hadn't found the other two men and notified them. So he hurried on. They could be fetching a dog to follow his scent. He had to rescue the children.

There was no trail here. This was uncharted territory. He was heading down a ravine. The trail leading into the village, the one they had come in on, should be just above him on his left, but he couldn't be sure. Nothing looked the same. He'd planned on going back the way he came, but things seldom work according to plan. He saw a tree and recognized it, broken off in the middle, hollow, barkless and bleached with a ragged-edged top. He nodded. Now he knew where he was. They were just a bit further up the valley. He trudged forward, peering through the leaves, expecting at any moment to catch a glimpse of movement through the branches, but saw nothing. He neared the rock wall. They weren't there. Where had everyone gone? His eyes darted about. Maybe he was mistaken. Maybe he had left them somewhere else—but this looked like the place. Had they been captured? He was standing in the exact spot where he'd left them, he was sure of it, and they were gone. *Tha-thump, tha-thump, tha-thump,* his heart pounded. *Oh God, why? Why? What now, Lord?* He could feel his face starting to flush, pinpricks of sweat sprouting on his lip. He flinched at the sound of a voice behind him.

"Señor, over here." Luis stepped out of the bush where he'd been hiding. "I'm glad you're back. We must hurry. Raúl moved everyone to a safer place, further away. But they will leave if you do not return soon."

Lonnie released a sigh and started to relax, but it was short-lived. His skin went taut and a flush of anger saturated his face. *Why would Raúl do such a thing?* He had specifically told them not to move. The boy couldn't wait ten minutes without challenging his authority. As soon as he was out of sight, Raúl persuaded everyone to disobey. He was probably hoping he wouldn't return at all, or if he did, that he wouldn't find them. This boy was trouble with a capital T. He'd tried to show faith in him. Lesson learned. He wouldn't do it again.

LONNIE WAS limping along in the lead again. He'd found the children unharmed, anxiously awaiting his return, which gave him a faltering sense of relief, however fleeting. If Raúl was trying to mobilize a coup, he'd failed. Unfortunately, Lonnie had thought to use the occasion to congratulate the boy on a job well done and thus lay a foundation of trust upon which to build. Instead, it was all he could do to hold his tongue and keep from saying something he might later regret. Every step he took reminded him of the pain it cost him to bring these children home. Nothing was going to stop him from making sure they were safe.

He was pushing the children hard. They were plowing through the woods, hoping to circumvent the town, climbing over granite shelves covered with moss, tangles of vines, and clumps of fallen trees, struggling up and down and in and out, like tunneling through piles of spaghetti. But though the children were his chief concern, his mind was occupied with another thought. His relationship with Nicole.

She was a lone traveler on the cerebral cortex of his brain, but why she was there, he didn't know. Well, maybe he did know, but didn't want to admit it. For three years they'd been seeing each other, even flirting, but not once had they ever breached the boundaries of friendship. He wondered if his thoughts weren't akin to those of a man contemplating adultery. Trudy had been his first love. Nicole was someone new. Emotions were fickle, shifting with the sands of time. He couldn't rely on his heart staying with Nicole any more than with Trudy. As much as it bothered him to think about it, he was better off with Trudy. At least that way he wouldn't feel so conflicted. She was, after all, the mother of his son. And he was sure of her answer. She'd marry him just to gain a larger stake in the company. It was a done deal.

He looked up at the cloud-stippled sky, the sun filtering through the leaves. It was time to venture back onto the path. He wasn't sure the trail was safe. He couldn't guess how many people used it during the day, but they couldn't travel by night, and they wouldn't be able to cover any real distance while tramping through the jungle. One way or another, he had to get back. He had to get these children home. He owed Nicole an explanation.

THIRTY-TWO

THE SUN, burning through the magnifying glass of the atmosphere, was scorching the earth. Father Paulo's heavy brown vestment turned dark under the arms. He was beginning to feel the weight of Sebastian's concern. They had retraced the route taken by the boy, over cobblestones and hardpan, leaving prints in the dust of rubber-soled huaraches and the serpentine tracks of the chair on wheels. Throughout the mission, the village, and door to door they went, the good Father rolling Sebastian along like a pushcart. The sisters in the hospital had only three patients, two with minor injuries suffered during the earthquake—a jar that fell on a woman's head, splitting her crown between her braids, a few sutures needed; a fractured toe received when a man slipped while chasing a bottle that had toppled over and was rolling across the floor; and one white-haired woman with so many wrinkles you'd think she was one foot in the grave, but who was recovering nicely after passing a kidney stone. About half the town's population were still at the coffee plantation. Behind the orphanage, children were playing games of jump rope and hopscotch hedged in by bougainvillea and ivy, the nuns supervising. But no one, not one single person, could recall seeing Nicole after the earthquake.

Now it was early afternoon and after half a day of inquiry with no results the priest was starting to fear the worst. Nicole was missing and they had run out of places to look. She had vanished, *poof,* disappeared. He couldn't discount the possibility she might have wandered into the rainforest, however unlikely. She was a nurse.

She knew the dangers of taking jungle excursions unescorted. She frequently treated those who engaged in such foolish forays. Or perhaps she'd gone to see if anyone at the plantation was in need of medical attention. He would call and ask if the phone lines weren't down, but he doubted she was there. It was a five-mile hike, and not one she would take without letting someone know. Which left only one other possibility. She had been in the church when it collapsed, but he didn't want to think about that.

Earlier, still convinced Nicole would show up at any moment, he'd commissioned volunteers to start moving the rubble, but so far the work hadn't begun. A few men were loitering by the pile but they appeared to be lost, wondering why they were there. It made no sense to be standing outside in the extreme heat of the day. The stereotype of the Mexican with his knees pulled up under his sombrero taking a siesta was spawned more out of self-preservation than lethargy. The southern sun forbade midday work, but they had come in answer to the priest's call.

He surveyed his former chapel, trying to keep a handle on his emotions. His heartache was akin to the way Jeremiah must have felt when he saw the temple in ruin. He could identify with the weeping prophet. But the temple was eventually restored and, as he looked out over the massive pile of rubble noting portions of the foundation were still intact, so they too would rebuild his church. At the top of the mound, because it was last to fall, he saw the old brass bell. Tarnished from years of use it lay three quarters buried in the dust and debris of crumbled stone. He raised his arm to point, his long looping sleeve sliding down to his elbow. "If you men are looking for something to do, I suggest you start with that bell," he said. "Let's at least save that."

Three men, their eyes shifting from one to the other, turned and started climbing the pile, and upon reaching the bell began removing the clay, broken brick, and pieces of wood surrounding it. They had to push, then pull, then push again, then pull, working it back and forth to set it free.

Sebastian tugged on Paulo's robe. "Father, what about Nicole?"

"I don't know, son. I don't know." And the good Father didn't. About all they could do was list her as a missing person. He'd barely finished the thought when the butterfly he'd seen earlier rose up over his shoulder, floating softly on a breeze, flickering red and blue in the sun. It was bouncing up and down on a current of air, wings flapping briskly, then pausing, then flapping again. It came to land on the very spot he'd seen it before. The butterfly, his metaphor of the resurrection, the very example of rising from the dead. Then he heard the bell ringing, loud and clear, freed from the heap of rubble, and a voice, audible only in his mind, saying, *"Roll away the stone."* Roll away the stone? The legacy of Lazarus. He stooped and picked up a brick, tossing it aside. The men on top of the hill began to descend, carrying the bell which now, with its clapper freed, was ringing loudly.

PERHAPS AS much as six feet below, Nicole heard something for the first time. It was muted, but it sounded like a bell. Deep in the tunnel of her chest, her heart skipped a beat, then picked up speed and started to race, making it hard to keep her breathing slow. She was hearing sounds. There was a world outside. They were alive, perhaps even sending help. She was still fighting to remain conscious, trying to stay awake, fearing if she let herself sleep it might be forever. It was the greatest struggle of her life.

But at least now she had something to think about. *Her rescue*. Perhaps now she could get her mind off Ryan. She had tried *so* hard, but the little pervert kept intruding on her thoughts. She shouldn't have gone looking for him. She should have stayed home...

She approached reception. The girl was new. Nicole hadn't seen her before.

"Hi, I'm Mrs. Jensen. I'm here to see my husband, Dr. Jensen."

The girl's eyes widened. "Oh hello, nice to meet you." She smiled, young and pretty, and then looked down to check her calendar. "Unfortunately, he's not here. He's stepped out. His next appointment isn't for another half hour. I think he's resting in his apartment."

"Apartment?" Nicole's eyebrows raised, not sure she heard right.

"Yes, would you like me to call and see if he's there?"

"No, that's alright." Nicole turned looking for a seat, thinking to wait, and then remembered there was no apartment. She must have heard wrong. She leaned over the counter, looking down on the receptionist. "I'm sorry. I work across town. I'm rarely able to stop by during the day, but I was in the area and, you know how it is, I thought I'd surprise Ryan and see if he had time for lunch, but I'm here so infrequently I've forgotten the suite number. Do you know what it is?"

"Yes, I think so." The girl's finger began running down a list. She turned a page. "Here it is, number 1200."

Nicole wandered down the hall to the elevator, already edgy because she wasn't sure how the news she'd come to share, the news that just couldn't wait, would be received by Ryan. Light coming from the window at the end of the hall spilled onto a pair of burnished brass doors. She knew the building had apartments. That was obvious. Only the bottom floors were used for business. She had passed several stores on her way in, all focused in one way or another on seniors. Senior comfort, senior travel, senior fashion and senior health. The top floors were condominiums. It was likely they too were designed for seniors. The doors opened and she stepped inside, eyeing the rows of plastic buttons, twelfth floor, right on top. She placed her thumb on the button and watched it light up. The doors *dinged* closed. She rode up in silence, contemplating how she would break the news to him. Maybe she was wrong. Maybe he'd love the idea. She waited, assuming the doors would open onto a long hall with rows of apartments, but instead they opened to a short hall with windows on either side, leading to a pair of double-hung doors with one brass number square in the center. Number 1200 appeared to be the entire top floor. *This can't be right.*

She traveled the short corridor to the door. The walls on either side were glass, the light streaming in, expansive. The entire universe could see her. She had the strange sensation of being naked. She raised her hand and started to knock but with her knuckles suspended midair, suddenly lost her nerve. No, this wasn't right. This place had to belong to someone else, and she was about to intrude on their privacy. What would she say if a complete stranger opened the door? She waffled. *Oh, go ahead and knock.* She lowered her arm. *Or not.* She turned, ready to make a hasty retreat. She could always discuss it with Ryan at home. She took three broad steps but then stopped, straightened herself, rolled her eyes to the ceiling, wiggled her fingers, and spun around again. There was probably a reasonable explanation. This was probably the apartment of one of his patients, someone too ill to come to him. He was probably making a house call. She raised her hand to knock again, but stopped short. The receptionist definitely said this was *his* apartment.

She reached for the knob, pausing with her hand on the cool brass to whisper a prayer. She gave the knob a silent twist and quietly slid the door open. Nothing could have prepared her for what she saw. Sophistication and elegance, a blend of wonderful plush carpets, decorative plants, artwork, cushy leather upholstery, and a glorious floor-to-ceiling view along the west wall of the entire LA basin. Her heart sizzled like a pan-fried egg. This had to belong to someone else. What if they walked in and found her standing there? How could she explain herself? Then she heard her husband's voice and, though startled, let go a sigh of relief. Her chest was pounding as she tried to determine where the sound had come from. The room with the door ajar spilling light on the floor? She started over, and then heard a second voice followed by a gentle laugh, soft, sultry and feminine. She was getting nearer and nearer, now hunching forward with her hands across her stomach, leaning to bring her ear closer to the door so she could hear better, but with each step more afraid of what she might find. She stopped just outside, waiting a second, her breathing rippled but deliberately slow, her heart thudding loud enough to be heard and hard enough to ruffle her blouse. She stooped over, listening more intently, aware she was eavesdropping but determined not to jump to conclusions. It might be innocent. She reached out and slowly pushed the door back—and her heart stopped.

THIRTY-THREE

BILL HUNG up the phone. "Oh my gosh." He spun on his heels. "Now what am I gonna do?" He looked out the window. The weather was dark and dank for the second day in a row. Snow flurries were starting to fly. He dropped into his derrière chair, the springs squeaking as he swiveled to face Angie.

"You heard that, didn't you? She's gonna scream, I know she is, but it wasn't my doing." He leaned forward, rubbing his palms together with his elbows propped up on his knees. He buried his face in his hands. Having been awake most of the night, he was tired, so tired he could fall asleep right there. His hands smelled like soap, reminiscent of a recent shower. He rubbed his eyes. He could recall feeling this way before, back-aching-tired, stressed. She was right. He was obsessing, only obsessing wasn't the right word. He was guilt-ridden, and he was worried, and the combination made him want to do something. Only up till now he'd been frustrated because there was nothing he *could* do, but that just changed and instead of feeling better, he now felt worse.

He raised his head. He no longer saw Angie, but instead he saw a coffin, and a room where he sat alone, trying make sense of his wife's death. At the end of each pew were flowers lining the aisle, and a podium replete with floral bouquets, splotches of color to brighten a colorless day. Death has no color, he realized. At least not for those on this side. Laurie would be there waiting when he crossed over, but for now their relationship had met its end, and all the platitudes about how it was time for him to move on and start over rang hollow, because he was the one who put her there. The once beautiful, vivacious, energetic, resourceful, smart-as-a-whip reporter was lying in that casket, cold and lifeless as stone because of him, and he would carry the guilt of that—forever. He'd put her in harm's way. He'd sent her in to fight the good fight. Be brave, good will triumph. He'd put the gun in her hand, but when she fell, he was miles away, and now, now when he should be repentant, atoning for his misdeed, he was perpetrating a second act, the armchair general sitting at home safe and sound, sending others in to fight. Something better not have happened to Daniela, God forbid, and yet he couldn't shake the foreboding feeling that something had. But now he had the prospect of doing something, only it meant hurting Mary, his second chance at getting it right, and he was determined not to blow it. She was right, his family had to come first, which is why he hadn't insisted on going. But she was also wrong. He didn't want to be part of the action. He wasn't some kind of white knight on a crusade. He was worried, that's all.

He felt a chill and rubbed his arms. Mexico would be nice this time of year. He should just pack up the whole family and take them with him. But that was out of the question. The boys needed their schooling, though Mary took care of that at home and could probably do it on the road, but no, it wouldn't be the same, and Angie didn't travel well. No, that was a nonstart. How was he going to explain this to Mary? He took a deep breath, stood, and walked into the den.

The room was warm. A fire flickered in the hearth, radiating heat and the woodsy fragrance of smoldering birch. Mary was sitting on the divan, reading a newspaper, enjoying a tea and bran muffin. Swirls of steam looped up around the rim of her cup. She brought it to her lips, looking over the rim as Bill entered.

Ah, good, he thought, at least she's relaxed. Bill walked over and sat down beside his wife. The couch was thick, wheezing as the cushions compressed under his weight. An afghan of pastel yarn was stretched across the back. He wanted to soften the blow, but he wasn't sure how.

Mary continued to read, the orange glow from the fire smoothing the lines exposed by the harsh morning light. Her brunette hair was wavy, rolling across her shoulders with wisps highlighted by the yellow flames. She was a handsome woman, a beauty, a natural. It was one of the things he liked about her most. Makeup was fine, a sweep of mascara transforming tired eyes into coals of fire, a brush of blush lifting and emphasizing the contour of cheekbones, and just a shade of pink breathing new life into deflated lips, but she didn't need any of that. Just a gentle hint of perfume was all she needed. Just a waft of Evening Rose, and he was hers to command. He who plucked the thorny rose was a fool—but worthy of blood was the fragrance of this gentle flower.

She folded the corner of her newspaper as if to see what was on the other side, and then looked up. "Did you want to say something?" she asked.

Bill hesitated. Flowers can't bloom in hard ground and, like it or not, they were about to cross rocky soil, but it was too late to turn back. "I, uh, you know what you said this morning about my going down to Mexico, about how I was being obsessive? I guess you were right. I mean, at least in the sense that I've been preoccupied. I can't seem to get it off my mind, but I wasn't planning to go down there, at least not seriously."

Mary's eyebrows arched.

"Alright, I don't have any other way to say it, but just to out-and-out say it."

"Say what?"

"I just got a call from my editor and, you're not going to believe this, but he's assigned me to cover the earthquake down in Mexico. You know, the one we saw on TV last night. Huge. You saw the damage. Another major quake is big news." Bill paused to let his words sink in, and then added, "Thing is, he wants me down there right away."

Mary placed her cup on its saucer, and turned to set the saucer on the coffee table. She folded her newspaper. Bill noticed the earthquake was the front page story, but all she said was, "Right."

"Honey, I did not call my editor. I did not plant the suggestion in his mind. He called me, right out of the blue. This has nothing to do with Pastor Lonnie or the missing children."

"I see."

"No, I don't think you do. He wants me to cover the story of the *earthquake*. Apparently it registered seven point five on the Richter scale, which makes it a major quake. It wasn't that long ago we had a tsunami, then the hurricanes in Florida, followed by an earthquake in Pakistan. A lot of people are questioning what's going on, everyone from environmentalists blaming global warming, to prophecy buffs declaring the end times. The birth pangs, you know, earthquakes, famine and pestilence, that sort of thing, but the point is people have a lot of questions, and that makes it newsworthy. Anyway, it's not my choice. He wants me down there."

Mary's face was void of expression, but Bill could discern a tightening of her skin, tiny crow's feet exploding as she crinkled her eyes. "So, let me see if I understand this correctly. Out of the blue your editor calls and wants you in Mexico, the very place you were mapping out this morning, so you have to go down there, but you're not going to interview that drug lord. You're not going to look for your pastor friend, and you're not going to try and locate Daniela or those missing kids. You're just going to go down there, cover an earthquake, and come home. Am I hearing you right?"

"No I didn't say *that.* I said my editor wants me there to cover the earthquake. Honey, look, the earthquake happened just outside Oaxaca, which happens to be where everything else is going on. You and I both know if there's any chance of getting a story about what's happened to that missionary and those kids, I have to do it." He wrapped his arm around the back of the couch, thinking to massage her neck and savor the softness of her hair, but she leaned forward, scooting out of reach.

"I need this," he pleaded. "This story has to be written."

She crossed her arms, twisting to face him. "I'm sure you mean the story about the earthquake, right? Because you already wrote about the Mexican kids and the increase in child trafficking. It's in print, been there, done that, old news. I mean, *why* would you want to rehash a story that's already been written?"

Bill pulled his arm back and leaned forward, lacing his fingers together with his elbows on his knees. "Because now an American is involved. No one paid attention before because they couldn't relate to something taking place in another country. There was no direct impact on their lives. But now an American's life is at stake. People will pay attention to that. Honey, what's going on down there has to be dealt with. Someone has to write about it. We have to get the story out. For the sake of children everywhere, for the sake of future generations, for the sake of our family."

"Don't," she raised her hand, "don't you dare bring your family into this. Don't you dare. If it was really your family you cared about, you'd stay home."

"Honey, I just can't sit by knowing things like this happen every day, and not do anything about it," though in trying to defend his actions, Bill knew he was avoiding the truth.

Mary turned and sank back into the couch. She picked up her paper and snapped it open, barricading herself behind its wall of pages.

"So, you're mad then."

She bent the newspaper, looking over the top. "Mad? No, I wouldn't say I'm mad. There's just nothing to discuss. You've made up your mind. You're not asking me. You're telling me what you're going to do."

"That's not fair. I'm being told to go down there. It's an assignment. I don't have much choice."

"Bill, you're a columnist. You write about what *you* want to write. Your editor rarely tells you what to do. Why is he sending you instead of one of his regular reporters? Associated Press has the story, why not get it there like everyone else? Why send anyone at all? All it takes is a few calls to verify facts, and a few photos off the wire. It doesn't require sending someone of your caliber down there."

"Because I've been there before. I have contacts. People will talk to me because they know me. That's what he wants, someone who can get in there, get the real scoop, and add a little local color. And

I'll have to write that story. The one he wants. I'll have to give them a complete accounting of the earthquake and all the damage and everything that's happened, including interviews with the locals. And that will keep me busy. And out of trouble."

Mary raised her newspaper, hiding behind its stately wall, feigning to ignore what he said. He stood. "I know this is bothering you Mary, but this is something I have to do. Try looking at it this way. I was curious about what had become of that missionary, but I didn't ask to go down there. I got a call from someone who doesn't even know about Lonnie, or his kids, and all of a sudden I'm being sent into the exact same vicinity. Coincidence? I don't think so. More like Divine providence. I think maybe God wants me involved in this, and if that's the case, you don't have to worry. He'll protect me. Now, I don't have much time. They booked me on a plane leaving at three this afternoon. I'm gonna need you to drive me to be airport so you'll have the car while I'm gone."

He waited to see if she would say anything, but she remained silent, staring at her paper. Bill knew what she was doing, the silent treatment, voicing her objection without saying a word. It was her way. She avoided arguments that led to hurt and put distance between them—*smart lady.* He admired her for that, no not *admired*, he *loved* her, loved her dearly, but that wasn't going to help, because this was something he had to do. His conscience was more of a tyrant than she was. It wasn't about to let him off.

THIRTY-FOUR

LONNIE SHIELDED his eyes with his hand as he looked up into a white sun, waiting for the glare to subside. Seagulls were spiraling overhead, their gray-tipped wings batting a cloud-laced sky. It was confirmation they were heading in the right direction. Just follow the sun. They had to reach the coast, eventually.

He was driving the children hard, though they had not eaten nor slept well the past two days. They were on the mountain ridge trying to maintain a vigorous pace, but his strides were longer than theirs. Their smallish feet were barely able to muddle along, let alone keep up. And their bodies were frazzled and worn. They had climbed out of a culvert formed by the face of two mountains, working their way up over ridges, rocks and rills, and around the tangled root systems of fallen trees. They had started where Lonnie found them, not the place of Lonnie's choosing, but where Raúl had hidden them after bringing into question Lonnie's leadership. That was okay, Lonnie could forgive him, but he was keeping an eye on the boy. They'd had to go through the jungle to circumvent the town before getting back on the trail. It had been difficult. The bush at times was so thick it was like slogging through a mop, but at least the ravine traveled in the direction they needed to go. When they reached a rock too big for the small ones to scale, Lonnie, now sure they had bypassed the town, grabbed onto Mariana, pulling her up, and set a new course up the side of the mountain. She was followed by Juanito and the others fell in line. Lonnie asked Raúl to keep up the rear and make sure no one fell behind or went missing. So far, it had worked fine, even when squeezing through labyrinths of brush and multitudinous vines dangling from low overhanging trees. Lonnie maintained a constant lookout for predators. Mountain lions and pumas were known to roam these parts, but it was the snakes they worried about most. So far they'd seen only a few, and they had quickly slithered away. Insects notwithstanding, for the most part the animals left them alone. He could only hope they hadn't trudged through some kind of poisonous plant that would have them itching and breaking out in hives, a much more subtle threat, but it did no good to worry about that.

It took the better part of an hour to break through the barricade of brush and seize the crest of the mountain, an hour Lonnie counted lost because it was an hour going up, not forward. An hour that made them more tired without moving them closer to home. An hour forfeit to the enemy. There was no doubt the men who had seen Raúl, or the man who'd seen Lonnie, would contact Miguel and report they were in the area. Learning about the reward only verified that Miguel had not given up the chase. They had to keep moving.

Lonnie felt a tug on his shirt. He looked down. It was Juanito.

"What?"

"Why do the clouds have flat bottoms?"

Lonnie looked up and saw the cumulus bounding across the sky. They did appear to have their bottoms flattened as though they were sitting on a plate of glass high in the sky, but he didn't have an answer.

Luis spoke up. "They're not flat. They're blocking the sun which creates a shadow underneath that blurs things so you can't see the bumps. They just look flat, even though they're not."

Lonnie turned. *Impressive.*

"My dad was a professor at the university," he said proudly. "He took me to work and I would read all day in the library. My dad said I was a genius, but..." He shuffled his feet, his eyes beginning to fill.

Lonnie crouched down. "Hey, look, my dad's gone too. I know it's hard." He gave the boy a hug and felt a moist puffy cheek against his own and rotund arms squeezing his neck. "Sometimes things just happen."

"What happed to the lady in the truck?" Juanito wanted to know. "Did she go away?"

Lonnie turned and nodded. "Yes, far away."

"She's dead. Just like my dad, your dad, and his dad. They're all dead!" Raúl intoned.

"My dad's not dead."

"Come on guys, lighten up. We have to keep moving." Lonnie started forward. He had a mental picture of where Posada was on a map. Even if they pushed hard, they couldn't cover twenty-five miles in a day. And that meant they were at least three, maybe even four, days away. Somehow, he had to inspire them to keep moving.

And there was something else—*Nicole. Why?* He had to stop feeding his lust! *Lust, lust, lust, lust, lust,* like rust corrupting the deep inner recesses of his soul. It was the way he'd previously felt about Trudy until Nicole entered his life, and the shift in his affections made him realize he was unstable, and he knew what God had to say about that. "Having eyes full of adultery that cannot cease from sin, beguiling *unstable* souls." *Ouch.* So he worked at keeping his mind focused on Trudy and how to forge a lasting relationship with her. He was determined not to fall.

Lonnie stopped, and the children drew up behind. Children in every sense of the word. The oldest was probably Sofía, and she was only thirteen. Probably next was Raúl, whom he knew was nine, and then Luis, whom Lonnie judged to be about seven or eight. The youngest was Mariana, at only five, though the one Sofía carried wasn't much older. Sofía had Juanito wrapped around her like a life preserver. He wondered how she kept it up. Even if the boy were only six and light as a feather, it still had to present a strain. Sofía was raw-boned and frail, with long arms and muscles that appeared stringy, much too gaunt to carry a flesh and blood load over mountainous terrain. And yet each time he tried to help by holding his arms out to take the boy, she pulled back as though he were trying to remove an essential part of her body—*please, sir, take my heart, but not my child.* Okay, *fine*, as long as she could handle it. Overall, the kids were behaving. Lonnie felt like a teacher with a group of second graders on a field trip. He had to keep his wards in line while avoiding unforeseen danger. They seemed to understand the predicament they were in. To keep their spirits high, he tried making it a game. *"See, we're the good guys, and the mean old bad guys are out to find us. Like hide and seek. We have to stay ahead so they won't be able to catch us."* And so he kept moving them forward, encouraging them, assuring them that everything would be fine as soon as they were home.

BILL SQUEEZED himself into the tight seat of the airplane. He was wearing his travel clothes, denim shirt and pants, with hiking boots to provide extra support for his twisted ankle. He settled in with his elbows on the padded armrests. A woman to his right blew her nose on a wadded tissue. He hoped it was an allergy. He didn't need to catch a cold. His knees were bumping against the seat in front of him. He was a large man and the legroom afforded by economy class was sparse. It felt like his knees were propping up his chin, but his employer wasn't known for wasting money on cushy travel. He pulled the seat belt across his waist and locked it in place. Didn't matter. He wasn't there for a comfortable ride. He was there to assuage his guilt.

The final numbers of those injured in the quake weren't in yet, but surprisingly there were no reported deaths, at least none so far, though there were bound to be, and Americans would be listed among them. Getting their names would have to be a priority. But his real concern was for Daniela and his new friend Lonnie. He identified with the man, crazy though he was. But now the whereabouts of both of them was unknown, and that made him nervous. How could he risk the lives of two people if he wasn't willing to go himself? Armchair general? *Nuts!* He hadn't learned a thing.

The engines were churning. The woman beside him smelled of pungent perfume. Her red hair was frizzed into an Afro globe around her face. She was checking her makeup in a compact mirror, applying a coat of lipstick. He nearly laughed when she puckered her lips and smacked the air with a kiss, but stopped short when her elbow almost popped him in the eye. He made sure not to look at her. He didn't want to talk. Bill leaned forward, struggling in the small space to store his laptop under his seat. There would be time for writing later. The seat belt sign was on. A blond flight attendant was going through the motions of showing travelers where they could find oxygen masks and puke bags. Her arms were choreographed, pointing this way and that, her movements as mechanical as a robot. The engines were done warming up. Bill felt the pneumatic breaks release with a *thunk.* His stomach tightened. No matter how many times he flew, he always felt anxious when the plane started to roll. The slate gray buildings of Portland International were moving back. He was on the aisle, but craned his neck to see if his family was by the window waving, ducking his head under the chin of the woman to his right. They weren't, or at least he couldn't see anyone.

Maybe Mary, once he got home, would see he'd acted for the greater good. She hadn't said a dozen words all the way to the airport, and standing in the boarding area with his daughter and two sons she looked like she was sucking ice cubes. He could feel the chill. The boys were unfazed. They were used to their dad taking business trips. It was all he could do to keep them from racing through the airport, knocking over other people's luggage. And Angie, well, she understood. Defending the defenseless was as much a part of her as it was of him. She was a girl of exceptional faith. She would trust God for his return. Mary, on the other hand, could only imagine the worst, and her emotions ran deep, causing her to fear what she couldn't control. But he knew her heart. She too wanted what was right. Her struggle was on the inside. Her sense of justice warred with her maternal instinct. He'd hugged her, transmitting all the reassurance he could muster, but it hadn't been enough. Their kiss goodbye seemed as artificial as the kiss of plastic dolls. He could always tell when Mary was mad. She didn't have to say anything. He could read her lips.

THIRTY-FIVE

PAULO'S HANDS were cut and swollen, heavy blisters starting to form. He regretted not having gloves but finding a pair would take too much time. He was thinking of quitting anyway. It was pouring rain, drops splashing in the dust, soaking into the ground. Every shallow on the landscape was now a muddy pool. Lightning blazed like a strobe light, *light-dark-light-dark-light-dark*, on a swirling backdrop of soggy sky. The murky air was filled with the roar of thunder. Father Paulo stooped to pick up another brick. He pushed hard, pulling back, pushing, pulling, pushing, trying to break it free. It was time to quit. His dark brown frock was soaked, weighing him down like a wet blanket. Those long looping sleeves restricted free movement even when the robe was dry, but now the heavy material was clinging to his skin. His hair was matted to his face with water running off his chin. He gripped the stone again, yanking it out and securing it in his arms, teetering backward as he stood, elbows flailing out as he settled it against his chest. He trudged a few feet and dropped it at the edge of the waiting pile.

His helpers had quit. They had stayed with him, unexpectedly working through the heat of the day, creating a pile nearly three feet high and ten feet across. But when the ground turned to mud, and the pasty goo stuck to their boots, they excused themselves saying they would return once the rain stopped. Paulo had watched, envious of their sanity, as they trudged off to the tavern to dry out and refresh themselves. He couldn't fault them. There was no rationale for digging in this kind of weather. He couldn't explain why he was still there, because he didn't know. He yanked and pulled and pushed and pulled at another brick, breaking it free, grunting as he lobbed it into his arms and stumbled backward. He moved toward the pile carrying the block of adobe, and dropped it, relieving himself of its weight. He couldn't explain why he was doing any of this, except *"Roll away the stone"* was echoing in his head. He could hear it loud and clear, though he had no idea what it meant, unless someone was down there—*Nicole?* But if she *were,* surely she was dead, so pushing himself didn't make sense. Yet something drove him to pick up another stone, and *another*, and *another*, and *another.* How could there be so many? He turned and staggered back to his work.

The butterfly was gone, having moved to drier climes. There were better places to weather the storm. Even Sebastian had abandoned him. The priest refused to solicit help. He felt awkward about imposing on anyone. He couldn't communicate the sense of urgency he was feeling, and therefore asking people to work through the heat of the day, let alone in a downpour, was absurd. He pulled another rock into his arms and looked up, the rain pelting his face. At least it was cool. He deposited his load on the pile, his skin itching under a mix of dirt, sweat and rain. He reached up to scratch, leaving a muddy smear on the side of his face. He stumbled forward, wiping his hands on his already muddy frock, and held them out with his palms turned up. Those cuts would hurt in the morning, but Christ suffered worse for him. Blisters and cuts could not compare with nails. So he walked back to the pile, taking another stone, pulling it back and forth, clawing at the dirt. He reached for a stick to scrape mud off the rock, and leaned into the task of trying to break it free. Once again he pulled it into his arms, tottering backward, turning and dropping it onto the pile. He didn't know how much longer he could keep it up. Maybe just one more stone, then he would quit. Moving the entire cathedral, one stone at a time, would take forever and for what? He still didn't know. He would have to quit soon. He didn't have the strength to go on. Maybe just one more brick, then he would quit. *Maybe just one more stone.*

AT FIRST, Nicole thought it was an aftershock and it terrified her. She thought the sand might shift and remove what little space she had, but as the repeated rumblings continued, sending vibrations through the ground, she realized it was thunder. Now her concern turned to worry that the rain might turn the dirt to mud causing it to seep in around her, or that she might drown if the water found its way into her tiny pocket of air. She was struggling to stay calm and keep her breathing slow and even. She tried to maintain an element of pragmatism. Perhaps a quick death would be preferable to the endless agony of the thoughts poisoning her mind...

The woman reached for a blanket, jerking it around her shoulders. The man beneath her raised his head and turned, noting the interruption. The eyes expressed surprise, then wrinkled in outrage at the intrusion. It was Ryan. He lurched forward, grappling with the covers while rolling onto his elbow to prop himself up.

Nicole stood there, her mouth agape, color draining from her face. She averted her eyes, embarrassed, hoping if she looked away she would awaken from this bad dream and the abhorrent scene would disappear. She didn't know how to react or what to say, so she focused on the furnishings. Low profile chest of drawers in high gloss, ebony black, pristine white statuary and vases, the expansive view of LA over the balcony, sun shining through the tinted glass. *Who is this girl, and what is she doing with my husband? And what's my husband doing with her?* Random thoughts swirling like bits of confused confetti. She glanced back at the couple and the nightmare returned. She blinked to clear her vision. They were still there, Ryan and the girl scrambling to cover their offense. She needed to say something, but words wouldn't come. Her husband was in bed with another woman. What could she say? Nothing came to mind. Her vision began to cloud. Then she remembered why she'd come.

"I'm pregnant," she said.

She turned, feeling hot and light-headed, her ears buzzing and the room growing dark. She staggered backward, leaning on the door frame for support. Her face burned, the color flooding back. She fumbled across the room, knocking over a lamp as she bumped into the table by the couch.

"Nicky Girl, wait!"

She heard the words, but they didn't register. She saw flickering shadows in the room as her feet scuffed the carpet, passing the table, the chair, the door, another chair, all in strobe light shades of gray.

Somehow she managed to reach the front entry and round the corner. The elevators were at the end of the hall. She was in the glass tunnel, the light from the windows exposing her humiliation for all to see. She smashed the elevator button with her thumb three, four, five, six times, waiting for the door to open—*Come on, open!*—but nothing happened. "Nicky, wait!" She looked to her left and saw a door with a glowing red Exit sign over it. She plowed through, entered the stairwell, and began pounding down the steps, *whump, whump whump. How many floors were there, twelve?* She could beat the elevator, easy. She pummeled toward the bottom, her hand on the handrail for support. The room echoed with the sound of leather shoes clopping on concrete stairs. The walls were a blur of barren cement, pockmarked holes, and spray-painted graffiti, a stark contrast to the suave decor on the other side. The walls resembled her soul, ravaged, stripped bare, and written about in rude language. She felt embarrassed, like she'd been caught in some indiscretion, not the other way around. He would pay for this. He would pay big time. *Whump, whump, whump.* Ten floors to go.

Her breath was coming in gulps. She felt anger, she felt rage, she felt betrayal, but she couldn't find her tears. *His apartment?* That couldn't possibly be. They didn't have that kind of money. They were living paycheck to paycheck, barely able to juggle the bills and keep the electricity on. Now she understood why he discouraged her from dropping by unannounced. "I can't be disturbed while I'm seeing patients." *Haw!* If she wanted to see him, she had to schedule a lunch, but the key word was, "schedule." He didn't want her hanging around the office. He would meet her. She'd only been further than the lobby one time, the day she'd been given a perfunctory tour of the facility, and that was barely a few days after he'd signed the mortgage. He'd wanted to show her what he'd bought. In all their years of marriage she'd only been to his office fewer times than she could count on one hand, partly because she didn't want to be there. He'd bought the cursed place without her consent, but only once had he ever asked her to stop by. Only once, and that was because his car was in for service and he desperately needed a patient's lab results for an afternoon appointment, and she was in the area and able to pick them up. But that was the only time. He'd made it clear that unannounced visits were forbidden. Eight floors to go. *Whump, whump, whump.*

At least she'd delivered her news. Let him stew on that for a while. He'd always insisted she use birth control. And she had. She hadn't become pregnant on purpose. She'd followed his instructions to the letter. Blame it on preoccupation, or distraction, or maybe good old-fashioned carelessness. She must have accidentally missed a day, it happened, but could one day make such a difference? She didn't know. All she knew was she'd started feeling ill in the morning and losing her breakfast a lot, so she bought one of those self-test kits because there was no other reasonable explanation. And there it was. Blue. She was pregnant. She'd tested herself three times.

She should've waited until Ryan got home to tell him, but he hadn't come home the night before, and she wanted so desperately to tell someone and he had to be first. It would be difficult financially. She'd have to take time off work, a few months at most, and it meant another mouth to feed, but this was their child, flesh of their flesh, bone of their bone. Once he got over his initial shock, he would love the idea. Six floors to go. *Whump, whump, whump.*

What was she supposed to do now? Divorce him? She had justification, but her child would need a father, and like it or not, that father was Ryan. *Why? Why? Why, Ryan? What did I ever do to you?* She felt humiliated. The nurses in his office must have known. People talk. Maybe not the receptionist. She wouldn't have sent her into the lion's den if she'd known. Four floors to go, *whump, whump, whump,* the clomping of her footsteps echoing off the walls.

She knew the woman, or at least she'd seen her before. She was one of Ryan's nurses. She remembered getting the look. A beautiful woman, enough to make her jealous, brunette hair flowing in long shiny waves, perfect pouty lips, cheeks dusted with just enough blush, stunning, but the eyes were cold, hard and glaring, a piercing look so sharp Nicole felt severed at the knees. She'd confronted Ryan about it, but he assured her she'd been mistaken. The lady was probably thinking about something else when Nicole caught her eye. She had misinterpreted the look she'd received.

She'd seen the woman one other time, at a Christmas party hosted by one of Ryan's peers. The gathering was for doctors and their wives. Nicole remembered wondering why Ryan's nurse was there, seemingly unescorted. She'd gone to powder her nose and come back to find Ryan talking to the woman. Once again Ryan reassured her it was nothing. They were just talking business. Right! That's probably what they were doing today, talking business—the business of a pro. The corner of Nicole's mouth raised slightly. The little tart probably charged for her service. She wouldn't call it making love. Two floors to go, *whump, whump, whump*.

She was numb. She hadn't even started to cry. Perhaps it was because she'd been there before. She'd gone to work early and was sitting at her desk slipping her brown-bag lunch into a drawer and setting her purse under the desk when her boss's wife Trudy walked in. She'd glanced up, startled. She wasn't expecting anyone.

"Oh, hi Mrs. Striker. I don't think Harlan's in yet. At least I haven't seen him." Her words, in retrospect, were said with that same innocence expressed by Ryan's receptionist.

Trudy Striker was strikingly handsome. She stood with the windows behind her, causing her auburn hair to resonate with light, a knowing look on her face, one of ambivalence, but also of tolerance for the pitifully uninformed. One thing could be said for Harlan—he liked his playthings pretty. They were bimbos for the most part, long on looks, short on brains, but definitely pin-up material, Playboy centerfolds, every one. And Trudy, though not as buxomly as the others, was a ten in the looks department, with her full lips, dusky hair, and those penetrating green eyes. Max, Harlan's right-hand man, had suggested Harlan put her in the movies, something Harlan flatly refused to do. The same way, Nicole now realized, Ryan made sure she didn't become his nurse. Wives should not be given a window into the private lives of their husbands for their own good. Better to live in ignorance than have to deal with truth. Why can't husbands be happy with what they have? Trudy was a looker, which was why Nicole remained jealous of her, even today. Lonnie had once loved this woman too, though she'd ultimately married his brother. When Harlan died and Lonnie inherited the company, he'd tried to resurrect their relationship. Trudy had been receptive, for a time, but it wasn't about love. It was about holding onto a lifestyle, the out-on-the-town in a chauffeur-driven limo to drop a thou on another vain outfit or hairdo. Latching onto Lonnie was about getting what she wanted, but not about love. Trudy stopped loving long ago, and much of it started that very day.

"Oh, he's here. He called last night to say he was staying in town, working late again."

"I wasn't aware of that."

"Nor should you be."

Trudy turned and stood in front of the heavy oak doors with raised brass lettering that read, "Striker Films, Harlan Striker, President." She started to knock, but hesitated with her hand suspended in space as though thinking about it, and then changed her mind and reached for the knob, turning it and throwing the door open wide. Nicole recalled it vividly. Long seconds passed while Trudy just stood there, not saying a word. Then she spun on her heel and walked out. A call from inside the office followed. "Trudy?"

Trudy reached the front lobby just as Harlan came hobbling out of his office in boxer shorts, his hand extended like a police officer trying to stop traffic. "Trudy, wait!"

Maybe that's why she didn't feel anything. She'd already seen the movie. Déjà vu. And with all the excuses Ryan made for not coming home, business weekends, medical conferences, the all-night operations. *Déjà vu. Déjà vu. Déjà vu.* That was the thing about men. They were totally unoriginal, they all said the same things in just the same way, and she'd always known—*always*.

She threw the door back, and walked hurriedly through the

basement parking lot, her heels echoing on the pavement as she fished in her purse for her keys. She scanned the garage looking for the hunk-a-junk Chevy she'd inherited when her husband bought the black beast, too distracted to remember where it was parked. The beast was there, groomed like a wild stallion in all its magnificent glory, corralled in reserved parking by the door, a shiny black and chrome steed. That was Ryan's bit. He always referred to the machine in terms of horsepower, comparing it to an animal. She stood over the car. The tinted windows were dark and in the low light her reflection was bright. She wasn't a bad-looking woman, perhaps a bit harried by the stress of the moment, but that was to be expected. Why wasn't Ryan happy with what he had? She walked around to the front, past the chrome grillwork and lights, on around to the other side. She didn't think about it. She dug her key into the paint and raked it along the side of the car, walking front to back, the sound of rasping metal echoing off the walls. Her heart was pounding. *Now that felt great.* She smiled. She crossed the aisle to her own car, used the key to let herself in, and sat looking straight ahead. Then the adrenaline rush dissolved exposing her to raw emotion. Her shoulders began to heave and her body to shake. She brought her face down to her hands and began to sob.

THIRTY-SIX

LONNIE STOOD at the edge of a cliff facing the Pacific, his hands resting on the shoulders of two brown-skinned, dark-headed children, one on either side, as his entourage gathered around. He was breathing deeply, his hair and clothes whipping in the wind, drinking in the compost of seaweed and brine, a smell as old as the earth. It reminded him of home. He doubted he'd ever seen a grander sight. The boundless plain stretched as far as the eye could see, with a bright yellow dab of sun on the horizon dividing the deep crimson of space from the bottle-green water.

For Lonnie, it was a sign. It meant they had made it. They had trudged through pounding rain, slip-sliding while holding onto each other until the trail finally leveled off and cut sharply to the right. And when the rain stopped, a fog rolled in so thick they could barely see their feet. As they felt their way through the windowless mist, the jungle came alive. Thousands of birds, frogs, and mosquitoes *cawed, crroooaked* and *eeeeinnnnned,* creating an eerie drone of marshland sounds that had them constantly looking over their shoulders. They were following waterways that ran off the mountainside, stepping into swampy muck that left their shoes filled with silt and their ankles fraught with leeches, moving steadily downhill and heading west. Lonnie could feel the ocean pulling him the way a wave is pulled back from the shore.

Miguel's men, if still in pursuit, were not to be seen. Perhaps they were waiting in the next village, or in every town along the route, but they didn't appear on the trail. Now with the sun sliding into the horizon, soon to be sucked into darkness, Lonnie had a choice to make. They could stay on the beach where surly waves were pounding the shore, or follow the path along the shadowy slope of the ridge in the direction of home. Posada would be in that direction. The town sat on the edge of a cliff much like this, a thousand feet above the ocean. But that was at least another thirty miles and, as anxious as he was to get the children back, they needed to rest. The wind was heavy, tousling his hair. Bullets of water stung his face as the cold wet air cut through his shirt. "Okay," he said, tweaking his voice up a notch to be heard above the wind-scathed ocean, "this is as far as we go for today. We'll spend the night on the beach and pick it up in the morning."

From where he stood, the cliff dropped vertically onto a tidal shelf, but the wall was riddled with outcrops of rock that could be used like steps to make their way down. "I'm going to go first and pave the way," he said. "Raúl, maybe you should go last in case someone needs help."

"I...I don't think I can make it," Luis complained.

"Sure you can. It's only thirty feet to the bottom. Just follow me." Lonnie stepped down to a lower shelf, turned and stepped back the other way, zigzagging back and forth till he reached the bottom. He stood with his feet in the sand and cupped his hands around his mouth calling back up. "See, it's easy."

Mariana hopped off the edge followed by Sebastian and then Sofía, their feet scuffing along, kicking gravel over the side, hundreds of pebbles bouncing against the rock wall.

"Go on, Luis. I'm not waiting all day," Raúl said.

"I...I...I can't."

"Yes, you can. Go on, get moving. You don't want to be left up here alone with all the wild animals. *Ohoooooo.*"

Luis adjusted his glasses and stepped down to the first ledge, looking back over his shoulder with a tepid smile, but seeming uncertain about where to go from there. He backed up, trying to see over his stomach, but went too far and when his foot found air instead of ground, he spun around and slipped onto his butt. Cries rang out from the bottom. Lonnie snapped his head around, craning to look. Luis had stumbled and now sat on the edge with his feet dangling in space. He started to cry.

"Shut up, Luis. Quit being such a baby." Raúl stepped down to the shelf. "Give me your hand."

Luis tightened his grip. "I...I...I can't."

"What are you gonna do, sit there and cry? Give me your hand."

Luis started to raise his arm but Raúl didn't wait. He grabbed him by the wrist and yanked him up. The boy was squirming but was able to get a foot on the shelf and finally stood.

From down below, Lonnie whispered a silent *Thank You.* He cupped his hands around his mouth again. "That's okay Luis, it gets easier from there."

The entire group was standing in a huddle with their backs to the wind, but even in his bulky sweater Luis shivered, and Sofía's long dress was wrapped tightly around her legs, flapping. The horizontal sun cast streams of yellow on their clothing, their dark hair highlighted with tints of red. Lonnie turned to Sofía. "I need you to stay here and watch the group. I'm going to try to find us some shelter."

He pulled off his shoes and headed for the shoreline. The surge tickled his toes as he entered the water, leaving heel and toe prints in the hard wet sand that crunched under his feet like granulated sugar. The waves were phenomenal. Translucent and bottle green arching with the sun at their backs, they looked like photographs he'd seen in surfer magazines. *"In search of the perfect wave."*

He walked to a jetty where waves driven by the wind were crushed against the rocks. He climbed aboard just as one hit with a *whoooooosh* sending spray fifteen feet into the air. Lonnie curled his shoulders and ducked as the rainbow of foam fell, soaking his back, the saltwater cutting into his wounds like a knife. *Ahaaaaa, oh, man!* He shivered and began shaking his hands loosely at the wrists. The rain had moved on and he was just beginning to dry. The wind and waves sloshed against the shore with the sucking sound of water gurgling down a drain. The cloudless sky was red toward the sunset, fading to blue in the east, but the wind was unabated. He wrapped his arms around himself, deciding it was time to head back.

MARIANA AND JUANITO stood on a bed of tiny shells overlaid with strands of washed-up seaweed. They twisted their feet, digging them in, and then sat down to examine the shells more closely. They sparkled with infinite color. There were blues and peaches, roses and tans, hazels and violets, aquas, greens, browns and yellows all beaming like rainbows across a surface of a million tiny oyster-shaped faces no bigger than a fingernail. Juanito's tie hung in the sand. It was loose, but he refused to take it off. He began digging, his hands excavating trails and building mounds. "The sand's so soft."

"It's really ground-up shells. See this?" Luis held up a pink fan-shaped shell. "The sea is full of these, and it's constantly churning and grinding them up until the pieces are so small they're like this." He dug his hand into the sand and brought up a scoop, letting it filter between his fingers.

Raúl got up. *Why is the sky blue? What makes it rain? Where do shells come from?* He'd heard about enough from the walking encyclopedia. He decided to do a bit of exploring on his own. He wasn't about to let his sister sleep in the cold. He rubbed his sleeveless arms as he meandered down the beach in the opposite direction from Lonnie.

LONNIE CRAWLED over rocks with sharp crustacean edges. He rubbed his hands together, massaging his palms to alleviate the pain as he crossed the sand, disappointed he hadn't been able to find anyplace better to stay than where they already were. They could make do, but it would be cold. He found the children huddled together down by the water, exposed to the onshore wind sweeping across the beach, trying to stay warm in the purple shadows of evening. He gathered them around him to explain.

"It's okay, señor Lonnie. Raúl found us a cave to stay in. See?" Luis pointed a chubby finger at a dark, gaping hole in the shadowy seawall, his sweater, laden with sand, sagging at the elbow. A wave crashed on the shore and the children scurried to escape its reach.

"We can't stay in that. When the tide rises, it will flood that cave."

Juanito dusted his jacket and tugged on Luis's arm. "What makes the tide rise?"

"It's a function of the moon and gravity. See, the moon's gravity pulls the water toward it, causing the water to swell in that direction. When the moon is directly overhead, that's when it's high tide." Then Luis looked at Lonnie. "It depends on how old the cave is. My dad says some caves are very far back because the waves have eaten away at them for years and now the water doesn't reach them anymore. It also depends on the seasons. The tides are different at different times of the year. The sand in this cave is very dry. I already checked. Raúl's right. This is an excellent place to stay."

Lonnie's shoulders lifted, resigning himself with a sigh. He was weary of competing with a nine year old. The opening was high and a good distance back from the pounding surf. "Alright," he conceded, "I suppose we should at least check it out."

THIRTY-SEVEN

WHAT BILL saw out the window of the plane on approach to Mexico City was not the tall vaulting towers of the modern megalopolis, nor the history suffused into the antiquated buildings composing one of the oldest cities in North America. What he noticed was the ugly gray cloud covering the city in perpetual gloom, the smog rising from the industrial sprawl, and the emissions of millions of vehicles trapped by the seven-thousand-foot mountains that bordered one of the largest cities in the Western hemisphere on three sides.

After landing, with his scuffed hiking boots planted firmly on the ground and a hand raised to shield his burning eyes, the view looking up was no better. *Skies should be blue, not brown.* He hated smog. That's why he'd left Detroit. The cool mountain climate of Oregon kept the air clean. He stood mopping his brow with a handkerchief. He hated the heat. He didn't mind working up a sweat with an axe and a woodpile, not if it came from honest toil, but the sweat that poured from a man as he hustled a taxi was the fruit of wasted labor. He sent the first two drivers on their way because neither could speak English. A flood of cars *beep, beep, beeped* down the crowded boulevard with drivers yelling and cutting each other off. He waved at another cab that whizzed by leaving him in a cloud of dust. He hated big cities.

A tiny beetle finally pulled to the curb looking like a sour ladybug—*lime green.* Of all the models in Mexico City, Volkswagens dating back to the sixties were among the most popular. They had to number in the thousands. Most of them were taxis crawling through the streets like bugs on blades of grass. Bill squeezed inside. A number of splits in the seat were covered with duct tape, others were not. He turned to sit down, then jerked his hand away, waving his fingers. A red welt began to rise. *Dang-busted blistering vinyl.* He sat with his legs pulled up under his chin, rubbing his palm, and melting in the heat. From a plane with no legroom—to *this.*

The hotel looked presentable. The white stucco walls were free of weather stains and the roof, characteristic of Spanish architecture, was shaped with half-moon rust-colored tiles. He stood tall, exchanging pleasantries with the man at the front desk in perfect English, pleased to see the travel agency had done their homework. He took the note handed to him, scanned it, and shook his head, squinting to make sure he'd read it right. The message directed him to call another room in the hotel. He curled the note in his fingers and hefted his bag, nodding at the clerk.

His route took him down a breezy corridor. Colonnades supported arches with potted ferns swinging from chains. Bordering the tiled walk were gardens sprouting clusters of oleander and bougainvillea. In the center of an open-air courtyard was a fluted fountain gurgling with foamy water.

Bill slipped his key into the lock and turned the deadbolt, feeling it snap, but the door didn't budge. He leaned forward with his shoulder pressed to the wood, forcing it to pop open. He had traipsed through the lobby standing erect, parading his full six-foot frame without a wince, but as he crossed the threshold into his room he let the pretense drop. He should have listened to Mary. He should have stayed off his swollen foot, but following good advice was never his forte. The flesh was red on the palm of his hand. He rubbed it, keeping the pink slip of paper lodged underneath his thumb. The note bore a simple message: "Call room fifty-three." His other hand held his only piece of luggage, a zippered nylon garment bag that he half pulled, half carried. *Wheels are for wusses.* He tossed the bag on the bed and sat down, *good firm mattress.* He reached for the phone looking at the piece of paper, *room fifty-three,* and punched in the numbers, biting his lower lip. It was answered on the first ring.

"Sí?"

"Uh, Bill Best here. I was asked to call."

"Oh sí, Mr. Best, welcome, welcome. Gracias. I was wondering, would it be possible for you to meet with me for a few minutes? I have something I, uh, I think you will find of interest."

"Who is this?"

"Oh, forgive me, por favor, I should introduce myself. My name is Santos, Santos Herrera, but of course we've never met. Please, if you'll allow me, I will explain, though I would much prefer to do so in person."

Bill hesitated. "Yeah, sure, mystery and intrigue, gets 'em every time. Three questions, señor. When? Where? And most of all, why?"

"Where? How about down in the hotel bar? And how about now? As to why, I'll explain that when we meet."

Bill bit his lip. Mr. Herrera, whoever he was, was in the loop. Must be some kind of correspondent. As far as he knew, only his wife and editor knew where he was staying, let alone when he would arrive. Someone was feeding the man information. He looked at his watch.

"Have I got time for a quick shower?"

"No, please, do not bother. This will only take a few minutes. I assure you, it will be worth your time."

Bill scratched his itchy scalp and rubbed the bags under his eyes. His bones were aching, his skin coated with dried sweat, and his beard hung from his jaw like a heavy mat. The last thing he needed was a meeting. "Sure. How about ten minutes?"

BILL WALKED into the bar, feeling the tension in his travel-weary back. He'd called Mary from his room but the phone hadn't been answered. She'd probably decided to stay in town after dropping him at the airport and would arrive home late. She didn't need much of an excuse to take Angie and the boys shopping.

He glanced around, his eyes becoming accustomed to the dim yellow light. A man was at the bar drinking with a woman who appeared half his age. They sat in the subhues of obscurity with their backs to the world, carrying on a muted conversation. It didn't appear they wanted to be disturbed—perhaps not even recognized. Behind them, a life-sized mural of a matador locked in a duel with a steamy bull was painted on the wall. Another man was seated by himself at a table in the center of the room. He wore a white sport coat and had a white Panama hat resting in front of him at arm's length. He fit the description.

The man looked up and caught Bill's eye. He sprang to his feet. "Mr. Best," he said, extending his hand. "Welcome. Please, have a seat."

Bill took a chair and leaned back, letting it absorb his tired body. It was padded black vinyl, a bucket shape that swiveled. He placed his hands on armrests that had scraped the table so many times white cotton poked through. The cushions wheezed under his weight. His host took a sip of a freshly served amber cocktail, his eyes visible above the rim of the glass. "Can I order you something?"

Bill raised his hand, waving him off. "Sorry, never touch the stuff."

The man raised his eyebrows. He set his drink down on a wet napkin and squeegeed water from the side of the glass with his finger, looking at Bill. "So, you're wondering who I am, and why I asked to see you. Fair enough. I'm a businessman, Mr. Best. I run a small import/export business, you know, bongos, donkey blankets, sombreros, just tourist items, nothing fancy, but I make a living. I have an office here in Mexico City and one in Las Cruces, New Mexico, so I operate on both sides of the border, but I'm here most of the time. That's why I asked to see you. I understand you want to meet Don Miguel Estrada."

Whaaat? Bill's eyes wanted to screw down on the man but he kept his face deadpan, trying not to let it show. *Okay, he's not from the newspaper.* Silent seconds passed. He sensed the man was waiting for him to respond, but in the parlance of negotiation, he refused to blink. He waited for the man to continue.

"Import and export are my chief concern, Mr. Best, or I guess by extension anything that has to do with international trade." He held his drink up and gave the liquid a quick flick of the wrist, spinning the ice cubes, then took a sip, pulled the glass away and smiled as he swallowed and set the glass back down. "This is risky business. Would you not agree we have to guard against an opening of our borders? Already it's hard to track things that slip by without notice. We can do this politically, of course, but governments change, social constructs, party loyalties, nothing stays the same. Even old dogs don't lie still very long." He raised his glass, took another drink and set it back on the table with a *clunk*, wiping his lip with a finger. "We have a saying: 'Only the past is more uncertain than the future.' This is why I asked to see you. Change is in the wind right now, even as we speak, and you need to know of it. I suggest you visit the west side of town. There's a place there, the El Diablo Hotel and Cantina, where men are gathering to discuss current events. They've been collecting there for two days, growing in numbers. You should go there. I'm sure you would find it of interest. Strictly, of course, from a writer's perspective." Señor Herrera looked at Bill again, waiting. He picked up his drink, poured back the last two swallows, and held up the empty glass, twirling the ice. "That's all I have to say." He wiped his mouth with the back of his hand, plopped the empty glass on the table setting the ice cubes clattering, and picked up the wet napkin to wipe his fingers. "It was a pleasure to meet you, Mr. Best. I'm sure our paths will cross again." He leaned over, sweeping his white hat from the table, slid it on his head and walked out, leaving Bill to wonder just what the heck *that* was all about.

POLICE CHIEF Maximilian Ortega sat at his desk with his eyes fixed on the wall, immobilized. His teeth were clenched, his compressed lips rendering a line of white where they pinched together. He held a pencil in both hands, rolling it between his fingers and thumbs. *This is not going to happen.* He snapped the pencil in two, his cheeks stiff as cardboard. Kids were taken from the streets everyday, but not his. *No—not his.* The others were back-alley children, and good riddance. They had to keep the neighborhood clean. The homeless propagated like rodents. Maximilian approved of Miguel, and people like him. They served a purpose. They were pest control, trash collectors, exterminators, but the unspoken rule was to leave children with families alone—and especially the children of friends.

It never occurred to Maximilian to follow up on the report filed by the priest who claimed several kids had been stolen in Oaxaca. It was out of his jurisdiction, thought missing person reports were routinely faxed to all state and local authorities and considered required reading. He'd buried his copy in the drawer with hundreds of others. They were looking for orphans, unwanted rejects, the dregs of society—not people. It wasn't his job to find throwaways. To the contrary. He was paid to look the other way. Only now, as he sat alone in his office realizing he might never see his son again, he saw a connection. The mission children had disappeared within a day of his son's abduction. It was likely they were on the same bus heading north, awaiting a similar fate.

Maximilian wasn't buying Miguel's version of the story. Not for a minute. He'd ducked the issue by pointing his finger at the competition. "I would not do such a thing," he said. The man was lying. Maximilian had been to the street where loosening lips meant cracking heads. Not that he was above the law, but a soft-spoken word bore little fruit and his more direct, heavy-handed approach got the job done. It was jurisprudence at a practical level. He'd always been a better cop than an administrator.

The folds of skin around Maximilian's eyes pinched into crow's feet when he squinted. He could feel the temple at the side of his head throbbing. He hadn't learned much, but what he *had* discovered pointed the finger directly at Miguel. Two witnesses had seen the abduction and both told the same story. The young man, still wearing his parochial uniform, had been standing in the schoolyard by himself when a lone assailant approached, picked the boy up, and ran for the fence with his hand covering the boy's mouth. It was a planned assault, carried out with determination on a specific target. The kidnapper had parked outside St. Mary's were he'd clipped a hole in the chain-link, gone in under the nun's noses, and ignoring the dozens of other children in the yard, pulled out Maximilian's only son, kicking and screaming. The description of the man right down to the cowboy hat and denim vest he wore, and the tattoos on his arms, to the vehicle that spit up clouds of dirt as he raced away—*the priest's report also mentioned the tattoos, and the dirty blue van*—fit only one man—Paco—a man he'd jailed several times. And Paco worked for Miguel, and no one who worked for Miguel did anything without the Don's blessing. Maximilian found himself with his hands balled in fists around the staves of broken pencil, his nails biting into his flesh. He pitched both pieces at the wall, but the splinters of wood were too light to make much impact. Not even a dent. He closed his eyes and took a breath. *The man's crazy.* Maximilian was determined to hunt him down. And God help him if they were unable to recover his son.

MIGUEL WAS PACING. He'd had to inform his client of the delay. They were reworking the schedule but at this point there was no way he could confirm a new delivery date. To expedite the order, he offered a substitute, but stopped short of saying the girl was missing. He should have known better. Suggesting a replacement only caused his client to dig in his heels. He had paid for *that* particular girl, and he expected to receive *that* particular girl. Now Miguel was backpedaling, trying to convince his client he wasn't pulling a bait-and-switch. Miguel turned and retraced his steps, his white shoes treading a groove in his twenty thousand dollar hand-woven carpet.

"I'm sorry, my friend. I have caused you a problem. I promise you will have your delivery. Yes, just a little delay. Sí. A minor inconvenience. The earthquake left us a mess, but soon as we get things cleaned up, we will bring the child to you. You have my word. Have I ever let you down? Good, I appreciate your understanding."

Miguel cradled the phone. He placed his hands behind his back, pacing the carpet with the ball of his thumb rubbing his cuticles. Those children better show up. He'd have them now if he hadn't left the job to farmers. Field hands made lousy mercenaries, but he'd rectified the problem. He'd dispatched his personal guard, a dozen highly trained professionals, to find the kids and bring them back. All he had to do now was sit and wait. The product would be returned, and more would soon be coming. And there would be no more screw-ups. Miguel's hands were wringing. Why was he sweating? He hated sweat. There was no need for it. The air conditioner was working. He could hear it humming in the background and feel its cool air chilling the moisture on his arms.

He had made a vow to the Blessed Virgin. It was a vow he intended to keep. Imagine stealing the child of the chief of police. *Another problem to be rectified.* Miguel felt his stomach wrench, releasing effervescent bubbles of bile. He brought a hand to his side and reached for his bottle of antacid.

He modeled obeisance. All the lighting of candles, his daily mantra of prayer, the genuflecting, they were sincere attempts to appease God whose retribution he feared. That place of torments he'd so often visited in his dreams. He would bow a hundred times, say a thousand Hail Marys, kiss each bead on his rosary, repeat a litany of prayers—*anything*—whatever it took to avoid perdition. *Please, my God, remember the good I do.* He popped the chalky tablets into his mouth and bit down.

But he had nothing to fear. Profit was the reward of labor, as punishment the reward of sin. He never exacted interest that wasn't due. He was determined, in all he did, to benefit others as much as himself. He was an entrepreneur, yes, but a philanthropist too. Was not his ulcer proof that he regretted letting so many people go? The families of the men he employed depended on him. It was only happenstance that caused the closing of one business to benefit the other. He would never sanction the laying off of men and have their families starve, just to flood the streets with more children. The very thought was ludicrous—though lucrative as well.

He abhorred the misunderstanding. The foolish missionary, like so many others, disparaged the work he did, but few were witless enough to refuse his endowment. Only those blinded by narrow-minded intolerance, who stumbled over minor transgressions while ignoring the greater good. He was doing what adoption agencies, bound by ropes of bureaucracy, longed to do, but could not—finding tens of thousands of children homes in the United States where they could partake in the best of everything. The men who bought these children were, aside from a few questionable quirks, basically good. They were wealthy—they had to be to afford him. It was their sexual proclivities that were misunderstood.

People should study history. Every society on earth had used children for sexual gratification, the Egyptians, the Persians, the Romans, the Greeks. And with the increased acceptance of homosexual behavior, man/boy relationships would soon find approval in North America as well. It followed logic. If children were allowed to have sex with each other, and men were allowed to have sex with each other, where was the wrong in letting men and children have sex with each other? Though for himself, he would vote to keep it illegal. Better for business that way. But there was certainly no harm in it. If starting young was what it took to gain a better life, then let the orgy begin. His children weren't being sold as slaves. They weren't imprisoned in unventilated sweatshops chained to sewing machines eighteen hours a day. It wasn't like sex was painful. Sex brought joy, ecstasy and pleasure. Where was the crime?

Miguel turned and started back across the room. His stomach was in knots, his forehead dripping. The dread he felt, that was Paco's doing. He couldn't risk selling the boy. They'd never get him across the border. Maximilian had the power to increase surveillance at every crossing. One slip-up leading to the boy's discovery, and—if he'd known who the child's father was—but it was too late for that. He'd let the young man see his face. Now the child had to be destroyed.

This, not the layoff of his men, was why sweat was rolling down his chest, never mind that electronic sensors controlled the climate in every room. This child had done nothing wrong. How could he light a candle and pray for the conciliation of a soul that had committed no offence? What would he say?

Miguel sucked in his cheeks. Something also had to be done about Maximilian. The loss of a loved one was a powerful, often unstoppable driving force. It was something he could no more understand than he understood the unfair opinion people had of him. A father's love was unfathomable, which was another reason he preyed only on the homeless.

Someday, maybe soon, he would retire to the coast of Spain. He had enough money. Another few years and he'd have more than he could spend. There were worse things than tanning on the deck of a gleaming white yacht. He crossed into his study, his spotless white silk suit rustling as his arms swung with renewed vigor.

The candles flickered, their tiny yellow flames dancing inside vases of red glass. He knelt and crossed himself in front of a bronze casting of Mary, opening his prayer book. "Oh Mother of Perpetual Help, grant that I may ever invoke thy most powerful name, which is the safeguard of the living and the salvation of the dying. Oh Sweet Lady of Guadalupe, let thy name be henceforth ever upon my lips. Delay not, Oh Blessed Lady, to help me when I call upon thee, ever repeating thy sacred name, and hear now my confession." He closed the book and stared into the statue's eyes. "I am innocent of this young man's blood, but I accept what is set before me. Is not the way of the cross that one should give his life for the sake of many? Sweet Lady of Guadalupe, I pray you wash my hands and purify me. Look down upon me with favor, for what I do, I do for the sake of your children."

THIRTY-EIGHT

THIS WAS no tourist attraction. There were no brightly colored crepe paper creations, trumpet troubadours, or spike-heeled dancers with flaring red petticoats stomping the floor in time with castanets. Not even hard rock, rap or disco. No, the Old Diablo Hotel and Cantina was an uncivilized puke-and-stagger watering hole for locals. The place was packed, hundreds of men standing shoulder-to-shoulder, drinking tequila in a haze of cigar smoke so thick it literally wafted to the ceiling and wrapped around the blades of the lazily rotating fans. If the building had an air conditioner, it didn't work. *Must be a hundred degrees.* Bill raked a denim sleeve across his forehead. The humidity hung like a transparent gauze, stifling circulation. There wasn't a man in the room who didn't have wet melon-shaped wedges under his arms. And the din was pervasive, the roar of men letting off steam, the rake and rattle of cutlery and clinking glasses, wood chairs scraping across wooden floors, all combined to make conversation unfeasible.

Bill looked at his watch—*after midnight.* He slid his finger under the flex band, relieving pressure on his wrist, and stood, ready to leave. He'd been there over an hour, and had yet to see why. The mood of the room seemed to waver between dejection and rancor, but that was probably the normal behavior of men who worked all day and drank all night. A few rounds of mescal would have Mother Teresa grumbling. Bill knew little Spanish. He'd keyed in on words like "empleo," *work*, and "dinero," *money*, but he hadn't heard anyone mention the name of Miguel Estrada, which was why he'd come. He yawned, covering his mouth with the back of his hand and pulled his shoulders up to stretch the kinks out of his back. Time for a good night's sleep. He'd had a long day, all the way from Portland to Mexico City, and he had plenty to do tomorrow. He reached for his wallet, removed several greenbacks, more than enough to cover his soda, and laid them on the counter. He turned to go, eyeing the door through the hot brown haze, wondering how difficult leaving would be. The bar's patrons seemed to increase by the minute.

Shouts erupted, then a scream. Bill turned and saw the entire crowd roll forward like a wave. A fight broke out at the bar. Two men had their arms flailing with glass mugs swinging as a bottle of Corona sailed through the air. A few bystanders jumped into the fray, while others worked to pull them apart. A man crawled up on the bar, shouting. The tide of men pulled back and the ruckus dissolved as quickly as it began. Walking back and forth on the bar, breaking the pandemonium in his stride, the man launched into a loud tirade. Bill sensed something familiar. *Right*, he thought, snapping his fingers. It was the man he'd met earlier, back at the hotel. Only then the man was well dressed and clean-shaven. This man was dressed like a peasant, in muslin pajamas with a black sash tied around his waist and sandaled feet. He had a large bristling mustache that reached across his jaw connecting with his sideburns, and wore a pair of black-rimmed glasses that were so thick they magnified his dark, piercing eyes. He paced back and forth shrieking so loud his voice kept the crowd at bay, while at the same time inciting them to riot. Their fists were raised, their voices mingled together as one, chanting and thunderous.

NICOLE KNEW pain. Not so much the pain she felt right now, the physical pain stabbing her body, she knew emotional pain, the pain that wounded her heart. She was surrounded by dirt, clinging to life though expecting to die, her arms and legs pinned and a shard of glass sticking through her cheek. Yet the pain she *felt* was the agony suffered the day Ryan walked out, leaving her for another woman.

The mute darkness enveloped her. Whatever sounds she'd heard earlier were gone, absorbed into the nebulous depths of the earth to be silenced by sand. For hours she had heard what she thought were muffled voices, though it was probably her imagination, and the thudding of rocks and pounding of feet—but they too had stopped. Now the world had gone silent, and her thoughts thrust her into a bad movie, one she was sorry she paid to see, and hoped to soon forget...

She drove home—alone—barely able to keep her car from swerving off the road, barely able to see through the blur of her tears. She jerked the steering wheel in response to warnings from horns on either side. She was determined to leave the past behind. She would get on with life. She didn't need him. She wanted him to follow her home. She wanted him to beg her forgiveness, and beg her to take him back. A ditzo blond, completely schizophrenic—just like he always said. Her body ached with the pain of his adultery. Seeing them together, that, that *tart* straddling him like that, seeing him take pleasure in that, whatever they called it. *Honnnnnk!* She pulled the wheel hard to the right, exploding at the accusing driver. She took a punctuated breath. She'd pushed him too hard. She shouldn't have been so frugal, but debt was bondage. And she was bull-headed, argumentative and stubborn, but so was he, and it took two to tango. She never meant half of what she said. It was just her sharp tongue cutting through her dull sensibilities. That was her problem. She couldn't control her mouth. Her battle rage and pillow talk co-existed within the same mind, even though they were complete opposites—air and water, sweet and bitter, black and white—they both lay hidden deep within the recesses of her subconscious, ready to spring forth and remedy the occasion. Pillow talk was better. She needed to keep the battle rage locked up, and let the pillow talk out more, but it was so much harder. And, okay, maybe she didn't throw herself at him. Maybe she felt like sex was a private affair, not some kind of circus act to be preformed in front of a live audience. Another horn blaring on her right. *Don't like it? Get off the road!* She wiped her eyes with her sleeve. Sometimes beds were for sleeping in. Okay, maybe she pushed him away a little too often, but she was tired, and marriage wasn't just about sex. Why couldn't he just tell her what he expected? She could have made it right. Now it was too late. They could never make love again. She would give what he required, but she would turn her head away and refuse to participate in the act. But that was if, and only if, he followed her home and begged her forgiveness. And she wouldn't do it for herself. She would do it for their child.

She pulled into her parking space. Alone! Was that her destiny? An old maid? Could she even survive? Her car hit the cement bumper, thrusting her into the wheel. She sat there shuddering, wiping her eyes on her shoulders. Her meager job barely paid the rent, but at least it was doing that. If she had to manage on her own, she probably could. In fact, she knew she could. Ryan contributed nothing. She took a fluttering breath, feeling the tremor in her chest. Her mouth hung open with strings of saliva clinging to her lips. She looked in the rear-view mirror, blotting her eyes with a tissue to avoid smearing her makeup. Slowly, she dragged herself from the car and made her way into the apartment.

The late afternoon sun was bleeding through the sliding glass doors, casting long shadows on the shag carpet. Her house was freshly cleaned, spotless and sterile, and now empty, abandoned and alone. She stood there, not even certain how she'd got from the car into the house, the walls closing in, her breathing faint. Such an austere environment. There weren't even pictures on the walls. She didn't want to spend the money, but there *was* one. She marched into the bedroom and took down their wedding portrait. The couple staring back looked oh *so* in love, a pair of glorious smiles, filled with hopes and dreams. A tear rolled down her cheek and fell, spotting the glass. She smashed the frame against the dresser and tossed it in the trash. Now she could get on with her life. Why did she feel so trapped? She felt handcuffs clasping her arms, manacles around her feet. This was prison, no frilly furniture, just basic needs, lock the door and throw away the key. She couldn't eat. She couldn't sleep. She couldn't read, watch TV, or listen to the radio. All she could do was crawl into bed, pull the covers over her head—and cry.

She rolled over. The glowing red letters of the alarm clock screamed 1:45. She lay awake, tossing and turning, her eyes toothpick wide, awaiting the dawn. But how could she expect to sleep when the man she'd given her life to, the man to which she was inextricably bound, the man she'd vowed to cleave unto forever, forsaking all others, was in the arms of another woman? She shuddered and felt the knife digging in deeper. She tugged at her pillow, turning it over, but the other side was wet too. She shoved it off the bed and reached for its twin.

He'd dressed a little nicer that morning than other days. His shirt seemed a little bit crisper, his tie brighter, his shoes shinier, his hair somewhat neater. She should have known. He didn't dress like that for her. But that morning—*that* morning—he'd been especially dapper. He'd brushed by, giving her an obligatory peck on the cheek, but the fragrance of his cologne hung in the air long after he'd slipped out the door. He hadn't come home that night, but she was used to that. It was only because her news was too important to wait that she'd gone searching and caught him in the act. He didn't look all that dapper then.

She woke up, startled, and realized she'd drifted off. She flexed trying to move the dirt, but without success. She was slowly suffocating and her lack of oxygen was affecting her ability to think. It was becoming increasingly difficult to separate the horror of her past from the horror of her present. She would die with Ryan on her mind. Wait! *No*, she would not! This grave was reality, this dirt, this darkness, this rarified air. *Please God, make it go away!*

She started drifting, and once again found it hard to separate one pain from another, the dark fear of her past from the dark fear of her present. She tried to stay awake, but her eyes were heavy, there was nothing to see, and eventually, she fell asleep.

She couldn't say for how long, or how many horrors slithered by in the passing of the hours—just that she heard a sound, and it startled her. In the fraction of a second between the recognition that something was wrong, and the opening of her eyes, her mouth was clamped shut and paint thinner, or acetone, or maybe it was floor polish, sallied up her nose and she went to sleep again, peaceful now, a desirable slumber from which she would not awaken until morning.

THIRTY-NINE

THE EVENING storm swept through on sails. To the west, Bill could see the sky rumbling cobalt blue with pulses of lightning flickering against the distant clouds. A mosquito buzzed his ear. He waved it off and slapped the back of his neck, then looked at his fingers. There was a veneer of transparent sweat, but he missed nailing the bug. He wiped his hand on his pants. He stood beside a giant avocado tree, watching a procession of vigilantes. The scene was right out of a Frankenstein movie, a lynch mob with torches demanding the doctor hand over the monster, only instead of a laboratory, they were surrounding a Spanish mansion.

The stone-walled villa was more than a home, it was a garrison, probably originally belonging to an early Spanish noble. How ironic that a court of pomp and splendor should become the burrow of a man who serviced pimps and pedophiles. But governance today was assumed, not granted, and nobility no longer charged.

Bill leaned against the tree and used his good foot to step on one of its massive roots to get a better view. Lights were on, but there was no movement behind the walls. The throng was pressing in. The man responsible for inciting the mob—was it Mr. Herrera? Bill couldn't be sure—was now standing on an egg crate off to the side, using a battery-powered megaphone to spur them on.

He stepped down, wiping green avocado dust from his hands. The peal of voices rolled like thunder. Alarm bells were ringing. They should move back. A drug lord like Miguel would employ a private army. He would not tolerate a riot. Already they were swelling like a flood about to burst the dam. The first wave had come straight from El Diablo, numbering in the hundreds, but as word spread the count increased to what now had to be well over a thousand. The man with the megaphone looked to his right, not more than a dozen feet from where Bill stood. His eyes, magnified through his thick black glasses, were enlarged with the violence of his words. He put the amplifier to his lips and continued his rant, his spittle flying, a spray of sweat creating a rainbow of light whenever he shook his head, working the crowd into a frenzy.

There! There was movement in an upstairs window, only a shadow against the fluttering of the drapes, but it set the crowd pointing and screaming, "There he is!" Someone threw a rock and the window shattered, exploding from its frame with shards of glass tinkling to the ground. The door flew open and four men armed with AK-47s stepped into the yard. Bill felt a change in the tide. The wave pulled back. He stepped on the tree's massive root to elevate himself, tipping up on the ball of his foot high enough to see over the heads of those in front. The armed commando unit moved forward, leveling their guns, pointing them into the crowd. The front line scrambled, backing up to get out of the way. Bill spun around, placing his back against the tree as one of the guns began sparking and smoking. *Pufft-pufft-pufft, pufft-pufft-pufft, pufft-pufft-pufft*, spewing rockets of light. He put his hand on top of his head and ducked. He wasn't an armchair general now. He was in the thick of it. Mary would kill him if he got shot. He tried to peer around the tree's massive girth. Three men were down, at least from what he could see. One rolled over grabbing his leg, scooting back out of the line of fire. One lay on his side, writhing, clutching his stomach, and the other lay in a pool of blood, his hand twisted behind him with his palm open, the nerves of his fingers twitching. The gates began cranking back, and the people trampled over each other, trying to flee.

The four armed militia moved into the yard unaware that dozens who had used the wall to dodge the bullets were now at their backs. Within seconds, the four armed men were bushwhacked from behind, forced to the ground and swarmed. They disappeared into a whirlpool of kicking feet. No longer visible, Bill could hear their screaming and the *thump, thump, thump* of flesh being pulverized and bones cracking. The night erupted with isolated bursts of gunfire. *Look who has the guns now, señor Estrada.* Windows exploded and doors were riddled, splintering chunks of wood.

The man on the megaphone continued screaming, and the crowd went into a frenzy as the mob charged the house.

MIGUEL WAS squatting behind a sofa, trying to stay off his knees to avoid coming in contact with residual dirt. "Get down here this instant!" he cried into the phone. "I want the entire police force down here, every man! There's a mob out there!"

Maximilian lay in bed, rubbing sleep from his eyes. "You want me to come there now?" He rolled over and picked up his clock, turning it to check the time. "It's two in the morning. Where are your security men?"

Miguel knew where they were, but he couldn't let the police chief question him about leaving himself exposed—not when his personal guard were dispatched to the Sierra Madre del Sur to capture the man's own son. In retrospect, the decision was rash. It left him with a security detail of just four men who could not possibly defend him against such a mob, but who could have anticipated this would happen? The people had gone muy loco. "My men are here with me, but there's a thousand men out there! I demand additional protection!"

"Alright, señor Estrada, calm down. It will take some time. I have to assemble..."

"No! I need you down here now!"

"I will do my best, but—" The sound of bullets could be heard strafing the walls. "You alright?"

Miguel cowered on his hands and knees behind a twelve thousand dollar hand-embroidered loveseat. "No, I'm not alright, estúpido! They've got guns! Hear that?!" A stray bullet ricocheted off a gold chandelier with a *ping*. "Hear that? Get me out of here—now!"

MAXIMILIAN HUNG up his phone. He should head down to the station and begin making calls. He should assemble an armed brigade. He should do a lot of things, but the man had ordered him to come without delay, *and*—he looked over at his wife. He'd had to give her Seconal to help her sleep. The loss of their son was tearing her apart. *You only get what you deserve.* He would mosey over, because it was required of him, but as an observer only. He stood, reaching for a pair of pants hanging on the bedpost.

His wife raised her head, her drug-laden eyes half-lidded. "Whooooo wash that?"

"No one. Roll over and go back to sleep."

BULLETS WERE pitting the walls, sprouting bursts of dust as they pelted the plaster. Miguel crouched, pulling his hands over his head. "Sweet Mother of God, have mercy on me! Send me thy salvation." He raised his eyes to implore a statue of the Madonna, but her ears were the work of a sculpture's hands and it suddenly occurred to him. They couldn't hear.

OUTSIDE THE chanting reached a fever pitch. From his position in the shadows, Bill scanned the road for police. An uprising like this would not go unnoticed. He expected to see whirling red lights or at least hear the wailing of sirens. If the authorities didn't step in soon, it would be too late. He caught a glimpse of a fireball streaming through the sky. The torch fell through Miguel's front window, lighting the drapes inside.

MORNING AND NIGHT had no boundaries in Nicole's mind. All was dark—her space, her thoughts, her life...

She hunched over in her rocking chair with the blanket around her shoulders criss-crossed in her lap. She wasn't cold. It just felt good to be under something. She wasn't rocking. She wasn't moving at all. She was listening to noises in the kitchen, but she made no effort to get up. Her eyes were oozing red, her hair a mat, and her face, though veiled in shadow, was lined with stress. Haggard, old and tired, that's how she felt. She was sure it was also how she looked.

Ryan was probably fresh as a puppy, showered and shaved, old Dapper Dan himself. She could see him screwing up his lips to kiss that pretty little face, while the little tart smacked her lips to get her lipstick oh *sooooo* even, and oh *sooooo* perfect.

She heard a chair scraping the floor. He was moving about in the kitchen, calling her name. "Nicky Girl, I'm home. Where are you?" By now he had seen her uneaten breakfast, toast with only one bite gone resting on a saucer amid a clutter of crumbs, the unpalatable bowl of cold oatmeal, milk sitting out and left to sour. Maybe he'd see the clutter, the mess he'd made of her life, and concede the pain he'd caused.

And then he was there, his angular frame filling the door, a black turtleneck over his black heart, covered by a cream-colored linen sport coat. He'd left wearing a suit and tie.

"Oh there you are," he said, pushing a sandy blond lock off his forehead. "Hey, Nicky Girl. Man, you look a mess. Hey, sorry I didn't make it home last night. I just couldn't after, you know. I didn't mean for you to see that."

The nerve. Nicole kept her jaw tucked but her eyes rolled up glaring at him. "I didn't mean for you to see that! Is that the best you can do? I didn't mean for you to see that!"

"Hey, relax. I'm mean, look, I'm sorry, okay? You're going to have to remain calm if we're going to have a conversation. I've been wanting to bring it up for a long time, but I've been afraid. Now it's out, so let's talk. I mean, we've been through a lot together, you and I. We've had some tough times, but we've had a few good laughs too. I think we can get through this, if we both try."

Nicole's eyes dropped to her blanket, burning. She was waiting for an apology, waiting for him to grovel. *On your knees sucker, plead, beg, implore me to reconcile and we'll see.* And for one flickering second she imagined he was saying they could work it out. Love conquers all.

"But I think you know we've drifted apart. I don't love you. Not the way a man is supposed to love a wife. I think you know that. And

I'm pretty sure you don't love me, either. I mean, you put up with me, but that's not the same thing, is it?"

Nicole closed her eyes, tightly, clamping her jaw, trying to block the sound of those horrible words, hoping to keep herself from screaming by focusing on something else. Behind her eyelids, she saw red. "How could you?—climbing in the saddle with that cow. You call that love?"

"You must have known. How could you not? I mean, it's not like I wanted this to happen. I didn't go looking for it. It's just we kinda dried up, know what I mean? I was so involved in my work I didn't have time to think about it, and it's not like I don't feel anything for you. You're a terrific person. You deserve better. And I still want us to be friends. Anyway, I'm saying this all wrong, but—Nicole, I want a divorce."

Nicole? Now he had the audacity to call her that? For years he'd refused to use her real name and now, just like that, it's okay because now he's talking about divorce? "You want *what?* "

Ryan raised his hands, palms out to prevent her from getting up, his long lanky body leaning over with elbows akimbo, the lock of sandy blond hair falling down over his forehead. "Hold on, Nicky Girl, calm down. I'm going to do right by you. Relax. Hear me out, okay? I know you said you're pregnant. I'm not sure how that happened. I assume you're still on the pill, and we haven't exactly been intimate lately, but I'm not questioning it. If you say it's so, it must be. But the problem is I'm not father material. I guess you saw that last night. But I know how bad you want to be a mother, so the thing is, the only way to solve this dilemma is to go our separate ways so each of us can live the lives we choose."

"That's it? That's your answer? Knock 'em up and leave 'em? Nothing about your part in all this? Like it or not, this baby's half yours, buster! What are you gonna do about that?"

"Yes, well, I guess you could always get an abortion. I mean, I thought about asking but, you know, I figure that's not going to happen. So, if this baby's going to be born, I guess I have an obligation to take care of it. And yes, I have considered my responsibility. I'm not a total cad, despite what you think. In fact, I've given it a lot of thought, and here's what I'm willing to do. I've been to my lawyer, and we've worked out a plan." He reached into the inside pocket of his coat and withdrew a document, holding it out, but she refused to take it so he laid it on the bed. "Believe me, it's fair. And it's the best you're going to get. It says you keep everything in the apartment. It's all yours, and the car. I don't think you'd want mine, the payments are too high, and besides, someone gave it a nasty scratch yesterday." The corner of Ryan's mouth curled up slightly. "At least the one I'm leaving you is paid for. The only other asset we could share is my office, but I'm heavily mortgaged, completely up to my eyeballs, and I know how you are about debt.

"So what I'm recommending is you keep what's yours and I keep what's mine and we go our separate ways. Except! Now here's the part you have to appreciate, Nicky Girl. I'll be taking care of your baby. You won't be left high and dry." He reached forward and opened the document, pointing at a specific section. "I think you should read this. It says I'm going to pay you a thousand dollars a month to support the child. One thousand is a lot of money. I'm not even sure I can afford it. But I'm obliged to make sure the kid has a fighting chance so I'm willing to do that. It's right here in writing. And you get full custody, no battles, no hassle. If you sign the divorce papers right here today, your child will be well taken care of.

"But if you're not willing to do that, you have to know I'll still get my divorce, only this deal will be off the table. You can hire a lawyer and we'll do this in court and probably end up in a costly, mean-spirited battle. Personally, I'm hoping we can end it amicably right here and now. You won't get a better deal because I'm already offering more than I have. My practice is in debt, I owe everybody. Who knows? In the end the judge may feel sorry for me and decide a thousand dollars is too much. But I can't speak to that. Ball's in your court, Nicky Girl. That's the offer. Take it or leave it." Ryan stood there, holding his pen out like an olive branch.

Nicole shook her head. Unbelievable. He thought this was about making a good deal. Like she gave a sweet juicy fig what kind of deal she got. She didn't want a deal—she wanted a husband! She wanted their child to have a father. I'll raise your bid by a house and a car and throw in the baby for good measure. The unmitigated nerve!

Nicole stood and snatched the pen from his hand. "You want out? Fine!" She leaned over the bed and started flipping pages until she got to the signature line and scrawled her name, the tip of the pen breaking through the bed's soft backing. "Fine! There! You've got your lousy divorce! Now get out! Get out right now!" she yelled, flinging the papers at him, a cyclone of white spinning around his face. "Get out! Get out! Get out!"

Ryan began scooping up papers quick as his hands could manage, tucking them under his arm as he backed toward the door. "Fine, good, I'll send you a copy. You may not think so now, but in the long run, you're gonna see this is best for everyone."

"Get out!"

"I am. I'm going," he said, pulling the door closed behind him. "But it's for the best. You'll see." His voice coming through the wood was muffled—just like every conversation they'd ever had throughout their entire marriage.

Nicole fell to her knees, clenching her fists, her arms rigid, her veins popping, her face tense and red. She crumpled into a ball and rolled onto her side, sobbing. If only he'd made an attempt to reconcile. He didn't have to promise forever. She didn't want him back. She just wanted him to acknowledge the pain he caused. If only he'd said what he did was wrong, instead of "it's for the best." If only he'd been contrite. *If only, if only, if only.* She lay there crying till her lungs ached and her nose dripped into the weave of the carpet. She sniffed and smelled the musty odor of a rug filled with dust. Like her. Dirt. No, she was less than dirt. She was nothing.

Nicole's eyes popped open. *Forget Ryan.* This was reality, the hole that would be her grave, where her body would dissolve and become one with the elements—just another mound of *dirt!* She could feel it starting to happen. Her eyes closed. *Ashes to ashes, and dust to dust.*

FORTY

FATHER PAULO was already moving rocks before the rooster began to crow. He turned, looking over his shoulder. "So it is my turn to wake you, eh mangy bird? Now hush, the town does not need to hear your complaints." He pushed his hand into his back and leaned into the task of removing another stone.

The rain had cleared, leaving midnight blue clouds laced with red ribbons hovering over the dark expanse of the ocean. He could see outlines and shadows through the dim purple of the predawn light, but it would be another few hours before the sun clawed its way over the mountain. There was only the faintest trace of illumination on the horizon. He hefted a rock into his arms, feeling the cuts in his hands, the blisters opening again, starting to bleed. He stumbled backward until he reached the pile.

He wasn't being noisy, nor was he being quiet. There was work to be done and he had to do it, but in the blue stillness of morning the sound broke the silence like clay jars dropped on cement. It wasn't long before heads were craning out of windows to see what the old priest was up to at such a pathetic hour. Smoke began to furl from breakfast fires, and one by one, the villagers struggled from their lethargy, joining him on the mound, many still rubbing sleep from their eyes. Work never began before sunup, but such determination begged questions and curiosity drove the townsfolk to action. Before he knew it, Paulo had a crew of about twenty workers, all lifting and moving stones. The pile began depreciating rapidly.

The sun rose in the sky, a sticky yellow lollipop, heavy and overbearing, inhibiting progress. Strain was compounded by sweat, and rests, by necessity, became more frequent. But no one abandoned the job, though he noticed a few workers staring off into the distance with an expectancy of rain, hoping for an excuse.

His excitement began to swell when they unearthed one of his vestments, though streaked with dirt. He was happy to see anything besides mortar and clay. A leather sandal, the chaplet he held as he prayed, and his chasuble—a prized possession given him by the bishop on his twentieth anniversary of making sacraments—which they gingerly removed, soiled, but still intact. He took a deep breath and exhaled slowly through pinched lips, then raised a brown-frocked arm to blot his brow. It wouldn't be long before they were mopping the tile floor.

With renewed vigor, he stooped over and grasped two fist-sized stones, one in each hand, and tossed them aside. The chunks were becoming smaller, mixed with powder and crushed gravel, and were getting easier to move but were far greater in number. He saw something dark and immediately recognized it as the drape that covered his table. He began clearing gravel, his hands working rapidly. He found his chalice, the one he used for personal communion with God. He worked it free and held it up, letting the sun glint off its gold rim as it turned in his hand. One small dent, but no other discernible damage. He set it aside and cleared away more dirt, scooping now with both hands. He came to a picture frame. The glass was broken, the photograph creased and dirty, and there was a cut where a sharp edge had sliced through the image, but it wasn't beyond repair. He brought the photo to his lips, kissing it, thanking God for preserving the last vestige of his family.

He placed the photograph beside his other prized possessions and continued sweeping the dirt away as he tried to remove the long green cloth, being careful not to tear its silky fabric. Now the entire surface of the table was clear, but there were still items missing like his prayer book and the crucifix. He scraped away the dirt, found the table's edge, and poked around beneath the lip till he could grip it with his fingers. He tried lifting, but it wouldn't budge. The legs were still buried. He sat down with his hands on his knees, panting in the overbearing heat. He wiped a sleeve across his forehead and turned looking over his shoulder, calling for assistance. Two men joined him. "Help me free this table, por favor," he said, pointing at the ebony wood surface.

The men scraped away the dirt around the table's legs. Others drifted over and began taking stones that were handed to them, passing them along to the next person in line until they were deposited on the pile. A gold crucifix found buried just outside the table's edge was passed to the priest—the risen Lord—*Roll away the stone.* He kissed it, and took it over to where his personal effects were beginning to accumulate. Another stone was removed revealing more shards of glass, and something else. Those who could see were horrified. There, beneath the rock, looking flat and white as a tortilla, was a human hand.

NICOLE'S STOMACH fluttered, which she imagined to be the baby, not nerves, but she couldn't help wondering if this was the right thing to do. Her eyes flicked right to left, glancing around the walls, examining the illustrated life of a baby floating in an amniotic sac at various stages of development. She closed her eyes. How could anyone look at this and call it a fetus?

She was hooked up to a machine with jelly on her belly and a monitor pointed in a direction only the doctor could see. He was rotating a paddle around her abdomen, though at this early stage, her stomach was still flat. She couldn't say she was showing.

She shouldn't have come. She couldn't afford it, especially if she wasn't sick—and she wasn't—at least not physically. Her problems were marital, not maternal. Her obstetrician might prescribe a pill, but that wasn't what she needed. No, quite the opposite. She wanted to know why she was feeling good. That was the problem. Nothing about it made sense. After Ryan departed with divorce papers in hand, she had run the gamut of emotional swings, one minute asking God to forgive him the error of his ways, pleading for his swift return, and the next, when he stubbornly refused to call, bringing down venomous curses upon his head. And afterward, feeling guilty about spewing both blessings and curses from the same mouth, she had castigated herself for the violence of her tongue, begging God for a second chance. She was humbled and crumbled and broken inside, a scrapped vessel without worth. But what troubled her was that in spite of all the turmoil she'd endured, her morning sickness had disappeared. The headaches had stopped, and so had the dizziness and vomiting. She couldn't sleep at night, or focus on her work during the day. Yet in the one area where she might expect to feel ill, whether Ryan was there or not, she seemed perfectly fine. Other than a slight cramping in her lower regions, she felt normal, which made her wonder if the baby was alright.

She knew undue stress could lead to miscarriage and other related complications, particularly with first-time mothers. If something like that had happened, she'd never forgive herself—or Ryan. How dare that self-serving, self-indulgent, narcissistic egomaniac bring grief to what should be a joyous occasion? She took a calming breath. She had to learn self-control for the sake of her child. She knew everything was alright. It had to be. If she'd miscarried, she would have known. But the baby could have died in her womb, couldn't it? No, that did not happen. She knew it, she just wanted the doctor's confirmation to put her mind at ease. She had enough problems to think about without adding to the load. She loved her baby and the child knew it.

She looked down at her abdomen. "See anything?" she asked.

"No, nothing. But that's not uncommon. You're not that far along. The fetus is probably too small. And sometimes they like to hide. I just thought I'd take a look while they're doing the blood test. Come over here. I need your feet in the stirrups to do an examination."

Nicole hated the stirrups, hated the invasion of her privacy, the lewd process of being on display, but she had to get used to it. That's how her child would be born. Obediently she crawled off the table and followed her doctor to another table and lay down placing her feet where instructed. She drew a deep breath and released it slowly. The doctor pulled a paper blanket over her knees so she wouldn't feel exposed and inserted a speculum to start the examination. "*Hmmmm*, interesting." He rolled back on his stool to look at her.

"Have you noticed any blood in your urine, or anything unusual on your sheets when you get up in the morning?"

"No, nothing. Why?"

The doctor nodded and continued what he was doing. Nicole appreciated him using the privacy blanket, but right now it was in the way. She wished she could see. He rolled back again. "I'll have to wait for the blood test to make a complete diagnosis, but you are showing minor abrasions in the birth canal, which would explain the irritation you said you were feeling." He removed the speculum, placed it in a basin, removed his latex gloves and threw them in the garbage. He stood to wash his hands and looking up over his glasses said, "Don't worry about it. I doubt there's any cause for concern."

BILL PLOWED another forkful of fire into his mouth, huevos rancheros dripping with hot sauce. He fanned his lips trying not to be obvious. It was his fault. He should have asked them to hold the Tabasco, but when in Rome. There were paintings of cactus and bottle-brush deserts hanging on the pale low-lit walls, and behind the bar a large mural depicting a coliseum filled with people pressing a matador to deliver the coup de grâce to a snorting bull. *Perfect, absolutely perfect.* He'd come in late and washed the sweat from his eyes with a cold shower, but the room's poor air conditioning had resulted in a wet night's sleep. And now, after fitfully sweating through the hours tossing and turning with his mind replaying what he'd seen and heard—the blood, the mob, the fists raised and the revolutionary cries, the torch, the fires—he had to have the slaughter of a bull thrust in his face. The whole scene brought to mind books written by Ernest Hemingway.

It wasn't a bad analogy. He reached into his pocket and removed a small notepad to jot down his thoughts. The images were disturbing, but it was a good story, and one he was compelled to write. Only now he had to focus on the earthquake because his editor would be expecting a preliminary report. That's why he was there, not to witness the undoing of a drug lord.

He was sipping coffee, organizing mental notes, reviewing background information, and trying to determine where to begin when the trader he'd met the day before walked in. Bill heard footsteps approaching and felt a vibration in the floor but continued writing, choosing to wait until the man's shadow crossed his plate before looking up. The man was clean-shaven, wearing a white sport coat with a black T-shirt underneath and a white Panama hat—but no glasses. His pants were black as were his leather shoes. He stuck out his hand.

"Buenos días, señor Best," he said.

Bill reciprocated and then leaned back, slinging his arm across a nearby chair. He stretched out, crossing one leg over the other, keeping his damaged foot on top. "Good morning, sir."

"Ah, I see you dared to try our breakfast. They put extra onion and jalapeno in those. Caliente. Sometimes it catches people off guard. Our spicy eggs can set the mouth on fire."

"Indeed," Bill replied.

"A bold choice for a gringo. Most would decline, but I see you are not one to run from danger. I trust you were able to get your story last night?"

Bill squinted, trying to see beyond the facade of business dress. "So that *was* you."

"If you mean in my hotel room, reading, sí. I spent the night catching up. I have a contract to negotiate. In fact," he looked at his watch, "I'm late for my meeting, but I saw you sitting in here and wanted to pass along my greetings."

"My mistake," Bill said.

"Sí. Happens all the time. I trust you will have a good stay while you are here in Mexico, señor Best. Perhaps our paths will cross again." He held his hand out for the second time, and Bill returned the gesture with a firm squeeze.

Señor Herrera turned to go, but paused and turned back to deliver a parting thought. "By the way," he said, "what you saw, that should be written about, if you have the time. Who knows, it might deter others from becoming involved in such business. Ah, but as for you and me, we never met, if you know what I mean." He turned and walked away.

"Son of a gun," Bill mused, nodding his head. His eyes were pensive, his mouth drawn back in reflective thought, but his lips held the faint trace of a smile. Last night he hadn't been sure, but now? He wondered if his editor knew. Probably not. He had to start writing his other story, but, well, let's just say there was more to this than appeared on the surface, of that he was sure. Someone from The Company had called in a favor. How in God's green earth could an earthquake be used to topple a regime, while at the same time providing justification for his being there to witness and write about it? How indeed? *Son of a gun.*

FORTY-ONE

HEARTS STOPPED. For a moment the air was still, filled with a cloud of yellow dust that settled as people stood silently gawking. Dirt matted Father Paulo's hair and covered the shoulders of his brown robe, and beads of sweat rolled down his cheeks making tracks through the dust, but his hands flew into the air. "Praise the Lord." The spell was shattered and the scene broke into pandemonium. Diggers began scooping the earth, spinning trails of dirt through the air. "Careful, careful! Take it easy! Stop!"

They had found Nicole, but alive—or dead? He reached down and swept loose gravel gingerly from between the fingers. They were cold, but not stiff. If she were dead, rigor mortis hadn't set in. He tried squeezing the fingers but there was no response. He slipped his thumb and forefinger around her wrist and continued brushing the dirt away with his other hand. He held his breath hoping for even the tiniest pulse. There was none. At least none he could discern. He laid the hand down and raised himself.

"Okay, you, you, and you, pull the dirt away from this table," he said, pointing at those he'd stopped only a moment before. "But be careful!"

A half dozen people, including one old woman, resumed clearing. No one bothered stacking the rocks in a pile. They burrowed like animals, flinging stones behind them as they tunneled into the earth.

"Careful, careful! She might be alive. Don't let the dirt cave in on her."

Two men at one end of the table uncovered blue material. They felt the fabric, then felt legs. Paulo recognized the clothing. Only Nicole wore Western dress like that. Several others excited by the discovery joined them in scooping the dirt away. From the placement of her hand the priest drew a line to ascertain the position of her upper torso and where her head might be, right about the middle of the table. He started to dig. Another man began working from the other side. His hands were those of a farmer, hardened from years of furrowing mountain soil. Dirt came away rapidly as he dug straight down, forming a smooth wall with a small chunk of the building stuck in the middle. He dug around the block and when he could grip it from both sides, he rocked and pried until it pulled free and fell into his lap between his knees. He had found an opening. He got on his hands, putting his eye to the hole, but it was too dark to see.

INSIDE THAT vacuous space air rushed in and lungs that had been existing on mere particles of oxygen exploded with new-found life. Nicole's body began choking on the excess. Her brain went *whomp* as the blackness flashed red, sizzled white as a sparkler, and then faded to black again...

Nicole hunched over with her elbows on her knees and her fingers laced, rubbing her palms together. Her head was bowed but she raised her eyes to study the windowless office. A jumble of books and framed documents covered the mint-green walls lacking any pretense of organization, and the desk was crowded with stacks of paper, manila folders, paper clips and coffee rings. She could feel pinpricks of sweat on her lip. She squirmed in her seat, feeling dizzy. She tried to sip in a breath and clear the confetti whirling in her head.

The man seated at the desk across from her wore wire-rimmed glasses and had a well-trimmed beard. His shoulder-length hair was pulled back in a ponytail and held in place with a rubber band. He looked like a Peter Pan hippie, a man caught in time who refused to grow up. Owing to her frugal nature she'd opted for legal aid, but frugality had its downside. The man was shuffling through a file but his eyes were moving so fast Nicole couldn't believe he was taking the time to read. The fluorescent lights emphasized the green pallor of the walls, adding to her nausea. She was ready to pass out. He set the papers down.

"Okay, here's what we got," he said. "This is a standard no-fault divorce. Your husband filed a petition, and you signed it, letting it go uncontested. Frankly, I'm wondering why you're here. Far as I can tell, your husband's lawyer did a fair job of listing the premarital assets and if you're not ready to contest it, there's not much I can do. The only mutual interest is the baby, which has yet to be born, and your husband has agreed to provide for the child in what appears to be an equitable manner. I don't see a problem. As long as you've agreed to split your possessions amicably, divorce in California is simple. There's no reason for a trial. Thus, you don't need a lawyer."

Nicole kept her head down, her hands folded between her knees. Her heart was skipping. She was trying to slow her breathing so she wouldn't hyperventilate. Her eyes rolled up under her forehead. "This is not about the divorce," she said. "I want my husband arrested. He stole something from me."

The lawyer frowned and leaned back in a chair with squeaky springs, folding his hands over a mildly rounded stomach. "What? Jewelry, a ring, personal mementos?"

Nicole kept her eyes down, shaking her head.

The right side of his mouth curled into an impish grin. "Oh, I get it, yep, well, the fact that your spouse stole your heart, or robbed you of your innocence, or whatever you want to call it, doesn't make him guilty of a crime. Emotional duress isn't a jailable offence." He picked up a pencil and began bouncing the eraser on his desk. "Hey, look, I'm not saying it's easy. Having someone cheat on you messes with your head, but it's not something you can litigate."

Nicole sat up, shifting uneasily in her chair. Her eyes darted about the room, trying to find the words. *Stop fidgeting and just say it.* "That's not what I'm talking about. Ryan didn't steal my heart. He stole my baby."

The lawyer reached for the file and began shuffling through the papers. "What am I missing here? I thought the child wasn't due till May. And if I'm not mistaken, your husband's granted you custody.

How does that translate into stealing?"

"He killed my baby."

"Come again?"

"I said, he killed my baby." Nicole was trying to keep calm, but she could feel the tremor in her voice. She closed her eyes, trying to hold back the tears. "He, he waited until I was asleep, then he drugged me and did an abortion."

The lawyer was now sitting up, paying close attention. "So you're saying your husband aborted your child without your permission?"

Nicole nodded. "That's exactly what happened."

"*Hmmmm*, your husband's a doctor, right? I guess he could have. Alright, maybe you have something." The lawyer pushed out his bottom lip, squinting. There were precedents, husbands responsible for the death of a baby while still in the womb had been tried for murder. "I'll have to get an affidavit from your family physician stating you were pregnant and that the pregnancy was somehow terminated, but how are you going to prove it was your husband? Was he with you the previous evening? Can your doctor substantiate when the abortion occurred?"

Nicole's eyes narrowed. "Don't ask me what the doctor can substantiate. Ask me what I know. I had a baby. I was pregnant, and now I'm not. Do you know what it's like to have someone invade your body and kill a part of you? He did it, and you know it. Look at the motive. It's right there in black and white. If I had his child, he'd be on the hook for a thousand dollars a month until the child was grown."

"Okay, but we still need to get an indictment, and for that we're going to need some kind of proof. They'll want to bring him up on criminal charges. Then we can launch a civil suit. I need to have your doctor release the test results validating your pregnancy. You said the doctor told you the pregnancy had been terminated."

"No, I didn't say that. The doctor never said the pregnancy had been terminated. He said I wasn't pregnant. That's what shocked me. I know I was pregnant. There was a baby inside me."

The lawyer raised his hand. "Whoa, back up the bus. Did the

doctor, or did the doctor not, know you were pregnant?"

"I did the pregnancy test at home, but it was valid. I checked several times. That's how I caught Ryan. I couldn't wait to tell him. I rushed to his office and found him..." The words stuck in her throat, dry and pasty as wads of cotton. She closed her eyes. In the blackness her head was spinning, but she sucked in air, held it, and forced her eyes open, willing herself to remain conscious.

The lawyer slid a drawer open and pulled out a box of tissues, handing them to Nicole. She took one and balled it in her hand to dab the bridge of her nose, and swallowed to lubricate her vocal cords. "He, he didn't take the news very well. He didn't want children. It was one of those things we never resolved. I walked in on them and he was with his nurse. She was in on it, that, that... She wouldn't want him to have another woman's baby. They did it together. I'd bet on it. I want him tried for murder."

"Mrs. Jensen, I hear what you're saying, but before we can prove your husband took the life of your child, we have to validate the child's existence. Who else knew about your pregnancy? Did your mother know? Did you tell your friends?"

Nicole wiped her eyes and shook her head. "No, no I didn't have time. I wanted Ryan to be the first. And then when I caught him with that other, you know, I just kind of went crazy. I spent the rest of the day in our apartment waiting for him, hoping we could talk, but he never came home. And I didn't call anyone because I didn't want anyone knowing about the affair. And that night they came and killed my baby."

The lawyer leaned back in his chair, the springs grinding as he relaxed. "I'm sorry, Mrs. Jensen, I really am, particularly if your story's true, but based on what you've told me, you haven't got a case. Even if you got a grand jury to listen, he'd rip you apart in court. He'd stand there and claim the only information he had about the pregnancy was what you told him, and that he agreed to the thousand dollars a month because he felt it was the right thing to do. But now he sees you were never pregnant and that you made the whole thing up to get more money and cause him grief."

Nicole jumped out of her seat. "He wouldn't dare!" But she stood too fast.

"No? I don't know your husband, Mrs. Jensen, but you just told me he's capable of murder, and you don't think he's able to twist this around to make it look like you made the whole thing up? He'll play the old, 'hell hath no fury like a woman scorned' song, and you don't have a shred of evidence to prove otherwise so he'll get away with it. Mrs. Jensen, are you alright?"

Nicole's eyes rolled to the top of her head and she suddenly felt empty as her legs turned to latex and she slid to the ground with the lawyer rushing around his desk, his ponytail flapping.

FATHER PAULO knelt in the dust beside Nicole, holding her hand while painstakingly brushing dirt from her face. They had removed the earth surrounding her without disturbing her position. The table now lay on its side at the top of the mound. He was careful to avoid the piece of glass protruding from her cheek. It was from his family picture, he was sure of that, but how that one shard got under the table while the rest remained shattered in the frame, he couldn't guess.

The sun overhead was as big and bright as a slice of lemon, causing him to swelter in his robe. He looked up, feeling a trickle of moisture run down his cheek. *Sebastian, hurry, por favor.* He removed the cross from around his neck and placed it in Nicole's hand, wrapping her fingers around it. "A cruce salus," he whispered in Latin—*from the cross comes salvation.* She was alive. For now, that was enough. But there was barely a pulse, and her breathing was faint, hardly discernible. He took his thumb and smoothed dirt from her unconscious eyes.

Sebastian had bolted shortly after Nicole's legs were discovered, racing his chrome chariot across the cobblestones faster than the priest had ever seen him move. He couldn't help with the digging, so he'd scurried off to find a stretcher and let the nurses in the hospital know they needed to prepare a bed. The dirt surrounding Nicole's body had been cleared away, but it would be a difficult move. They had no way of knowing if she'd suffered broken bones. Paulo was particularly concerned about the possibility of a fractured neck or back. She would have to be moved with the utmost care. He let everyone know what was expected. It wasn't going to be easy, but it had to be done.

Paulo caught a glint of chrome out the corner of his eye and heard the metallic clatter of wheels approaching. True to promise, Sebastian had the stretcher, a long flat board with straps for holding the patient down. It was fastened to the back of his wheelchair, supported at the base by the wire basket he used for moving things. Someone must have helped him tie it on, someone who could have just as easily carried it and come a lot faster, but Sebastian would have insisted he be allowed to bring it. He had to contribute something. Paulo stood and saw light flicker at the edge of the woods, a glint of color, red, blue, red, blue, red, blue, but it might have been his imagination.

BILL SAT on his bed with his heel propped up on the frame, lacing his hiking boot. There were probably better, more comfortable shoes to wear, but in this case he found his ankle needed the extra support—*can't keep a good man down.* He slid his foot to the floor and slapped his knees, ready to go, satisfied he was back on track.

He'd called his editor, ready to make excuses about not having a story to break, but before he could open his mouth, his editor up and apologized for sending him on a wild goose chase. Apparently, initial accounts had been exaggerated. The earthquake was centered deep in the Sierra Madre del Sur and API was now reporting surrounding cities had few casualties and only minor structural damage. Bill assured him it was not a waste of time and that he would bring back a story one way or another, but it was agreed he should abandon the news feature and focus on human interest.

His first call had been to Mary. He was happy to hear her voice, though he could have done without the gentle reproach. She was peeved he hadn't called sooner, but he reminded her he had, and that he'd left her a message, but *she* hadn't been home. It was a moot point because she was still able to scold him for not trying again until now. He should have called last night but so much happened—*the mob, the guns*—things he didn't want her to be concerned about. And besides, by the time he got back to the hotel it was too late, so he took her reprimand in stride.

He took a few minutes with each of the boys, and spoke to Angie, who, though she couldn't speak, let him know she was listening through a distorted series of grunts and groans. He told them he was just starting to gather information about the earthquake, purposely avoiding the events of the previous evening. Any mention of gunfire and mobs would have caused needless worry, and the rest of the story had yet to be written. He'd let them read about it once he was safe at home. Today his focus would be on the earthquake, so he let them know about that, and then turned the conversation to what they were doing and whether they were behaving themselves. It was long distance so they kept the conversation short. He signed off, saying how much each of them was missed, and that he'd be home soon, hugs and kisses all around.

He climbed inside yet another Volkswagen, giving new meaning to the old phrase "packed like a sardine." With his knees under his chin, again, relaxing was pointless. He gave the driver the address, and considered how to approach Daniela. He didn't want to catch her off guard, but when he'd tried to call a man had answered, and since their relationship was clandestine, he couldn't leave a message. Better in person anyway. She'd want to know about the events of the past evening.

Bill stared out the window through glass coated in brown dust, or was that smog? It was hard to tell. He couldn't see the horizon for the buildings sweltering in the haze. Waves of corrugated heat rose from the pavement. The sardine can was an oven, but at least—he rubbed his palm—the seat covers were made of cloth, not plastic. Hundreds of cars weaved and bobbed in and out, changing lanes without indicator lights or regard for safe bumper distance. The streets of Mexico City were a glut of traffic. American drivers, complain though they might, didn't know how good they had it.

The cab pulled to the curb in front of a small market with stacks of hand-woven baskets feigning Mayan and Aztec designs, and wood crates filled with bushels of beans, peppers, onions, mole, hibiscus and quesillo cheese. The sign on the storefront read, "El Tomate Rojo," with huge green serif letters painted on a burgundy background. *The Red Tomato. Yep, that's the place.* Bill climbed out and paid the driver, half expecting the air to be filled with the fragrance of fresh produce, but what greeted his nose was the smell of exhaust fumes and rotting garbage. He looked up at the sign again. He hadn't actually been here before. Daniela was paranoid about being watched. He couldn't just walk in and start talking. He might try passing her a note, but if he were seen it could mean trouble. The best way was to pretend to be a tourist. He looked at his arms. He was still wearing denim. Tourists were more likely to be in sport shirts with loud prints, but in broad daylight he didn't look Mexican. He would ask how to find the El Diablo Hotel and Cantina and make up some story about meeting a friend at seven. It had been a few years, and he'd grown a beard, but hopefully she'd still be able to recognize him and once over her shock, would pick up on his meaning.

The building didn't have a door. A hinged iron gate hung to the side of the arched entrance, ready to form a barrier at the end of the business day. Bill drifted into the small building, pausing to shuffle through postcards and piles of shell jewelry—a typical sightseer fresh off the bus. Two kids were quickly at his side, bouncing up and down like jumping beans. They didn't have to speak English. Bill knew what they wanted. Their hands were extended with palms out while they squealed the Mexican equivalent of "gimmie, gimmie, gimmie."

A man emerged from behind a donkey blanket hanging at the back of the counter. He flicked his hands in front of him, shooing the kids away. Bill watched, feeling a little sorry for them. He walked to the counter with a pack of chewing gum in his hand. He knew they'd be waiting the minute he stepped outside. He reached down and placed a few more packs on the counter, and then added a few candy bars.

He turned toward the man, pushed the items forward indicating he was ready to purchase, and took out his wallet, removing several bills. He had no idea what things cost, or what amount to offer. The man took the money, put it in a coffee can under the counter, and began counting out change. Bill debated whether or not to ask about Daniela. There was only one way to frame the question, but playing the part of a love-sick sailor was repugnant.

"Perdón, señor, dónde está Daniela, the woman who's usually here? I know her from another time. She told me if I was ever in town to look her up."

The shopkeeper stared at him blankly, which Bill took to mean he didn't speak English. His hair was cacao thatch and his eyes dark and shadowy like those of a man who wrestled in his dreams. He stood eyeing Bill up and down, his head floating and bobbing like a stork's. "Daniela ha muerto," he finally said.

Bill stepped outside, more confused than ever. His Spanish was weak but as far as he knew the word "muerto" meant "dead." The kids, now more than half a dozen, came clamoring up, squealing with their hands outstretched, but he looked straight ahead, handing the paper bag to the one closest. He stumbled off the curb as the shrieking pack ran after the lucky recipient, demanding their share of the booty.

It made no sense at all. He'd spoken to Daniela only a few days ago. She'd been fine. The shopkeeper must have misunderstood. It was obvious he spoke little English. Maybe he meant to say Daniela had taken ill. There was one sure way to find out. He stood in the street and raised his hand to hail another taxi. *Bless my socks,* he thought, *I got myself a Lada.*

FORTY-TWO

HAD NICOLE been conscious, she would have reveled in the crisp, starchy feel of those clean hospital sheets. But she was not conscious, nor was her condition stable. Her body lay surrounded by penguin-suited nurses monitoring her vital signs. Her pulse was touch and go, but there wasn't much they could do. They weren't trained medical professionals. Truth be known, the closest one to having any textbook knowledge was Nicole herself, and she was in no position to help. The sisters were volunteers. When called upon to provide treatment they had about as much expertise as candystripers. They could tape sprained ankles, administer salves to burns, or disinfect open wounds, but real medicine, the diagnosis of a disease or writing of a prescription, they left to the doctor. Unfortunately, the doctor was in another village delivering a baby that, with all the excitement of the earthquake, had decided to come early.

An inch-long incision marred the side of Nicole's face. Father Paulo said it was from a piece of glass, but it must have fallen out on the trip over. No one saw it after Nicole was delivered to the hospital. Sister Fatima had been known to administer sutures, but the cut wasn't bleeding and after careful washing it was determined a butterfly bandage was sufficient to keep the wound closed. She didn't need little white needle marks adding to her scar

Sebastian rocked back and forth in his chair. "What's she doing now? Is she awake? Isn't there *anything* we can do?"

Fatima turned to acknowledge the young man who sat in the corner, watching. "I don't think you should be in here, Sebastian.

This room is supposed to be sterile. Have you washed your hands? I didn't think so. The doctor would not approve. You could be contaminating the environment. But to answer your question, no, I'm afraid not. It's hard to tell whether she's in a coma, or just fainted. Until the doctor returns, all we can do is keep her comfortable. As long as her heart keeps beating, she'll be fine. Now you should probably leave before the doctor returns and catches you in here and we all get in trouble."

BENEATH THE deliberate and determined conscious mind is a surreal world where fantasy and reality are mixed, and where events that happen, though occurring at random, seem somewhat more real than those that can be known experientially. This was the realm in which Nicole now existed. In the darkened theater of her mind she saw images played out like motion pictures on a screen. From her perspective, she was fine, and required no further rehabilitation. There was no coma to drag herself back from. She languished on the familiar plain of memory, however loosely defined, and within that existence felt a balance of pain and peace common to the human condition.

IF THERE existed a dictionary definition for the way the troops looked as they reached the top of the hill, that definition would be found in the word *exhausted*. They were so sluggish it appeared they were walking underwater, pushing one foot forward and dragging the other up from behind in a kind of smoothly choreographed fluidity. They'd traveled fifteen miles, and fifteen miles on short legs was twice as far, though Lonnie, Sofía and Raúl took turns carrying the little ones. He'd pushed them hard. He couldn't help it. He was being driven by some unseen force. He had to get back to Posada. All his life he'd sought to know the will of God, to hear His voice with the clarity of a prophet, but the workings of God remained a mystery. It seemed the best he could do was muddle through life trying to do what he thought was right, and hope it somehow lined up with God's plan. But such were the ruminations of a madman. He hadn't slept well. Every muscle, tissue, fiber and bone in his body pulled, strained, tore and ached, but none of that really mattered. He had to keep moving.

Oddly enough, the only one complaining was Raúl.

"Why are you pushing us so hard?"

The change in Raúl bewildered Lonnie. He'd been the one saying they had to hurry. Now suddenly he was complaining they were moving too fast. But then Raúl always seemed to row against the tide. Lonnie turned to face the boy.

"What is your problem? You don't have to question everything I do. Why don't you just try to get along?"

"Why did you let them go? You wouldn't be pushing us if they were dead. I had them!" Raúl spat on the ground. "You're a coward! That's what you are!"

"What? Killing someone makes you brave? They were trapped in a car, unable to defend themselves. That's not justice. That's murder. It makes you just like them."

"Nooo, youuu..." Raul's hands balled into fists. "You take it back!"

"What?"

"Take it back!"

"Take what back?"

"I'm not like them. They killed Mamá and Papá. Take it back—now!" Raúl ducked his head and rushed Lonnie, head-butting him in the stomach. Lonnie lost his wind, falling backward, and Raúl jumped on him in a cyclone of fists. Lonnie raised his hands to block the blows and protect his already bruised face. He tried to roll Raúl off but the boy stayed with him, fists flailing wildly. The others stood there, frozen, their eyes wide. Then Luis stepped in and wrapped his chubby arms around Raúl's waist. A loose elbow knocked his glasses askew, but he was joined by Juanito, Mariana and Sofía, and between the four of them they were able to wrestle Raúl off and pin him to the ground, though he was still thrashing.

Lonnie propped himself up on his elbows. Raúl's tears were a river flowing through the dust-bowl of his cheeks. "Let me go! Let me go!

Let me go!" Lonnie pulled himself to his feet and stood, holding his stomach. He nodded at the children. "Let him go," he said. "You may not understand this, Raúl, but those men will pay for what they've done, that I can promise. I can't say when or how, but I do know it's not up to you or me to be their judge. That's up to God."

Raúl was already crawling to his knees. He pulled himself to his feet and stumbled into the bush, wiping his eyes as though ashamed anyone should see him cry.

The kids stood around with their hands on their knees, panting heavily, their chins raised looking at Lonnie. Lonnie scanned the purple twilight. The collapse of the sun had left the trail subdued in blue shadows, and though they could find their way by moonlight, it wasn't fair to make the children keep moving. They needed their rest.

"Alright, I guess everyone's a bit on edge. We're just overtired. We need to get off the trail and find a place to bed down," he said.

Lonnie began herding the children down the side of the mountain. It was rocky and steep and the light had faded quickly casting the trail into shadows making it hard to see, but the hilltop had been too exposed. They stumbled along for another quarter mile before finding a dish formed by two adjoining bluffs covered in tall sawgrass. It would suffice.

"Okay, this is as good as it gets."

Sofía and Juanito dropped where they stood, disappearing into the knee-high green. Lonnie was pleased to see the wisdom of his decision. They would never be seen from the trail above. A line of trees crested the hill, their dark shapes looking like the silhouettes of cotton balls balanced on spools of thread. Raúl would come back. He wouldn't leave his sister. Thank God for the return of her voice. If it weren't for her, they'd be long gone. The rest dropped one by one to the ground, dusty and spent. The wind picked up, rustling the grass and clattering leaves on the trees like bits of tinfoil. The briny smell of saltwater saturated the air, but it seemed normal now that they were moving along the coast. Lonnie took it in, breathing deeply. Along the side of the hill the wind would be less severe. He stared into the opal twilight, listening to the sound of the night crawlers beginning to wake. With Godspeed, they'd be home this time tomorrow. The terrain was becoming familiar now. He'd hiked this part of the trail before, but because there was no reason to, he hadn't fixed any particular landmarks in his mind, so how much further they still had to go, he couldn't say. All he knew was home was just ahead. He could feel his excitement growing with each step.

Home. He doubted there was a more beautiful word in the English language. Home—where the heart is. He stopped and made sure he was thinking about Trudy. If he was lucky, her answer would be waiting, and they would marry, and together they would make a beautiful new home. He'd have to build something nice. Not just nice, something special, the grandest house anyone had ever seen. Trudy would expect no less. One thing was sure. He wasn't going to move into his brother's Malibu mansion. It didn't matter where the home was as long as the heart was there, but he didn't want his heart sleeping in Harlan's bed. But why he was thinking of that? This was about the children.

He looked over his shoulder. The kids were nestled in the grass, probably already asleep. Crickets were beginning to chirp, mosquitoes to buzz, and fireflies to glow, tuning up the nocturnal choir.

For the first time Lonnie allowed himself to think they'd made it. A breezy walk in the park tomorrow and they were home free. He brought his hands up and pressed his palms to his eyes, not rubbing, they were too tender for that, but dabbing the fatigue away. He wondered if they were still bruised blue. He tipped his head back, gently pinching the bridge of his nose, thankful it no longer felt broken, and slipped through the bushes trying to be quiet, hoping to find a place where he could kneel before God. A rock perched on the edge of a bluff overlooked the moon-dappled valley. It was the altar he sought. He eased himself onto his knees. Stars were flickering on the blue velvet curtain of night. He looked to the sky and as he raised his hands, he recognized once again how insignificant he was.

How odd that the Designer of a universe so vast and so complex would care about the plight of a handful of ragamuffins camped on an escarpment along the southern coastline of Mexico. There were billions of others to take care of on the planet, many of vastly greater importance, and many in much greater need. And yet, while he recognized the scope of his unworthiness, he also knew God held them in the palm of His hand. Imagine God using an earthquake to set them free, or having Daniela's truck right there at the right time. And there was the rotten tree God provided for a bridge, and Raúl escaping men too drunk to give chase, and Luis slipping from a cliff without being hurt. Too many inexplicable things to call it coincidence. God had been with them every step of the way.

He pulled his elbows forward, tweaking his shoulders and reveling in how much freer his movements were and how much less pain there was. Why him and not Daniela? It seemed so unfair. He hadn't had much time to think about her, the surprised look on her face, her lifeless eyes. Maybe he just wanted to forget. He bowed his head. She'd given her all. *Greater love hath no man, than he lay down his life for a friend.* He looked up again, probing the stars. *Daniela, you did good.* His eyes swept across the host of heaven, soft and luminous through a veil of tears. He wiped his cheek on his sleeve. Daniela was up there. Whether she had visibility into the temporal world was not for him to say, but he hoped she did. He wanted her to know her sacrifice was not in vain. God used her to save the children, and then called her home. At least now she could rest. But God had left him, which meant *his* work was not yet done.

THE DEEP purple of dusk had faded to black by the time Lonnie made his way back to the children, but the moon wove silvery threads into the tall grass, enabling him to see. The *nic nicking* and *whoooo whooooing* of night accompanied him along the way. He wasn't expecting anyone to be awake and he didn't want to disturb their rest, so he stepped lightly through the bush counting heads. They were all there, even Raúl. The dome of a large smooth rock rose in the moonlight above the thickets. He sidled over and sat down. He would try to stay alert. He trusted God implicitly, but God told the children of Israel to keep a watchman on the wall.

Then he heard it. It was so faint, at first he thought he imagined it. *No*, there it was again, soft and sad, like wind whistling through a canyon. Someone was crying. Lonnie put his hands on his knees to help himself stand. He listened again and followed the sound. It was Sofía. He swept the grass aside and sat down, stroking her shoulder. She flinched. He drew back and wrapped his arms around his knees. She curled into a fetal position, crawling into her shell. He didn't say anything. The tears on her face were shining in the blue velvet light, but she kept her eyes closed. "You...you don't know what they did to me," she whispered. Her lips were purple, wet, and *trembling*.

FORTY-THREE

A LONG sustained drone burst from the machine.

"We're losing her!"

The nurses scrambled. A crash cart slammed against the bed and bounced back, rattling. Sister Gabriela hit the switch and the defibrillator buzzed with two hundred joules of heart-popping electricity. Isabel grappled with the ECG recorder and Fatima squeezed conductive agent onto the paddles. Sister Gabriela placed one paddle at the apex of Nicole's heart and another at the clavicle to the right of her sternum.

"Clear!" Gabriela shouted.

The nuns took a step back. Gabriela glanced over her shoulder, making sure the indicator light said fully charged, and then pressed the paddle buttons simultaneously, holding them down until the current was released. Nicole's body jumped. Gabriela stood back with her arms raised, her sleeves billowing like the wings of a large black bird. The process was familiar. She'd done it before, several times, but always with the doctor present. This was the first time any of them had tried it unsupervised. The heart monitor continued to drone. Flatline.

"I hope you know what you're doing," Sister Isabel said. "What if you're doing it wrong? I wish the doctor were here."

Sister Fatima leaned in close. "It's okay, Nicole, you're safe now. Come on querida, it's okay, please don't leave us. Please come back."

Father Paulo was also in the room, just in case. He stood with his back to the wall, trying to stay out of the way. He wasn't sterile either.

His frock was smudged with chapel dust and his hands and face wore a film of sweat and grime, but he didn't dare leave to wash. He prayed he wouldn't be called upon to give last rites, but he was there if needed. Nicole wasn't Catholic. He was pretty sure she would have made her own confession, but if her soul was determined to enter eternity, he would do whatever it took to help her go in peace.

IT WASN'T the paddles Nicole felt, nor the electric shock. It was the turbulence. The plane bounced, slamming people toward the overhead bins and jerking them back by their seat belts. Outside the window it was dark but green forks of stroboscopic light sparked against the clouds. The rain ran horizontally down the length of the fuselage. Wasn't rain supposed to fall? Or was the rain actually falling and the plane along with it? The thunder cracked, and the sky lit up again. Nicole leaned into the window. A plane's wings should be straight and rigid. These were flapping like a bird's. The plane dropped another ten feet and the passengers were thrust toward the ceiling, their arms flailing out. A pair of glasses went flying. In that moment, Nicole knew she was going to die. *Not now, Lord. You know how long I've waited. And You, You made it possible. Don't take it away now.*

This was Nicole's launch. Ryan was her past, this was her future. She'd been christened a missionary, heading into a dark, unexplored world of indigenous natives to minister the gospel of Christ—at least that was how she romanticized it. She'd stood at the airline counter unable to believe it was actually about to happen. Her heart flittered when they announced boarding, her jitters growing as she took her seat on the plane, a window seat just over the wing. It wasn't necessarily about seeing Lonnie again, though that excited her. She'd worked with him for a short time after his brother died and knew this was where he was stationed. It was more about knowing she'd finally obeyed the call.

Through all her years of marriage, and most of the years that followed, she'd struggled to compensate for a deep lack of fulfillment. She couldn't say she'd been entirely submissive to Ryan—Ephesians or not, most of his demands were unreasonable—but she *had* allowed him to hold her back. For the sake of marital peace, her dream of serving on the mission field dissipated the day she said, "I do," though for a while she hoped they'd one day take a short-term mission trip together—doctor and nurse immunizing a nation of unwashed peoples—but that idea was shelved when Ryan stopped going to church shortly after they were married. It wasn't long before it became evident there would be no peace at all as long as she conveyed a life in Christ. Ryan wasn't ready to acknowledge his need for God, and until he was, he wanted her Christianity put on hold.

Part of her cried out in lonely desperation, but she kept it locked inside. She only made it to church when Ryan was out of town, which was most Sundays anyway. But she still wanted to be a nurse. That wasn't unreasonable. She could worship God in spirit, and find fulfillment in helping people. The shock came when she realized Ryan wasn't going to allow even that. And it wasn't about money, as he'd claimed. It was about control, about keeping her in a box. He didn't want her to have a life of her own. She could only wonder how many women he had entertained in his private suite all those nights he failed to come home because he was called to assist in a last minute "operation."

But that was history, over and done. She didn't want to dwell on that. Her life was ahead, a new adventure waiting just around the corner in the mountains of southern Mexico. She'd spent the past two years in a nursing program energized by the awakening of her dream. She'd filled out the paperwork, supplied references, completed the interviews, been accepted by the Missionary Alliance, and had specifically requested a nursing assignment in Posada. It was a no-brainer. She had the administrative skills obtained from her years at Striker Films, and the hospital was in permanent need of nursing staff. She'd received immediate confirmation, providing of course she could pay her own way.

Now, here she was, cruising at thirty thousand feet, the fulfillment of her lifelong dream just over that dark cloudy horizon, and she was about to die—*oh ye of little faith*—this turbulence, this storm, it was just an allegory of her life. She'd get her feet on the ground, one way or another. Would Lonnie be standing there with arms open wide, waiting to welcome her arrival? Or would he be too busy to take notice and send an emissary to pick her up? Surely he'd been told she was coming, though she'd not had the courage to contact him herself. *Wham!* The plane hit an air pocket and bounced hard...

"Clear!" Nicole's body lurched forward. Sister Gabriela had the defibrillator cranked up to three hundred joules. The nurses held their breath, hoping to see blips on the monitor, but the machine refused to comply. The obnoxious whining continued.

"I'm going to three hundred and sixty. Lord Jesus, please. Okay, stand back!" Once more the paddles were applied to Nicole's chest...

For a moment, the plane lost power. The lights in the cabin went out but the electrical system kicked into emergency mode and they flickered back on. The plane slammed into another air pocket and lost altitude. Nicole was beginning to think she'd never see Lonnie again. The plane was falling apart. She was going down with the ship.

BILL STOOD outside Oaxaca International Airport, trying to negotiate a ride to Posada. He wanted to haggle for a flat fee, but the first few drivers demanded too much. Never mind, he had little choice. He needed to be there. He had to find out what happened to Daniela. If, God forbid, she *were* dead, was the preacher dead too? He needed to see Lonnie.

LONNIE PAUSED and looked around. The stream provided a tranquil place to rest and refresh themselves, but it was also a good spot for an ambush. The dense low-lying thickets could contain a dozen of Miguel's men waiting to pounce the minute they settled in. His eyes scanned the horizon. But why would they wait? If they were there, wouldn't they have already shown themselves?

The kids needed to rest. He'd awakened them an hour before sunup in the predawn haze. A fog had rolled in from the ocean, covering the valley in a cloudy mist. The blanket was so thick he'd had to use his hands to fan wisps of vapor away, trying to locate where each child slept. They pulled themselves up and encircled him, hungry and cold, their eyes droopy with sleep, but nary a complaint. There had to be something supernatural about the strength these kids displayed. But of course it was supernatural. He himself had been whipped and beaten. He should be in a hospital, not conducting a cross-country expedition with a ragtag bunch of kids, but instead of pain, he felt the intense anticipation of a horse heading down the home stretch. He took a deep breath. The air was saturated with the smell of seaweed and ancient water. He could describe the landscape with his eyes closed. They were less than five miles from home, and there hadn't been a single sighting of Estrada's men. Dare he hope they'd called off the search? They were down to the wire, the finish line just ahead. If they pushed hard, there was a good chance they'd make it by nightfall.

RAÚL DISAPPEARED into the bushes. The padre said they'd be home before dark. Time was running out, but he couldn't let them take Mariana. He would take care of his sister. She would be raised by him, not some stranger. He had to scuttle her away before they reached the orphanage. He scuffed sand, walking between bladed tufts of grass. The stream meandered down from a heap of red boulders that became a mountain speckled with trees on the horizon. The sky was a robin's egg blue. Clouds piled up in clumps, blazing white in the sun. Even if he could convince Mariana to stay back and slip away quietly while the others trudged on, they'd eventually notice them missing and come back looking, and there was nowhere to hide.

LUIS AND MARIANA finished splashing water into their parched mouths and collapsed. There were few large rocks and little shade, and the morning heat was unrelenting. Sofía and Juanito found a pool and took refreshment in sips. Lonnie watched, curious about the symbiotic relationship they shared. Sofía had a strong nurturing instinct. She had finally shared what was troubling her. How could men be so cruel? It was one thing to beat a grown man.

At least a man could withstand pain. But what they did to Sofía was unthinkable—robbing her of her innocence one after the other in succession while standing around laughing as they egged each other on—all in good fun. It was hard to believe such evil could exist. And he'd only heard part of the story, only as much as she could tell before she broke into tears and the sobbing made her words intelligible. "Their hands, señor Striker, I still feel them. They crawl over my body like worms." For the first time Lonnie felt hate for those men. They could have beat him to death and he would have looked up and said, "*Father forgive them, for they know not what they do,*" but he couldn't look at Sofía without wanting to put his hands around their necks and squeeze—and it made him realize he was no better than Raúl. Lonnie felt his face turning red. He mopped his cheeks with a bloodstained sleeve, hoping the others would think it was the heat, but he knew otherwise.

Sofía sauntered upstream to find a rock big enough sit on and hold little Juanito. She would make a fine mother. She was strong. She'd get over the trauma. The secret was in being able to forgive, but since he wasn't ready himself, Lonnie could understand how difficult it might be for her. She'd gone back into her shell. Her eyes were darker and more vacuous than before. Lonnie had hoped that once she shared her pain, she'd feel release.

Mariana rolled over in the sand with her arm under her head. A small mouse skittered away, startled by the intrusion. Lonnie saw the bush behind her shudder as a breeze danced through its leaves. He heard the rustling. Then he saw it. He rushed forward, yanking Mariana up, pulling her into his arms, and spun around to leap back—but it was too late. The snake clung to his ankle as he jerked away. He thrust her into the arms of Luis and began hopping on his other foot shaking his leg, but the snake refused to let go. Stomping his foot down, he stooped over and squeezed the snake behind the jaws until he pried it loose. He stood there with a three-foot asper, writhing in his hand. Its jaws were open wide, its beady black eyes coals of fury, its inch-long dagger fangs fully extended. It was a muscular beast, twisting and flopping every which way, trying to break his grip.

Lonnie knew if he didn't get rid of it, it would succeed. He began spinning the serpent like a lasso, letting gravity straighten the beast out until he had enough momentum to get a bit of distance. Then he let go, flinging the snake into the bush a dozen feet away.

Luis set Mariana down and leaned over placing his puffy hands on his knees to examine the bite.

Lonnie had experience with snakes. The venom of the asper could be deadly, but not if treated quickly. He had but minutes. He grabbed his shirt, pulling it over his head, and used the sleeve to tie a tourniquet around his calf. *Come on, God!* Now was *this* His will? To handicap him and slow progress when they were so close to home? There was a part about leaning not on his own understanding that he *really* didn't understand. He pulled the knot as tight as possible. "Luis, I need a stick. Find me one? A good solid stick," he urged, through gritted teeth.

The boy turned and put a finger to his glasses holding them in place as he bent over to pick up something. He threw it down, and picked up something else. "Will this do?" he asked. "It's not really wood, it's a dried skeleton from a cholla cactus but it's very fibrous, and very strong. I'm not sure what it's doing here. Cholla usually grows in drier climates. Maybe a trader brought it with him. It's used a lot in aquariums, for lizards and things like that, and I've seen them make lamps out of it too."

"Yes, yes, thank you, Luis, that's good." Lonnie took the stick. It was hollow and full of holes, but Luis was right, cholla wood was strong. He tied it into his knot and gave it a twist.

"Make it tight. You have to cut off the circulation."

"I will. Thank you, Luis." Lonnie took the other arm of his shirt and tied it around the stick so it couldn't unfurl, and then slowly let go to see if it held. He relaxed.

Raúl, hearing the commotion, came running back. "¿Qué pasa? What's happening?"

Lonnie took hold of his ankle and squeezed. The bandage seemed to be holding tight. Slowly he stood. "Nothing, me and a snake had a difference of opinion, that's all, but I won."

"A snake bit señor Lonnie, a Bothrops asper, about a meter in length I would think. Poisonous too."

Raúl stepped forward. "I don't believe it," he said. "We're almost home and our leader has to get bit by a snake. Do you not see this as an omen? He's going to slow us down. He'll probably die, and leave us out here to die with him."

Mariana's eyes pinched in. Her nose wrinkled and her lips puckered hard. She squeezed both her hands into fists, stomping the ground. "Shut up! Just shut up! Raúl, you are the most stupid boy I know!"

All eyes went to Mariana. The little five year old had never so much as raised her voice at anyone, let alone her brother.

"He did that for me, estúpido! That snake was coiled, ready to eat a mouse, and I scared it and it was about to eat me, but señor Lonnie grabbed me and that bite—that was meant for me!"

"Look," Lonnie said, "we don't have time to worry about who did what for who. If we're lucky, we've got some time before I pass out, but I don't know how long. It doesn't matter how hard I tie the tourniquet, some of the venom is going to get through. Raúl's right, I probably won't make it. I'll go far as I can, and I'll try not to hold us up, but it's likely I'll pass out sometime. When that happens, someone has to run on ahead and find help. This path leads right to Posada. Stay on the trail, but if you see anyone, avoid them. Don't trust anyone until you reach Posada. Then ask to see Father Paulo, and if he's not there, talk to Nicole. If you can't get hold of her, find one of the sisters, or anyone who'll listen. Don't waste time. Get a few men to come back with a stretcher. You'll need it to carry me in. If I don't get to the hospital in pretty quick time I'll end up losing this leg, or..." Lonnie stopped short. He wasn't going to die, not now. Maybe it was leaning on his own understanding, but he knew God would never do that. "Alright, let's get moving."

THE CAB, the cheapest one Bill could negotiate, albeit another Volkswagen, let him off in the center of the village. He leaned in and paid the driver in American dollars. The driver took the money, stuffed it in his jeans, and without stopping to let the engine rest, did a U-turn around the plaza heading out of town, the little Volkswagen whining and grinding and sputtering its way down the cobblestone road. Bill stood in the middle of what looked like the town square, next to a well with a cistern for a base and a long wooden handle for pumping water. He raised his arm and wiped his brow. All around the perimeter were stalls and bins where vendors would meet and hawk their wares, but the kiosks were empty. Trading wouldn't begin until the cool of evening. Where to start? He looked around and saw the white-painted adobe walls of what looked like a convent and the damage done by the earthquake. Judging by the remains, the collapsed building had been a cathedral. Several people were standing beside the pile of bricks talking. He walked over. "¿Hablas inglés?" *Do you speak English?*

The men shook their heads in unison. Bill turned, looking down the narrow row of buildings. The village was completely surrounded by jungle except on one side where an opening dropped off toward the Pacific. The lane he'd come in on left the town at the other end dividing the town in two. A sign over an arched entry read "Posada." Maybe the proprietor spoke English.

Bill walked through the doors, noting how much cooler it was in the dark room. He made his way to the desk and popped the little bell sitting on the counter. No response. A pair of bull horns mounted on a green velvet plaque was nailed to the wall. He rang again.

"There's no one here."

Bill turned to see a boy in a wheelchair.

"Oh, gracias, thank you. I appreciate you letting me know." Bill walked over and squatted down on his haunches to converse eye to eye. "You speak good English, son."

"I had a good teacher."

"That so."

"Sí, all the children in the orphanage, we all learn English from señor Striker."

"Well, dang bust. You know señor Striker? Good, 'cause that's just who I'm looking for."

"He's not here either."

"Do you know where he is?"

The boy shook a head that was disproportionately large compared to the rest of his body. His hands were squirming in his lap. "Nobody does. He left many days ago and has not come back."

Rats. "Have you heard from him? Has he called or tried to get in touch with anyone?"

Again the boy shook his head. "No, señor."

Bill nodded and stood. "Is there anyone I can talk to who might know something?"

"You can try Father Paulo. He runs the mission, but I don't think he's heard anything either."

"And where can I find this Father Paulo?"

The boy turned his oversized head, looking over his shoulder. "He is in the hospital, señor."

"Oh. Is he ill?"

Sebastian cranked the wheels of his chair, turning it around, and began rolling toward the door. "No, señor, but one of the ladies in our village, my friend, la señorita Nicole, was buried alive in the earthquake. For three days she was underground and now we found her, so now she's in the hospital and they won't let me see her. And she's my friend."

Bill walked beside the wheelchair, keeping pace. "But your friend is alive?"

"Sí, she is alive, but they don't know for how long."

It was a pale day, almost white. Bill stepped outside into the glare of the blistering sun, following the young man in the wheelchair whom he supposed was taking him to the hospital. It smelled like wet beach sand, or the combination of rain and dust. The workers he'd seen earlier were stacking bricks. Who said the earthquake didn't cause any structural damage? That church was a pile of powder. And if the boy had his facts right, the woman who survived was a miracle. Bill had a sudden premonition. He was where he was supposed to be. He would wait until Lonnie returned. After all, he'd just been handed another dynamite story.

FORTY-FOUR

LONNIE WAS not at the airport with arms open wide. The plane touched down, skimming water from the wheels, but the passengers were thankful just to be on the ground. No one complained when they hydroplaned halfway down the runway before coming to a stop. Someone was there to pick up Nicole, someone Lonnie had sent on his behalf, but the letdown was more than she wanted to show, and made worse when she was told Lonnie was attending a board meeting in Hollywood where she imagined he was sitting around sharing tea and crumpets with Trudy.

Nicole had met her substitute escort on one other occasion. When Striker Films was in financial trouble, señor Enrique Ramírez, the local coffee plantation owner, had left Posada and come all the way to Hollywood to bail Lonnie out, a gesture that pulled the tailspinning company out of an imminent crash landing. He stood on the other side of the customs gate, umbrella in hand, welcoming her with a smile big as sunrise. But of course there was no sun, only rain, and a hard-driving rain at that, which in spite of Enrique's good intentions made her feel cloudy inside.

He took her by the arm, brimming with gentlemanly charm, and escorted her to his dated Mercedes where he introduced her to his wife and two sons. Señora Ramírez wore black lace with a net bonnet covering the top of her long flowing black hair. She was a Spaniard, through and through. She sat with a lattice fan cooling herself despite the fact the car's air conditioner was running the whole time. Nicole thanked the family for going out of their way to pick her up, but they made little of it insisting they had other business in town anyway. Señor Ramírez said he wouldn't have missed the opportunity to see her again for the world. She tried to understand why Lonnie couldn't be there. He had a film company to run, but couldn't he have missed just one board meeting, or have moved it to another day? Wasn't that the least he'd do for an old friend—or was she less than that? She was obviously too insignificant to warrant a rescheduling of his time.

She decided not to go out of her way to see him. Let him make the first move. See how he liked it. She dove into the business of administration, which the Alliance listed as her chief duty since this was what the hospital needed most. It would take many months to clean up the mess she found. She worked hard, frequently not retiring until after midnight, and had on more than one occasion found herself still shuffling paper when the rooster crowed at dawn's first light. Yet she asked for as many nursing duties as they could accommodate. She did her best to put Lonnie out of her mind. She wasn't there for romance, she was there to serve. It wasn't long before she earned the title of head nurse. The sisters, who never considered themselves medical experts anyway, gladly deferred to her for advice.

Other than from a distance, she didn't see Lonnie for more than a month. He didn't go out of his way to welcome her to Posada. He went on with his life as if she weren't there. And while his involvement with the locals took a fair amount of time, and even considering he frequently took off to remote villages where he ministered for days on end, there was really no excuse for not at least stopping by to say hi. She wasn't expecting a welcome wagon, a simple howyadoin' would have sufficed. They weren't complete strangers. This was nothing more than purposeful avoidance, which in her mind meant only one of two things—either he was being standoffish because he possessed secret amorous feelings and was shy and afraid of stammering like a fool in front of her, or he had the self-elevating conceit of a megaloid narcissist and believed she was *sooooooo* in love with him, he had to avoid her to keep from letting her down. Either way, she was determined not to give him the satisfaction of making the first move. She had earned the right to work in this town, and for better or worse, they would be working together. If he had a problem with that, too bad.

Ignoring him paid off. Lonnie finally came around, apologizing for not stopping by sooner and inviting her to church. His church. She was just waiting for him to ask, but patience was a virtue and hers had worn him down. He no longer felt threatened by her presence. Weekly Sunday meetings eventually led to a standing Thursday night dinner, which quickly became the most exciting part of her week. They would sit in the waning shades of evening, the lights in the arcade soft and the air warm. Roving minstrels would stop and entertain them as though they were lovers, even though Lonnie waved them off, cautioning them not to get the wrong idea. And though the conversation all too often revolved around Trudy and the otherworld of Hollywood, Nicole still basked in the thought that his eyes were on her. The prolonged stare that stayed perhaps a little longer than it should, and the casual touch of hands that logic said shouldn't have been. He had to feel some emotional connection. She was convinced he was fighting to suppress feelings he wanted to pretend didn't exist.

She just wished she had the courage to confront him. She would present him with an ultimatum: me or Trudy, make up your mind. But if he chose Trudy, what was she supposed to do, leave? She didn't want to leave, even if he wanted her to. Better to live in the fuzzy world of self-delusion than face the reality of rejection.

Then this whole thing with the children came up and he rushed off to save them, leaving her—again.

He'd only been gone a day when the letter came. She'd stood in the hotel lobby, actually on her way out the door, when she saw an envelope with Trudy's return address. She picked it up. She wanted to open it, but knew she couldn't, or toss it in the trash, which she couldn't do either, so she just stood there waving it in her hand. She brought it to her nose—perfumed! Why would Trudy write Lonnie a perfumed letter? She wasn't aware they were corresponding. She laid the letter back on the counter and walked outside.

She decided to ask Father Paulo if he'd heard anything from Lonnie. She walked across the courtyard, past the Portico of Saints, and into his office. Suddenly, the floor shifted under her feet. She stood for a second, watching as the tiles popped out of place, then turned and looked out the window. The bell tower was crumbling at its base like a carpet had been yanked out from underneath. The monolith came crashing down. She had but a second to react. She dove under the table, rolling onto her back and reaching out to keep the legs from collapsing. Then she heard the earth-shattering sound of the walls crashing around her, and everything went black.

LONNIE PLODDED along, his tennis shoes dragging dirt. Without the protection of his shirt, the merciless sun broiled his pasty-white shoulders red. He rubbed his face with his open palms. They were climbing now. The trail that led to the coast was now steadily rising as it crawled its way toward Posada, a thousand feet above the sea. The wind was driving in hard from the ocean, tearing at their hair and clothes and sending threads of red sand sailing away as Lonnie scuffed his feet. He stepped on a sharp rock and stumbled but recovered quickly, straightening his back and swinging his arms to give the appearance of normalcy. He was falling behind, though Sofía walked beside him with Juanito in her arms. Lonnie refused to look at his leg. It was numb, but if it was swelling or turning purple, he didn't want to know. *I need to keep going. Please God.* His head was buzzing—loud—like a chainsaw ripping through wood. Beads of sweat dotted his forehead, his hands felt moist and clammy. He knew what was coming. The blue sky, and sand, and palm trees, and grass began to swirl. He reached out to steady himself, but there was nothing to steady himself on. "Okay, I think I've gone as far as I can," he said in a hoarse whisper that no one but Sofía heard. "It's time for one of you to run aaahea..." but his legs disappeared. They were there one minute and gone the next. He fell face forward in the sand.

Sohpía turned and dropped to her knees, rolling Juanito aside. Her hand began pushing Lonnie's shoulder. "No, señor Lonnie, get up! You must get up! Get up!" Her hands went to her face. "No, Get up! Get up! Get up!" whereupon she broke into tears. Juanito crawled to his feet and stood, still wearing his parochial school blazer which he dusted off before combing a knot of curly hair with his fingers.

The others were a good ten yards further up the trail, but they spun around and seeing Lonnie and Sofía in trouble, rushed back.

Sofía's tears were gushing. She pulled a wet strand of hair from her mouth. "He's gone! I think he's dead!" She started pushing on Lonnie again. "Wake up, señor Lonnie, wake up,"

Luis leaned over with his hands on his knees. "He's not dead. He told us he'd pass out. That's all it is. Look, see, his chest is moving. His lungs are filling with air. He's still breathing."

The wind kept Sofía's black hair dancing around her face, pushing it into her mouth when she tried to speak. She pulled a handful away, pressing it against her neck. "Are you sure? I mean, absolutely sure? Because..."

"Look for yourself. You can see him breathing. Dead men don't breathe. The Bothrops is a bad snake. Its venom can kill you, but it's rare. Still, he needs a doctor. It is time to do what he said. Someone must run ahead and get help."

Each of the children looked at someone else, but in the end, all eyes came to rest on Raúl.

"Not me. I'm not leaving my sister. You go, Luis."

"Me? That's silly. By my calculation, I would take twice as long as you. I don't run. See, my legs are too short. I can't cover much distance, and my body mass is too heavy. There's more wind resistance for one thing, and it takes more effort to propel myself forward, and..."

"I cannot leave my sister."

Sofía put her hand under Lonnie's head. Her eyes welled, a single drop falling onto his face as she leaned in close, her hair brushing his cheek. She wanted to hear his breathing. She wanted to make sure he was alive. She listened and in spite of the pulsing wind, heard the hollow labored sound of deep sleep. She closed her eyes, swallowing the warm saltwater of her tears.

Lonnie's leg was twisted behind him, the ankle fat and discolored. Mariana took his pant cuff and slid it up as far as it would go. The limb looked twice its normal size and was bruised purple-green. It must hurt, but he hadn't said anything. She let go and glared at her brother. "Then I'll go." She turned and marched off down the trail. Raúl reached out to grab her arm but she tucked it in, eluding his grasp.

"Mariana! Wait!"

"Wait!"

It was the second, "Wait," the one from Luis, that made Mariana stop.

"I have a better idea."

Mariana crossed her arms and turned, her eyes urging Luis to be quick with his explanation.

"Señor Lonnie said we'd be home by dark and the sun is well past its zenith. Look, I would say it is past four." Luis raised a stubby finger and pointed at a flat afternoon sky. The haze had moved in, making the sun look fuzzy, like a yellow tennis ball bouncing off the green court of the ocean. "I figure we only have another few hours, and so far he hasn't slowed us down, at least not much, so we're probably right on schedule."

"Get to the point, Luis."

He brought his arm around and continued to point. "See those palm trees? Look around the bottom. See the fronds? I say we gather a bunch of them together and use them to make a stretcher and take him with us."

The trees were bending in the wind, their heads bobbing and ducking. Raúl shook his head. "Luis, I swear you are truly nuts. I'll go with you, Mariana."

"No! We can strip the fronds. They peel. They use them sometimes for making baskets. I read somewhere they even make hammocks with them. They're muy fuerte, strong. And the fibers make excellent string for tying. We can lace them together and make a mat. Then we just roll him on it and pull it like a sled.

"He's too heavy."

"There are five of us. If we all use our weight it will distribute the load and make it light. He only weighs about one fifty, and that means we only have to pull about thirty pounds each. That should be easy. The secret is in combining our strength, like horsepower. Many horses can pull a bigger cart than just one. If one of us runs ahead, it will take two, maybe three hours to get to the village, find someone to help, and then the same amount of time to get back. And then señor Lonnie will still have to be carried into town, which will take another three hours, even with grown men, and that's three trips, and probably at least ten hours. He could he dead by then. Even if it takes twice as long for us to pull him as it takes us to walk, it will still be faster, and we won't have to split up." His eyes darted from one person to the next, seeking affirmation, but finding none. Sofía's tears had begun to dry but her face held about as much expression as a sheet of paper, and Mariana's eyes were wide and empty. Raúl shook his head, shrugged his shoulders, and walked away.

BILL STOOD at the edge of the world, enjoying the vista of God. He could see for miles. The bottle-green bounty of the Pacific rolled and undulated and above it the vault of heaven could not contain the boundless blue. He inched his toes out to the rim. *Just don't look down.* It was a sheer drop of a thousand feet. Why would a tribe build its dwelling on the edge of a perilous cliff? Only one reason he could think of—human sacrifice—toss a virgin over the brink and appease an angry god. Where there weren't any volcanoes, you had to improvise. He ventured a peep over the side. *Brutal!* It might look like the body would hit water, but factoring in the onshore breeze, it was more likely to slam against the rocks. Thank God for Christianity. He may not have understood Catholics all that much, but at least they'd come preaching a God who offered life. He could imagine Lonnie using this as a point of inspiration. He knew that's what he would do. All that water bespeaking the infinite nature of the Creator. If nothing else, it was certainly a good place to pray.

ACROSS THE plaza, past the primitive fountain and the bazaar of wooden stalls with floors covered in hay, further down the town's time-worn cobblestone road where burros still brayed and chickens clucked while scratching for seeds, stood a incongruous building less than three years old. And inside the concrete facade of that building were some of the best technologies and latest medical advances known to man—none of which were of any use to Nicole.

The nurses were frantic. Fatima locked her fingers, pounding on Nicole's chest, once, twice, three times. They had to get her heart started again. It was intermittent, pumping one minute only to stop the next. Sister Gabriela reached for the paddles. She didn't know how much more Nicole's body could take. The doctor would only try three times, increasing the settings, and if that didn't work, give up. But Gabriela refused to lose hope. She had to do something. "Clear!"

One minute Nicole was standing in the sun, concerned about trivialities like Lonnie's whereabouts and the nature of his relationship with Trudy, and whether or not she should confront him about his inability to choose, and the next, she was under five feet of crushed brick in a dark world, wondering if her real concern shouldn't have been about what she would say when she saw the face of Jesus. There would be no room for Ryan on that day. All memories of Flyin' Ryan, alias Lyin' Ryan, cum Cryin' Ryan and Dyin' Ryan, would be gone. The slate would be wiped clean. So why, at this, the moment of her death, did he still dominate her mind?

FIVE CHILDREN, ranging in ages from five to thirteen, had accomplished what most adults left to fend for themselves under similar circumstances would never attempt to do. They managed to transport an object much heavier than themselves up an incline and over great distance, on a sled made of thatched palm fronds that they themselves had made.

The idea put forth by Luis proved incredibly resourceful. By placing a frond against each of their backs with the spines pointed up, hacking off those at the base of their necks, and wrapping the ones remaining around their shoulders and tying them off, and then using the stem of the frond hanging down to connect with the sled, he had ingeniously fashioned a harness for each of the children. Sofía was practised in the art of basket weaving, a craft passed down from one generation of women to the next, and was skilled at twining the fronds together. She assigned each member of the group to a project, securely fastening the yoke and the thatch mat upon which Lonnie would ride into a single cohesive unit. Raúl was the only one who complained, but he quit when he saw he was outnumbered. As the crazy idea began to take shape, and started to look like it might actually work, he pitched in to do his part, and following Sofía's lead, tied the assembly together.

They were stomping across a sandstone ridge, keeping to the path, plumes of red dust billowing up at their feet, but plowing ever onward. The wind coming in off the ocean scathed the bramble on either side of the trail, but they refused to let it slow them down. Even Juanito and Mariana pulled their weight. Between the five of them the load was surprisingly easy to manage, but Luis wasn't saying, "I told you so." He knew better than that. They moved together, pulling as a team, one foot in front of the other. They may have only covered a mile since Lonnie fell, but that was a mile closer to the village. There couldn't be many more to go. Following the edge of the cliff, the trail ran consistently uphill now, but it was reasonably smooth and thus far they hadn't found any obstacles they couldn't get around.

The sky had grown dark and heavy with ominous blue-gray clouds threatening rain. A rumbling could be heard in the distance. They could feel the wind spitting in their faces, and it gave them impetus to quicken the pace.

Lonnie remained unconscious. They couldn't ask him if they were heading in the right direction, but he'd told them to just keep going, so that's what they did. Maybe he was being optimistic, but he'd thought they'd make it by nightfall. They were counting on his being right. They wanted to avoid traveling by night, especially if it was going to rain.

AT A LOCATION hidden beneath a canopy of deep green foliage, new pens were being built. The digging of postholes and the unraveling of chain-link and reels of razor wire were evidence of preparations underway for a new generation of children. The flow of merchandise would not be stopped by the dismantling of the plantation, nor by one measly group of waifs who had disappeared. But that group *had* to be found. Badger cursed, flinging the stub of his cigar to the ground. Stringing lines for phones and computers was low priority, even if it meant being out of touch. Having a place to hold the kids took precedence. A new shipment would be arriving any day, and they couldn't very well shackle them to the trees.

To obtain information he was having to rely on a military issue long-range radio. He'd made sure the portable units were carried by every team on the mountain. He put the handset down, gritting his teeth, holding back the curses he wanted to scream to maintain an element of control. Every report he'd received delivered the same information. No new sightings.

The sky rumbled overhead. Great, and now it was going to rain. In an area boasting three hundred days of sun a year, the great escape had to take place during the rainy season. A military tarp with a camouflage pattern of browns and greens was stretched overhead to keep him dry, but even with a blockade of trees the wind still buffeted the canvas. It whipped and snapped, tearing at its grommets. His stumpy body leaned over the table, his arms spread out like anchors to keep the corners of his map from lifting and blowing away.

Only two sightings had been reported, the first right after the earthquake but the fugitives had fled up a hill and vanished. Even the turncoat Daniela hadn't been found, and there was proof she'd been shot. Blood was splattered on the dashboard, the seat, and the window, but there was no trace of her body. However unlikely, he couldn't discount the possibility she was still alive and traveling with the group, but if she were, she had to be slowing them down, and you'd think her blood would leave a trail to follow.

The second sighting came from Peñasco were two former workers had caught one of the children stealing garbage. At least they were desperate for food. They had to be getting weak from hunger, which would also slow them down. Unfortunately, the locals had bungled the capture. The boy had wrested himself from their hands and escaped into the night. In some ways being out of touch was a blessing. It meant he didn't have to listen to Miguel's polite but not so veiled threats. If they couldn't bring the missionary and the kids in, there would be nowhere on this green earth for them to hide. Miguel was not a forgiving man.

He had to conclude they were lost. Oaxaca was far north of their location. It would take them several extra days to get back, and they had to get to Oaxaca to return the police chief's son and secure protection. There was a time when Maximilian could have been counted on to turn them in, but with his own son bundled for sale with the rest—Badger glanced at Paco seated in a chair across from him, toying with that infernal knife—his loyalties would likely have changed. Badger had four men stationed outside the police station around the clock to intercept any attempt to bring the children in.

"Only two sightings. We have no idea where they are, and you sit there cleaning your nails."

Paco didn't look up. He sat beneath his straw cowboy hat with his denim vest hanging open, his vulgar tattoos on display. He mashed the blade against his cuticles, curled his fingers, and brought his hand up to examine his nails. "You worry too much, mi amigo. They have nowhere to go. You have offered a reward, and the peasants are afraid of Miguel. They won't cross him. We just be patient and wait. They show up soon enough."

Evil is addictive. For the totally depraved, nefarious behavior becomes so matter-of-fact, it's hard to recognize. But Badger saw evil in Paco. Maybe it was just the green cast given off by the tarp, but Paco's eyes looked yellow like those of a snake—or a demon. Even without the tarp, Badger would have called Paco's gaze malevolent—*look at the way he fondles that knife*. "I wish I had your confidence. You'd better hope they're not heading for Pochutia or Huatulco. I don't have enough men to cover every city on the map. And I don't know if the authorities in those places are loyal to Miguel."

Paco stood, the heels of his pointed-toe cowboy boots kicking the chair behind him, scooting it back. "Don't worry about Pochutia. I know we're covered there, and Huatulco's too far. Where you say they been?"

"Somewhere between here and the coast," Badger said, poking a stubby finger at the map.

Paco nodded. Pochutia was where he'd first met the boy and his sister, but the house was destroyed along with their parents. They had no reason to go back. On the other hand... "I know where they are," he said. He took his knife and stabbed the map, leaving it *twanging* back and forth, marking the spot.

FORTY-FIVE

NICOLE WAS floating. She didn't know how she got there but she found herself suspended from the ceiling and it made her feel dizzy. It was like the room had turned upside down and she was lying on her back looking up, only she was looking down. She viewed the setting from an abstract distance, not part of the scene itself. It was more like watching a video, a prerecorded segment of a day in the life of an emergency room nurse. Her friends Gabriela and Fatima were frantic, scurrying about the room in a tizzy. She hadn't seen such intense patient care since señor Alverez fell from a ladder, hit his head, and remained unconscious for three days. Something had them in a panic.

She felt like she should be down there helping. They were trying to save someone's life. There was a chrome rollaway bed, and white linen, and someone lying on the bed covered with blankets, and a monitor was droning *on and on and on*. The poor person was dead, flatline, game over, slip a toe tag on and cover the face with a sheet.

Gabriela raised her arms, revealing gigantic wings as she brought paddles down on the patient's chest. "Clear!" she yelled, as the body lurched forward. Her hands raised again. The wings folded back. They were folding in and out and changing color, first red, then blue, in and out, red and blue, in and out. The red made Nicole sad in a way she couldn't explain until Gabriela turned around. Inside those red wings she saw the visage of a man, her Lord in His passion, His blood outpoured covering His lifeless body as He hung on a cross. Her eyes grew misty and her heart faint, but as the wings folded in, the color changed to blue. Now she saw Christ in his glory, radiant and alive, shrouded in a blue-white light so bright she had to raise her hand to shield her eyes—red, blue, red, blue, passion, glory, passion, glory, as though the two were inseparably one, a composite forming a single color—royal purple. And in that moment she saw Jesus, not an image of the risen Lord, but God in the form of a man, the One who had died and was alive forevermore. When the color change stopped, she was looking into eyes that blazed with fire. He was calling her name.

"Nicole, do you believe My blood was shed for the remission of sin?"

"You know I do, Lord."

"And, for Ryan?"

"I...I...that's different. You saw what he did."

"You want to move on, yet you carry the weight of your past. Forgiveness comes to those who forgive. Give Ryan to Me."

"I've tried, Lord. You know I have. I've tried."

"With man it is impossible, but with God, all things are possible. Come unto Me all ye who labor and are heavy laden, and I will give you rest."

Nicole could feel her eyes flooding, tears clear as crystal tracking down her face. She saw her hands reaching out.

"Come home, Nicole. Enter into My rest." His arms were open wide, ready to receive her. He was motioning for her to follow, and for one brief second she felt like she was ready, but her mouth opened involuntarily and without thinking her lips said *I...I...please, Lord, can't I just say goodbye?*

THE RAIN fell in torrents. The five children struggled in their wet harnesses with their wet clothes sticking to their wet skin, the wet fabric pasted to their arms and legs placing a drag on their movements. Their hair was plastered to their faces. Streams of water poured off their noses, earlobes and chins, and ran down their bodies. The sharp wet edges of the thatch cut them to the bone, yet they struggled on.

Raúl unofficially assumed position as team leader, marshaling strength in an act of focused determination. His foot slid out from beneath him. He landed on his knees in the mud, but picked himself up and continued pulling. It was dark now, with visibility down to half a dozen feet. The mountain around them had turned into a river of slippery silt, but following Raúl's lead the children refused to call it quits, even though they pulled against futility. The criss-cross thatch of the mat behind them was like a grater, scooping up the sodden earth until the mat bogged down and came to a halt, caught on its soggy bottom.

Raúl dropped to his knees and looked up into the murky sky. He wished he were a bird. He wished he could sail up and over the mountain and see how far they had to go. If a mile was just over five thousand feet, as Luis said, and if with each stride they covered at least two feet, then with every few thousand steps they should cover a mile. They must have traveled several miles by now. Luis said they only had a few miles to go when they started out. But it didn't matter. This was it. They couldn't go any further. They were stuck in the mud.

If Raúl *had* been a bird, he would have seen they were only a few hundred yards from the village. He would have seen little yellow dots of light and been encouraged by how short the remaining distance was. But he was not a bird and not able to soar above so he could not tell that with all the progress they'd made, they had less than half a mile to go.

"HEY BABE, how's it goin'? Uh huh. No, actually, things here are pretty quiet. Uh, not so good, it's raining cats and dogs, but it's supposed to let up by morning. Look, I can't talk long, I'm on a private line, but I thought I'd better let you know I won't be staying at the hotel tonight, just in case you tried to call. No, it's not that. Uh huh, the accommodations are fine, I'm just trying to get a handle on the earthquake story. Turns out most of the damage was done in remote areas, so I'm out traipsing around the country looking for something to write about. Right now? Uh, well, I ended up in a little town called Posada. Yes, that's right. Yes, yes, where that missionary lives, but that's totally separate. It just happens the earthquake was centered in his area, so I thought, being as he lives here, I'd kill two birds with one stone and stop by and say hi. No, I couldn't. He's not even here. Oh, while we're on the subject, you should pray for him. He hasn't been seen in days, not since he stayed with us. Un uh, no one knows. I suspect he's alright, but people here are worried, and I don't blame them. Nope. Nothing about the children either. Yep, that's right."

"I'll probably end up staying a few days to write about the earthquake, though. You should see it. They've got a convent here, a church and a school, the whole nine yards, and the whole thing went kaput. I mean there's part of a wall and some rooms around back still standing, but the bulk of it bit the dust. Darn shame too. They say it was over a hundred years old. Apparently one of their parishioners was trapped inside and survived almost a week underground. She's in the hospital right now, fighting for her life. You could say a prayer for her, too. I think her name is Nicole. If she lives, it will be a miracle. I'm getting lots of photos of the damage and, uh huh. Okay, put the boys on."

THE CRY could be heard—but only barely. It was the voice of panic, the voice of alarm, like a ghost in the night. But the sound was muted by the rain and what may under ordinary circumstances have brought quick response was now ignored.

"Help! Someone, please! Please help us!"

The boy's lungs were raw. He tripped over a branch and slid elbows first in the mud, but picked himself up and kept going. He couldn't actually see what lay ahead. The moonless night was black, and if that weren't enough, his vision was further reduced by rain seeping into his eyes. He only knew he was on the trail because he wasn't plowing through bushes, which is what happened whenever he veered off.

He stopped short, out of breath, standing before a massive granite wall. He'd come within a foot of plowing into it. He reached out to take hold, leaning on the rock, breathing hard, staring at the monolith. The size and shape of the slab was vaguely familiar. The cliffs in Posada had granite outcrops, but this one was blocking the path. He turned to his left and saw orbs of fuzzy yellow light. He had reached the town. *Gracias a Dios. Thank You, God.* He took off running again.

"Help! Someone help us!" he blubbered, wiping the rain that dribbled from his chin. He continued to run. He was looking for the priest, that's what the preacher said to do. He had a pretty good idea of where the mission was supposed to be, but it wasn't there. He stopped, putting his hand to his chest, panting. Where else could he look? He started running again, past the fountain, past the stalls, until he came to the only place within reasonable distance that was lit—the tavern at the inn. He approached the entrance but hesitated, pausing outside the door to catch his breath, shivering and dripping water. The last time he raided a tavern at night, Miguel's men were inside, but this was life or death. He'd escaped before, he could do it again—if he had too. He stepped inside.

Heads turned, wrinkled faces glazed orange by the low-watt lamps. A hand brought a jalapeno pepper over a chin and dropped it into an open mouth. The rest paused from their frijoles and beer, waiting for an explanation from the mud-covered wretch.

"Ppa, ppa, please," he wheezed, "someone, help me."

BILL CAME down the stairs, his hiking boots thudding on the wood. The inn only had two floors, no need for an elevator. He was hungry, and with the street vendors calling it a night on account of rain, the Cantina was pretty much the only place to get food. He bounded off the last step and turned right, moseying under the arch that led inside, and ran smack dab into a bunch of murmuring patrons. They were grumbling about something, their voices agitated, their hands antsy, continually moving about. He sidled up to see what was going on. Curiosity might kill a cat or two, but journalists weren't cats. The crowd was surrounding a young boy who was soaking wet and smeared with mud, talking a mile a minute in Spanish Bill could not understand. The townspeople turned toward each other, fidgeting in a manner reminiscent of the mob he'd seen in the El Diablo. The boy turned, pointed out the door and started to leave followed by more than half the men. Bill watched as the boy stepped beyond the curve of light cast by the open door and fled into the darkness. He did not want to follow. It was pouring out there, for one thing, and his ankle was still sore.

"Does anyone here speak English?" Bill asked in a voice loud enough to be heard over the ruckus. He turned away, avoiding the press of men squeezing out the door. His eyes scanned the few people remaining at the tables. A dried-up apricot-faced woman with a braid of gray hair answered from the back of the room.

"Sí, sí, I speak un poco inglés," she said, raising her hand with her thumb and finger pinched together.

"Gracias," Bill said, moving to the table. "Gracias. My name is William Best. I'm a journalist. You know, I write for the newspaper, el periódico, sí?"

The old woman wore a mask of thick wrinkles. She nodded, her eyes weepy with age.

He waved his hand at the now empty door. "¿Qué pasó? What was that was about? Where are they going?"

The woman puckered her face, her lips bunched in wrinkles. "The boy say our padre hurt. They go to help."

Bill sucked in a breath, then nodded. "Gracias," he said. He turned and walked back to the door, stretching his hands across the opening, gripping both sides. The men were heading across the plaza, following the boy who was starting to sprint, and within seconds was in full stride, running until he disappeared into the darkness. Bill continued to watch until the last man disappeared around the corner. Then he placed a hand over his head and ducked into the rain, his boots splashing through the puddles as he half hobbled, half ran to catch up.

DAWN STOLE softly through the window. Nicole's eyes opened, looking at the ceiling. She took a long sustained breath, enjoying the familiar smell of a morning after a rain—the humid smells of damp clay and soggy grass. For a second she imagined she was in her own bed. She rolled her head toward the window and saw the curtains ruffle translucent in the sun, but it wasn't her window, and it wasn't her bed. Her muscles tensed, then she smiled. She was in the hospital. She had survived! She brought her hand up to finger the sheets, but it was wrapped in a bandage. She used the soft gauze to touch her cheek. A bandage there too. She tried raising her head and realized she hurt just about everywhere and especially—she took a deep breath—inside, but *oh my*, she thought, *I've been rescued.* She wanted to shout for joy, to leap from her bed, to scream *Hallelujah,* but it hurt *so* bad. She took a deep breath and tried to pull the blankets up under her chin. It *hurt* just to move. But she had made it. She tried once more to toss the blankets off, but her arm cramped. She raised herself on her elbows trying to sit up, but couldn't, and fell back, her head crashing to the pillow. It occurred to her that while she was alive and thankful for it, it would likely be some time before she was able to move about freely again.

At least the window was open. She could hear birds crooning in the woods, the hoofs of a donkey clopping on the cobblestones, and the squeaky wheels of a cart crossing the plaza. Somewhere chickens were fighting over seeds sown by their keeper —sounds she knew well. The sun streaming through the open window was vibrant, painting a yellow stripe on the floor.

She brought her head around to look the other way. Another bed was off to her left, filled with the lumpy shape of someone sleeping. She wasn't the only victim of the quake. The hospital was probably full. In the corner Fatima sat in a chair, her head nodding forward in sleep. Nicole smiled. Just like Fatima, to be there when she woke up.

It was a beautiful day. She stretched, rolling her shoulders, and reveled in the most radiant peace.

LIGHT ADVANCED on the Sierra Madre del Sur, stretching long shadows of mangrove and cocoa palm across the road as the van sped down from Oaxaca. They wound their way around the treacherous face of the mountain with a view overlooking the flat plain of the blue-green Pacific, releasing the color of the midnight sky. The oil and dirt highway was made for slow travel, or perhaps no travel at all, but it was not built to accommodate speed. That didn't stop the driver. The van hit a pothole at forty-plus miles an hour, throwing the occupants to the ceiling, all except Paco who flopped around like a rag doll in a cowboy hat with its hands tied to the steering wheel.

"Watch it! You're going to break our necks if you don't slow down."

Paco's eyes were pinched, partly from the glare and partly from his hostility. "I break more than that if you don't shut up."

Badger ground his teeth on his cigar, staring at the dashboard with one hand glued to the door's armrest and the other gripping the underside of his seat. He was too short to see the road ahead, so he couldn't tell what was coming, or prepare for a bump. He just had to take it when it happened. He tried to remain calm. For the moment, he needed Paco, "You don't slow down, *none* of us will get there alive."

"Sí, and if I *do* slow down, the missionary will collect the kids and be gone."

The van bounced over a series of washboards, tossing Badger and the two mercenaries who were clinging to the ripped mattress in the back from their seats.

"Maybe, but the way you're driving, we'll be lucky to get there at all."

BILL SENSED the presence of someone. His eyes popped open with a start, the abrupt light blinding him until his pupils could adjust. The silhouette took the form of Sister Fatima. She was hovering over him with her hands folded across her apron and a Mona Lisa smile on her lips.

Bill stretched and yawned, extending his legs to improve circulation, his portable computer sliding off his lap. Around him, other heads were starting to bristle with sleepy eyes fighting their way open. He was surrounded by children, all of whom had fallen asleep on each other's shoulders. The mud-caked urchins had insisted on not washing or going to bed until they learned what became of señor Lonnie and no amount of persuasion was able to change their minds. They were in the hospital sitting on a scruffy couch that had been donated to the mission. Perhaps not as comfortable as the waiting room of a big city hospital, but it sufficed. Bill's long arms were stretched out across the back encompassing them all.

Sister Fatima nodded. "He's going to be alright," she said. "He's still unconscious but we've been able to bring the swelling down and siphon off most of the poison. Were flushing the rest with a mild saline solution. He's been resting comfortably for the past few hours. And Nicole is awake now. I thought the children would want to know."

Everyone began talking at once. Bill glanced around at the bobbing heads. These kids were something else. He'd heard some of what they'd been through, including what the missionary endured to bring them back, and the sacrifice made by Daniela—what a tragedy. She had died while the armchair general was safe at home. But someone was missing. "Where's the young lady?" Bill asked.

Fatima smiled, unconcerned. She woke up a few minutes ago. I found her in the hall and told her. I think she's gone outside. I'm going to find Sister Gabriela and let her know the good news."

FORTY-SIX

EVERY CAR engine bears a distinctive mark. Call it the car's fingerprint if you will, a sound as unique and identifiable as DNA. Nicole's father once said he could tell more about the health of a car by listening than by running diagnostics. After he died—she was only eleven at the time—she found herself paying attention to what engines were saying, and with so few cars in Posada, she had it down pat. There was the *hummmmmm-varoooom* of señor Ramírez's Mercedes, and the *cough, sputter, grind* of the mailman's Jeep, and of course the *wheeeeze* and *hisssssssss* of the old school bus. Each had a unique voice, but the vehicle she heard now she didn't recognize. It had a high-pitched ticking, a *tap, tap, tap, tap, tap* that indicated the valves were dry. The breaks *squealed*, and with a *clunk* the sound stopped. Two hollow tin doors slammed. She heard men's voices, and another door creak open. She wanted to lean out the window to see who it was.

PACO AND BADGER held the rear doors of the van as two militia crawled out. Their eyes immediately roamed the market square. They turned to retrieve their AK-47s, and stood, if not at attention, at least on alert. They were mercenaries, part of Miguel's elite personal guard. They were commissioned to find the children, and the missionary, and bring them back.

The wind blew in from the ocean, sweeping across the cobblestones, tearing at their clothes. The short one threw the stub of a cigar to the ground, sending sparks flying. "Okay, Paco. You're the one who said they'd be here. Where are they?"

Paco shrugged, his tattoos rising and falling. "I say they be in this town. I didn't say where. But this man is the padre. I say we look for his church."

Four sets of eyes scanned the plaza. Off to the left was what looked like a bombed-out cathedral, piles of brick and stone and the remains of a collapsed building with two domed towers at the rear. A large bell stood upright on the ground. A brown-robed priest with his hands folded behind his back, and a sister in black, stepped out from behind a partially crumbled wall that looked like it had once connected the building to a row of structures further down.

Badger nodded at the soldiers.

They were enforcers, built like mastodons, with steroid muscles corded and veined, and expressionless faces that responded like robots. Miguel's elite. One was six inches taller than the other. The short one had gray hair combed straight back, riding long on his shoulders, and the tall one had a shaved head with a mustache that covered his lip and feathered down both sides of his chin. They pulled their weapons over their shoulders and took off in the direction of the priest. They didn't engage in pleasantries, nor did they invite the priest to join them. They simply grabbed the priest and nun, each by an arm, and dragged them over to Badger.

"Hey, hey. Perdón! What's going on?"

"Excuse me, Father, forgive the abruptness of my friends. We mean you no harm. We are looking for someone, *sniff,* a man they call the preacher."

"There must be some mistake..."

"Do not be difficult. He has something that belongs to us and it's imperative we get it back. If you'll tell us where we can find this man we'll be on our way, and no trouble will come to your village." Badger wiped his nose on his sleeve.

Isabel shot a sideways glance at the hospital. "I think you're in the wrong place," Paulo said. "I'm the only priest in this town. If you want me to hear your confession, I'm at your service. Otherwise, I'm afraid I can't help." He took Sister Isabel's arm and turned to leave, but the mercenaries stepped forward, blocking his path.

Badger smiled, his buckteeth yellow as a gopher's. "There is no mistake, Father. The man we are looking for lives here. He runs an orphanage. I'm sure you know who we mean."

"I have not seen him. He's been gone over a week."

Isabel stared at the ground. Her hands were folded in front of her apron with her fingers entwined, but she was rubbing her thumbs together. Paco grabbed her by the arm. "And what about you, Sister? What do you say?"

She grabbed at Paco's hand, trying to tear it away, but shook her head, keeping it bowed beneath her headpiece, hiding her eyes.

"What? You saying you don't know either? Somehow, I don't believe you."

Paco slid his eyes to the man next to him and raised his chin toward the priest. The mastiff responded by putting his gun to Paulo's head. Paco turned his attention to Isabel again. "I think you will tell me, or the good Father will be in heaven before he blinks."

The priest's eyes widened. He sucked in his cheeks, puckering his lips, and for a moment his face was gray as cardboard. Then he closed his eyes and when he opened them, his face was relaxed. He smiled and crossed himself. "She has nothing to say. You may shoot your gun, señor, but what you said is true. I *will* be in heaven. And you will damn yourself to perdition. But that is between you and God. I've made my peace."

Paco nodded, his cowboy hat dipping in the sun. He grabbed Isabel by the elbow, slammed her against the van, and reaching down, slipped his knife from its sheath. He held it against her back. "What about you, Sister? Are you ready to meet your Maker?"

She turned her head toward Father Paulo, looking for support. Her face was drained of color, her lips quivering. She scrunched her eyes, now filled with tears, and mumbled something, but Paco took her wrist and slammed her hand on the hood of the van. He leaned against her using his weight to hold her in place, and brought the butt of his knife down, smacking her knuckles until her closed fist was forced to open. He was breathing heavily, keeping his mouth close to her ear so she could feel his breath. He slid the blade down over her knuckles and applied pressure. "Tell me what I want to know, Sister, or three seconds from now you won't have a finger, and three seconds more you be missing two, and three seconds after that, eh, until there be no fingers on your hand. Uno."

"Wait!" Paulo said.

"Dos."

"Don't do it!"

"Tres." Paco started bearing down on the knife.

"*Nooooo!* Please! He's in the *haa, haass*, hospital!" Isabel's face gushed. *"Pleeeeeease!"*

Paco eased his grip, spinning her around. He pulled her in close, bringing her head under the brim of his hat, panting into her face, his breath moist and fecund. "Thank you, Sister." He let go and slipped his knife into its sheath, looking over his shoulder at the two commandos. They nodded and took off, pounding the earth as they thundered toward the building.

Badger combed back wisps of hair that were sticking out from the sides of his head. "Forgive us, Father, but these things are necessary. I promise you, the children will not be harmed."

BILL HEARD the commotion. He got up struggling from the cushioned depth of the sofa and went to the door, limping more from his foot being asleep than the sprain. He was stepping outside just as two men entered brandishing weapons. Bill recognized the make—*Russian*. He raised his hands shoulder high as an AK-47 was leveled at his chest, forcing him back into the room. The four children were still squished together on the couch, lying atop one another. He glanced around for his computer, but it had slipped behind a cushion out of sight. The men spoke in Spanish. One with a flowing gray mane crossed the room and went out the other door. Bill heard his feet pounding up the stairs. The one who stayed behind was Bill's height and built like a brick. Bill outweighed him, but he'd grown soft, and this guy looked like he ate steroids for candy. Plus he had a gun. He'd have to catch him off guard to take him. The gun was pointed at the children. Bill didn't need to speak the language to know what he was saying. The kids began to line up and move toward the door. Bill tried to intervene but found the weapon aimed once more at his chest. He raised his hands again and started to back up, but the man swung the gun around, clipping him under the chin. Bill felt a rupture of bone and tissue. The lights went out for a fraction of a second, but he willed them back on. The man swept his gun toward the door. Bill didn't hesitate. He turned and followed the children out. They were herded into the street where an emaciated man, looking like a lizard dressed in a cowboy suit, and a shorter, thicker man like a hog walking upright, were waiting beside the priest Bill met earlier and one of the nuns. The short one addressed Bill in English. "Who are you, señor? What is your name?"

Bill waggled his jaw and slipped his arm up to wipe blood from his chin. "Bill, Bill Best. And you, compadre, who are you?"

"I will ask the questions. What is your business here?" He smiled, wiped his nose, and pushed back his thin hair.

Before Bill could answer, the other thug appeared in the hospital's second floor window. He yelled something to the men in the courtyard. In the short exchange that followed Bill knew they had found Lonnie. The tall baldheaded goon handed his weapon to the snorting hog-man and took off in the direction of the hospital. The man fumbled with the weapon holding it awkwardly. Bill doubted he knew how to use it. The skinny cowboy with large tattoos on his thin arms walked around to the back of the van and opened the doors. He looked at the kids, his eyes slithering back and forth from one child to the next. Two of the boys began climbing in but the one they called Raúl held back. He grabbed his sister's arm keeping her at his side. The skinny one snickered and leaned in to say something to the girl, but Raúl hocked up phlegm and spat in his face. The man froze. His eyes tightened till they were slits under the brim of his hat. He reached for his knife, but the stocky one said something that made him pull back. His arm relaxed. He let go of the knife and smiled at Raúl, using his shoulder to wipe his cheek.

Lonnie was being dragged across the courtyard. The two hired guns held him under either arm and dropped him at the hog-man's feet. Bill couldn't understand what he was saying, but the little bucktoothed man seemed to grow increasingly impatient and finally kicked Lonnie in the side, sending wisps of hair flying. The sister's hand flew to her mouth, and the priest reached down to help. Bill took a step forward but got the butt of a gun jammed into his ribs. He lost wind and grabbed his waist, doubling over, gasping for air. He tried to straighten himself, his hand reaching out for something to grasp. He was choking. Through tear-filled eyes he saw the priest on his knees, holding Lonnie's hand. Couldn't they see the man was too weak to stand? The sawed-off runt said something. The goons pushed the priest aside and grabbed Lonnie under the arms yanking him to his feet leaving the priest sprawling in the dirt. Lonnie's head lobbed forward. His eyes were open a sliver, but he looked unconscious.

"Well, señor, you have led us on, what is it you Americans say? A wild goose chase, eh? But now we must go back and finish what we started. Okay, we have four here, where is the other one, the older girl?"

Lonnie remained limp. They held him upright, but it was like propping up a scarecrow.

"Ah señor, I warn you, do not ignore me. Refusing to talk can be most unpleasant. Mi amigo here has a very sharp knife, isn't that right Paco? Sí, sí. Most unpleasant. Perhaps he'll cut out your tongue and feed it to the ravens. Then you will have an excuse for not talking. Sí? You know we mean it. We've been through this before. Why not save yourself all this pain, eh? Do not worry, the young lady will not be hurt."

Lonnie's head continued to hang motionless. Paco shrugged. He grabbed Lonnie's hair and pulled his head back, raising his knife, his snake eyes glinting. He started to bring his knife down but Raúl screamed, *"Noooooooo!"* He let go of Mariana and rushed forward tackling Paco around the waist.

Paco's reaction was instinctive. His knife rose over the boy's head and started to come down but Bill staggered forward grasping the arm, stopping it midair. With lightning speed, Paco brought his left hand up to take the knife and thrust it forward, piercing Bill in the side. Bill froze, still holding the empty hand, his eyebrows raised in complete surprise. He stepped back, looking down at the blade stuck in his gut, unable to believe he'd been stabbed—*not an armchair general now.* His hand came up to cover the wound, blood seeping through his fingers as he stumbled backward, tripped and fell to the ground landing on his seat. Then he fell over with his knees curled up under him like a sleeping child.

Isabel screamed and covered her mouth, tears gushing. Paulo struggled to his feet. He looked at the man on the ground putting his arm around Isabel's shoulder to console her, but she pulled away.

Paco relaxed. He put a foot on Bill and reached down to dislodge his knife, wiping it on his leg before slipping it into its sheath. He looked up at the nun, but she quickly averted her eyes and redirected them to a spot out by the cliffs. For a second they grew wide, and she sipped in a short breath, then they darted away—but it was too late.

Paco raised his chin and motioned to his left. The men pulled Lonnie's unconscious body to the vehicle and lugged him inside. Then he picked up Mariana who squealed, kicking and screaming as she was tossed into the van and Raúl, unwilling to leave his sister, scrambled in behind. Paco slammed the doors with a sad finality.

On the other side of town, between two granite boulders perched on the edge of a cliff, stood the one they were looking for. Sofía's hair was being tossed by the wind, lifting and swirling around her face, her long dress snapping like a flag. Paco took off in her direction. She stood there, frozen in place, pulling the hair away from her eyes as she watched the man get closer and closer, one step at a time. There was no place to run, nothing behind her but heaven and a vast expanse of water. Paco was within a few feet, reaching out to take her hand almost as if he were being polite and offering to help her down.

Suddenly her arms floated out, extending so that her silhouette formed the shadow of a cross against the pale sky. "Soy una mariposa. Tengo alas para volar." *I am a butterfly. I have wings to fly.*

Then she turned and sailed over the side.

FORTY-SEVEN

"OH LORD, *oh God. No, oh God!*" Nicole slid down the wall, melting on the floor like a puddle of butter. Just a few minutes ago a man had entered the room carrying a gun and walked straight to the other bed, ripping off the covers. It was Lonnie. She hadn't even known. *How long was I out?* She had no concept of the number of days she'd been underground. Lonnie had returned. Had he found the children?

The man ordered Lonnie to get up, but he was obviously sedated. Why was the man yelling? Lonnie was in no shape to respond. The man reached out and slapped his face. Lonnie moaned but couldn't raise his head.

The man had walked to the window and called down to someone in the plaza, his eyes warning Nicole to stay put. A minute later he was joined by a second man. They went to the bed and took hold of Lonnie, hauling him to the floor and then across the room. She heard the *whump, whump, whump* of his body being dragged downstairs. Using what little strength she had, she tried to swing her feet around to roll off the bed, but when her toe became entangled in the sheet, she tripped and found herself lying on the ground. She tried to get up but pain shot up her arms and she collapsed to her side. She eased herself to her knees, wobbling, and crawled to the window. She threw her gauze-wrapped hand over the sill and pulled until she was elevated enough to peer into the courtyard below. Father Paulo and Sister Isabel were standing by four men, two of which were holding Lonnie. A fifth man lay bleeding on the ground—*dead?* The two men who held Lonnie opened the rear doors of a faded blue van and thrust him inside, and another man, a greasy Mexican cowboy, began walking in the direction of the cliff. Nicole tracked to see why, and—*oh no, he's after Sofía!* She was standing at the sharp edge, arms outstretched as she'd seen Lonnie do so many times. The man wore a denim vest over his bare skin. He reached out to take Sofía's hand, but she calmly stood there with her eyes raised toward heaven and sang out something about a butterfly, and then turned and dove over the side.

Oh God, no. Pleeeease, have mercy.

The four men climbed into the van and with wheels spinning drove away leaving Paulo holding onto Isabel, and the dead man lying in a pool of blood and cloud of dust.

THE VAN was bouncing across ruts in the road, the tin walls shuddering, but at least Paco was driving sanely now. He'd accomplished his mission. He'd done what he'd vowed to do. He'd recovered the children. He alone had known where to find them, and how to get them back. He was already spending his reward—there was a new cock he would buy, the greatest fighter in all Mexico with the quickest spurs ever, and sharpest, like razors in the gut. No opponent could survive that—and then he would make even more money.

"See amigo, I told you we would find them."

"Sí, but not all. We lost la chica. Miguel will not be pleased."

Paco's mouth scrunched into a knot, looking like a head of cabbage. Under his hat his eyes were narrow. He slid a sideways glance at his pompous partner. The little man was all chest, like a gunny sack stuffed with cornmeal. No, a pompous sack of donkey dung. Paco smiled thinly. "Fool! Miguel did not want that one. I took her on my own. We have the two, the brother and sister. These he wanted. He sent me after them, and the policeman's son. And don't give me no stink about that one. His old man disrespect me and I could not let it pass, okay? Anyway, he is young. These lions, they like their meat tender, eh? He will bring a good price. But that tall skinny chica, she was too old—and that other fat one, muy gordo, already he is a problem. Miguel does not care about them. He only wanted them 'cause they see his face. La chica's death will not cause him grief."

Badger pulled a fresh cigar from his yellow teeth. "Her death was his decision to make, not yours. Are you willing to forfeit her price?"

Paco wiped his hand on his chest and brought it away glistening with sweat. Even with the windows open, the musty van sweltered in the morning heat. He looked up just as they hit a bump, bounced, and ran over a half dozen limbs before he was able to slam his foot on the brake, the metal screeching as the van skidded to a stop. Badger was thrown forward against the dash and the kids and men in the back went flying. A curtain of dust swept across the road.

"What is this?"

A tree lay across the narrow dirt track making it impossible to pass. It had not been there when they'd come down the mountain traveling the opposite direction. Paco felt a moment of apprehension. He looked right and left out both windows and checked his mirrors. Nothing but trees and bushes bending in the wind. It must have blown down. "Get out and move that log," he said over his shoulder. He shifted his eyes to Badger who was already climbing out to open the rear door. The soldiers, holding onto their guns, crawled out and *blamm, blamm*, the wind banged the doors closed behind them. Badger returned to his seat up front. The men moved along the side of the van, walking cautiously. Except for the sound of the wind, the jungle bordering the road was quiet. No cawing ravens or twittering birds. They looked around, set their guns against the side of the tree, and began to push.

IN THE SHADOWY back of the van, Raúl contemplated an escape. The doors had slammed one after the other but not in the right sequence and the locking mechanism hadn't engaged. He turned and found his sister also studying the crack of light. She'd know what to do. They weren't bound. He could kick the doors open and, *zip*, be gone. They wouldn't be able to catch them all, especially if they split up and ran different directions. The woods were thick. Slowly, he turned to see if the others were with him, but they seemed clueless. *Ay caramba*, Luis wouldn't get ten feet. He could waddle, but not run. Someone would have to pull him along, like before, and that would slow them down. *So what?* It was every man for himself. But Mariana and Juanito had short legs. And they'd have to leave the missionary behind. For the first time, and for reasons he could not explain, Raúl felt a twinge of hesitation. *Why?* The man was unconscious. They couldn't be expected to carry him. Movement up front caught his attention. His head snapped around.

THE FRONT doors were flung open simultaneously and armed men filled the gap, pointing pistols at Paco and Badger. Several uniformed men stepped out of the woods with rifles pointed at the men pushing the log who immediately raised their hands.

"Get out, por favor," someone said.

The rear doors opened, but there was no one there. Slowly, a man with a rifle raised shoulder high crept around the back of the van. He stayed a good distance back, moving warily as though expecting someone to start shooting from inside. It took a second for the children's eyes to adjust to the light, but when they did they saw the man was wearing a dark blue uniform with a gold badge on his chest—*la policía?* The children scrambled to climb out, but the last of them, little Jaunito, didn't make it. Before his feet hit the ground he was scooped up by a tall man who held him out at arm's length.

"Ah, my son. It is good to see you. You had your mother sick with worry." The man also wore a blue uniform but his had boards with stripes on the shoulders, and a row of stars pinned to his collar. His dark sunglasses rode under the broad bill of his cap. He walked around to the front. Raúl followed but stopped at the rear corner of the van just far enough back to be able to run if necessary, but close enough to see. The other children grouped around, hugging the taillights and craning their necks to get a better look.

Maximilian turned, handing his son to one of his officers. The boy clung to his neck, fighting fiercely to hold on. He made a last grasp at his father's collar before breaking out in tears as he was pulled away. "It is alright, my son. I'm right here. I'll be taking you home. Just give me a minute alone with these men, por favor."

Paco, Badger, and the two henchmen were now standing in a line surrounded by a half dozen uniformed officers with guns at the ready. Maximilian walked over and stood in front of the group. The enforcers were equal to his size, but he was taller than Paco, cowboy hat and all, and Badger only came to his chest. He began pacing back and forth. "I want to thank you, señor Badger. You found my child and, as I can see, you were bringing him back to me. Gracias."

Badger's face brightened momentarily, not enough to say he was smiling, but enough to show relief. He resumed his mask of seriousness, removing his cigar. "Sí, we found your son mixed up with these we were sending to school in the U.S. but we realized our mistake and were just on our way to return him to you."

Maximilian looked straight at Paco. If eyes were bullets, Paco would be dead. "Yes, that is what I thought. Miguel would not to be so foolish as to take my son. Such a mistake would have grave consequences."

Paco's lips curled and he spat on the ground. "You sack o' donkey feed. Miguel ever hear you talk like that, he have your head. You touch any of us, or threaten us, you won't live to see another day."

Maximilian nodded, his bottom lip puckering. He looked around as though silently counting his men.

"They won't help you. There's not a man here who's not on Miguel's payroll, including you."

Maximilian spun around and smiled, his copper face bright as a new minted coin, his teeth perfect and white. "What was that? Did I hear you say my men are being paid by Don Miguel? There must be some mistake. None of my men would take a bribe. No, I do not think so." He shook his head, his hands planted behind him as he rocked on the heels of his shiny black boots. "I suppose we could ask Don Miguel. I'm sure he could straighten this out. Ah, but alas, no, we cannot. Perhaps you have not heard. There's been an unfortunate accident." Maximilian resumed his pacing. "Yes, most unfortunate.

Miguel's house caught fire and burned to the ground and sadly the Don was inside and did not survive. Very sad. But you are still my friends, are you not?"

From his place behind the van Raúl broke into a grin. He stared at Paco, his thoughts plainly visible—*a fire. Perfect justice. You pile of garbage!* He eyed the pistol in the holster of the officer standing beside him, but felt Mariana's hand slip into his own, preventing him from reaching for it.

"Sí, we are friends," Badger interjected. He dropped his cigar to the ground, crushing it under his heel. "I have mucho dinero. Don Miguel paid me well, but gave me no time to spend it. And what can I do with so much? I'm sure we can work this out. How much you..."

Maximilian swung around. "Do not speak of such matters in front of the children." His tone was harsh, but then he smiled. "Come, let us talk in private." He extended his hand like a man inviting guests to enjoy an after dinner cigar. His officers followed as Maximilian led his party down the road, all but the one holding Jaunito. He stayed behind. Raúl assumed he was there for their protection. But what if Jaunito's father worked a deal with the bad men? Would they still have time to run? He stepped out from behind the van. Off to the right the trees were only a dozen feet deep bordering the edge of the mountain beyond which, through the boughs, the blue Pacific could be seen shining in the sun. That way led to a cliff. They would have to go left, up the mountain. The men continued down the road until they disappeared around the bend.

SITTING IN the sun, without air circulating through the open windows, the back of the van had become insufferably hot. Lonnie began to wake from his stupor. His forehead was beaded with sweat. He rolled to the side and tried sitting up, and then, still groggy and not entirely sure of where he was, pulled himself to the door. He leaned against the opening and swiveled his legs over the rear bumper. Raúl felt the movement.

"¿Qué pasa?" Lonnie whispered, as Raúl's head swung into view. Off in the distance a gun went *pop, pop, pop*, like someone shooting a tin can. Lonnie wrinkled his nose, looking confused, and the children craned their necks to see, but the burst was short and ended as quickly as it started. The children surrounded Lonnie, taking turns hugging his neck. Lonnie grimaced, his sunburn and lacerations still tender. He straightened his back and looked both ways, counting heads. "Where's Sofía?" he asked.

"She isn't with us. I don't think they found her," Raúl said. "I think maybe she got away."

Juanito's father and his cadre of uniformed officers turned the corner coming back into view, but instead of walking, they were now riding in a column of Jeeps, three of them in a line, and the others were missing. Raúl's heart began to race. *Had they escaped? Wouldn't the police chase them? Or were they paid off? Did they let them go?*

The column came to a halt. One of the policemen held a pair of shiny cowboy boots in his lap. The tall officer got out. His dark shades, uniform, and crested hat with its gold emblem lent an air of authority. He approached Lonnie and stuck out his hand. A dozen dress ribbons and other accommodations were pinned to this chest. "Ah, señor Striker. So we have the opportunity to meet. It is good to find you sitting up. Allow me to introduce myself. I am Maximilian Ortega, chief of police of Oaxaca. I have been told you saved my son's life."

Lonnie nodded groggily. He hadn't done all that much. He'd run like a scared rabbit, just like everyone else. How do you take credit for that? God had more to do with their safe return than he did—*and Daniela.*

Juanito climbed down from the arms of his guardian and pulled on the leg of his father's trousers. "What happened, Papá. What happened? We heard guns. What happened?"

"Ah, a most unfortunate accident. These cliffs are very dangerous. We were talking to the men who were with you and the wind, very strong and most unexpected, came up and swept them over the edge. My men tried to save them. One even reached out with his rifle to give them something to hang onto but it accidentally went off. That is what you heard. It happened so quickly there was nothing we could do.

"But now we have other things to think about. Let us return to Posada. We can talk more there. You kids hop in the Jeep with my men. All except you, my son," he said, stooping down to pick up Juanito. I want you and señor Lonnie to ride with me." He held his son in one arm and slipped the other around Lonnie's waist, offering to help him walk. "One of the good sisters at the mission called me last night to let me know you had rescued my son. I tell you, I couldn't sleep, but my wife has been ill and I had to stay with her, you understand. I wasn't able to leave until first light, but then on my way here I received an urgent call from your village saying you and the children had been taken hostage, and that you were headed this way..."

FORTY-EIGHT

THE ARTICLE left on Bill's laptop was found by Paulo and brought to Lonnie while still in the hospital. The computer of course had been shipped along with Bill's personal belongings back to his home in Oregon, but not before Lonnie had a chance to read what Bill had written. He blushed. The flattery was undeserved. It was Bill who deserved the accolades, not he. He was neither brave nor courageous, and he most certainly was not great. He was weak, and broken. If he had any virtue at all it was that he was obedient. At least Bill had the grace not to mention his name. Part of him hoped the article would never see print, but that would probably be determined by whoever had commissioned Bill to write the story.

> I've known greatness—not the kind you typically think of when you see men of power and influence. I'm talking about greatness of the inner man, or greatness of the soul. The accumulation of great wealth, the requisitioning of land through conquest, the power 2 of politics and the wheeling and dealing in the board rooms of corporate business, all leave the superficial impression of being great, but what I'm talking about is the antithesis. It's when a man is ready to forsake all he has, to give everything, including his life, for the good of someone else. True greatness is seen in what a man is willing to give, not in what he has.
>
> Until just recently I'd experienced that kind of

greatness only once before, in Vietnam. I was with three other troops. We were dug in behind coils of barbed wire when a grenade came sailing over the rice paddies into our bunker. The four of us all saw it at the same time, and we knew we were going to die, yours truly included. But one man, John Swyburn, jumped on that grenade. Three people are now alive because John believed the death of one was better than the deaths of four. He gave himself that we might live. The Good Book says, "Greater love hath no man than he lay down his life for a friend." That's true greatness.

A while back I wrote a series of articles about a heinous evil that has quietly grown among us like a cancer, deadly and unseen. Many have heard it discussed, but only in passing conversation. It is rarely debated in open forum and few have an inkling of how big the problem is. In most cases, it doesn't affect our families, or our jobs, or our day-to-day lives, so we are hesitant to become involved or even be concerned. I'm talking about the buying and selling of innocent children.

Unlike the trafficking of drugs, which visibly destroys a person's life and wreaks havoc on society, leaving our politicians no choice but to keep it contained, or weapons trafficking, which lays death at our feet and forces us to demand measures be taken to ensure our families are safe, human trafficking is done invisibly. Its victims, mostly children, come across our borders holding the hands of those claiming to be their parents, or by busloads feigning to be school tours with authorization to visit American historical sites, in trucks moving across the borderless desserts at night, and in freight containers shipped across the oceans. Those who survive to adulthood are so degraded, or have themselves become so deranged, they rarely speak of the physical and emotional abuse, so the crime is rarely reported, and few know it exists. But the truth is, in excess of a half million people are brought across international borders and sold into the savagery of the sex trade every year. Little children, innocent ones, sold to pimps who market their bodies for profit. A fourteen year old found in a bar in Florida was forced to service thirty grown men a day, while young boys sold to pedophiles are passed around from one sadistic ring to another. Think of it—half a million kids every year and nobody knows. So it continues unabated.

It's not that governments aren't aware, or aren't working to limit the scope of the problem. They are. After the tsunami in Indonesia, eight brothels catering specifically to pedophiles were discovered and shut down, and for a time the government cracked down on child prostitution rings. And in China, a man convicted of child trafficking was recently sentenced to death.

Efforts are being made. Only two countries continue to ignore the problem, Japan and Mexico, and international pressure, some of which will undoubtedly be brought to bear after the publication of recent events, will eventually make them also do their part. But until the world's citizens stand up and cry "enough!" only minimal tax dollars will be allocated to address the problem.

We should all take to heart the oft-quoted words of Edmund Burke: "The only thing required for evil to triumph is for good men to do nothing." We cannot afford to stand by and watch while opportunists profit from pandering to the depraved at the expense of the innocent. We must stand up and say, "No more—not in my country, not in my town, not in my backyard."

Whether you know it or not, you have the power to bring about change.

I recently had the pleasure of meeting a missionary who refused to let evil triumph, an unassuming, self-effacing man, but imminently courageous and strong, who found children being bought and sold right under his nose. To protect him from further repercussion, I will leave his name anonymous. Suffice it to say the story took place in Mexico, in an orphanage where several kids under his care disappeared. He went to the authorities and was told there was nothing they could do. Abductions were being reported with increasing frequency, especially among street kids and orphans. A local crime lord was known to be responsible, but the police refused to get involved. The missionary was faced with a choice. He could turn and walk away, and perhaps vow to keep a more watchful eye on his kids in the future, or he could take action. This man chose to do the unthinkable. He single-handedly went after the entire cartel.

Such an endeavor usually comes at great cost. At least one person lost their life trying to save the children, and the missionary himself was severely tortured, whipped and beaten. He, like my friend in Vietnam, placed the lives of others above his own. Because of his willingness to sacrifice himself, they are alive. But he'll bear the scars of his actions the rest of his life.

When I see greatness like this, it brings to mind the words of men like Patrick Henry who in arguing for independence said, "Is life so dear, or peace so sweet, as to be purchased at the price of chains and slavery? Forbid it, Almighty God! I know not what course others may take; but as for me, give me liberty or give me death!" He would, I'm sure, have fought

> for the freedom of enslaved children as well. Also Nathan Hale, a young patriot who at the age of twenty-one stood before his British executioners and said, "I regret only that I have but one life to give for my country!" That's the kind of self-sacrifice that makes a person great.
>
> It doesn't always mean death. Sometimes our greatness is revealed by the way we live. Think of the people saved by the self-sacrificing efforts of Albert Schweitzer and Mother Teresa. They could have chosen easier lives for themselves, but they sacrificed their own comfort for the well-being of others. They took the biblical view that to be great in God's kingdom, you have to be a servant.
>
> Few among us will have the opportunity to acquire much of this world's wealth, but anyone can choose to be great. It's not about how much money, land, or power you accumulate. True greatness can only be measured by how much you're willing to give.

LONNIE STOOD in his favorite spot in the whole world, on the extreme edge of a thousand-foot drop with his arms outstretched to embrace the setting sun and his heart wide open to embrace his God. Most of his weight rested on one foot. He was still limping but was getting around without a crutch and gaining more strength every day. He'd only been released from the hospital that very afternoon.

The letter had been found on the hotel's registration desk. Few received mail in Posada, the post office only delivered twice a week, and since no one thought to tell him or bring it by the hospital, he didn't know it was there. According to the postmark it had left Malibu shortly after they talked, which surprised him. He would've thought such an important decision would take more time. The fragrance flooded his head with memories. Trudy was a beguiling woman. He was nervous about opening it, apprehensive about what it might say. He kept the envelope sealed in his pocket, at least for the moment.

He needed time to pray.

He took in the smell of seaweed and saltwater, a fragrance he'd come to love even more than the smell of Trudy's perfume, though she'd probably take exception to the thought. But it was the smell of all things familiar, the smell of peace and tranquility. It was the smell of home. The view was spectacular. Multicolored rays zoomed out from the horizon—magenta and blue, peach and purple and orange, with fleecy clouds absorbing their light. He wondered if Sofía had imagined such a display of color before leaping into the arms of Jesus.

He would disagree with Father Paulo on this one. He would never sanction suicide. Killing yourself was wrong—period! But he had to believe the real Sofía had been murdered long ago by violent men. Her body went through the motions, but her spirit had fled. All that remained was an empty shell. It wasn't about lacking the courage to go on. It was about a lifeless body refusing to be used by necrophiliacs.

He felt his eyes burning, his vision starting to blur. He'd been told of her swan song, the words of her final cry. He recalled a conversation they'd had. He'd shared with her how in Christ she was a new creation, and likened it to a caterpillar leaving its cocoon as a butterfly. He could only hope she had cried out to Him and received mercy. It might be poor theology, but he chose to believe God had given her wings to fly.

He would order markers made as soon as possible, cement slabs with names, "in memory of," to be planted in the cemetery, a place to post flowers and remember. Not for Bill. He and his personal effects were put on a plane and flown home. He wondered how his wife and kids were taking it. Lonnie lowered his arms, his chest heaving, heavy tears gushing down his face. Two markers, one for Sofía, and one for Daniela. They deserved recognition, though their graves would remain forever empty. Perhaps in heaven every question would be answered, but in this man's world, the whys would remain.

Life on earth was fleeting. King David said man was but a flower fading in the grass. He comes from seed, he grows, he withers, and he dies. And all too often he's plucked out unexpectedly. Lonnie took comfort in knowing death was not an end. Death was a beginning. *God hath given us eternal life, and this life is in His Son...that if we confess our sins, He is faithful and just to forgive us our sins and to cleanse us from all unrighteousness...*

He struggled down from his perch, no longer able to enjoy the evening's ambiance. He slipped the envelope from his pocket. His was in a mournful mood, not the right frame of mind for reading the letter in hand. He wanted to feel excited, filled with hopeful anticipation, but he felt only dread. Yet he knew he had to read it. The letter contained an answer, one he'd waited twenty years to receive. He found himself thumping the envelope against his palm. It was an answer he was afraid to face. Either way it would mean closure, and that in and of itself would be worth it.

He pulled his shoulders back, straightening himself. The wounds were still sore, but not like before. The doctor had returned and administered thirty-seven stitches. On the smaller cuts, scabs had formed and were already beginning to peel. He touched his face. He couldn't feel any swelling, and the discoloration was almost gone. He hobbled off toward his hut. The sun had dropped below the horizon, and the dusky gray that surfaced would make it difficult to read. Stepping into his cabana he stooped over to light a match and ignite the Coleman lantern hanging on a peg by the door. He'd never desired to live anywhere else. With a cot for a bed, and a small table and chairs, what more did he need? He couldn't bear the thought of Father Paulo taunting him, but he hadn't taken a vow of poverty. He chose to live like the locals to better identify with their plight, but it was voluntary. If she wanted a bigger house, she would have it. He carried the lamp to the table and set it down. The room was bright in the glow of its light. He pulled back a chair and settled in, removing the envelope again. He slipped a fingernail under the glued flap, opening it, and shook out the folded piece of paper. The air filled with a blend of Trudy's perfume and Coleman lantern fluid. He began to read.

Dearest Lonnie,

As promised, I said I would consider your proposal, and I have. I know how anxious you are. You wanted me to answer you on the spot, but I didn't dare. There's just too much at stake and I wanted to be sure that whatever answer I gave, it would be the right one, and well thought out. You and I have a long history. The best of times, and the worst of times, as they say. But there's one thing I know about you. Your faithfulness is second to none. I'm glad for what you've taught me. You are so right. Love is not a feeling. Love is a commitment. I wish your brother Harlan could've understood that. He never failed to say, "I love you." But then he had what he called "urges" he had to satisfy. Purely gratuitous sex, that's what he called it. No passion, no romance, nothing whatsoever to do with love, just physical, an unbridled lust he couldn't control. He always claimed I had what really counted—his name, his fortune, and his arm at every social gathering. *Ha, ha*, what a joke. I was a laughingstock and everyone knew it, the brunt of cruel gossip, but I chose to drink myself into oblivion rather than risk losing the life I'd become accustomed to. Of course we did share intimacy. But it wasn't love. You taught me that, Lonnie. Love is something you commit to, and hold onto, even if it means giving up something else you desperately want. You do it sacrificially. But that wasn't Harlan's way. He never denied himself anything.

Anyway, I don't want to talk about him. This is about us. I know you would make a good husband. You have that kind of single-minded faithfulness. We don't have much in common, you and I. I couldn't possibly be part of your ministry. I just wouldn't fit in. Nor could you accommodate my social calendar, or accompany me to political events with any degree of comfort. These hurdles are just too high for us to clear.

But if love is about choosing to be faithful, come what may, then I choose to love you!

I guess what I'm trying to say is, I accept your proposal. I say, YES, *yes, yes, yes, yes, yes.* Nothing would make me happier than spending the rest of my life with you. I'm not worried about those other things. We'll work it out. I think we can keep the things we had before separate. We'll just refuse to let them get in the way.

Please call me as soon as possible. We need to set a date and start making plans. I think June is the perfect month. Maybe it's just the romantic in me, but I always wanted to be a June bride. I didn't get the chance last time around, you know, because the pregnancy forced us to act fast. Not this time. We're going to make this work, Lonnie, you and I, together

With all my love,

Trudy

Lonnie laid the letter flat on the table. He leaned back, staring out the window, his face as dark as the night. His eyes began to mist. He should feel buoyant, walking on air, but the events of the past week weighed him down. His eyes scanned the letter again. He couldn't deny his change of heart. It was all he could do to keep it bottled during the few days he'd shared with Nicole in the hospital. But that was temptation. He had sinned, and sin came with consequences. There was a debt to pay. No one said following the right path would be easy. He had prayed, "Father, if there be *any* way, let this cup pass from me. Nonetheless, not my will, but Thine be done." Now he had his answer. God had spoken.

FORTY-NINE

THE SUN scorched the hard pan of the courtyard leaving the earth parched and dry. Rock gardens survived interspersed with cacti and bougainvillea, and lizards camouflaged themselves on stones to hide from the hawks circling in the sky. Mariana skipped over a rope held by Luis and Raúl as it whirled over her head and skimmed under her feet, *faster, faster, faster.* She was good, hopping about quickly, kicking up puffs of yellow dust with each pass, counting *ninety-two, ninety-three.* She was determined to quit at a hundred to give Jaunito a try.

Jaunito was now part of the mission family. He'd been unable to return to St. Mary's, too many unpleasant memories. He'd never made friends there anyway. Luis, and Raúl, and Mariana, they were his friends. They possessed an inexplicable bond that came from shared experience. And Luis never grew tired of answering his questions.

Jaunito's father agreed to let him attend the mission school during the week as long as he could be home on weekends. It was a logical decision. His wife was ill, and in the aftermath of the failed cartel, he was too busy cleaning up the streets to be home much himself. Only one pretender to Miguel's throne had been foolish enough to approach him with an offer of special favors. Purporting to take over where Miguel left off, he'd vowed to increase the salary of every man on the force, and offered Maximilian a new house and his choice of car. Maximilian baited him by requesting a driver, then asked that little flags be mounted on the fenders to give the vehicle a look of "importancia," and when the man smiled and agreed, he had him arrested on the spot. Maximilian's men were warned he would no longer tolerate their accepting graft, though he knew it still went on, and like flesh, drugs and arms smuggling, always would. Wherever there was money to be made...

"...ninety-nine, one-hundred," Mariana spurted as she ran from the rope, giving Jaunito a turn. He gauged the rope's rotation, his face strained with uncertainty, waiting for just the right moment to step in.

Strapped to his chrome chair, Sebastian watched. It hurt knowing Sofía had carried Jaunito over miles of mountain terrain and saved his life, and then chose to end her own. He'd never had a chance to see her again. It hurt that she was gone, but he found refuge in the others who shared her loss, and they welcomed him into their trust. Now they formed five points of a star, inseparable.

Jaunito tripped over the rope on its first pass, spilling himself on the ground. Raúl reached to help him up but he scrambled away. Luis dropped his end of the rope and joined in the chase. Jaunito knew they wanted to tickle him again. He ducked behind Sebastian's wheelchair and spun it around to hold them at bay. The dust plumed and the five children circled and laughed and giggled and teased, a fray of unsullied kids—innocent as a newborn day.

THE SUNSET was big and surreal, a painting in bolder-than-life-color stretched across the sky. Brush strokes of dark blue saturated the top half of the canvas, fading to purple, then to magenta, and finally to orange. Nicole languished in the warm evening, wondering why sunsets in the city never seemed so grand, and why coffee enjoyed in the open air always seemed so much more robust. She was doing fine. *No*, all things considered, she was doing *great.* She was relaxing in front of a panoramic Technicolor sunset without a care in the world. Well, maybe one, okay maybe two, but she would resolve the Lonnie thing tonight, and the sleep deprivation thing would pass with time. It was hard. She was having trouble letting herself drift off knowing she might wake in total darkness, as she had the other night, and be tricked into thinking she was back underground, buried alive. The chest pounding sweat of the adrenaline rush had darn near caused a seizure, but she'd get over it. The fear would pass with time. Just being able to think of Ryan without regret was conciliation.

She paused, holding her cup in both hands, watching the steam rising off the molten black surface, and then took another small sip, muy caliente, *hot*, but *oh soooooo gooood*, brewed from beans grown locally. She held the cup close to her nose, the aromatic vapor misty and warm. The plantation owner, Enrique, was truly blessed. She'd been invited to take a tour of his new farm and was looking forward to seeing what God had done to restore what the locusts had eaten. The government had located the marijuana fields formerly belonging to Miguel Estrada and had seized his assets. They set fire to the remaining crop and sold the acreage at auction. Enrique won the bid and was now reworking the fertile valley to grow avocados for export to the U.S. The warm climate, irrigation, and well-furrowed soil were perfect. Miguel's former employees, upon hearing the farm was under new management, had returned in droves. They were farmers, skilled at planting, growing and harvesting. With employment, they would continue to provide for their families.

Nicole stirred her coffee listening to the marimbas and watching buyers and sellers haggle over the price of chickens and beans. The warm breeze tickled her arms. She was waiting for Lonnie. They hadn't talked about getting together, but she knew he'd come. It was their standing Thursday night date. They hadn't had a chance to sit and talk since before the earthquake. Before the children disappeared. Before the board meeting with Trudy. But that was a lifetime ago.

She could see him out across the plaza standing at the edge of the earth with his arms outstretched, a dark silhouette against the blaze of sunset, communing with God. It was just one of many things she loved about him—he served God first and the trickle-down effect was that he served man. She would be his helpmate. She had her best outfit on, the dark blue slacks and crisp white blouse opened at the neck to look relaxed, but not too provocative, and her blond hair washed and shiny resting on her shoulders in loose waves with just a touch of perfume, enough to be alluring but not sensual. Her hand came up lightly fingering the bandage on her cheek. She prayed he wouldn't be put off by the scar.

No more pussyfooting around, she was determined to lay it on the line. Ryan was behind her, forgiven and forgotten. Lonnie was the future, but she was tired of waiting. Tonight she would present her feelings clearly and wait for his response. There would be no more guessing about where either of them stood.

She looked up and saw him limping toward her, holding something in his hand. She turned and sipped her coffee, pretending not to notice until he stood at the edge of the table, too large to ignore.

"This seat taken?" he said.

She reached out with a white open-toed sandal and pushed the chair back. "It is now."

He laid an envelope on the table and eased himself down slowly to minimize the pain. Nicole had heard his story. They had shared the same hospital room enabling the limited staff to provide better care. He hadn't been forthcoming, hiding for long periods behind the curtain that gave them privacy, but two days of confined quarters got a lot of questions answered including one she dared not ask but had been curious about for a long time. *Praise God, Lonnie didn't snore.*

"Beautiful evening, isn't it?"

"Yes," she said, leaning back and relaxing in the waning shades of color. "It's nice to get back to normal."

"Indeed. Have you ordered?"

Nicole shook her head, her hair dancing lightly on her shoulders.

Lonnie sat back and grimaced.

Nicole seized the moment. "You know what you need, buster? You need a good woman looking after you."

Lonnie nodded. "Yes indeed. Fact, that's something I wanted to talk to you about." He reached for the envelope and removed a piece of paper.

Nicole beamed. *I knew it.* "Talk to me? About what? Go ahead, I'm all ears."

Lonnie handed Nicole the letter. She took it, looking perplexed. She wrinkled her nose at the smell of perfume as she began scanning the page. She didn't have to read far. "Dearest Lonnie..." Her face stiffened and lost its color. "You asked her to *marry* you?"

"Uh, yeah, I figured it was the right thing to do. I've been stringing her along for a long time. I abandoned her, twice actually, once when I left her with my brother. Then, you know, after we salvaged the company and were supposed to run away together, I walked out on her again. I figure I have to make it right."

Nicole tried to keep her fingers from trembling as she laid the letter down. "Sounds like guilt to me."

"It isn't. You have to understand, I loved her deeply, once. And all marriages have highs and lows. But like she said there, love is a commitment, and I guess I'm just ready to make that kind of commitment."

Nicole fought to keep her emotions in check. She wanted to lash out and expose Lonnie for the fool he was. She wanted to weep and wail and beg him to change his mind—but she couldn't. She brought a hand up to cover her cheek and backed the chair away from the table to stand.

"I'm sorry, I'm not feeling well. You'll have to excuse me. I...I have a headache. I think I need to rest."

She turned and walked away, the tears sprouting from her eyes unabated as she rushed to her room without looking back.

FIFTY

Hear the bells ringing, they're singing...

THE BELL of St. Christopher's resounded throughout the Sierra Madre del Sur. Over green leaf jungle, coursing down waterways, echoing through the valleys, and spilling out over the ocean, everywhere, the sound of celebration. Come one, come all. *Hear the bells ringing, they're singing...*and yes, methinks, the bell does indeed toll for thee.

And why not? It was the grandest wedding Posada had ever seen. From every town and village for miles they came, some walking for days to be there. They would not miss the joyous event—their own Pastor Lonnie, getting married.

Posada wasn't big enough to accommodate such a crowd. Many were forced to sleep along the road. The sellers were hawking their wares in the plaza, brightly colored crepe paper piñatas and flowers. And for the hungry, tortillas stuffed with peppers, onions, beans and cheese. The town was caught in fiesta frenzy. There were rumors circulating that the day was to be named a holiday, which Lonnie knew was just plain silly, though he was flattered by the thought.

Crowds swarmed the plaza, circling the well and cistern, every head turned toward the side of town facing the ocean where two granite outcrops rose like giant guardian angels carved from solid rock. Father Paulo Ceylon, in his frugal brown robe, stood in Lonnie's favorite spot, with his arms extended out from his sides, opened wide to welcome the bride and groom.

There was an abundance of color. For the past month the ladies of the town had stayed up late creating crepe paper butterflies of all sizes. The mariposas could be seen everywhere throughout the village in as many sizes and colors as the mind could imagine, but as you moved closer to the altar, there were only the agrias colored in red and blue. Being sensitive to her feelings, Lonnie asked Nicole for her permission to use the display. He still considered her his best friend, something he promised wouldn't change even after he was married. He saw the butterfly as an avid demonstration of how God used the simple things of the world to confound the wise. God had used a beautiful but fragile insect to save his best friend's life—not just once, but twice. Once when He used the colorful agrias to inspire Paulo to dig, and a second time when the gentle creature appeared in a dream and made her want to live. She'd told him to go ahead and do whatever he wanted, but she'd turned away so he'd missed the expression on her face.

Hand-woven wicker vases were filled with flowers and stationed along the matrimonial route. Two ropes formed an aisle down which the bride would walk, led by children throwing flowers. The blue cornflowers and red daisies would be scattered at her feet, the red would be distributed by Mariana and Juanito would be tossing the blue. Mariana's little dress made her look like a princess and Juanito's miniature tux, though he kept tugging at the collar with a finger, made him a prince. Posada didn't have an organ, but the marimba band volunteered to play the wedding march. It took a vivid imagination to conceive Wagner's Lohengren played on wooden bars with small mallets, but the harmonic results were surprisingly good.

Lonnie stood at the front, waiting beside his "Best" man, Bill Best, now fully recovered from the wound that had laid him up for over a month. Bill carried the ring in his vest pocket just over the bandages that girdled his waist. His doctor said he'd cheated death by inches.

On the other side of the raised plywood platform, constructed by local tradesmen to ensure the audience could not only hear but also see Lonnie make his vows, were two bridesmaids waiting for the bride. Gabriela and Fatima practically fluttered with excitement, their dark eyes glittering with flashes of light as the marimba band struck the chords of "The Wedding March." Lonnie looked up. He tried to swallow, but his mouth was dry and it ended up looking more like a grimace. He was glad to be there, glad to be doing what he thought was right, but there was no guarantee he'd be able to keep the vow he was about to make. It would require a commitment to God first. Then, and then alone, would he be able twenty years from now to look his wife in the eyes and still say, "I love you." But it was too late to back out now, down came the bride, one slow pace at a time. Heads turned, expressing awe as the procession began, the long cream-white train flowing behind.

Bill's wife Mary, and their two boys Ted and Josh, sat in the first row along with a whole pile of other kids. But of all the people who came to witness his marriage, those he admired most because their lives were a powerful demonstration of victory over adversity, were the three parked in a chrome gallery of wheelchairs—Angie Best, Sebastian, and his son, Quentin, all of whom wore Cheshire smiles as his lady took his hand to step up on the dais.

And when Paulo instructed Lonnie to lift the veil and kiss his bride, Lonnie was so captivated by the welcoming ocean of her deep blue eyes, he never even noticed the inch-long scar on the side of her cheek.

EPILOGUE

Please do not be hurt, Mamá. What I do, I do for the sake of Mariana. She needs someone. And the school is teaching us so many things. My teacher, she say I can be as smart as Luis—if only I learn to read. But you will always be our mamá. We will not forget. Oh, and if you see God, would you thank Him for me? The men who hurt you are dead. I have thanked Him myself—the padre showed me how—but it would be nice if you could say it to Him in person.

LONNIE STOOD at the edge of the world watching the moon spread its smile across the evening sky. He was there to concede the sovereignty of God and acknowledge that God's will and Divine plan, though frequently misunderstood by man, were nonetheless always right.

He'd returned to Malibu on a cool November morning with the clouds covering the sun in gray gauze, shoulders heavy, dragging his feet, feeling like the Dickens—*It is a far, far better thing that I do than I have ever done.* It seemed so appropriate. He was fully intending to do what he believed God wanted. He was committed to sitting down with Trudy and setting a date for the wedding. He had never been intimate with anyone else so he was certain this was the union God would bless. God had taken him to the mountain, like Abraham, and had tested his faith and willingness to obey, but at the last minute God revealed a better plan.

Lonnie hefted his travel bag onto the bed and saw the hand-written note on the pillow. Trudy hadn't met him at the door or welcomed him home with hugs and kisses, but that was fine by him. He felt more relieved than disappointed. It didn't surprise him Trudy wasn't there. He'd come to attend the board meeting, a monthly routine, but he hadn't let her know what time to expect him to arrive. He should have called, but wanted to avoid getting into discussions until it was necessary. At least now he could take a hot shower and relax before they began negotiations. His idea of a simple wedding was bound to be a far cry different from hers. He turned and glanced over his shoulder toward the door making sure he was still alone. The room was bigger than his whole house in Posada. It was his habit to stay at his brother's mansion. There was no point paying for a hotel when he could visit his family, but this time he found himself thinking he might be better off somewhere else. It was a silly thought. He'd never be able to explain such a move. The place was huge, and a private suite was always reserved for him. It was just that this was Harlan's house, and it made him feel on edge.

He leaned forward, placing a hand on the frilly pink bedspread as he reached for the letter assuming Trudy had placed it there for him to read. He recognized her handwriting, written on her letterhead, pink and embossed with her scrolled initials, TAS, Trudy Anne Striker. At least she'd left it unscented this time.

Dearest Lonnie,

By the time you read this, I'll be over the Atlantic on my way to Greece. You remember me speaking of Stefan Papazikos, that wealthy friend of mine, you know, the one I always refer to as "that curly haired rascal," though his hairline seems to recede a little more each time I see him. Anyway, I think you know we've been seeing each other on and off for years, at least you would have if you'd been paying attention. "Poppy." That's what I call him. He gets such a kick out of it. Poppy is your typical jet-setting tycoon, too busy making money to settle down, and frankly I figured he wasn't serious about me anyway, so when I received your proposal, I decided it was for the best. Well, ever since I said I'd marry you, Poppy has changed his tune. I've received cards and flowers, telephone calls and e-mails begging me to reconsider, and goodness gracious me, you know how it is. I'm a sucker for romance. Can you imagine, Trudy Papazikos, isn't that a hoot?

Now on the other side of the equation, is you. I don't want to see you hurt, really I don't. Please believe me. I just don't think I'm right for you. All your missionary stuff would probably drive me crazy and there's just no point in pretending otherwise. And I've noticed you've changed too. Every time we talk about setting a date you tactfully change the subject and before I know it, you're gone again and nothing is settled. You're supposed to be faithful to me, but I think your work will always come first. And Poppy swears he'll never be with anyone else, so maybe he'll be faithful too.

I care about you deeply, and I know you'd make a fine husband, but Poppy likes to travel and wants to take me on a tour of the world. That's my kind of honeymoon. And you should see the ring he bought me. Four carats. Diamonds truly are a girl's best friend.

I do appreciate your offer, but after giving it careful consideration, I think it would be better for both of us if we just remain friends.

Love,

Your dizzy, soon-to-be ex-sister-in-law,

Trudy

Talk about getting the desire of his heart. Lonnie was smiling all the way down to the last line, and with bags in hand was on a plane before the letter hit the floor.

THERE WERE scattered clouds on the horizon, but they billowed in the moon's radiance and left the wealth of space to shine with a nebula of stars, pink and blue. He had cause to celebrate, and cause to be sad. Saving a few children shed light on how many he couldn't save. But that wasn't his calling. In saying goodbye, Bill reminded him that Corrie ten Boom hadn't been able to save all the Jews—but she saved some, and God used what she did to focus the attention of the world on the tragedy. Because of what Lonnie did, God was using the media to do the same.

The evening was warm and mellow. Were it not for his duties he would stay out late, but his new-found responsibility was calling him home. The doctor claimed the damage suffered by Nicole at Ryan's hand meant she would never have children. But he too was wrong. The adoption papers for Mariana and Raúl were already in place. Lonnie was a proud husband *and* father. He could not have asked for more.

He looked off into space. The moon's light around the edge of the clouds ruffled like lace and the blue Pacific frolicked in its glow. *"For as the heavens are higher than the earth, so are My ways higher than your ways, and my thoughts than your thoughts."* God did work in mysterious ways. The starry host began to gently blur. *As high above as the moon and stars*. The moon's glow was soft and elegant, a misty multilayered pale green slice of melon in the sky. He took in the sultry brine feeling the wind combing through his hair and listening to the surging sea, the sound of many waters, like unto *the voice of God.*

If you want to share your comments about this book please write myview@coltonpublishing.com

Recent Praise for Above The Stars by Keith Clemons

Winner – 2005 Canadian Christian Writing Awards – Best Contemporary Fiction
Honorable Mention 2005 IPPY Awards – Religious Fiction

"Wonderful...a great plot...unexpected twists and turns...awesome character development."
Alice Gray – Best selling author: Stories for the Heart and The Worn Out Woman

"A convincing writer...rings with authenticity...a social giant in the guise of a riveting novel"
Anne Severance, Writer, Consultant and Editor of CBA Best Selling Classics

"What a great book! Five stars! And God is above them all!"
Pastor Rod Hembree, Producer and Host of TV's Quick Study Bible Program

"Considerable writing and storytelling skills...an enjoyable page-turner."
Gary Hassig, "CBA Marketplace" (Christian Booksellers Association)

"A fast-paced story of intrigue and betrayal...the characters are well painted and believable."
Barbara Brennan, "Maranatha News"

Recent Praise for If I Should Die by Keith Clemons

Winner – 2004 Canadian Christian Writing Awards – Best Contemporary Fiction

"Gripping...could not put it down...an amazing book...I hope he does a lot of books like this."
David Mainse, President, CrossRoads Television, TV Host, 100 Huntley Street

"A wonderful story...a real must read"
Ron Hembree, President CornerStone Television, Host, Quick Study Bible Broadcast

"Creative excellence...I highly recommend this book."
Paul A. Webb, Publisher & Chairman, "Head to Head"

"Clever, brave, insightful and compelling...one of those novels that demands to be read."
Michael Coren, Author & Television Host of Michael Coren Live

"A very moving novel...makes you care about the characters and what they're going through."
Virginia Boreland, "The Christian Herald"